FOOL'S PARADISE

AARON BRAWLEY

FOOL'S PARADISE

KUDU
PUBLISHING

In loving memory of Rashaud Graham.

Dedicated to that little boy from twelve years ago, and anyone like him: who sees a secret world that keeps him awake at night, with dreams that bleed over into the day; whose mind is filled with countless fantastical realms where things make sense, and where it's okay when they don't.

ACKNOWLEDGMENTS

To Phill and Jacob, thank you for the countless nights, tireless discussions and all of the help you lent me when you could've been doing anything else. I never would have imagined I'd meet two of the most creative people in the world at a military college in South Carolina. But it would seem kindred spirits travel intersecting roads. Thank you for falling in love with the characters and world I envisioned and helping me to really look under every crevice and curtain to discover all of its secrets. Thank you for believing in the message of Fool's Paradise and its subsequent installments, and the necessity of that message. Most of all, thank you for seeing the value and affirming that to me and locking arms with me to get the story out and not fall prey to perfectionism. I will always be grateful for your support and contributions.

To Chantelle, Brandon, Arsenio, Neliann, Uncle Steve, Mom, & Nan and Pop, the first explorers on the continent of Gia and the land of Assyr, thank you for reading my story. Do not be surprised if you notice bits of yourselves in this book or future installments; after all, each of you have shaped who I am in some profound way and therefore this book. Your feedback, encouragement and excitement have been invaluable to me. They were the currency I needed to push through to the end of this book.

To Dad, who told me that "done is better than perfect" and to stop starting over. You were right.

Debbie, Sarah, and John, thank you for all of your hard work on this book: phone calls, strategy sessions, and countless zooms. Thank you for wanting this book to succeed as much as I do.

To George, your artwork blew me away and it was so great working with you. I can't wait for the world to see what you can do.

Martijn and Amy, thank you for taking a chance on this unconventional story. Thank you for believing in *Fool's Paradise*, and me, and for giving me the opportunity to share it with the world. I will be eternally grateful.

To Adeline, my wife, thank you for your patience on the countless nights I stayed up until two or three, writing this and not coming to bed; your grace has not gone unnoticed. Thank you for supporting my passion for this world that I speak about as if it were real. Thank you for understanding that, to me, it is. Most of all, thank you for your commitment to me on this wild ride we've taken together and for never leaving my side. I love you.

Finally, thank you God, for ordering my steps. There have been many detours over the past twelve years but you've used this book to show me that, when I follow You, every detour becomes a straight line. Thank you for the experiences that shaped this book into what it has become, and that shaped me right along with it.

✳ ✳ ✳

"OUR ENEMIES ARE NEVER
AS EVIL AS WE IMAGINE, NOR
ARE WE EVER SO PURE."

✳

PROLOGUE

Some dreams hold people for a lifetime. And sometimes, it is the dreams of others that are held, binding souls to paths they did not choose. . . .

This dream—*or was it a memory?*—always began the same way.

It was a small home. The howling winds of a blizzard beat against scrap metal walls, made from a ghastly amalgamation of plywood, plastic, and tin.

There was always the same woman in the dream. Clay knew it had to be his mother, Lena, but she was unrecognizable.

Lena was young—younger than Clay could ever imagine or remember. Even beneath dirt and frost, there was a beauty to his mother, the kind that years of hard living would come to completely replace with darkened, gnarled skin and a grime that could never be washed away.

From the looks of it, she was in Ombada, for there was no other region in Assyr known for its devastating winters like Ombada. Residents there had a saying: "Life is what occurs between the spring and summer months, but there is only death to be found in the winter."

The four walls of the tiny shack were touched by frost on the inside, only saved from freezing completely by a pile of burning trash, made up of any loose junk, towels, and frozen food Lena could find. She crowded the fire intimately and tightened her blanket.

Nestled in her arms was an infant. She caressed his bald head.

"My sweet boy," she said, hugging him tenderly against her breast, guarding his warmth with hers.

The child began to coo as he awoke and stretched out his arms.

The unforgiving gales of wind beat against those tin walls, its howls intensifying with the storm. But Lena heard none of that now. No, at this moment, she was simply entranced in the eyes of her baby boy. All else began to fade away.

The boy was enraptured by the blaze of the fire. He turned to it. Its embers littered his golden irises. With all the courage he could muster, he wiggled his arms out from Lena's embrace, braving the taste of cold air and stretching his fingers towards the flames.

"I want to tell you a story," said Lena, her voice hoarse but not yet cracked with age. "In times like this, my grandmama used to tell me a story that her grandmama told her, and now I'm gonna tell you."

Clay's hands still reached for the fire.

"Of a land called *Mohi'ri* . . . A home far, far from here . . ."

No longer was it Clay's hands that reached for the fire, but a young girl's reaching for the sun, its rays slivered between splayed fingers yet to be calloused and scarred.

"Untouched by war, hunger, slavery . . ."

The girl looked down and the walls of the frosted Ombada shack fell one by one. Gone were the blistering frosts of the slums; now, she stood in a field. To the left were children playing in the grasslands of the savanna. Boys and girls running about, laughing, singing.

Clay had never seen a landscape so golden, not outside fiction. But he could not shake the gut feeling that this place was *real*.

To the right was a cityscape unlike any other, not built by competition but by cooperation. Pyramidal towers, fashioned of warm-toned stone, reached for the sky. Sunlight played in murals of stained glass across the towers, refracting rainbows of color that shimmered and danced throughout the city's walls and streets. Even from here, where the city met open fields of golden grass, Clay saw godlike figures depicted in those leviathan panes of stained glass, stamped on those pyramidal skyscrapers.

He marveled over how much those figures looked like him.

Surrounding the pyramidal skyscrapers were orderly city blocks of smaller buildings, each structure different from its neighbor: some roofs were elegantly curved, some stabbed for the sky like obelisks, and some were flat; some were small and rectangular, their shapes sturdy and strong, while others bore elegant struts and flying buttresses; some had stained glass while others had no windows at all. Though the buildings showcased an explosion of architectural ingenuity, they were all contained neatly in squared city blocks. Horse-drawn carts and silhouetted figures flowed through wide smooth roads, and not a single person appeared hurried or rushed.

The city was a monument to and by humanity.

Straight ahead in the distance were oases and fountains. Animals of all colors, shapes, and sizes drank without fear: birds the size of elephants—their plumage iridescent, each feather catching a different color with each shift and movement—roosted and preened; herds of tall stilt-legged creatures pranced and hopped across the gentle golden hills, their fur a gentle white, their giant antlers brushed with gold; colorful primates played and splashed beneath the fountain spray and groomed one another in the shallow oasis waters; and all manner of creatures too distant and small to be detailed flowed around one another in this ballet of harmony.

Not a one prowled, stalked, or hunted; not a single beast feared for its life.

A gentle breeze rustled the grass, shaking it with a calm *shhhhhh*. A gust of wind swept around Lena, creating a gentle cyclone that lifted her hair and kissed her skin. Where before there were the demonic howls of a raging storm, now there was only the angelic hymn of a song she's known all her life, tucked away deep but never forgotten:

I once was asleep on a long journey,
Off in the land of Mohi'ri.
I had a dream of bad luck and slave-ry,
But we're safe from it all in Mohi'ri.
Uxsata hi n'gwanali.
Basa Xi gon do, Xi gon do-'li.
The bad child runs from the safety,
But the rivers sweep me back to Mohi'ri.
I ate from the fruit of the forbidden tree,
But I always kept the seeds of Mohi'ri.
Cata ino Xhusa uma gon'ri.
Zuma Hoka hey en Mohi'ri.

It felt as if the land itself breathed the words, whispering them into the furthest reaches of Lena's heart. She closed her eyes and let the melody permeate her soul. A tear carefully slid down Lena's cheek. She could stay here forever.

But in this accursed world, the rightful place for dreams is in fantasy. It is the destiny of man to trek this world without them.

The four frosted walls of the Ombada shack arose from their lowly position, one by one, to corral Lena in again. Imprisoned, she was again met with the exhausting heat of the trash-fire. She had been staring absent-mindedly into the flames for some time now. It'd be going out soon. The smoke had begun to make her eyes water. She got up to get more fuel for the fire.

She looked around for anything else she could use. No such luck. It was an empty lot, stripped down to the bare essentials of four walls. Everything must have been looted long ago.

Lena looked to the body on her left. The woman was slumped over in the corner, drink in hand. Nearly an icicle, Lena patted down the body for anything she'd missed the first go-around. She pulled at the corpse's coat, frozen to the woman's body. Along with a few ice crystals, she tore off a pocket inside the jacket. Inside, she found a small lighter. It had a little bit of fluid left inside of it. *Thank the gods.*

The storm had finally seemed to simmer down. Lena approached the window and exhaled. She rubbed her fist against the steamed glass, revealing what lay beyond.

It was a wasteland. Gone were the playful children roaming the savannah. Instead, there were men, women . . . children, frozen beyond recognition, their bodies too small to keep them warm enough to breathe.

Some people huddled together, some with their fingers still wound tightly around a piece of bread they thought would get them through to tomorrow.

Lena looked at Clay. "Oh, what a world I've born you into, my sweet boy." Lena was trying not to shake the boy too much with all of her shivering. "I promise, it won't always be this way."

The baby recognized the pain in his mother's eyes. His eyes clouded with tears and, soon enough, he was crying, greatly distressed.

Out of options, she did the only thing she could think of doing. She sang:

"Uxsata hi n'gwanali,
Safe from it all in Mohi'ri."

ONCE FORGOTTEN PROMISES AND LONG REMEMBERED DREAMS

I

CLAY

In the stillness of evil, a single proud footstep can shatter dread.

Truth be told, before that moment when *he* walked into town, Sally Smith had never cared for that line—came straight out of one of her favorite books, but it had never felt realistic.

Well, it sure felt realistic now.

He was a tall sort, striding into the besieged town with a cool bravado that defied the sticky desert air. The spurs on his boots rattled and clanked, announcing his arrival to all in town: the terrified villagers, the gun-toting and ugly bandits—even the fresh corpses seemed to stir when he broke the silence.

And he was making his way straight towards the trio of bandits, straight towards their leader: the weasel . . . the . . . the wicked . . .

Crap, what's a good title for him?

Hmm.

Ah, got it!

... straight towards their leader: *the Worm!*

Sally squinted against the setting sun, her eyes still raw from the tears. The lone man was covered almost head to toe in a long duster, and his wide-brimmed hat was tilted down so that his face was obscured. She couldn't see much more, silhouetted as he was against the sun.

Billy and his two goons raised their guns, a low chuckle rising from Billy's throat at the audacity of this lone man.

The lonesome man splayed his hands, almost mockingly, but his pace didn't slow one bit.

Sally didn't see a single weapon on him: no six-shooter at the hip, no lever-action slung over the shoulder—not even a knife strapped to his boot!

Oh, her hope fell flat. No way would this unarmed fella take out Billy the Worm. Sally would've buried her face in her hands then and there, but the way he was walking—that confidence wasn't shaken one bit, not even with three barrels staring him down.

"Stop right there!" the Worm yelled, his scratchy voice almost as ugly as he was.

The lone man stopped, just a few paces from Billy and his two goons.

"Show us your face, fella—I like to see the fear of death in the eyes of those I kill," said the Worm, cocking the hammer of his revolver.

The lowered hat started tilting up real slow-like. Sally caught a glimpse of lips drawn tight—she couldn't tell whether from anger, fear, or focus.

Those lips were all she saw.

The man ducked, the sunlight behind him flaring up as he did, shining right in the eyes of the Worm and his goons.

The lone man moved so quick that Sally couldn't make sense of what had happened until after it happened: by the time everything stilled, it was just the lone man standing above three unconscious men, holding three revolvers in his hand.

The Worm had been defeated! Their town was saved!

A great cheer went up from the hostage villagers, and Sally—along with many others—rushed towards the man, cheering, "Our hero! Our—"

✳ ✳ ✳ ✳ ✳

The bedroom door rattled out as Lena almost battered it down with her fist. "Caius Cassian Ntuli, you better not make me call your name again—you better not still be sleeping when breakfast is warm!"

Clay sat up ramrod straight; the fear of death slipped into his soul—was never good when his mother called him by his full name.

"I'm not sleeping, mom—I'll be right out," he called, making sure to keep his voice neutral. If Lena caught a hint of anger or annoyance—well, it'd be a bad way to start a day, especially a school day.

Clay's mouth twisted up at the thought of school. He looked at the plastic figures laid out before him: the hero, Lonesome, with his duster and hat, the mayor's daughter hugging him, and the three goons splayed around them, their cheap limbs twisted almost to the point of breaking.

The boy scooped his bookbag off his bed and began zipping it up—Clay paused halfway, looking at the lone hero figurine on the floor.

Always good to have a little courage with you, he thought.

Clay scooped up the figurine, sliding him into his bookbag before rocketing out of his bedroom.

Uneven planks creaked beneath Clay's feet as he stepped over the wood rot. A portly, lazy gringafly flew in with the breeze, slipping through a tear in one of the mesh windows. Sturdy, well-made furniture adorned the house: tables with chipped corners, a couch with a small sewn rip, a bookshelf with dust-sprinkled tomes. A small television, its screen no larger than Clay's splayed palm, filled the room with the low conversations of black-and-white characters from a sitcom.

Lena was under the kitchen sink with a wrench, trying to appear busy. Next to the sink was the gas stove, one of the four burners alit. Flames licked a small bowl: Lena's own breakfast.

His mom was probably just under the sink to keep Clay from seeing the worry peppering her gaze.

"Sink leaking again?" Clay asked.

"When is it not leaking?" she responded. "Bowl's on the table."

Clay sat and took his first scoopful. The oatmeal tasted dry, and silence lingered in the modest kitchen.

"Why don't we just call a plumber? Mister Janus could look at it."

"Mister Janus . . ." she said in between grunts ". . . is a pervert . . . and I ain't giving him an inch past the threshold of this house."

"Okay, then can we call a real plumber? That thing's been busted for weeks."

"As soon as you get 'real plumber' money, I'll happily give them a ring. Until then, sit and eat your food. It's going cold," Lena said. And Clay knew that was the end of that.

"Whatever," he said, doing his best to shrug it off.

Clay knew this wasn't really about "plumbing." Ever since Clay had come home with a black eye a few days ago, a thick tension had permeated almost every morning, and the oatmeal seemed tougher to swallow with each passing day.

Lena glanced at Clay, her mouth ajar with a question that had been living in her mouth for days. They both noticed the sudden lack of grunting. Lena swallowed the question and turned back to the pipes.

She took a deep sigh. "Sorry."

"It's fine."

She put the wrench down and sat up from under the sink. "No, it's not."

"Yes, it's fine."

"No, Clay, it's not," she said emphatically. She sat in a chair at the table, leaning over towards her son. Clay didn't even look up from his bowl of oatmeal, which he was just stirring over and over. "It's not, Clay. This ain't us. Barely talking. All snappy-like." Lena looked to his face, where the fading welt had begun to settle. "I know you didn't come out of me with that thing."

"I don't want to talk about it."

"Why not? Clay, we've always talked. About everything. What makes this any different?"

"You wouldn't understand," Clay mumbled.

Lena paused for a moment. She had a fire in her soul that seemed muffled as of late—no, much longer than that. At one time, she'd have wrangled Clay for those poor fools' names, gone up to the school, and wrangled those kids too, Ghoula Codes be damned.

But that was a long time ago.

When Clay came home with a black eye, she tended to it, iced it, but said nothing. Things would have been different when Clay was younger, before he and Lena arrived at Ruka. For some time now, it seemed to him that Lena had found her groove in staying under the radar and keeping her head down. The passion of youth had long been subdued by the wisdom of obscurity. The fire just wasn't there anymore. So, she swallowed her words and again said nothing.

Clay finished his bowl, stood up, and placed it by the sink. When he made eye contact with his mom, he almost winced—he hated that look in her eye. Pity. Worry.

"I'm going to uh . . . go," Clay muttered.

Lena looked at him, her eyebrow quirked. "Not without a hug, you fool," she said, her tone warm.

The two embraced.

Clay, just recently thirteen, only came up to his mother's sternum. Lena was a tall woman, wiry and corded with the strength gained from a lifetime of odd jobs and harsh labor in all manner of conditions. Nowadays, she had a good job with the local head of state, a Quaestor of the Empire. Still, though, she looked older than she should have. People said Clay took after her some, but Lena said that he was the spitting image of his father—had his blocky jaw and sharp eyes.

Not that he'd know.

"Try to learn something at school," Lena whispered, her eyes closed and grip still tight around her son. "But don't forget to have a little fun, too."

"Okay, mom," Clay said, pulling out of her embrace and hiking his backpack up on his shoulder. He walked to the door, his head hung low and arm dangling from a backpack strap.

"And Clay?" said Lena, her voice still low and soft. He looked to her. She hesitated for a moment, as if fighting the urge not to swallow this too. "Make sure you're home before curfew and. . . . don't let those kids steal your light," she said, with a gentle smile.

Clay smiled, his eyes still dull, and left.

II

CLAY

Though Virtue Cradle Junior High was not far from Clay's house, it was no short journey.

Ratty sneakers crunched along paths long since worn to dirt by Ghoula feet. Other Ghoula schoolchildren walked near Clay, but only a few traveled to Virtue Cradle; most attended the various Ghoula-only schools nearby. Far as Clay knew, Virtue Cradle was the only junior high with an integrated Ghoula and Assyrian population in Ruka.

The chatter and laughter of nearby children only deepened Clay's sense of loneliness. Many of them knew he attended Virtue Cradle, and so many of them didn't speak to him, especially since their paths diverged so soon. Friendships were hard to build five minutes at a time, and Clay's mere association with Assyrians was enough to make other kids avoid him.

Clay stepped over a line of pebble ants crossing the path single file. Each one was the size of Clay's finger. They carried various bits of food and pebbles back to their colony. He paused to watch one of the ants, lain upon its back, its legs twitching. The other ants paid no heed as they walked by.

Though Ruka, Clay's home for the better part of a decade now, had plenty of paved roads and a half-decent infrastructure—for this part of the Empire—Ghoulas were consigned to snaking dirt paths that wove around the outskirts of town. People like Clay could only walk on paved roads when accompanied by someone of Assyrian descent; otherwise, they could only travel along unkempt paths, just as they could only buy from shops that were connected to the Ghoula paths.

The Ghoula path that ran from Clay's home to Virtue Cradle Junior High circumvented the town entirely, making what could have been a five-minute jaunt into a twenty-minute trudge.

Before long, the rush of low voices fell to nearby stillness. Wind whispered across the forest's eaves. Distant chatter arose from the town square as it awoke. A few old cars, backfiring as they were fired up for the day, rumbled along Ghoula paths and cobbled streets.

He tried, as he did every morning on these paths, to find something to look forward to. He hoped Ayala showed up at the end of the school day—spending time with his best friend felt like the only good thing in life lately.

One nice thing about the Ghoula paths is that Assyrians avoided them like the plague. It was frowned upon for one of their kind to tread the paths, and so they were one of the few places where Clay could feel safe and didn't have to worry over the correct salutations, honorifics, or etiquette.

With each passing day, the journey felt shorter and shorter.

Clay regarded the dark stone angles of Virtue Cradle Middle School with a knot in his chest.

He stood there, hands white-knuckled around his backpack straps, took a deep breath, and took his first step forward.

And then another.

And another, until he was entering the back doors of the prison they called "Junior High."

✳ ✳ ✳ ✳ ✳

Backed against the cliffside, the warrior-king gazes down upon the battlefield below. His second-in-command tends to his arm; she draws the bandages tight over the stump where his hand once was, but the king's eyes do not betray the pain. His focus lies on this battle, this turning point—as every battle had been so far.

He smiles a grim satisfaction. The Harrakas are losing—they are surrounded and being pushed back, closer and closer to this cliff. The warrior-king glances back, peering over the side of the earth and to the jagged rocks and turbid surf below.

They were outnumbered and technologically outmatched.

Finally, it was an even fight.

He shares his reaper's smile with his second-in-command.

"A blood-day then," she said, gripping her khopesh with a crazed glimmer in her eyes.

"A miracle of blood and death: here we stand again, upon the precipice of history." The warrior-king jams his greatsword into the nearby rock and grabs the horn about his waist. "And this day, we reclaim our history."

He brought the horn to his lips and blared the siren-call of war. Thunder ushered forth across the field, stilling the desperate death-dance before him for but a moment. The gazes of all turned to the warrior-king, bloodied and debilitated: to the warrior-king who stands tall and proud, the crimson haze of death lingering about his visage.

"TODAY, DEATH FEASTS!" thundered the warrior-king.

"HOKAHEY!" called all those Harraka warriors below, slamming their bloodied blades and spears against their rent shields.

Boom, boom.

"TODAY, DEATH RAGES!" called the warrior-king again.

"HOKAHEY!"

Boom, boom.

"TODAY, DEATH ERUPTS!"

"HOKAHEY!"

Boom, boom.

"WHO ARE WE?" The warrior-king raised his bloodied stump. Spittle and blood flew from the Harrakas.

"DEATH!"

"HOKAHEY!" cried the king, ripping his blade from the earth and charging down the hill.

"HOKAHEY!"

"Hokahey," whispered Clay, staring upon the poorly drawn stick figures in his journal with a giddy smile.

"Clay?" asked the teacher, drawing the eyes of all in the classroom to the boy. "Do you have something you'd like to share with the class?"

Clay shot up from his reverie, finding a mob of harsh violet eyes surrounding him, and shook his head as if he were trying to decapitate himself—which may have been preferable right now. "N-no, sir, Magister Darrow, sir."

"Then how about you sit upright and pay attention?" Magister Darrow's voice was sharp, as it always was when speaking to the Ghoula kids. "And maybe you can answer the question while you're at it, Mr. Hokahey?"

A derisive chuckle arose from the class at Clay's new nickname. Clay glanced to his friend Paul, who sat on the other end of the class. Paul was the only other Ghoula in the class and the only person who wasn't laughing at him.

A tightness crawled into Clay's chest—he had no clue what the question was. To his right, a freckled face furrowed its long eyebrow: Billy with that smirk of his, probably dreaming up more insults to add to his list for the day. Clay wondered what they would be this time.

"Um—"

"'Um' is not an answer, Clay, nor is it the proper honorific," said the Magister. He looked to the rest of the class, his words half-sighed. "I know there are many places you'd rather be than here but do try to pay attention. This is important history we're covering. Now, Clay," he said, returning his gaze to the boy, "the question was: 'What was the final campaign of the Shadow War called, and who was the Legatus leading the campaign?'"

Clay smiled. He may be a daydreamer who'd rather be playing with mines than be in this classroom, but if there was one topic he loved in all academia, it was this one. He revered the Harrakas, even if associating with them was punishable by death.

"Magister Darrow, the name of the campaign, sir, was The Forest Conquest, and the Legatus in charge was Samael of the Kota, whose brutality was legendary, especially during The Forest Conquest, where he would gather any women, children, and elderly Harrakas and—"

The teacher cut Clay off with a raised hand, his narrow features more uncomfortable than before. "You've answered the question, Clay—no need to dive into the nasty bits." The teacher then looked to Billy and said, "See, William? Clay wasn't even paying attention and he got it right."

Would have been kinder for the teacher to just shoot Clay right then and there.

Suddenly, the gaggle of laughter was no longer focused on Clay but on Billy. As soon as the teacher walked away, Billy leaned over towards Clay, his violet eyes aflame with fury, and he whispered, "You're dead, *Ghoula*."

The teacher kept talking, but Clay could only hear the rush of blood and fear in his ears.

By lunchtime, Clay kept his eyes peeled, watching. He knew if there were a time for Billy to get him, it'd be either now or just after school. Wherever he could find a crowd. The Billy's of the world always wanted a crowd. He'd be looking to recover his pride after the embarrassment from earlier. Clay half hoped he'd just get him now; waiting was the worst part.

"Hey, earth to Clay."

Clay unglazed his eyes and looked across the table, where his friend Paul was looking at him. Paul's eyebrows were bent in a funny way.

"Daydreaming again?" Paul asked. "I thought Magister Darrow snuffed all that out earlier," he jested.

Clay shook his head, trying to fling off thoughts of Billy and just enjoy lunch. For once.

"Sorry, what'd you say?"

"I was asking if you had caught up on *Revolt*."

Revolt was a comic series. Clay wasn't really close to Paul like he was Ayala, but they bonded over media in a way that made it easy to forget about anything else. Paul was also a Ghoula, one of the few at their school—it was natural that in a sea of kids with platinum hair and violet eyes, the few without such distinguishing features would gravitate toward each other.

A smile came to Clay. "Oh yeah, I finished volume 8 last night."

Paul's face split apart with a gap-toothed grin and he leaned back from the table. "That fight between Horus and Kaiser?!"

Clay couldn't help but mirror Paul's energy—his excitement had always been contagious. His leg started bouncing up and down beneath the table. "You kept talking about it and building it up and I didn't think it'd live up to it—"

"But?" Paul interrupted, leaning forward again, eyes growing wider.

"It freaking rocked, man—I didn't expect Lonesome to show up at the end there. Can't wait to see what happens next." Clay's hand rested on his backpack, where the figurine of Lonesome was. His mind flashed to images of Lonesome beating up Billy the Worm, and his smile grew even toothier.

Paul punched the air, making *Bam* and *Kapow* noises as he did so. "Slick as always, man—slick as always."

"When's the next volume coming out?" Clay asked. Paul was always up to date with nerd stuff like this; hell, he lived for it.

Paul's demeanor shifted; his mouth corkscrewed, and he threw his hand. "No one knows. The creator's been getting flack for *Revolt* since volume 1, and with how 7 ended, people aren't happy that she showed the Harraka character winning."

"No kidding."

"Yeah—doesn't matter that the creator's Assyrian too. They say that she's had to move to a new place a few times just to escape the—" Paul cut himself short, his gaze flicking to something behind Clay. All animation and hint of passion fled Paul's posture, and he said in a hushed voice, "Hey, watch out. The Worm's heading this way."

Clay didn't even have time to look—a stinging pain flared up at the back of his head from where Billy slapped it.

He sat down right next to Clay. Two shadows fell over the table: Billy's idiot friends, content to let Billy be their mouths and minds, were standing right behind Clay.

The young Ghoula boy looked to the upper deck of the cafeteria, to where the teachers were gathered: all Assyrian. One was looking right at him; no doubt they saw Billy slap him, but the teacher didn't move. Didn't even have the decency to *look* sympathetic.

There was no help to be found here. They were on their own.

A second sting to the back of his head forced his attention back to the table. "Think you're better than me, mutt?" Billy's face was mean, his eyes so wide that Clay could see his entire purple iris.

Clay forced the words through the blockage in his throat. "No, I . . ."

"You're what?" Billy said, leaning closer and lowering his voice to a venomous hiss. "A dumb good-for-nothing Ghoula?"

Clay was silent, keeping his gaze on his lunch tray. In his periphery, he saw Paul doing the same.

Don't let those kids steal your light.

Lena's voice popped into Clay's head. He placed his hands under the table so that Billy couldn't see his fists. Clay was glad his nails were chewed-down stumps; otherwise, they'd be digging into his palms.

"Billy . . . I didn't mean to—"

Billy's eyes grew even wider, his scowl deeper. "To what?"

Clay grew silent again. *Nothing good to say. Anything I say will make it worse. So I will say nothing.*

He glanced to the teachers' table. Jokes and laughter fluttered between the adults; no one was paying attention, not even the one who saw Billy approach earlier.

Billy pushed his tongue against the inside of his cheek. Craning his head at one of his cronies, he said, "Look at them. Scared shitless. Hey, Brass?"

"Yeah?" one of his minions answered.

"My dad told me that Ghoulas shouldn't even be able to read. 'Evolutionary deficiency,' he says."

Spell "evolutionary deficiency," Clay thought.

"My dad told me something similar."

"Hey, did you hear the one about us being descended from rats?" Clay chimed in. "Used to live in sewers. That's why we smell so bad." He pinched his nose for additional effect.

Billy looked to his cronies, confused. Clay wasn't supposed to join in. Takes all the fun out of it.

After a few beats of confusion, Billy made his predictable attempt to regain control: "Yeah, you're just a sewer rat!" His cronies followed suit in the name-calling.

"Sewer rat!"

"Look at his fat, rat nose!"

"Stupid, filthy, stinky rat face!"

"That's what I've been trying to tell you," Clay added. Paul let slip a soft chuckle.

Billy's wheels were visibly spinning. Looking at him, Clay almost felt sad for the poor kid. Almost.

This wasn't going anywhere. It clearly wasn't having the desired effect they had hoped for.

Finally at the end of his rope, Billy made one final desperate lob for power. Clay knew it would be the big one: "You know what we do to rats in my house, Brass?"

Clay went silent, bracing himself for the worst of it.

Billy leaned over the table, picked up a carton of milk, and poured it over Paul's head. Paul stayed still, hunched over as the white liquid splattered over his hair and drenched his shirt.

You pour milk on rats? Clay thought, though such words would never see the light of day.

Both Ghoulas remained silent beneath the laughter of Billy and his friends. With his leg, Paul quietly shifted his bookbag beneath the table so that the milk didn't drip on it.

Billy tipped the carton up before it emptied; there wasn't much left now. He spun to face Clay, pulled his collar, and splattered the inside of Clay's shirt with what was left.

It was cold.

And it smelled.

The carton now empty, Billy placed it back onto Clay's lunch tray far too gently; the Assyrian teenager turned to Clay, his eyes slivered now, and said, "You'll find out after school today, *rat.*"

Then, finally, Billy and his friends walked away.

Don't let those kids steal your light.

Clay met Paul's eyes—though they were swimming with tears, Paul forced a smile.

"You okay?" Clay asked.

Paul's chin started to tremble and his smile wavered.

"I should have something in my bag to help that dry," Clay said, his voice still hushed with indignity.

Billy's laughter rose above the din of the cafeteria again, and the dam shielding Clay from his own emotions broke. Something white-hot began frothing and pulsing in his chest.

He tried to smother it—Ghoulas had no place to fight back, to talk back, to complain, to do anything. No matter what happens, Clay would be blamed for it and then he'd be expelled. Maybe worse. And then what? His mom had worked hard to get him into this school.

Clay bent down beneath the table, opening his bag and looking for the handkerchiefs he kept stashed. They were great at mopping up sweat, blood, and milk.

And then Paul spoke. "Spent three weeks saving up for this shirt." His voice was cracked with tears yet to be spilled. "Was excited to finally own something clean."

Clay never found those handkerchiefs—no, his hand instead grasped a small plastic figure: Lonesome.

Don't let those kids steal your light.

Billy's laughter was cut short when a milk carton exploded against the back of his head, and the cafeteria went silent.

III

CLAY

*B*illy *whipped around to see Clay now standing, his fists so tight that the white of bone peeked through skin.*

Clay held his bully's gaze and hoped that Billy couldn't see the tremor in his hands.

The cafeteria was still silent, watching the milk drip down Billy's clothing. Even the teachers were too shocked to move.

"Apologize to Paul," Clay said, shocked by how strong his voice sounded.

Truth be told, Clay was freaking out.

He's never done this before, never been all heroic and ballsy.

No way this'll turn out well, not in the short-term or long-term.

Billy's shock turned to fury. He swiped his milk-drenched hair back from his face, splattering milk droplets on a group of cute girls sitting nearby. As they shrieked, Billy's face grew even redder and he began advancing, pushing his sleeves up his arms.

"I'll apologize to him at your funeral, rat," Billy said.

Brass and Brutus, his minions, rushed at Clay too, their expressions and posture a crude imitation of Billy's.

As Billy stomped and sloshed towards him, Clay was surprised at how his fear seemed to melt. He glanced to the teachers and the stock-still students and realized that he was already done for.

That today was as good a day as any.

Billy moved into Clay's personal space.

Clay rushed forward.

Raised his fist.

And as he slugged Billy across the jaw, he realized two things: punching someone in the jaw freaking hurts, and he must be a lot stronger than he ever gave himself credit for.

Because Billy's head snapped back, and his eyes rolled back in his head, and he fell hard to the floor.

His friends stopped short, looked at Billy's unconscious form, looked to Clay, and then raised their hands, backing away ever so slowly.

And Clay stood, breathing heavily, looking around the entire cafeteria as if daring someone else—even a teacher—to approach.

For the first time in his life, Clay stood triumphant.

✳ ✳ ✳ ✳ ✳

Were it so easy to overcome oneself.

Billy, dry and unharmed, laughed his way back to his lunch table with his two friends, and Clay and Paul sat with their heads hung low.

Clay's fantasy was just that: fantasy.

That frothing fury that had built up . . . well, it seemed to just break in half. Clay could feel himself retreating further into his own mind, growing distant from all his surroundings until it felt like his body was nothing more than a distant puppet.

Mechanically, he reached into his bag, his hand brushing by cheap plastic Lonesome, rummaging around until he found the stash of dirtied handkerchiefs.

As if from a distance, he watched his hands unfold the handkerchief, watched as he helped Paul dry his once-clean and once-new shirt as much as two poor boys with nothing to their names could.

Didn't even bother drying his own shirt.

Didn't see much point in it.

✻　✻　✻　✻　✻

Not a second too soon, the final bell of the day rang. The Assyrian children made their way to the front doors, near the buses and main routes, while the Ghoulas made their way to a pair of double doors located in the back of the school.

A teenager hovered by the Ghoula path that skirted the nearby wood. She was in her normal spots, hugging the tree line and wandering around, plucking berries from bushes with a casual boredom. She was tall and lithe; toned forearms that peeked out of rolled-up sleeves. Her hood was down, and long, silky—but messy—hair framed her brown, freckled face and spilled down her shoulders. Her eyes, amber and harsh, glimmered beneath the shade of the forest. She walked like someone who grew too tall too fast; her steps were short and stuttering, giving her the impression of an adolescent bird yet to grow into its gracefulness.

Clay stood with Paul at the entrance to their school. The two boys hesitated, meeting each other's eyes with a sad knowing smile.

Paul pinched his shirt. "Do it all again tomorrow?" he joked.

Clay smiled; it was nice to see Paul's exuberance begin to return, even if it was an inch at a time. He knocked knuckles with Paul.

Paul nodded, his smile with more teeth in it now.

And then the two parted ways.

Clay hurried from the confines of the school, bounding across the trimmed grass and beveled pavement, enjoying the midday breeze.

The sky blanketed in a thin grey cloud. Sunlight was weak and diffused, settling over the land with a timid touch. The orchestra of nature and life buffeted Clay; from dusk till dawn till dusk, the forest sang its song: birds hooting and chirping and singing, beasts rushing and hunting and fleeing, trees and trunks bristling and swaying. It was a tune that Clay had known all his life, one that bore more comfort than the sterile air-conditioned halls of Virtue Cradle Junior High.

He glanced around, searching for Billy and his goons.

They weren't in sight—Paul and Clay's final class let out early, so maybe he had enough of a head start to get away from the Assyrian brat.

Clay was safe. For today, at the very least. Thoughts of tomorrow were best left for tomorrow: today, school was out.

When he came within speaking distance of the girl by the tree line, she noticed him, and Clay felt the ball of tension in his shoulders unknot and roll away.

Ayala's eyes flickered between Clay and his shirt; her eyes slivered with knowledge of the stain's origin.

When the two met, Clay offered greetings and Ayala prodded her finger against his chest.

"Got something here," she said. Her voice was hoarse and scratchy with the creak of a girl in puberty who prefers to be alone. Present company excluded, of course.

Clay looked to his shirt, and Ayala's finger flew up, flicking him in the nose as he did.

He couldn't help but to chuckle, and with it he felt the last vestiges of the day's tension dissolve.

"Billy get you?" Ayala asked, her smile at odds with her serpentine eyes.

Clay nodded.

She shook her head. "I would've kicked his butt if he tried that."

"Yeah, well, you're also taller and older than him. And you go to a different school. Some of us have something to lose."

An odd look flashed across Ayala's eyes, and Clay worried that he said something wrong for a moment. But that expression disappeared as quickly as it showed up.

Ayala looked around the school grounds, probably searching for Billy and his goons. Maybe they had detention. Or they had found another Ghoula kid—their amusement didn't begin and end with Clay but extended to all students without bleached platinum hair and violet eyes.

Satisfied that they weren't within butt-kicking range, Ayala began walking to the edge of the forest. Clay followed.

"Sounds like excuses, milk boy," she said, her tone light and teasing. She glanced over her shoulder, amusement flecked in her hazel eyes. "Don't tell me you cried, man."

Clay scoffed. "Really? Crying—"

"Over spilled milk," Ayala said along with Clay, though her words were with a smile and his weren't.

"Ha ha," Clay deadpanned.

A light drizzle picked up, pattering miles of forest canopy and streaming down broad green leaves. Clay's ratty sneakers squelched in the mud beneath the tightly woven grass; raindrops beat a staccato rhythm on his canvas bookbag. He glanced at Ayala's old boots, which were fraying at the seams. The sole of her right one was loose, flapping like a tongue with each step.

They passed beneath the forest canopy, now surrounded by the drumbeat of raindrops on leaves. Even with a light shower, the noise was so abundant and the foliage so close that it felt as if the rest of the world bled away, and they were just two kids going to their favorite spot to play. They trekked through hair-thin paths, moving with a confidence gained only by repetition and familiarity. Before long, all traces of civilization had vanished but for one dilapidated sign they came across.

NO TRESPASSING peeked through the foliage in faded red letters. Ayala brushed aside the leaves crowding the lower half of the rusted metal sheet, revealing the secret the jungle wished to hide: UNEXPLODED ORDINANCE AHEAD.

She chuckled. "How long's it been since we found this place?"

Clay exhaled, shaking his head slightly. "Shoot, I don't know. Five, six years?"

"All that time, and we still haven't found a mine that actually works," Ayala said. She glanced over her shoulder again, a scoundrel's grin slanting her lips. "Maybe we'll get lucky today."

Clay scoffed; he, for one, did not share Ayala's fascination with unexploded ordinance. "You'd just blow yourself up the moment you found one."

She shook her head, confident. "Nah. I'd disarm it."

Clay laughed. "You don't even know how to drive, Ayala."

She looked back to him, her face screwed up. "Hey, driving a car and disarming a mine are two totally different things."

"Alright, let's say you disarm a mine—now you have a mine. Ain't like you can sell it. Moment a peacekeeper spots you with one, your fingers are getting broken."

Ayala's eyes widened a touch, but with excitement rather than fear. "Nah, I'd just chuck it into a lake and watch it blow up." She rapped her knuckles, calloused and woven with tight-knit scars, against Clay's chest, right where the milk stain was. "Or I'd leave Billy a surprise."

Clay chuckled. "If only."

Clay and she had been wandering the old paths for five years now—since he was eight and she was ten—and they had never found a single mine that worked. The handful they came across were old, broken, defunct, or covered in so many cobwebs that they should have already detonated. Nowadays, they stuck to the paths that they knew were safe—their days of intrepid exploration were long past them, ever since one encounter too many with a giant, territorial Glade Spider.

Ayala walked past the sign, giving it a good-natured pat.

This area of the forest was silent; animals had long since learned to avoid these old paths. The oldest people in the region call this area the Wraithwood. The geezers didn't believe that it was the scent of undiscovered seismic concussion mines that kept the animals away: they believed it was the vengeful spirits of fallen warriors, those whose essence infused the old paths with an energy too bitter for most forest creatures, especially the noisy ones.

Clay and Ayala had also never found a vengeful spirit in all these years. Only Glade Spiders—venomous dog-sized arachnids—and insects lived in the Wraithwood.

Metal carcasses peeked out from the nearby undergrowth, fallen remnants of a battle long forgotten. But still the rusted beasts remain, adamant to be remembered by any who dared to tread the Wraithwood. The woods have long since claimed these carcasses as their own: Vines spiral around crumbling girders and struts; hornets and small spiders build nests and webs amidst the rusted bones.

The old paths formed their own web in the forest landscape; they overlapped and crossed, interweaving without a rhyme or reason. Some may have been used by wandering animals long ago, others by ancient villagers traveling between towns. Nowadays, only two children leave footprints against the soil.

As is, many modern towns and villages stand on the perimeter of the Wraithwood, connected by these old forbidden paths. Cutting through the old paths, Ayala could reach Clay's home in a third of the time it would take to walk around the taboo zone.

Ayala and Clay meandered from bush to bush, picking those berries that were safe to eat.

They would stop by ponds and look at their reflections, skip stones across the still dark surface.

Ayala would pick a flower and stick it in her hair, gaze upon the interwoven canopy of vine and leaf: all that which could calm her mind and chase away the voice in the woods that had haunted her dreams the night before. As it had the night before last, and the night before that.

Only Clay knew about those recurring nightmares—he was the only one she felt open enough with to share such a thing.

They did not stray from the safe and known paths, though they would stop and stare at the paths that were swaddled in giant ropy spider webs, marveling at the intricacies of their designs.

The two of them sat upon a log overlooking a stream, enraptured by the blissful orchestra of the water and the trees and the hum of insects, blended in beautiful harmony. Clay took the opportunity to take his first free breath in what felt like ages. He inhaled liberally through his nostrils and let the cool forest air fill his lungs.

"Hey, Ayala," he said in almost a whisper, as if to not disturb the serenity of the woods.

"Yeah?"

"Why don't we just stay here?"

She laughed. "You sound like you almost mean it this time."

"I mean, just look at this," he said, pointing to the majesty before them. "How could someone ever think of leaving all this?"

"Well, I'm sure the mines were a reason. But I know what you mean. . . . it's unreal."

Clay looked to Ayala. "Never too late to run away. They'd never find us here."

"I don't know if you know your mom like I do. But she always finds out. Always. It's kind of freaky, actually."

Clay chuckled. "Yeah. Speaking of which, sun's getting low. We probably should head back soon."

"I guess so."

Ayala made a move to lift herself off of the log before Clay grabbed her hand. "Hold on. Just a few more minutes."

The two sat down together, watching the sun's rays hover over the water, creating a kaleidoscope of colors that scattered through the stream.

It was ever quiet here. Ever peaceful. A place of almost sanctimonious respite from life.

At least, it was until the explosion.

And the boy.

And all that blood.

IV

LENA

What distinguishes a dream from a nightmare?

There is a popular Assyrian folktale about a woman in prison who dreamed of being free. She was serving a life sentence with a chance of parole. She'd been there so long, she forgot what she even did to end up there. Waiting out her sentence, she often found herself dreaming while awake of the smell of freshly cut grass, or the humidity of the air after fresh rain; of dreamed beaches that stretched along the curvature of the earth, as far and wide as the eye could see. She often wondered what she would do if she ever saw the sunlight again and was free to come and go as she pleased.

Her days became preoccupied with these thoughts. The prison allowed her to collect books on the objects of her obsession, of the world beyond. The days and weeks went by, lost in the years that consumed them. Every year, they'd dangle hope and freedom—the carrot—just out of reach. Yet, release would not come. Still, she kept her head down, lost in the prison of routine: of scrubbing and brushing the finest crevice of the prison, taking each beating in stride and eating the sludge they disguised as meals—bearing it all with smile. A smile that, over time, began to decay. Until the look of her was that of a hollow shell. And though she eroded slowly, painfully, she'd never lost hope, no. . . but she did let it go. Like a butterfly, it flew further beyond this prison—this body—to a place with the warmth of the sun, and howling winds, and a beach vast as the ocean beyond it. But she never cauterized the wound, so it bled her until she was dry.

✳ ✳ ✳ ✳ ✳

Lena had never seen the inside of a prison. Thank the gods for that, as Assyrians were known to have especially cruel prisons. No, she did her best to stay out of the way. She kept her head down, fortunate to have made it out of Ombada and to find a decent place for Clay to live. She used up her good looks while they lasted and then made out while the getting was good. She counted herself lucky that she'd made it out at all and with scars that, fortunately, couldn't even be seen when she was fully clothed. She wasn't strung out on drugs like so many others on their street, on that new "Luna" or whatever they called it now. And she had a steady, stable job. One that put food on the table for Clay and paid for school. For this, she also considered herself to be extremely lucky. She was doing well. She was *surviving*.

Why, then, was there this knot in her stomach? The whole way to the Estate, her stomach turned and churned something fierce. *What is it, girl?* Something about that conversation with Clay—she just couldn't get it out her head.

The boy comes home with a black eye and you tell him not to "let them steal his light"? What kinda crap is that? Looked 'im right in the eyes and told him to keep letting them whoop his behind, with a smile. Some mother you are. . . .

Self-deprecation was a new experience for her. She'd never questioned herself, not once in all of these years. Mama had said it was her sixth sense. She'd always known the way to get by. Didn't matter what it was, she could see the tide in the distance and had the good sense to get on it before building too deep in the sand. That's how she survived everything she'd seen.

She never thunk too deep and she *never* questioned her gut. Not when she was living in Ombada, or was out whoring, or was running off in the dead of night across Assyria. And if her gut told her to jack up a snarky Assyrian brat messing with her son, well, then that's the way it was going to be. She'd find a way out somehow. And she didn't question it.

Think and die. Move and survive.

It was too late. A dangerous question was forming in her head already:

What was she surviving for?

This line of thought ping-ponged its way about her head as she walked on the sidewalk, hands in pockets, up to the gate of the Estate. While it usually housed one dismissive guard or another, she was surprised to find that it was completely empty.

This was a first. She looked at her watch. *It is still a bit early, I suppose. Must be in the middle of a shift change,* she told herself. After waiting a few minutes in the damp morning cold, no one came. Eventually, she grew tired of shivering. Checking over her shoulders first, she finally mustered the courage to lean into the booth and press the button beneath the window. There was a click then a beep and before she knew it, the gates spread themselves with open arms.

She strode past the gates onto the concrete aisle that led to the back entrance. Past the maze of shrubbery and past the images of Dominus himself.

Still, she found it far too silent. Even when the Quaestor was away, servants busied themselves on the grounds and in the manse itself.

She moved past all of Reggie's typical workstations, also devoid of life. It wasn't like him to be late. This early in the morning, there weren't usually many others on the grounds, but Reggie, the groundskeeper, was always around for a wave and a smile. He always started his work at sunrise, "just as all the plants wake up to greet the day," he would say.

Lena considered the old man to be one of her few actual friends here, even though he was Assyrian.

And his calloused features were nowhere to be found.

Lena sighed with a bit of disappointment but continued on her way. The wooden heels of her shoes rapped against the concrete aisle, digging the already-snug shoes into the back of her ankles.

As she neared the back entrance, the shadow of the enormous estate fell upon her. Familiarity had long replaced rapture at its massive, esteemed grandeur. Past the maze of shrubbery, the tips of pointed arches and grand doors became more apparent in the morning fog. The Estate itself was made from a blend of brick and wood, abandoning the usual Assyrian stylings of marble, cement, and gold for the remnants of a long-forgotten era—a remarkable style, once referred to as "Shadowspire," although Lena had no such barometer for the word and therefore simply considered the whole appeal to be above her comprehension. The mahogany stain on the wood never faded, as Dominus Gratus demanded an extensive polish of the wood every six weeks.

Still, the Estate had an ethereal chill to it, one that even she couldn't help but notice, especially on mornings like this one. No, today it contained a coldness that felt unnatural. *Chilliness to the bone*. It was almost hypnotic. A calling, reminiscent of a trance that invaded all the precious places of one's mind. Before Lena knew it, she had reached the back door.

And it was open. Cracked.

Lena paused.

There was a sickly feeling in the air, a thickness that bunched her shoulders.

It had been a long time since she felt that tingle in the back of her skull, the kind that traveled down and settled in her gut like a length of bone in the wrong place.

Gently, she pressed on the door, so that it wouldn't make a sound.

The house was a wreck. Looked like some wild animal had turned loose upon the inside.

As manager of the house, she felt inclined to follow the wreckage and assess all the damage.

Dominus was known for his wild parties, but as far as she knew, he was out of town last night, and no party had done anything quite like *this*.

She followed the trail of broken portraits and shattered marble sculptures to a hall that led toward the basement. But as she turned into the hallway, a familiar scent made its way into her nasal passages.

The scent of blood and feces.

She covered her hand to her mouth to keep from retching.

Lena looked up and stopped short.

Bodies lay before her.

There were four of them, scattered about the Ghoula entrance. She had seen death before—rare was the Ghoula who hadn't, but she had never seen wounds like these before: where limbs were bent and crumpled, and flesh was ripped apart, and bluish smoke unfurled thereabouts.

It bent and wavered from the slit throat of the new guard, the one who had accosted Lena just the previous day, as if he had something to prove. A crimson canyon slashed across his peach-fuzzed cheek, the blood dried and caked onto his fair skin at its seams.

The guard captain himself, she found cratered into the wall, as though stuffed into it. A thick cloud of the pale blue smoke surrounded the stump where an arm once was. She found his arm a few steps away, adjacent to the body. The entirety of his torso was depressed, as if caved in by a massive sledgehammer or something of the like. Beneath his pale mustache, so often turned downwards with sternness, his mouth was popped open in some final moment of surprise.

The third guard's eyes were rheumy and unfocused, and Lena recognized her as one of the few who had treated her kindly. She couldn't bear to search the body for wounds.

And last was Reggie, his hedge clippers still in hand and flecked with blood. Even in death, his crow's feet were prominent, and if it weren't for the wounds across his chest, he might even look asleep.

Lena's hands curled into fists. Reggie was a good person, one of the best she had ever known, Assyrian or Ghoula, and he hadn't deserved to die like this. *Why didn't you run, you fool?*

She turned her gaze to the *Ghoula* entrance: The doors were open, the guard captain's key still lodged in the lock. She knelt next to Reggie's body, prying his fingers from the hedge clippers. They came away easily enough.

It was illegal for Lena to take one of the guard's weapons, but it wasn't for her to take Reggie's old clippers, still warm around the grips from the memory of him.

She took in a deep breath, staring at the open doors and summoning the strength she had relied upon in her youth.

And she pressed past the scent of death and decay.

It'd been some time since she felt that spark in her heart; her feet seemed to move of their own volition, her instincts having shoved her mind to some distant corner.

Some far-off part of her felt surprised at how easily the Lena of decades past took charge. The Lena who wasn't afraid to pull a knife on a man who thought he could get away without paying after using her. The Lena who choked a man out for beating on a friend. The Lena who knew how to play in the shadows of society, skirting the bounds of the law and doing what was required to survive.

Inside the manse, it felt even quieter. Stiller, like the whole house was holding its breath.

Stepping lightly, rolling her feet gently from heel to toe, Lena followed the thin trail of blood that marked the tile. It trickled through the mud room, winding out towards the hallway and snaking into the kitchen.

Déjà vu settled over her: padding in the same manner down a dark alleyway; scissors in hand, gripped by the blades to better jab into an eyeball; the husked memory of cigarette smoke in the back of her throat; eyes darting around, searching for any flicker of movement from the shade or the steam that billowed from pipes.

Yet these marble halls were a far cry from those bloodied alleys perpetually shrouded in night and death; the detailed stone figurines in stark contrast to the huddled bodies of dead and dying Ghoulas; the paintings of distant landscapes and endless beaches bore slim resemblance to dried blood, urine, and vomit.

Lena glanced to the blood on Reggie's hedge clippers, and she tightened her grip.

She listened a moment, trying to glean any hint of the intruder.

Nothing but silence and the lingering scent of corpses in her nose.

She padded into the kitchen, where a trickle of blood spread to dispersed droplets. She followed the drops to the counter, where they conglomerated in a thin puddle amidst disturbed kitchen rags.

Whoever had broken in had mended their wound here—no more blood trail to follow.

Lena sighed and looked back the way she came.

She was fooling herself if she thought she could take down whoever had killed three guards and poor old Reggie. Thinking that her bones and joints were the same as decades ago.

She could die here.

Slashed to pieces like Reggie.

And it'd be her corpse with smoking wounds that Clay would see, and he would have no one left.

A cold sweat drenched Lena, extinguishing that long-forgotten spark that had leapt up in her chest.

She could keep going on. She could do this for herself. For Reggie. She could risk her life as the manager of the house, as the avenger of a kind old man.

But she couldn't risk her life as a mother.

She placed the clippers on the counter, turned back the way she came, exited the mansion, and screamed for help as loud as she could.

V

CLAY

Blood, painted across the path—flecked on leaves, smeared across the grass.

Turning around the corner, and there he was—a man with black, tail-like braids, indigo eyes, a face covered with sweat. His eyes fluttered, delirious and pleading for help.

Clay had never seen this person before.

The bloody man's hands were clamped around his thigh; Clay looked and regretted it immediately.

Splinters and mangled flesh and blood, all blended together and vomiting crimson. A strange steam, colored a soft translucent blue, billowed from the wound and all the others on his leg.

Bile crawled up Clay's throat—he couldn't look at the leg without imagining his own in that state, without imagining the pain and shock.

Clay froze.

The hole in the man's leg burbled audibly and gushed out blood. He had since fallen aback, eyes half-closed.

"Oh gods, it sounded like pasta," said Ayala, her voice choked with nausea.

Clay swallowed the feeling rising in his own throat. He wouldn't stand here, paralyzed like in the cafeteria.

Lonesome wouldn't just stand there and watch a man bleed to death.

Clay's legs moved before he willed them to; he pulled himself to the boy's side.

Ayala stood there a moment, her hand pressed against her mouth, looking across the blood-soaked foliage with widened eyes.

"Ayala! Help—it's bad—like, really bad."

Snapped out of her daze, she rushed over to her friend's side and looked at the leg.

"Oh man, it's really not better up close. What happened to him?"

"I don't know, but it's still bleeding!"

From a distance, the leg had looked mangled, and up close, it was an absolute mess: the most egregious wound had been the giant splinter the man just pulled out—the hole it had left was vomiting blood about Clay's hands, which were pressed against the wound; wooden shrapnel peppered the rest of the man's leg, leaving it an indiscernible mess of splinter, trouser, muscle, and blood; skin hung off the inner side of his calf, shredded and perforated; and the boy's ankle hung limp in his boot, which looked as if it had been chewed by three dogs.

"What do we do?" Ayala all but yelled, her fist jammed against her mouth.

Blood and blood.

It just kept bleeding and steaming.

"I don't know!"

The man was still upon the ground. His chest pumped up and down, though his eyes were closed.

"Blood here needs help," Ayala said.

"Yeah, no crap!" Clay felt like his brain was short-circuiting; all he could do was stare at the leg.

Lights formed at the edges of their vision—amorphous forms, like they had forgotten their shapes long ago.

A knot formed in Clay's throat; every time he tried to look at one directly, it faded from sight.

Wraiths.

After all those rumors, he'd never once seen them; yet, here they were, hovering around the half-dead man with a stark intensity. He shoved their presence from his mind—now wasn't the time to think about anything other than the man and this blood and that leg.

But what could they do? They were just kids.

Clay perked up and caught Ayala's eye. "Mom."

Ayala spread her hands, her eyes bug-eyed. "Look at him—Blood here's gonna bleed to death before we get to your house."

Clay was already standing, his blood-soaked hands gripping the man's ankle. "Just help me!"

"Alright, damn."

They started dragging the boy, and Clay couldn't ignore the path of blood left in his wake or the wraiths that clung and watched and judged.

VI

BLOOD

Blood. How easily the moniker had slipped over him, how quickly he had embraced the name himself. It was appropriate. It was his life. His purpose. His past. His future.

He was Blood.

He was standing in front of the orphanage. He felt the heat on his back: the fire crowded the orphanage, billowing upwards and outwards in flame and smoke.

Good. Let it burn.

A scream came from amidst the flames and crackling wood. Male. Adult. The Overseer.

Good. Let him suffer.

Blood stood outside, lined up beside Uxiah. He watched with no small amount of satisfaction as the orphanage's "caretakers" were executed before his eyes.

Hatred and satisfaction conflated in that moment.

It felt strange—to hate. He had almost forgotten the feeling.

Uxiah, a giant of a man, executed the last caretaker.

Was it only him and Uxiah who caused this mess?

It's been too long—Blood couldn't remember if others had raided the orphanage alongside the two of them. Maybe they had and he just forgot them. Wouldn't be a surprise. Memories from those years were blurred; the intensity of moments like this all but repressed anything else.

Uxiah faced the orphans, huddled together. Some of the children cried, others looked glad, and some simply had emptiness in their eyes.

"Do you hate me?" asked the giant man.

His answer was the crackling of flame, the fading whimpers of those still trapped inside. All the orphans were outside; Uxiah had gotten them all out before setting the place ablaze.

Blood had helped; he climbed the wall and unlatched the second-story window, stealing into the bunkroom and rousing the orphans, leading them to safety. Promising them freedom and a life of revenge, should they want it.

One of the few times he felt like a hero.

Uxiah nodded, a pleased look on his face. "You're free now, all of you. Free to pursue a life under the Empire—to toil and sweat and beleaguer your existence away until you're an unmarked grave visited by no one. Or you can make something of yourselves and live a life of steel and blood; come with me and you shall be remembered. Come with me and your grave shall be a monument."

Blood held nine winters at the time.

The vision began to fade—a dull off-white crept in from the edges of memory.

Those orphans didn't hesitate for a moment. They chose their path.

It was then years later, and Blood stood before Uxiah. Both of them were being watched over by one of the old guardians: a large head that stuck out of the whistling sands, its stone eyes regarding the two of them as if they were its progeny.

"There is a power in your blood, boy," said Uxiah, a heavy hand on Blood's shoulder. "Do you wish to unlock its potential? I warn you: It is not an easy path."

"If it is within my power, I shall do it," said Blood.

"You will be broken."

"I will become whole." Blood puffed out his chest, still sore from the last day's exercises. "I am ready for whatever it is I must do."

Uxiah nodded, his features blended between pride and sadness. He took his hand from Blood's shoulder and stepped back.

"Forgive me, then, for what I must do," said Uxiah.

The vision faded to a bone-white before the worst of the memory came.

Nothing comes without its price. Nothing. The scars upon his back are still tight. The burnt flesh on the soles of his feet still ached after a long day.

Such was the price of power, willingly paid in pain and blood.

He had held twelve winters then.

Then came the sight of a sunset forest, the shadows of the canopy distended and splattered across the thick undergrowth.

Wraiths floated along the path. Their forms would stoop near to the ground for a moment, as if studying something, and then they would float off to another area of the path.

He felt some odd connection to these wraiths. Somehow, he knew these were the souls of warriors. Those who had fallen in battle.

Were they like him when they had breathed this world's foul air?

The two kids who had stumbled upon him, just before he lost unconsciousness, followed those wraiths. Both the boy and the girl were dragging a great sheet of metal, on top of which was a half-conscious Blood.

He watched, a disembodied spectator to his own near-death, as the wraiths led the pair of children down these mine-filled, spider-infested paths. The faint-blue ghosts seemed almost like an escort. Though their forms flickered and pulsed between a coherent shape and an indiscernible mass of light, Blood felt a dutiful energy from them, as if they would lay down their second lives to ensure he lived.

He had no clue why.

This vision came and went, and ivory flashes often shifted him from one area of the jungle to the next.

Sunset lasted only for the first vision; it was night come the next, and the children were still struggling Blood's body along the path, guided by the dull blue-white light that came from the wraiths.

Blood noticed a curious steam unfurling from his wounded leg.

He should have felt grateful that it was keeping him alive.

Shouldn't feel this slight disappointment.

The wraiths stayed near to the children, as if they were protectors.

The girl had a battle-look on her, as if she had thrown up strong walls against her emotions. He knew that face well.

The boy struggled in contrast: His features often shifted between fear and pain; his eyes strained with the struggle of a long labor. A few more days like this, and the boy would lose the last of his baby fat. He's had a soft life—the girl, maybe not so much.

Guilt came upon Blood. He had no desire to yank someone from their soft baby-fat life. He hadn't meant to. These Ghoulas were good people. Better than he was. Than he would ever be.

Pale light bled his vision into something else.

Her face came to him then—as he last saw her, not as she should have appeared. Bloodied, her ear singed and her arm a mangled mess. She had been reaching up to him with her good hand, begging her to take her with him. But she would have slowed him down, enough for him to be caught. She was the last of their crew, and he had left her behind for the carrion.

These kids should've done the same for him. It was no less than he deserved.

A lifetime of peace and compassion couldn't make up for his mistakes.

He wondered if the Holy Man would ever forgive him for what he's done.

Once again, the scene before him changed.

In this quiet moment, watching the children heave this unconscious stranger through a darkened jungle, wraithlight their only guide, a sadness came upon Blood. He felt . . . doubt.

He wasn't quite sure what he doubted. But the feeling was strong, and it intermingled with a regret-tinged lament at . . . at what?

Childhood. That was the first word to come to mind.

He never had a childhood. And now here he was—robbing two more kids of what was left of theirs, even if they didn't know it.

Another ivory flash.

It was deep into the night. The taller wraith was floating alongside the girl and the boy. The light of the other one came from ahead on the path.

To Blood's surprise, the girl was speaking to the wraith. Not in the mother-tongue either—in common. Not just speaking—laughing. Dour laughter, born more of exhaustion than of mirth, but laughter nonetheless.

The wraith shifted about to the front of the children, facing them and floating backwards down the path.

Blood moved closer, trying to figure out what the other wraith was doing. It was in the canopy, amongst the web-strewn limbs, guiding a giant spider away from the children. It did so calmly, as one might lead a horse across a river, and the spider followed the wraith, captivated by its otherworldly light.

An ivory swath crept in from the edges of Blood's vision.

A numbness came to the tips of his fingers, and a calming sensation swept through his body.

Blood closed his eyes for a moment, and when he opened them again, a wraith was standing before him—the same one that had shepherded the spider. It was looking right at him. The wraith raised its hand, its palm facing Blood, and lowered it. The calming wave intensified, and an incredible feeling of peace heralded an off-white film that blanketed everything.

VII

LENA

Lena wrung her hands beneath the cool water. She had stopped scrubbing them half an hour ago and was now just mindlessly folding her palms and fingers over each other, again and again and again. They had long since pruned, and there was a slight sting prickling across her hands from her earlier scrubbing.

It was the kind of day to fall back into old habits.

Living in Ruka for so long, she had forgotten the lingering slime death left on the soul.

Dominus had questioned her when he returned. Interrogated, more like.

Even after years of dutiful service, of acting so impeccably that she rose above her station to become manager of the house, she *still* wasn't trusted.

Being the only one left alive was suspicious in and of itself, it would seem; some of the guards rationalized that she had let the killer in, that she had shown whomever-it-was to the vault and *allowed* them to steal the "item."

Lena had never heard of the "item" and never even knew it was in the trophy vault, but the look on Dominus's face when it was declared stolen . . .

She shivered and rubbed her thumb over a knuckle.

If she hadn't served so dutifully—if she wasn't so loved by Dominus and the staff—well, she feared that he would have killed her then and there, just to let out his frustration.

Gratus was not a kind master, but he was fair and level-headed. Lena had only seen him in such a mood once: the night of his father's death.

Ghoulas died that night; such wrath burned bright and quick, and consumed all left in its wake.

Lena hadn't begged like that since . . .

Her wringing hands paused.

She couldn't remember. So readily had she thrown away her pride and dignity, to grovel at the feet of men who could decide her death on a whim. She hadn't even thought twice about it.

She started scrubbing again. Water spilled over the edges of the washbasin.

Embracing the indignity of her station, she ranted through tears and begged. She swore that she called for help, that she had been a good *servant,* that she had never committed an infraction against the house or Dominus—anything to cause his anger to relent.

It wasn't enough. After more than a decade of obedience and excellence, she was fired. All for being where she was supposed to be when she was supposed to be there.

And even then, that damn Guard Captain—that balding ass whose son Lena suspected of bullying her own—had the gall to call her *lucky* to escape without punishment, that she should have *gratitude* for Dominus's mercy.

And to top it all off, Clay still wasn't home.

She had one rule for her boy: Come home before night fell.

The Curfew Man would come soon and if Clay wasn't here . . .

Every integrated town like Ruka—where Ghoulas and Assyrians lived together—had a Curfew Man. Typically some Assyrian hardass. Every night, around the twenty-first hour of the day, the Curfew Man went to each and every Ghoula residence to make sure that every family member was there for the night. Officially, it was meant to dissuade crime, but no one really bought that story.

If every family member wasn't accounted for, there were punishments. With each offense, the punishment grew: The first time, the family is levied a steep fine; the second time, the absentee Ghoula spends a few days imprisoned; the third time and onwards, they take a finger. It wasn't uncommon to see Ghoulas missing fingers in the Empire.

Clay had never missed curfew before, but Lena still worried—he'd stayed out past sundown before, but he'd never been out so close to curfew.

Lena eyed the clock's pendulum—it was almost the twentieth hour.

She paused scrubbing her hands, faintly noticing how they stung and cried with relief, and peered out of the kitchen window. The candlelight within the house was dim enough for her to see clearly into the night. She squinted her eyes, scanning the nearby woods for any hint of movement.

But it was cloudy tonight, and the trunks only loomed silent and still.

Lena withdrew her hands from the basin, planted them on its rim, and took a deep breath.

Clay must've been with Ayala. It wasn't uncommon for them to play in the woods past dark. And with everything happening at school, she couldn't blame him for wanting to keep the day alive as long as he could.

But dammit, why did he have to pick today to stay out late?

Lena felt her anger slough into anxiety, and her eyes glued to the window. Absent-mindedly, she moved to the washrag and gently dried her aching hands. The thin rag passed over and under her hands, and she stared into the thick shadows of the forest. Searching. Waiting.

And then a dim bluish light appeared deeper in the woods.

✻ ✻ ✻ ✻ ✻

For a moment, it was too much: wraiths at the edge of the forest, their otherworldly glow reflecting in the trail of blood that led to her front door, the bluish steam rising from the blood itself, the tall boy slung off Ayala's shoulder, his features diffused by the steam clinging to him, Ayala's distant expression, and then her little boy in the doorway, his hands stained crimson up to his elbows, his eyes so wide and wet that she just wanted to kneel and hug him.

Clay's words tumbled out. "Mom, we found this guy in the woods and I think he stepped on a mine and his leg is—"

She cut him off with a raised hand, still trying to get her senses in order. Ayala was still limping toward the house, and the girl even offered Lena a tired smile as she brought the strange man closer.

She took a deep breath, and she willed away the panic and confusion that had been clouding her mind.

She looked over Clay from head to toe—he was drenched in sweat but looked and acted unharmed.

She glanced at Ayala, seeing that she was in the same way.

Then her gaze followed the steam billowing from the strange man's leg, where blood trickled beneath mounds of mangled flesh.

He should have bled out already, she thought.

Then she pushed the thought away; regardless, this man needed help now.

She caught Clay's eye. His throat convulsed with a nervous swallow, and then his heavy breaths came again.

"Clear off the dining table," Lena told him.

She rushed out of the house, trying to avoid looking at the ghosts lingering at the tree line. They worried and terrified her, and it was easier right now to pretend they didn't even exist.

Lena met Ayala and shrugged the boy's other arm over her shoulders.

The steam rolling off the boy's body was warm.

Was he attacked by the thief from the mansion too? Lena thought, eager to examine him once they got him inside.

Ayala side-eyed Lena and, through laboring breaths, quipped, "How's it going, ma?"

Lena huffed. "Not now, Ayala."

Together, the two women trudged to the house, angling the body between them through the narrow doorway and into the kitchen. Clay rushed to help them with Blood once they entered the home. They maneuvered to the kitchen table, now cleared, and hoisted the limp form atop its surface.

Now bathed in the candlelight of the kitchen, Lena got her first good look at him. His frame was tall and athletic, with broad shoulders as if he had spent his formative years working on a farm. She scanned him from head to toe, her worry and panic growing with every inch of detail she absorbed.

His eyes moved back and forth rapidly, as if he were trapped in a nightmare. Sweat and blood glued his dark hair to his face. Tattoos crawled up his neck, pointed swirling designs laid out symmetrically.

Lena's mouth twisted. These were . . . not from anywhere within the Empire. She had never seen spiked curling designs like these.

Her eyes lingered on his hands. His knuckles were scarred and calloused, as if he'd spent his life punching splintering wood.

Most curious of all was his face. Underneath the sweat, blood, and muck—the gaunt cheeks and sunken eyes—was just a *boy*, not a man. A *boy*, no more than a few years older than Clay.

Lena turned to Ayala, "You see that cabinet over there? There should be some gauze way in the back. Clay, bring the rubbing alcohol and that kitchen towel. I'll look for something to treat these splinters."

Ayala turned to go retrieve the items, but not before bumping into the table, causing it to shake. Blood let out a shrill cry that shook Ayala before going limp once again. She stared blankly at the boy, frozen.

"Ayala, hurry!"

She snapped out of it and got to work looking under the cabinet. Equipping herself with gloves and a pair of pliers, Lena returned to the boy's side. The children dropped their items off.

"Is that it? What else can we do?" asked Clay.

"You can go in the other room and wait. I need to focus."

"But I can help! I want to—"

"Clay!" she snapped. "Please, just go in the other room. We don't have time for this."

"C'mon," said Ayala, hooking her arm into his own and pulling him into the living room. He relented and followed her.

Lena tore her gaze from the children's backs and studied the blood-covered boy.

70

The leg was in tatters, as if tattooed with birdshot. Lena didn't have the knowledge or skill to fix this mess, but she'd try her best.

It took an hour to find and wrestle pieces of shrapnel and wood from pockets of meat along the leg. The boy had succumbed to shock, so resistance wasn't an issue.

At this point, most of the large pieces were taken care of, save for one large bastard of a piece that was too stubborn to come out. Now, there was just the smaller pieces of debris to deal with. She realized that soon she'd have to decide between retrieving every piece peppering the leg or treating it to prevent infection. Understanding time was not on her side, she opted for the latter. She found a topical antibiotic from within the bathroom cabinet and rushed back to Blood's side. But by then, something strange was already occurring.

A faint blue glow radiated underneath the wound. Although clearly unconscious, the boy was exerting a large amount of energy, straining himself to manifest . . . whatever it was she was seeing. Within a matter of seconds, his flesh began to pulsate and tighten around the bastard piece. It moved to and fro, coaxing it further outward until it was protruding almost entirely out of the boy's leg.

Lena allowed herself five seconds to be surprised before springing into action yet again. She grabbed her pliers and pulled the piece out, casting it aside onto a pan along with the other trinkets she'd recovered. Immediately, the boy let go and his body went limp yet again.

What the hell are you? Lena pondered as she studied the wound, watching as the glow retreated until there was no evidence of the phenomena she'd just witnessed.

She continued with the application of the ointment and finally to the bandages. As she did so, she gave herself permission to study him again. Her eyes traced his body, scanning for anything she'd missed, from his feet and grisly leg wound up to his waist and finally his shirt. That's where she'd noticed it.

A second wound had leaked through the shirt.

She rushed to the wound, rolling his shirt up until it was visible. This was not the same as the other wounds. It was succinct and more precise.

She knew a knife wound when she saw one.

The good news: It had already been treated and no longer posed a serious threat. She figured it had healed rapidly, just like what she saw with the leg. All that was left was a thin gash, already stitching itself together.

The bad news: A few inches above the gash, on the boy's oblique, was a curious symbol. A brand, more like. A shield with a sun in its center, its rays carved like hooked blades, flairing outward in every direction. There was only one meaning, no mistaking it:

HARRAKA.

And she just invited one into her house.

VIII

LENA

A *Harraka.*

The first in fifteen years, and her damn fool son brought him into her home.

She paused a moment and braced herself against the counter behind her. She placed her hand on her stomach, pressing her diaphragm, trying to force herself to breathe again. Lena looked from the boy—the terrorist—to the blood that painted her house. To the bluish steam that rose from his wounds.

He hadn't been attacked by the mansion thief: He *was* the mansion thief.

And here she was, tending his wounds. Saving his life.

She almost cursed her son for his kindness.

She caught herself and instead damned the world they were in.

Lena studied the boy's face again.

I could kill him here and now. Slit his throat. Act like he broke in here too, looking for shelter or a place to lay low, she thought.

It would be an act of protection. Of mercy, really, before the Assyrians caught up with him. And maybe she'd protect herself, her son, Ayala and . . .

The thought of killing this boy, her own kind, felt unabashedly wrong and sent bile crawling up the back of her throat.

But what other choice did she have?

Lena went to the knife block, sliding out the largest she could find.

With a white-knuckled grip, she approached the Harraka's throat.

Her mind was scrambling, looking for alternatives. Her survivor's instinct blared loudly, telling her that this was the only way to protect what she'd built, all that she'd sacrificed to ensure she survived. *That Clay survived.*

If not, then what was it all for?

She touched the blade to the Harraka's throat, pressing down enough that bluish steam curled around the metal, already mending where it split his skin.

Lena hesitated.

She's been here before—knife to a sleeping person's throat, the tang of blood, the way she'd scrub her hands raw, repeating to herself that *I did what I had to to survive.*

And where did surviving get her? A cozy cell in a world where just being at the wrong place at the wrong time is enough for her to be punished, where even after decades of dutiful service—of being a *good* Ghoula—she's still the first to be threatened with the lash and rod, the first to be let go "for security measures."

And her boy and even Ayala . . . lord, this was just an act of kindness, and it would spell their deaths. All because they saved the life of a stranger.

She could kill this boy beneath her blade.

A flick of the wrist is all it would take.

And what would change?

Tomorrow, she might again find herself in the wrong place at the wrong time, and she was all out of luck.

Tomorrow, Clay might act like a good person should and still find himself facing the gallows.

Tomorrow, the crushing boot on the back of her head will weigh no less.

But this boy's tomorrow . . . it was different. It had hope in it, even if he's the kind to kill a poor old soul like Reggie to reach that dawn.

There's a purpose beyond just surviving to him. To all Harrakas.

She looked at this struggling boy. He was a fighter—that much, she knew for sure. Even now, barely hanging onto life, he was still fighting. For what, she wasn't sure, but it reminded her of the woman she used to be, or maybe the one she thought she would've become. A woman with a flame in her soul. A woman with a *dream*.

This boy was literally steaming, so dedicated was he to his own purpose.

And here she was with a knife to his throat.

"Dammit," she breathed, tossing the knife onto the counter.

She couldn't kill this boy.

Then what could she do? Ghoulas have been killed for much, much less than what she's done here. And there would be no mercy for Clay or Ayala.

She scanned the kitchen and foyer: blood up to and on the door, blood across the rug she'd spent a month saving up for, blood on the corners of walls, blood on the ever-dirty kitchen tiles, blood on the counter, blood on the kitchen table. She looked up and saw the Harraka's bluish steam misted across the ceiling.

If they started scrubbing now, all hands on deck. . . .

Lena checked the clock and cursed.

Half an hour until the Curfew Man came.

Not nearly enough time for all this blood.

She then looked out the northern window and cursed again. Torchlight broke the dim of dusk, a cloud of amber light just past the zenith of the hill separating her home from Ruka proper. Too much torchlight.

Of course.

They wouldn't just send a Curfew Man, not after what happened at the mansion today—no, there'd be an inquest traveling from home to home, interrogating Ghoulas and searching for the slightest hint of suspicion.

And Lena had much, much more than just a hint on her kitchen table.

The Harraka roused.

Twitched.

Bolted upright on the table, eyes wide and wild.

And he was quick. Lena never took her eyes off him, and in a blink, he was standing on the other side of the table, the knife she held earlier in his hand. His stance was half-crouched and almost feral, and though he favored his good leg, the boy held himself with a warrior's ease.

"You were going to kill me," he growled, his voice low and steady, hoarse with pain and disuse.

She didn't know how he could know that. She didn't care.

Lena pushed her tongue against the inside of her mouth and cocked her head. "Should I have?"

His breathing was heavy and focused, and his legs were bent, as if he was about to leap over the table and plunge the knife into her chest.

He inched a foot forward, but he stopped short when Lena pointed her finger at him.

"Calm down, boy," she said. "I just saved your life, and I'm about to save it again, so sit still and open your ears." He hesitated, then, to her surprise, the boy lowered his guard, almost as if against his own will. It was almost childlike in a way. Lena decided she would use that to her advantage.

"See that torchlight in the distance?" she said, nodding her head to the window.

Still tense, the Harraka whipped his head to glance through the window, and then returned his gaze to Lena.

"That there's the Curfew Man and a Citizen's Inquest. There'll be peacekeepers there, and they'll be armed, and they'll be looking for Ghoulas to lynch for what you did at the mansion today."

The Harraka was stone, no muscle bending to her accusations.

"Yeah," Lena said. "I know what you are, what you've done." She took a step forward, and just then noticed the sting of her nails digging into her palms. "That groundskeeper was a good person— you put that knife on the counter, boy."

His jaw clenched and she thought she could hear a low growl emanating from him. He pointed the knife directly at her throat.

She raised her hands, slowly. "We really don't have time for this."

The Harraka placed the knife on the table, still within reach, though his unblinking eyes watched her closely. "The guards attacked me, so I killed them," he said. There was a simplicity to his words, a matter-of-factness that was defensive in its own right.

Lena looked through the window. It looked as if sunset were repeating itself; she could spot silhouettes among the amber glow now. Lots of them. She knew this was just the beginning. They'd never stop hunting until they found their pound of flesh.

"Listen," Lena said, "I don't know you from Adam. You may still kill me after all this. But if you're a Harraka, then my guess is maybe we have the same enemy."

Lena pointed to the back of the house, towards Clay's room. "Those are good kids. One of 'em ain't mine, but. . . . she might as well be, and I'll be damned before I let my kids die because they had the heart to save you."

His arms tightened around each other, the knuckles showing white through his dark skin. He looked down.

She studied him a moment, the torchlight in the distance growing stronger. Those men had a purpose, just like this boy with his cold blue steam and strange powers.

Purpose. What an elusive concept. Had she *ever* had one?

Maybe not, she realized. It occurred to her that her entire life was the sum of fleeting impulses and instincts—of running, hoping, searching for something worthwhile. Something worth waiting for.

That would be Clay's inheritance: a life of survival and fear.

Wait. . . . maybe . . . there could be one more thing. . . .

"I need you to save them," Lena said. "Get them out before that . . ." she pointed to the growing torchlight ". . . gets here. Get them to safety. Get them to the Harrakas."

Blood's hard exterior dropped for a moment, his eyes shying away from her wanting gaze. "It doesn't work that way."

"I thought you guys were supposed to help those in need? What kind of hero wouldn't save two kids?"

"You don't know what you're asking. I'm no hero."

There was a shocking vulnerability behind his words. Lena didn't have time to care.

"I *know* my kids are walking freaking corpses so long as they're in the Empire!" Lena took a breath, looked to the window, and tried to center herself as much as possible. "So, you *are* going to take them with you. You understand?"

He nodded.

"I don't know what's going on between you and the wraiths, but the Wraithwood's your best chance of escaping."

His brow furrowed slightly and he glanced at the window which faced the woods. "I would've thought you'd leave me to the dogs. Be a lot easier for you."

"Yeah, would be. For today. But our real troubles would still be there tomorrow."

Thoughts seemed to roil beneath his gaze. Then he looked to the western window, where distant wraithlight still lingered in the wood . . . watching, waiting.

"What about you?" His tone was level and low, tinged with apathy though with a hint of care.

Lena pushed her tongue against her cheek. She expected to feel fear, some kind of terror, but she didn't.

She looked to the fire on the horizon and felt something ignite within her chest. She moved around the table, toward the kitchen. "I think I'll stay." If they came across an empty house, it'd only give them cause to search the area. But if they verified that someone was here . . .

The Harraka tensed and crossed his arms again, though he didn't move away from her as she stepped by his side.

Lena picked up the knife, the same one she had considered killing the Harraka with. The same one he had considered killing her with.

Lena slipped the knife into her belt, and for a moment she felt like a teenager again. "I'll buy you whatever time I can. Got it?"

"Yeah." He almost sounded sad.

"Look at me."

He did so.

Lena pointed to the back of the house again. "Clay and Ayala. Those're the names of the kids you owe your life to. Repay your debt to me by saving them, but your debt with them ain't squared by this. Got it?"

He nodded.

"Alright," she said. His eyes seemed genuine enough. "I'm gonna . . ." her voice broke. She swallowed, took a breath, and tried again. "I'm gonna go talk to them. You linger by the door, in the hallway. I don't want you out of sight or hearing until I see you running away with them kids. Got it?"

"Hmph," he grunted. But he moved as instructed.

Each step hurt, and Lena channeled that pain into something sharp. Something that can cut through all that fire approaching.

This'd be the last time she saw Ayala.

That she'd see her little boy.

Oh, she was going to wreak hell on those Assyrians. For every year of being treated like something less than a human, used like a mule, cast out like an animal.

I'll show them what kind of teeth a cornered animal has.

And then she was outside Clay's door, and she could hear him and Ayala talking within, their voices hushed and rushed with worry.

She lingered a moment, just taking in the door.

It was little more than wooden planks nailed together, slim gaps from where the wood's been weathered by time. The handle was a steel knob which would never tighten right, no matter how many times she twisted that screw.

Seemed like the strongest door in the world right now.

"They're getting closer," said the Harraka, jarring Lena back to the present.

She didn't even look at the window; she grabbed the flimsy knob, twisted, and stepped into her son's bedroom. Clay and Ayala's conversation came to a quick halt, and both kids looked to Lena and then beyond, to the Harraka lingering in the hall with his arms crossed. Clay sat on the edge of his bed on the left side of the room, and Ayala was sitting against the right wall, her arms looped around her knees.

"Blood's better!" Clay said, his eyes and smile wide.

Blood? Lena thought. *Is that what they call him?*

Ayala looked more confused than relieved, and she narrowed her eyes at the strange boy.

Lena approached her son as he said, "How'd you fix him that quick, ma?"

She knelt in front of him and hugged him tight; with some hesitation, he wrapped his arms around her too.

Where do I begin? Lena thought.

She had never felt so powerless.

She pulled back from the hug, stood, and turned so that she could see both Ayala and Clay. In the beat of silence that followed, the air grew thicker, and Clay's smile fled; concern mounted in both children's eyes.

"I need you both to listen to me, and don't speak until I'm done talking. Alright?" Lena said, her voice measured and calm.

Both kids nodded.

"We are going to have go away for a while, and quickly. The Curfew Man is going to be here any minute now and we can't be here when he arrives. Pack a bag. Only bring what you can carry. We'll have to move fast and for a long time. I know you've got questions, but for now, I really need you two to trust me."

The two children turned to each other and shared a look of shock and confusion. They must've been waiting for the punchline.

"Move it. Now!" she shouted, clapping her hands.

The kids hopped off the bed and sprang into action. Clay emptied the books and binders from his bookbag and began looking for items to stow. They rummaged—panicked—through all the dirty clothes in his hamper and the pile splayed out on the floor.

"You've got two minutes. I'll meet you by the backyard door," Lena said, grabbing a shirt from the pile and handing it to Blood, closing the door behind her.

The children came clumsily down the hall clobbering the wooden planks with their heavy footsteps all the way down.

"Got everything you need?" Lena asked them.

They nodded.

"Good. Now, we'll have to be moving. We still have a few m—"

She was interrupted by a tug on the sleeve of her jacket. She looked down to see Clay looking up at her, his round eyes big and wide.

"Mom," he said, "did we do something wrong?"

The look in his golden eyes cut right through her. A lump caught in her throat, and a white film crept in from the edges of her vision. She knelt beside the two of them.

When she struggled with the words, she shook her head. "Absolutely not," she said finally. "I wish I had the courage to do what you two did. It's too easy nowadays to pass a person suffering in this world, to keep going by. I'm proud of you."

"But we still have to run?" asked Ayala.

"Afraid so."

"Why? What did we do that was so bad?"

Lena opened her mouth to answer, but Clay beat her to it. "It's . . . it's because he's a Harraka, isn't it?"

Lena folded her lips, blinked, and nodded. "How did you know?"

"I heard him say it, when he was going in and out earlier," said Clay. His eyes fell to the floor, avoiding her gaze. "But I didn't think it'd be like this, mama. I swear!"

The echo of a far-off knock reverberated throughout the house. They were next door. Time was running short.

"They're already next door," said Blood. "We gotta go now!" And he'd already begun to move. Turning toward the door, Blood wedged himself between Lena and the kids, pushing them toward the door.

There wasn't enough time to say all she wanted to. A billion things raced through her mind and none of them seemed right. Lena pulled away from the kids, a hand on each of their shoulders. She squeezed, trying to memorize the feelings of their shoulders: Clay's, sloped and soft; Ayala's, thin but corded with muscle.

"Go on; get out of here," she said, nodding her head to the Harraka, who was already lingering at the back hall.

"What about you?" Clay asked, looking back past Blood's broad shoulders.

Lena glanced at the window, then faced her son again. "I'll stay behind to distract them: draw them away and slow them down. Then I'll meet the three of you at the river."

She glanced to the Harraka, who met her gaze knowingly. He nodded, as if he approved of her lie.

She wouldn't give Clay or Ayala time to digest it. She pushed them—maybe harder than she should've—towards the Harraka and out of the house. "Now go, and don't stop running. I'll see you soon."

Lena backtracked out into the hall and squared her gaze on Blood.

"You better guard them with your life; you hear me?" Blood's eyes met Lena's with a steel resolve.

He nodded. "Yeah."

"The river is just past the Wraithwood, on the other side." Lena made a shooing motion with her hand. "Now get out of here! Go!"

They went, their footsteps heavy against the cheap wooden floor, and Lena almost couldn't bear to look as a fugitive ran away with the two people she loved most.

What a world.

When they reached the far end of the hall and Ayala went for the door, Lena felt that she should say one last thing to those two children who had been the happiest parts of her entire life.

But nothing came to mind.

And then they were gone, and she was alone, and it was quiet.

There was no time to grieve. She immediately went to work.

Darting toward the kitchen, Lena ran to the stove. Cranking each of the four coils far as she could, she smelled the thick musk of kerosene as it filled the room. She swiped the long red lighter next to the stove and aimed its tip beneath each stovetop. She listened as the antique oven struggled to ignite, clicking as it tried to catch flame.

Click, click . . .

No flame yet.

Three sharp cracks rumbled outward from the foyer: They had arrived, and they were knocking.

Click, click . . .

Still no damn flame—she should've replaced this old lighter years ago.

Click, click . . .

"Hey! Anyone home?!" called a gruff voice from the door. The knocks grew more powerful, and a flimsy door like that wouldn't hold up to a kick.

Click, click, click—fwoom.

A plume of blue flame leapt from the stove top, its yellow fingers flickering wildly as it reached up toward Lena's face. She didn't dare let go of the lighter's trigger, keeping the flame alive as she transferred it to each of the four burners. Eventually it settled onto each of the four stovetop eyes.

Quickly, Lena burrowed beneath the kitchen sink, scavenging for every dishrag, cloth, and alcoholic substance she could find.

Once again, she felt her mind shoved to some distant corner, her movements guided only by instinct and desperation. In what felt like only a moment, she had a bundle of rags in her hands, drenched in alcohol and anything else she thought would feed the flames.

It sounded like someone was just beating the hell out of that poor front door, and beneath the pounding was the steady hiss of the stove.

"Open up! Citizens' Inquest!"

A harsh voice, drenched in impatience and loathing.

She dumped the pile of alcohol-soaked rags onto the stove. Flames leapt onto the ranks of rags and trash so quickly that they caught her hands and forearms too, running across where the alcohol had dripped from the rags onto her hands.

She had never been burned before, yet even now, as she beat the flames melting her skin out, the pain felt distant. She didn't even bother looking at her hands and arms once they were freed of flame.

She focused all her will upon the stove, watching and ensuring that it would grow and flourish as she needed it to. She watched, and she was captivated.

The beating of the door, the yelling and cursing, the pain screeching across her hands—it all began to fade, warping into echoes in the wake of the ever-growing fire.

She remembered the young girl, the Lena of years' past, in Ombada. She who stared into that flame all those years ago. Her eyes had begun to water from the smoke, but as with now, the pain then was distant and insignificant, for Clay had cozied into her breast, his nose red and wet in the cool winter air. He hadn't begun to walk and venture off on his own yet.

It seemed so easy to keep him safe back then.

She wanted to tell her younger self to squeeze him tight and never let go.

That younger Lena thought she could get it all right. Back then, she had something worth fighting for. A promise, carried on from her mother and her mother before her.

Mohi'ri.

She would never get to see that promise come to light. Another generation waiting for light and fading into darkness.

But she took solace in knowing the dream would continue.

Burning the house would provide the perfect cover for their escape. By the time they finished scavenging the house for bodies and identifying them, Clay and Ayala would be a day's journey away. They'd get farther faster without her, and they'd be harder to track. She hated to lie to them, but Clay would never leave her behind. It wasn't much, but it would have to do. She'd have to trust Blood with the rest.

Fire had protected Clay then. Fire will protect him now.

After consuming all of the burning trash and alcohol, the fire spread to the countertops, up to the ceiling and down onto the floors. It was ready. As was she.

"What in Cyrus's name is going on in there?" she heard him say. "Open the door this instant!"

At one time, the Curfew Man's shouts frightened her. But as she listened to him, all she could hear now was trembling insecurity, masked beneath panicked cries.

"That's it—we are coming in!"

There was a crash from the front door. They were in.

"Right on cue," she thought. She checked the knife beneath her shirt, just to make sure it hadn't gone anywhere.

Lena took a few shallow breaths to get herself worked up, and then she ran to the foyer, seeing the Curfew Man at the head of a mob of platinum-haired, violet-eyed men. The Curfew Man had stopped short in the foyer itself, looking around wild-eyed at the blood and the flames.

"Oh thank heavens you're here!" she said, wailing emphatically. "My house is on fire! Please, I need you to help me. My son is trapped!"

IX

CATO

Salty mist splattered the young woman's face, stirring her from slumber. Her eyes fluttered open, and she looked around, seeing naught but ocean in all directions—so, they were still in the Catalian Sea.

She took a moment to absorb her surroundings. She saw the beading sun hanging amidst the sky, surrounded by nimbus clouds that were eager to hide its light. Lightning tumbled in the distance, growing closer. Turbulent waters fought fiercely against the rhythmic strokes of the boatman's oars. The sea beat the rowboat as though it had some kind of vendetta, and it was clear that the thin man was struggling to keep the boat from capsizing.

She grabbed her briefcase, flecked with saltwater, and feared that its contents were ruined.

"Ah, missy 'wake," he said to her, in the singsong rolling lilt the Venitane locals in this region often carried. "Bad wata's. Very bad."

Totally focused on her heavy silver briefcase, she ignored him. Unlatching the sturdy box, she flipped it open and saw, with relief, that its singular object was unharmed. It was a thin small box, no bigger than what a fine necklace would be packaged in. Its rich dark wood hadn't been scoured by the sea spray, and its surface was bare of details except for golden latches and a peculiar symbol etched on a corner. The wooden container was surrounded by paper packaging that filled the briefcase, ensuring that it would not be jostled or harmed on the journey.

The boatman muttered a prayer under his breath.

She then looked to the boatman and saw that his arms were trembling. "Is it going to be a problem?" she questioned.

"Ah, for you? No problem. For me? Big problem. Storm comin'; look, storm comin'," the ferryman said, pointing to the gathering clouds above them.

"How far until land?"

"Ah, not far, missy, not far."

Cato scowled and eyed him down. "My name isn't 'missy,' and it sure isn't my title, *Ghoula*. It's Sergeant Nemoida—got it?"

The man's gaze fell to the floor of the boat. "Yes, Sergeant Nemoida."

The girl sat back. With her eyes closed, she reclined against the wooden board that was the tail of the boat. She took one deep inhale and pressed it out in a measured pulse, trying to get rid of the frustration that *missy* had brought up. She hated being treated like some little girl. She hated being stuck in this sea.

"I hate the water," she muttered. Unfortunately, there was no other way to get where she was going. The Emerald Isle was a giant island off the southern coast of the Imperial Heartlands, and she wasn't allowed to charter a hovercopter for this operation. *"Too high-profile,"* her handler had said, offering no further explanation.

"Wata' hate you too, mi—Sergeant Nemoida."

She flashed a glare at the taxi driver, letting him know that she hadn't wanted his opinion.

He spoke to ease the tension: "It's bad omen, ya know?"

His guest didn't bother to reply.

"Wata' always nice. Always smooth. Now, three days, black sky come and wata's angry. Very angry. Dunno why," he said, and he trembled, mumbling another prayer in hushed tones to calm the angry tempest.

Great, she thought, *just my luck.* She reached into her left breast pocket, pulled out Ukkadian bourbon, uncorked the lid, and took a much-needed swig.

The rough waters and a simpleton's superstitions were the least of Cato's concerns right now. There was only one bad omen she concerned herself with, and she was headed straight for him.

✳ ✳ ✳ ✳ ✳

She did not hurry to the vehicle waiting just beyond the dock. Her feet fell into a slow plod as she marched down the wooden steps. Each step closer felt like leading the procession to her own funeral.

Raindrops slid off leaves, down trunks, through drainage pipes, and into storm drains. Cato took her time walking, reveling in the feeling of rain on her skin. She didn't worry about her uniform in the rain—it was made of a hydrophobic weave, and so the water beaded and rolled off the fabric. The weave was a recent invention, one allowed by the technological renaissance the world was entering, and Cato was one of the first to wear such a uniform.

She basked in the sights and sounds of the port town and greenery—broad-leaved bushes, knotted trees with sprawling leaves and dark wood, thick clumped grass—coated the cliffs that hugged the shore. Even in the rain, landscapers were busy trimming the nearby jungle here and there, keeping it away from the classy Assyrian town. Sloped rooftops, colored blues and oranges, topped wood-and-stone buildings. The constant hum of crystal machinery—dock cranes, cars, trucks, temperature units—suffused the air, fading quickly to the background of workers calling to one another, vehicles rushing by, and the indeterminate clanging and clinking of a town at work.

She caught the disparaging expressions of a few people at the outdoor bar. Cato grew all too conscious of the color of her hair and her eyes; unlike many Assyrians caught up in the latest fad, she hadn't bleached her hair platinum and she didn't wear violet contacts. She was a Cynical Ranger, and she couldn't care less about fashion. Yet, too many Assyrians did, to the point of seeing anyone without such hair or eyes as volunteering to be ostracized and shamed. They could seemingly smell that she did not belong. The rich, retired snobs made sure to stop their conversations and card games to convey the message.

She was familiar with the stares—recognized their pitiful and embarrassed looks—but she reminded herself that she had nothing to worry about. *Go ahead, have a look.* There were no cracks in her foundation, and Cato had spent most of her life making sure of that.

She reminded herself that she was an Ace in the Assyrian military, a sharpshooter credited with over eight confirmed kills with no signs of slowing down. As a woman at the humble age of nineteen with only a few years in the service, that made her a prodigy, and she was damn proud of that fact.

But her accomplishments weren't painted on her face, sprinkled around her eyes. It was always the first thing a stranger noticed and the first thing a stranger judged her by: her *Crystalli Squamae*, her scales—the rubine crystals flecked around her eyes, embedded in her face as firmly as her eyebrows. Not only did they mark her as something 'other,' a creature not to be trusted, but they also shouted to the world that she, Sergeant Cato Nemoida, Cynical Ranger, was born to a family who meant nothing to the world.

Being a commoner born to some forgettable parents in some backwater town was a big chip that didn't go away easily, especially in the Empire. Strangers loved to remind her of it.

Even in uniform, she couldn't escape such judgment. For her, the sharp white-and-red outfit was a shield, a crisp warning that she was untouchable to all.

Cato knew that the uniform kept people stabbing her with only sharpened glares and not knives. It was common for children born with *Crystalli Squamae* to find themselves alone in the woods with no way home, for adults with the crystalline scales to find themselves bleeding out in an alleyway for no reason except for how they look.

She refused to give them the satisfaction of seeing her squirm. She rolled her shoulders back, held a soldier's gait, and stared them all in the eyes until they uncomfortably averted her gaze. She'd slit all their throats if she could.

As delicious as that prospect sounded, Cato still couldn't believe she'd let them get to her. Normally, such a pathetic attempt at intimidation would not have scathed her so. In fact, she craved it, using it as fuel to propel her to the top.

But today was not a normal day.

✳ ✳ ✳ ✳ ✳

Her cab was nice; whoever was running this operation had connections. It was a newer model, powered by crystals rather than fuel, and as such it was quieter than most other cars. Since there was no engine, both the front and back of the car were trunks. A backup wheel was connected to each side of the cab, near the driver's door and the front passenger's door. The driver of the ebony vehicle, a sleek four-door car with an obsidian-like paint job, greeted her as she rushed in, just in time to beat the downpour of rain.

He *should* have opened the door for her since she was a Cynical, and especially since she was holding a briefcase. It was common sense to laud the agents of the Empire with the utmost respect.

She grunted to herself, surprised that she was even thinking about something that trivial—she wasn't normally the kind of person who was so arrogant as to care about something like that.

Maybe she was still rankled from those nobles' stares.

She shook her head: It wasn't that.

The car idled, its purring engine humming beneath rainfall's drumbeat. "You know where we're going?" she asked the driver.

He glanced to her in the rearview mirror, his dark eyes lingering on the crystals around her eyes and—for fear of being caught staring, most likely—he dropped his gaze, muttering, "Yes, Cynical."

"Then why are we still here?" Cato asked, unable to keep the exasperation from her voice. It had been a long journey—by train, then by boat, and now by car.

"Yes, ma'am," said the driver hurriedly. His hand went to the center console on the dashboard: a flat-surfaced panel with only a dial in its center. Embossed in the dial's face was a smooth polished crystal, its hue rubine and sparkling even beneath a cloudy day; it looked the bigger sibling to the smooth crystals that flecked Cato's face.

She pressed a button by her seat, rolling up the partition between the back and the front.

She hated being reminded of her face every time she was in a car. Or a train. Or a city.

Anywhere that wasn't on horseback in the wild, really.

She gazed out of the window, observing the landscape. As they traveled, the tropics crowding the shore thinned into rugged hills and rolling terrain. Mountains rose in the distance, so far away that only their silhouettes loomed above the horizon. Many of the hills were claimed by vineyards and farms, which partitioned the land neatly into lines of trees, crops, vines, and roads. Smoke rolled out of few-and-far-between farmhouses and estates. Both farmers and their trucks rolled lazily over hills and through valleys. Clouds hung thick across the sky, and the rain lessened the further they drove from the shore.

A sickly feeling agitated the pit of her stomach. It wouldn't be much longer now. Normally, Cato met the end of travel and the beginning of a mission with excitement.

Though, normally, she wasn't traveling to meet a legend. Not just a legend, but also her own personal hero—her god.

"And whatever you do . . . don't look him in the eyes."

It was a curious order, she had to admit. Though the whole thing was awfully strange from the get-go.

Her orders were opaque, her mission an enigma that few people were privileged to know. Even fewer people knew the details of said mission. Unfortunately, Cato could not count herself among that number. It was off the books, possibly outside the bounds of the military at all. It wasn't uncommon for Cynicals to perform covert unofficial operations—the Cynical Order was as much a shined sword as it was a shadowed dagger, and its agents went where they were needed when they were needed. All she knew were her orders and that was enough.

"The fate of the Empire rests on this. Do not fail me."

And then there was him, her mysterious benefactor, the very person who ordered her here. He gave her a bad feeling, a chill in her spine that felt foreign to her nowadays.

Cato only met him once, and then only briefly. He had lingered in the shadows, wearing a Cynical's uniform and a mask that distorted his voice. Every other time she was given directive or orders, they came through a messenger, and a different one each time—one time it was an urchin; another was a corporal in the army; and one was the owner of a cigar shoppe. Not one of them knew the contents of the letters they passed her; each seal had remained unbroken. Whomever her superior for this operation was, his web was vast, and many were caught in it.

Cato looked at the briefcase, resting in the other back seat. She didn't even know what was in that little box, only that it was leverage. She had never seen the strange symbol etched on its surface before—not in the Cynical headquarters, the Imperial palace, a private corporation—nowhere. It was strange that she should travel halfway across the Empire with this box in a briefcase for reasons unknown. Why not simply ship it by hovercopter? The Empire dominated the skies, and she was a Ranger—acting the courier was below her station.

Then again, the recipient of this package was no normal person.

As Cato sat in the backseat of the cab, she couldn't help but feel a sense of nervousness creeping in. She had a mission to complete, and she couldn't let anything stand in her way. She closed her eyes and took a deep breath, trying to steady her nerves.

The cab was making its way through the countryside, and Cato couldn't help but be awed by the scenery. Rolling hills stretched out as far as the eye could see, dotted with olive groves and vineyards. During her reverie, the rain and clouds had broken, and the sun now shined on the fog-brushed landscape. Cypress trees stood tall and proud, their branches reaching towards the sky. In the distance, she could see a small village perched on top of a hill, the terracotta rooftops glinting in the sunlight.

As they drove, the cab turned off the main road and onto a gravel path that winded its way through a copse of cypresses. As the car bumped and rocked along, Cato's nerves grew more rattled. . . . he was just around the bend now.

The tree line broke into a wide-open field of golden grass, swaying softly all the way to the mountain range sloping up the horizon. A dozen strong, tall horses grazed and trotted across the field, their coats still shiny from the rain and glowing beneath the sun's warmth. A large corral, its gate open and its stables well-maintained, sat between the field and a two-story cabin. Half a dozen horses grazed and lazed in the corral itself.

Cato was normally comforted and even excited by the sight of horses, but not this time. She knew, by their proud strength and size, that they were bred for one thing only: war. She knew who cared for them, and she knew that they too carried the deaths that clung to *him*.

Cato knew that this was his homestead, the removed sanctum of retirement for the warrior known as the Grim Reaper of Assyria. The former Knight-Commander of The Cynical Order. She took another deep breath and prepared herself for what was to come.

Cato was an accomplished soldier, with a reputation for being fierce and determined in battle. But as she approached the door of Samael's cabin, her anxiety heightened with each falling step. She had grown up on stories of his prowess in battle, of how he had single-handedly decimated entire armies. But she had a mission to complete, and she wouldn't let anything stand in her way.

The cabin was humble and rustic, with a thatched roof and a chimney that sent tendrils of smoke into the air. The front door was made of thick oak and had a brass knocker in the shape of a lion's head. Cato knocked and waited.

A middle-aged woman answered the door, her long, jet-black hair tied back in a bun, her crow's feet creasing her cautious eyes as she studied Cato from behind the threshold of the home.

✳ ✳ ✳ ✳ ✳

A young woman stood at Gabrielle's doorstep, her strawberry-blonde hair cut sharply to frame her face, her brow furrowed. Rich crimson scales, bearing the sheen of rubies, freckled the skin around blue eyes, which were leveled coolly on Gabrielle.

Her uniform was dreadfully familiar. Sure, they had removed a few pockets and added a few buttons, but Gabrielle recognized the dress uniform of a Cynical: crisp ivory overcoat, emblazoned with black buttons and with a cape over the shoulders; a red ascot peeking out from the lapel of the overcoat; sleek black trousers tucked into shiny knee-length black boots. Gabrielle looked to the young woman's shoulder, catching the crimson horse-shaped patch: not just a Cynical, but a Cynical Ranger. The young woman held a sturdy silver briefcase in her left hand.

Gabrielle grimaced, and she ensured the Ranger saw it. There was no justifiable reason for a Cynical to be here—her husband was retired, and she didn't like that an agent from his old Order stood on their doorstep.

Her husband had become a better man away from the clutch of Cynicals and Assyrian politicking, and Gabrielle didn't want to see him regress.

"Can I help you?" Gabrielle asked shortly, her tone husked with an edge which implied that she did not want to help this woman.

The Ranger's harsh look disappeared and her face split into a bright smile. "Good afternoon, ma'am. I am Sergeant Cato Nemoida of The Cynical Order." She offered her hand.

Gabrielle didn't shake it, staring at it as if it were a trespasser in her home.

Cato took her hand back and continued, "I'm looking for your husband. Perhaps I could speak with him, if he is around."

"I'm sorry that you came all of this way, but he doesn't see visitors," Gabrielle said, beginning to close the door.

Cato shoved her boot across the threshold, blocking the door from closing. "My apologies for interrupting your day, ma'am, but I'm afraid I must speak with him," she said, her voice still bearing that cheerful politeness.

Gabrielle did not move nor speak.

Cato's smile fell and a cold look entered her crystal-shrouded eyes, and when she spoke next, her tone carried the same edge Gabrielle had heard from her husband when someone pushed their luck with him.

"I'm not leaving until I do."

Gabrielle looked in her eyes and realized that this Ranger scared her. She relented, realizing that if the Empire wanted her husband back, then the Empire would get her husband back.

No matter the promises that were made . . . no matter the promises that would be broken.

Gabrielle stepped outside, closing and locking the door behind her. "Fine. Follow me."

✻ ✻ ✻ ✻ ✻

Cato followed the woman out of the cabin and towards the corral. Cato had the indistinct sense that the Grim Reaper's wife didn't like her; she almost stomped her way towards the stables, not looking back at Cato once to make sure she was following.

She knew that the wife couldn't hear her footsteps. No one could. She was a Ranger, after all, and Rangers were fabled for their silent movement.

A few of the horses, both in the field and in the corral, looked lazily at the two figures as they approached. A few sidled closer, and Cato sensed both curiosity and wariness in their sharp black eyes.

The Grim Reaper was of the Kota, a race long since assimilated in the Empire as Ghoulas. As they approached, Cato thought of the myths surrounding the Kota and their horses—how they seemed to share minds and even thoughts—and the fearlessness of their steeds when protecting their riders.

Cato had never imagined how it'd feel to be trampled to death until now.

The wife stopped at the gate of the corral. She faced Cato, her arms crossed, and said, in a low voice, "He's in the stables. Don't sneak up on him. Announce yourself at the door. And don't—"

"Look him in the eyes," Cato said, too anxious to summon that faux smile she had earlier. "I know."

The wife opened the gate and, with what looked to be a frustrated resignation, gestured for Cato to enter.

With every step, Cato felt like she attracted the attention of more horses until, by the time she reached the dark open doors of the stables, every single horse had its gaze trained unflinchingly on Cato.

She tightened her grip around the briefcase, focusing herself and settling her nerves. She stepped forward, allowing her eyes to adjust to the dimness of the stables. She lingered a moment in the doorway, scanning the inside for him.

He was on the other side of a great pale horse, its coat shimmering even in the dim stables. A single stripe of black fur ran down its head and nose. Its dark eyes loomed reddish in the low light, and its left one seemed to be looking through Cato as she stood.

He was brushing its coat, his face hidden behind the horse's muscled neck. Cato saw his rough hand, marked by callouses and scars, and she marveled at his gentle touch while grooming the horse.

The horse snorted briefly, as if ushering a warning.

The rough hand stopped brushing the coat.

If there was a time to speak and make herself known, it was now. The irrational fear that she'd be greeted by a knife to the throat popped into her mind.

"Gree—" she cut herself off, willing her voice to be louder and stronger. "Greetings, sir. I am Sergeant Cato Nemoida of—"

"I know what you are." The man hadn't moved from behind the black horse, his features still hidden from Cato. His voice wasn't as she'd expected: deep, yes, but soft like a summer breeze. "Why are you here?"

Cato's nerves bundled in her throat. She adjusted her grip on the briefcase. She had to make sure it was him.

"You're Knight-Commander Samael Tashunka of The Cynical Order?"

The man sighed, patted the big horse on the neck, and stepped back. He moved toward a tool rack further back in the stables, his back to her and the brush in hand. "What of it?"

He wasn't the towering, grizzled figure she'd imagined. Instead, he was a man of below-average height who looked like he kept in decent shape. Silver streaks ran lines down his dark hair, which was draped over his shoulders. He was dressed simply, in a plain tunic and leggings. He stood tall and proud, but there was a sense of meekness about him that did not match his fabled reputation.

Samael was more than the old Knight-Commander of The Cynical Order: He was a role model, a hero, a Ghoula who could stand tall in a room of Assyrians, a reaper with more blood on his hands than the Empire had even seen.

And Cato was there to tell this man the last thing he wanted to hear.

X

CLAY

*D*on't stop running.

Their only hope now was the dark web of the forest—that desolate place called the Wraithwood. A caravan of disfigured spirits lay hovering in wait for the three of them at the curtain of the forest.

One hundred meters lay between them and the edge of the forest.

At first, they were all running. Ayala in the lead, followed by Clay, with Blood quickly falling behind. Every few steps, it seemed like Blood's leg would lock up or give out, no matter how much he tried to hide it. It was clear that his leg was still very stiff, too stiff to bend properly, too stiff to support his weight . . . too stiff to run. There were violent shouts coming from the house, like a wild animal was let loose inside of the home. Then, Clay heard a cry come much closer behind him. He dared a glance backward.

Blood's leg buckled—his eviscerated knee shot backward in a jarring hyperextension, causing him to tumble forward in a violent volley.

There was no way he could outrun whatever was coming for them.

For the second time that day, Clay moved without thought.

His legs quickly pivoted backwards, running to Blood and lifting him off the ground. He didn't care that there were people coming behind him, didn't care about Blood's disgruntled protests. All that mattered was that they reached the Wraithwood. He'd figure out what came next after.

He hoisted Blood up, bearing the man's leaden weight as he draped his arm over his shoulder.

Blood, for his part, managed to keep up the pace of a hurried skip, launching forward on his good leg, keeping the other held off the ground.

Clay's heart was pounding against his chest, about to burst. Overactive lungs filled his rib cage as they fanned open and shut, searching for breath in the chilly night air. As fatigue spread to the calves and thighs, his gait grew messier.

The wraiths, still at the edge of the woods, looked antsy, wavering and shifting back and forth, as if they had wanted to rush out from the trees and save Blood themselves.

Finally, they had reached the woods.

The disfigured caravan of Wraiths was waiting for them. They entered a dim ethereal cloud of blue light, emanating from the wraiths and coating their surroundings like resin.

Clay tried to catch his breath, pushing his legs to keep running further into the darkness, with only wraith-light before him to light his path. He could hear Ayala, too, her exasperated breaths drawing loudly in the otherwise silent night.

Clay's overactive senses revealed every fine detail of the world around him like the brushstrokes of a fine painting. Out of the darkness, he spotted a familiar White Oak. It was the one where he and Ayala had spent many afternoons playing, climbing, and hiding in its nooks and crannies. Tonight, it was just another artifact in the growing graveyard of childhood things.

He urged the others to rest behind it. He sat Blood down on one of the many large roots extending from the giant tree.

Then Clay felt a strange, inexplicable feeling: His muscles tightened almost to the point of cramping, and a fierce tingling sensation coated his skin. He collapsed to his knees, almost curling in on himself, and grunted with the near-pain that almost paralyzed him. It felt as if he were on fire, but he didn't even know what that felt like—this wasn't exhaustion or fatigue. He didn't know what this was . . . only that it was awful. As suddenly as it came, it went, and all the tension left his body at once. He felt emptied, as if there was now nothing left of him.

"Clay!" Ayala rushed to him, breathing heavily, shaking his shoulder with her hand. "You good?—Oh, by Cyrus, please be okay."

"I'm fine; I'm fine," he said, forcing a smile through his sweat and pain. Maybe Ayala could see through the lie. With her help, he stood again.

"We've gotta keep moving," said Blood, his voice weak with exertion.

Coarse shouts and yells emerged from behind, closer than before. The snarls of bloodhounds entered the mix. Amid the chaos, one voice rose above the others.

"Hey!" he heard them call, "I think I saw someone headed that way!"

We're slow, too slow, Clay thought to himself. He knew that once the inquisitors caught up to them, Blood would be the first to go. And as tired as Clay was, he wouldn't fare too much better.

The intense drumming of his own heartbeat filled his ears, drowning out the ambient white noise of the opaque night. This cadence wasn't broken until he heard the angry snarling of the bloodhounds—they had caught their scent.

"She's got something!" called a voice in the darkness. "I think there're people in the woods!" A cloud of white *lumins* turned, whipping in their direction.

Ayala's eyes were wide with terror. She refused to run, said there was no point.

The footsteps grew closer.

"This is it. We are going to die," she said, sitting down on a tree trunk. She had her hand on her throat, trying to catch her breath. "How did everything get so screwed?"

It was a disorienting feeling, seeing her like this. *She* was always *his* rock, the sword to his shield, not the other way around. But everything was upside down right now, and Clay knew they had to act fast if they had any chance of surviving. He would have to be strong for her: the rock she needed in this moment of fear. Sword and shield. If he faltered, they would both be lost.

He took her hand and pulled her close. Looking at her, he said, "Ayala, listen to me. We can do this; we just have to stay together like we always do. You have to be strong."

Could've been talking to himself just then.

"They have dogs! And Blood's hurt. . . . there's no way we can outrun them."

Watching as they were, the wraiths looked at each other. Though their mouths didn't move, Clay heard foreign words quietly pass between them. They sounded far off, like an echo.

And with that, the wraith's turned back toward the entrance of the forest.

It was quiet for a few minutes. Then, noise broke through the night once more—an incessant cry came from the hounds, all at once.

"Come on, you stupid mutt! What's the matter with you? Get in there. What're you so afraid of?" he heard one say.

"Leave 'em," shouted his companion. "We're losing them!"

"Hold on, isn't that the Wraithwood? Maybe we should think about this. . . ."

"Yeah, try telling Dominus that you let that crook get away 'cause you're scared of ghosts that don't exist!"

"We've gotta go," Clay said to her, offering his hand.

Looking Clay in the eyes, she took a deep breath and took his hand.

Clay glanced in the direction the wraiths had headed toward, where the voices were coming from. Their cloud of blue light receded into the trees, growing more splintered and faded until it disappeared.

Branches broke and twigs snapped as the inquisitors continued into the forest. It wasn't but a few moments later that a loud roar erupted, unlike anything Clay had ever heard; though loud, it felt hushed, as if some great beast was hissing rather than screaming. The inquisitors shouted and screamed, begging for mercy. Then, there was silence, as though a supernatural vacuum had consumed every living thing.

"We need somewhere to hide," said Clay, his voice shaking with the terror of what they just heard. "The wraiths have done all they can to give us a head start."

"They'll be afraid of the woods now," Blood replied, speaking through his teeth and keeping the weight off his bad leg. "It won't keep them forever. But this is our best chance to create some distance."

"Blood, you can barely walk. I don't know how much farther I can carry you."

Blood flashed a look at Clay, then, out of options, cursed his lame leg.

"I know a place," replied Ayala. She pointed into the darkness. "It's just beyond the creek over there. Come on."

As they continued further into the dense forest, Clay did his best to ignore the smoky amber haze illuminating the sky behind them. His heart had the sickly feeling of being underwater, gasping for air in the open sea. But his adrenaline kept him focused on the present moment.

They continued forward into the darkness.

"There it is," Ayala announced.

Before them lay a craggy mound of sharp rocks, covering a small pit, stacked onto one another and forming something resembling a dome.

"Where's the entrance?" asked Blood. He let go of Clay, intent to stand on his own.

"It's not far, just over here," replied Ayala. "It's a small crawl-space I found years ago, perfect for hiding and—"

She stopped short, held at bay by Clay, who had lifted a finger in the darkness. He walked toward the noise, following the faint sound around the bend of the dome. Under the murmur of forest eaves, howling owls, and the rustling of trees were the sounds of three familiar voices.

"Man, I can hardly see my own piss out here," said a rather childish voice.

"Hurry up," said another. This voice made Clay's heart somersault into his stomach. "I want to find those rats before our dads do." The boy snickered, then locked eyes with Clay. "Holy crap! Fellas, look what we have here."

Clay couldn't believe his luck.

Billy, Brass, and Brutus: all three idiots gathered in one place. As if his day couldn't go any worse.

"What the hell . . ." Clay said, still not believing what was happening.

"Fellas, I must be lucky or something!" Billy said. "I'd know that ugly rat face anywhere. I was sick I couldn't give you a licking after school. And now here you are."

Ayala came around the corner and stood by Clay's side.

"Oh, and he brought his knight in shining armor with him!" They all jeered. "Two birds with one stone. This is gonna be fun."

"Say, Billy," interjected Brutus, "you don't think these are the punks our folks are looking fer, do ya?"

"Ooh," Billy said, his eyes growing, and unibrow lit with excitement at the prospect. "Hey, Clay, that wouldn't happen to be you, would it?" And he took one step forward, his eyes scanning Clay's sweaty skin, dirty clothes, and wild fearful eyes, his expression corkscrewing with some sick satisfaction. "After all, it's past Ghoula curfew, ain't it?" Billy passed over Ayala the same way. "So even if you're not who they're all looking for, we're still within our rights. . . ." he trailed off with a wicked smile.

Clay glanced back, and he didn't see Blood.

He and Ayala were alone.

Billy, Brutus, and Brass all took a leering step forward.

Then another.

Clay was frozen. He felt naked under the sterling glimmer of the moonlight. Its spotlight was on him, unblinking. Yet Billy was hidden, almost entirely eclipsed by the darkness of its shadow. It hid his features and all the normal piggishness of his appearance. He was now larger, murkier . . . scarier than he ever had been.

Clay took a step back.

"Why don't you go ahead and toss up whatever it is you stole before we get to hurting you too bad?" Billy said, his tone offering a sense of mock sincerity. Still, he inched closer.

"Take one more step and I'll make sure you're flossing with jump-rope." Ayala interjected, stepping up to meet the boy.

Billy looked over his shoulder to his goons. "Payback time."

They moved to intercept her.

She struck the first one pretty good, square across the jaw and knocking him off balance, but Brass grabbed her hand before she could load up a second strike.

They grabbed her and bound her arms, pulling her away from the action.

It was up to Clay to act. This wasn't the cafeteria—there were no rules. No one was watching. Nothing to lose. Nothing to stop him this time. Well, except himself.

He wondered how he had put up with the gang's terror for so long. Was it fear? There was always the lingering fear of disappointing his mom, getting kicked out of school, and making all of mom's sacrifices worthless. But that wasn't it.

As he stepped closer, Billy's eyes emerged from the darkness into the exposing moonlight. And it wasn't until this moment that he discovered another, hidden reason: *pity*.

His eyes were far less confident than his hefty body and lofty presence would convey. There was a powerlessness beneath it all, a deep insecurity that Clay had instinctively felt kindred to.

Still, the night would end poorly for someone, and Clay decided it would not be him.

Win, lose—it didn't matter. It was time to end this.

He did what he had seen all his favorite heroes do: He spread his feet, balled up his right fist so tightly his hand trembled. He narrowed his eyes, ready to give Billy everything he had.

But seemingly from out of nowhere, a blue flash appeared between them.

Like a clash of thunder, a loud *crack* reverberated in the air as Blood's fist made contact with Billy's face. His body went limp; his eyes rolled backward into his skull as his head collided with the dirt. His nose deformed, like it was doing an impression of mashed squash. The lights were out, and no one was home.

And that was only the first punch.

Blood lurched on him, continuing to ravage him with an array of punches.

Clay looked over to Ayala and it was then that he realized: Blood had already knocked out the other two goons.

They watched in horror as Blood continued his assault.

"Blood, that's enough." Clay yelled. "BLOOD!"

The grizzled teen shook his head, as though he were waking up from a long nap. He blinked his eyes, and he was back.

Blood stood over their unconscious forms, shaking out his bad leg. Clay and Ayala stood, stunned.

"What?" he said with raised eyebrow.

"What was that?" Clay asked.

"They attacked us," he said simply, as if he were just asked what color the sky was.

"Blood, he's just a kid."

Blood's face distorted slightly as he pondered Clay's words. Then, he spoke.

"We need cover. Come on," Blood said, and he limped to the cave.

Clay and Ayala shared a look, then followed him.

Silence settled like frost.

XI

CLAY

The first rays of light crept through the rocky rotunda many hours later. Clay had his head between his knees, only pretending to be asleep so as to maintain the silence.

There hadn't been any noise outside for quite some time.

His mind raced between two different but potent thoughts: The first fixated on the fight. Clay couldn't stop thinking about how it all had gone down. He had to admit that he was mesmerized by Blood, that enigmatic figure—his swiftness to action, his strength and ferocity, and the steely resolve in the face of danger. He had to admit he envied all these traits.

He constantly replayed the encounter in his head over and over. Rehearsing every move, slowing it down, speeding it up and everything in between. The frenetic pace of it all reminded him of his favorite stories come to life. In some ways, it was a dream come true. Still, it did little to assuage the stifling uneasiness settling in his gut.

He could still remember the look in Blood's eyes as he attacked Billy. His eyes were stone, unblinking and focused. It seemed almost . . . inhuman. Clay imagined it was like the way a hammer looked at a nail. And that look when he came to . . . dispassionate, and innocent, as though he wasn't sure if he'd crossed a line.

His second preoccupation was less colorful but equally as consuming: a mounting concern for his mother's well-being. Hopeful questions of how she could've made it out of the house, or if she would know where to find them once she did were only the tip of the iceberg. It grew progressively darker from there, a looming pessimism of the realities that could be waiting for him. And, throughout the night, strange and painful sensations settled in his bones and along his skin, a brief and sudden tingling that seemed to tighten his muscles and cramp his body. While it wasn't exactly painful, it was incredibly unpleasant, as if he were experiencing an excruciating memory over and over again. He did not know why it happened. He did not know how to predict it, stop it, or prevent it.

He didn't even begin to know how to unpack it all. And so, he found it easier to focus his energies on what he had seen and where he was now.

He looked over his knee to his left, finding Ayala. She wasn't sleeping either and wasn't pretending to be. Arms crossed, she had a glare on her face, a scowl pointed directly at Blood that Clay assumed she likely wore all night long.

She wasn't the most trusting of people—or trusting at all, really—so he wasn't surprised by this. Blood didn't seem too surprised either, but he didn't bother to pay attention to it. His eyes were laser-focused, scanning the pit's opening for any signs of life or movement outside of the cave.

"Good, we're all up," he said, without looking.

"Um, yeah. I couldn't really sleep," Clay replied.

"Could be the last chance you get for a while."

The man, or child rather, was garbed in black from neck to toe but for the large, shredded section of his left pantleg, where his dark leg could be seen—the skin was still shredded and coated with dried blood, but it had begun to heal since the prior day.

There was an empty sheath on his leg, presumably where a dagger once was. As Clay watched him, he noticed that no matter how Blood moved, one of his hands hovered over it, as though his blade might magically appear.

"Do you even know how to get out of here? Out of the Wraith-wood?" Ayala asked.

Blood shook his head. "Do you?" The question was softly spoken and genuine.

Clay looked at Ayala. She knew these woods well—much better than he did. If there were a way, she'd know of it.

Her gaze floated across the rocks beneath her for a moment, and then snapped up to Clay. "You remember a couple years back, when we were playing tag? You slipped and fell into the creek, and then we decided to just follow it wherever it went?"

Clay nodded, not quite sure where she was going with this.

"It came out to that river, yeah?" Ayala said.

"Yeah." The memory of finding that river, crowded by foliage and murky and probably filled with all kinds of creatures and diseases, flashed through his mind.

"Think that boat is still there?" Ayala asked.

"Boat?"

"Yeah, there was a ratty little boat on the shore. It looked old, but it seemed sturdy." Her tone shifted, growing more wistful. "I always wanted to explore the river on that boat with you, someday."

Clay did not remember seeing a boat. But he trusted Ayala. "Do you think it's still there?"

Ayala shrugged. "Probably. No one lives near there."

"A boat would be good," Blood said. "No tracks." He looked at Ayala. "Do you know the way?"

"Yep."

"Then we should get moving," Blood said, already shifting to get up.

Clay contemplated this for a second, then, feeling that this might be the last chance he'd get in some time, asked, "Do you think there's a chance my mom made it out?"

Blood took a deep breath, stopped getting up, and said nothing. Ayala narrowed her eyes at him. He didn't look at her. "We should keep moving." Blood had a soft voice, low as if he'd only spoken in whispers his whole life. But it carried well and clearly, and the dismissive edge in his words wasn't lost on Clay.

Ayala shook her head. "Nope. I'm not going anywhere with you until you answer the question." She met Clay's eyes briefly, and he was glad for her support.

Clay looked up earnestly into Blood's eyes. Blood stared back at him without emotion; the Harraka was clearly hiding something.

"She's right," Clay said. "You know something."

Blood took a breath and sighed. He looked to Clay.

"Why are you asking me a question you already know the answer to?" he said.

Clay quirked his head. "What do you mean?"

"You know what I mean," Blood said. He would not look Clay nor Ayala in the eye; he kept his gaze to the mouth of the cave, showing only half his face.

"Why don't you spell it out for us?" Ayala said, her teeth clenched.

"Fine. Your mom is dead," he said dispassionately. "I don't think she ever planned on getting out. She set the house on fire so we could get away. I'm sure you two could smell the smoke. Feel the scratching in the back of your throat. I can still taste it."

Blood, feeling the threat of death aimed at the back of his skull, turned around and faced Ayala. He raised an eyebrow, waiting for her to say something.

Ayala's eyes were wide; she seemed to be so furious that she was paralyzed.

"So, she lied to us?" Clay asked, his words barely a whisper. Were it not for the stillness in the cave, the wind would have carried them away. There was a lump in his gut and what felt like a fist in his throat.

"We should keep moving," Blood repeated. He pushed his tongue against his inner lip again, and for a second Clay noticed a flash of emotion in his eyes. "Those wraiths will only keep the men away for so long. They'll come back, and I don't intend to be here when they do. I made a promise to your mom that I'd get you to the Harrakas. You don't have to like me, but you have to trust me, because I'm the only one that can take you there. Otherwise, you'll die. Now come on. We should—"

"Keep moving," hissed Ayala, rising to her feet. "We got it."

Placing his hand on the pallet of rocks beside him, Blood steadied himself onto his feet. Then, reaching out onto the soil beyond the small exit, he dug his hands into the ground and shimmied himself out of the pit.

XII

AYALA

A thick veil of obscure fog settled over the marshy bog like the essence of a phantom presiding over its aquatic abode, marking its domain. Gray, milky residue coated the frosty morning air. Visibility was low but every noise was amplified. Ayala listened. All around were the eerie sounds of the morning: ravens cawing over the carcasses of the recently departed, water burbling underneath the boat as if gasping for air, swirls of wind bending gentle salt grass. Together, they created an iridescent hum around the children, an uneasy ambiance. Added to the thick humidity, it all created the feeling of being watched—that the danger had yet to pass.

The boat had been exactly where she remembered it, maybe two dozen paces from where the creek fed into the river, somewhat obscured by a brambly bush. It was an old, weathered dinghy, but it survived time and disrepair well. The three of them barely fit in the vessel; both Clay and Ayala shared the singular bench, while

Blood rowed at the tiller. Their packs were shoved beneath their feet; there was no room for them elsewhere. Though it looked older than time itself, it must have been well-built; they had been on the river for almost hours now, and no water had seeped into the dinghy.

The sun peeked timidly through the dense haze. Faintly, she saw Blood, his silhouette rowing through the curtain of fog before them.

Ayala watched him closely as he rowed, rarely taking a watchful eye off the enigmatic figure. She hadn't noticed before just how grimy he was, with a dirt ring girdling the underside of his neck and muck in the beds of his fingernails. His oily hair had begun to unwind as frizzy hair rose from frayed braids. She studied how the muscles of his arms twitched, as if weary with fatigue and overuse, yet unrelenting; he continued to row in slow, measured breaths. Bluish mist still rolled off his bad leg, squeezing between the gauze that Lena had wrapped around it. Where dirt and grime hadn't colored the bandages brown and black, dried blood marked crimson splotches. She examined the dark circles that swelled underneath his eyes. Occasionally, their eyes would meet. His were as impenetrable as the morning fog, his gaze a shallow stare that never focused on one thing for too long. There was no light in them and his dull expression rarely, if ever, changed. Even with all of this, she knew the single-minded attention and precision he placed on any given task, even rowing, was more than she had ever given one thing in her entire life.

Made her wonder which danger she should be more concerned about.

"You've been doing that for a while," she said, breaking a silence that had become as much a staple as the bubbling waters. "Why don't you let someone else try?"

"No," he said. And that was all.

"It's been hours, you have got to be tired. Come on, let me try." Ayala leaned forward, reaching past Clay to the oars he had in each hand.

Blood stopped. He shot a look at her, eyes narrowed.

A warning.

Ayala returned the look, gnashing her teeth. But she sat back on her side of the boat, arms crossed.

Blood continued his rowing.

She waited a beat, then said. "You know, you don't have to do everything yourself."

"Better that way. Prefer it that way."

"Yeah, sure, is that how you ended up with your leg blown halfway to hell?" She didn't know why she was arguing with him; after all, she didn't disagree with him. She just knew that it felt good to pick at him. He was arrogant, and she didn't like how he weaponized silence. Truthfully, she liked it alone too—that is, whenever Clay wasn't around. People were problems.

Blood seemed unfazed. He continued rowing.

"You know," she started, "you never did get around to telling us exactly how you ended up there. Alone? In the Wraithwood?"

There was no response.

"Come on," Ayala said emphatically. "After everything, we deserve an explanation. Why were you hiding? Why was your leg misting up like that? Can you do magic?"

Her answer was the hum of the morning breeze, the breaking crests of river water.

Ayala pretended not to care. "The Empire's out looking for you. You're probably scared shitless."

Still no response.

Her brows furrowed. She stuck her tongue in the pocket of her mouth, trying to restrain her agitation at his silence.

Nothing got under her skin more than being ignored.

"Too scared to answer a simple question. All you can do is run. What a coward," she said, dismissing him and looking over the water.

Color returned to Blood's face; his dark cheeks flushed with a hint of rubine tones, eyes drifting up slowly to Ayala. ". . . Coward?"

"Yeah," she said, doubling down on the bait. She still wasn't sure why she did so. "That's right."

Blood's teeth grit together, his eyes unmoving. "What do you know of cowards? Of honor?"

Ayala was silent, but she didn't break his gaze. She met it with a challenge of her own, despite her racing heartbeat. Her hands folded into her lap, knuckles tight, ready for any escalation that might follow.

"You know nothing of honor," Blood continued. "It is because of honor that you are still alive."

Ayala sat up, leaned in. "Save the speech," she said. "You'd be dead without us. That means *you* owe *us*. Don't forget that."

Blood bared his teeth, which were grit together so hard Ayala thought they might break. Then, after a few heavy breaths, his anger dissipated, and Blood returned to the same dour look as had been his *modus operandi*.

They rowed on a bit further in silence. Ayala looked at Clay, checking for even the minutest change to his condition.

Still the same.

Clay's knees pressed against his sternum on the bite-sized canoe. It was ill-fit for three passengers and Clay was nearly curled into a ball. His head lay backward against the side of the dinghy, tilted at the sky, but his eyes remained closed. Closed as they were, Ayala knew he wasn't sleeping. She didn't really know what he was doing; she hoped he hadn't fallen into a kind of malaise. She wanted to reach out to him and touch him—let him know that he wasn't alone and that she was hurting too. But even the thought felt wrong, and she didn't have any words that could reach him.

She wasn't Lena.

Her stomach growled, gnawing at her insides, reminding her how long it had been since she'd had a decent meal. She hadn't had a proper meal since the day before yesterday; she had been planning on Lena's cooking to hold her over last night. She placed her hands on her belly, massaging it to quiet its roars. She reached inside Clay's bookbag, hoping to scrounge up enough to take the edge off. It was a pipe dream. All she found were breadcrumbs and a half-empty glass of jam. Desperately, she stuck her finger in the jar and allowed it to glide over the glass, collecting what little was left and hoping it'd be enough to hold her over. It was bland, its consistency watery, and it mostly just made her feel even hungrier.

Ah well. Hunger was familiar.

"I will give you one," said Blood begrudgingly.

"Huh?" said Ayala, her fingers still scraping the jar.

"One question," he said. "One answer."

It had been so long since she'd asked, Ayala had already forgotten. But Blood was deadly serious. When she looked in his eyes, she could see that he hadn't stopped thinking about her words.

The gravity of the moment sunk in. There was so much she could ask, but what *should* she ask?

Finally, after much consideration, she was ready.

She began slowly, warming herself up to it. "Whatever you are caught up in, whatever you did, Clay and I helped you, so that makes us . . ." she paused, the word lying on her tongue like black soap ". . . accomplices."

He turned his head in, waiting for the question.

"I guess my question is . . . what was it all for? What did Lena die for?"

Clay, for the first time since they crawled into the rickety dinghy, opened his eyes. He peered at Blood, watching and waiting.

Blood took a deep breath, absorbing the question and clearly trying to find the best way to explain something so unforgivable. For a second, Ayala thought she saw sadness on his face—there for a moment but gone like a flickering candle. She wondered if it was fake.

He stopped rowing. The boat rocked as it settled in the middle of the waters.

"I can tell you why they are after me, why the empire wants me dead; but . . . why she had to die . . . I do not know."

He paused for a moment. His face distorted briefly, like the thought of the ordeal caused him physical pain. His poise returned and he continued.

"It's all because. . . . I stole something," he said, cautiously. "Something everyone in the Empire wants."

Clay and Ayala glanced at one another. Clay shifted, raising his head.

"Well?" Ayala prompted.

Blood's hands went to his lap, where they flexed into fists and relaxed again. He wiped his hand across his chin. "That's it. There's your answer." As if the conversation was closed, he grabbed the oars and began rowing again.

"Oh, like hell it is," Ayala said, leaning forward. "That's no answer; that's a cryptic tease—you owe us more than that."

Blood did not acknowledge Ayala, but instead rowed with an infuriating steadiness. Clay lingered upon the athletic teen, waiting for a word with his eyes glazed over.

"Come on, man," Clay said, his voice low, hushed, and thrumming with a pain that wrenched at Ayala's core.

She glanced down, noting that she could see the whites of her knuckles, and she felt her jagged nails digging into her palms.

"I promised Lena that I'd keep you two safe," Blood said, his voice softer. He met Clay's gaze, not deigning to meet Ayala's. Her throat grew cramped with the urge to throttle this guy.

"I need you to trust me—"

"You're not giving us many reasons to," Ayala interrupted.

Now he met her gaze, and there was a look in his eye that dulled Ayala's anger: It was something close to guilt or sympathy, and it was the most human she'd seen the Harraka.

"I know," he said. "For what it's worth, I . . ." he paused, swiping his chin with his hand again. Something near to vulnerability flashed in his features, and then they hardened again. "The less you know about what I carry, the safer you'll be. At least for now."

Ayala shook her head and leaned forward on her knees, glaring at Blood. He didn't meet her gaze and continued rowing.

"The wrong person died back there," she said, crossing her arms and leaning back again, throwing her gaze to the passing bushes and trees. She glanced at Clay, half expecting him to admonish her, but he was curled up again, his eyes closed and head face down in his arms and knees.

Blood said nothing, and silence settled.

Soon, the curtain of fog began to dissipate. Gradually, their new surroundings came into full view.

The river itself flowed between regions. The remnants of woodland growth crowded the water's edge; wide-fanned leaves and braided roots spilled over the shallow embankment.

As twilight transitioned to dusk, the river grew darker and more claustrophobic. Shadows clung like velvet to the forest, draped along the riverbanks and melting into the water itself. Birdsong faded to insect white noise, and the rustling leaves took on a dreadful tone.

Ayala slept fitfully that night, her dreams scattered and incomprehensible. She woke many times in a cool sweat, her back and neck aching against the harsh splintering wood of the boat.

Dawn finally broke after what felt like the longest night of her life. Ayala awoke to find Blood curled against the far corner of the boat, his arms crossed and his eyes moving rapidly beneath closed lids. Yesterday, the mist that roiled around his leg was thick enough to be smoky; today, it was thin and translucent, its tendrils almost hair-thin.

She looked to Clay and let out a small noise of surprise; he was awake and in the same exact position as when she fell asleep—knees tucked against his chest, arms wrapped around them, his empty features staring blankly ahead.

"Ayo, Clay," Ayala said softly, her voice still hoarse with sleep. He looked slowly in her direction; darkness crowded his half-lidded eyes, his lips were cracked, and his brow seemed fixed at a pained slant. They needed to get to shelter soon; they were almost out of food and water, and it wouldn't be long until they were forced to drink the river water and all the diseases it carried.

In her periphery, she saw Blood twitch and then settle back to sleep, his breathing measured and steady.

"Did you sleep?" she asked, sitting up and scooting closer to her friend.

He didn't say anything at first. She gently slapped his arm with her back of her hand, saying, "Come on, Clay, I'm getting enough silence from that thing over there." She cocked her head towards Blood. "I can't have you going mute on me too."

Clay blinked rapidly, and then his lips parted. "I felt what ma felt."

Ayala's face scrunched. "Huh?"

"It's like . . . when we were running away, I felt like I was set on fire for a second. It was so hot, like I was melting. And then there was nothing—just this, like, empty feeling."

"You talking about when we heard the explosion?" Ayala asked.

Clay's brow furrowed. "Explosion?"

"Yeah. There was a distant explosion and then you just fell to the ground; you looked like you were in a lot of pain." She almost grabbed his hand but stopped herself. Instead, she looked away. "You scared me, man."

"I'm sorry—I don't . . . really, there was an explosion?"

Ayala didn't know how he hadn't heard it; it shook the ground and leaves even fell. "Maybe you didn't notice it because you collapsed. Because of that burning feeling, yeah?"

He looked at her, his eyes wide with terror and pain. "I couldn't sleep because of it. I can't stop remembering that feeling." He looked at Blood. "Even when he told us that she was . . ." His voice faded, and Ayala felt like her throat was clamping up alongside Clay's. "I think I already knew, Ay." He looked at her then, his eyes growing red and misted. "It ain't Blood's fault that mama's gone. It's mine." His chin trembled and he tucked his face into his arms. His hands gripped his arms, tighter and tighter, and his entire body began tightening in on itself; a thin pained yell threaded through gritted teeth, and Ayala felt like it was happening again—that he was burning alive.

How did she sleep through that—how did she not notice this before?

She grabbed his shoulders and started shaking him, trying to break him out of this trance. "Hey, snap out of it!" she said, prying his hands apart from his own arms—she had always been stronger than Clay, but she struggled to untangle him from himself. It was like he was strangling himself, his grip so tight that it felt like straightening a stiff dead man. "It's not real, man—it's not real."

Finally, he loosened and went slack entirely. His eyes closed, and his breath grew measured. He had passed out.

Ayala lowered him gently to her lap, nestling his head against her. Sweat coated his face, and, not knowing what else to do, she began singing one of mama's lullabies.

Later that day, Blood fell unconscious. Throughout the day, he barely ate or drank, offering his rations to Clay and Ayala, and with each passing hour, the mist emanating from his wound thinned and thinned. When the smoky blue vapor ceased entirely, Blood passed out, crumpling and dropping both oars.

Ayala and Clay settled him against the boat's stern, trying to situate him as comfortably as possible as Ayala let loose a few choice words about the uselessness of the Harraka. Once again, she felt an odd disappointment when Clay didn't admonish her—he'd always been quick to defend others before, even his bullies at times, but now he barely even registered what she said.

Ayala settled at the boat's prow and began rowing, surprised at how difficult it was to push the boat along the slow-flowing river. Within an hour, her arms screamed and ached. She pushed through the pain, the image of Blood stolidly rowing forefront in her mind; if he could do it without complaint, she could too.

Even when an oar broke, she bit down her anger and rowed on, alternating sides with the one oar left. It came as no surprise that the oar broke; like the boat itself, the oars were old, and the stress of hours of travel like this was bound to catch up to the fraying wood.

Blood slipped in and out of consciousness throughout the rest of the day, his few waking moments defined by guttural screams; he screamed his voice hoarse, passing out once there was no breath left for the yells.

Clay tried to wake him up many times, but to no avail. He even tried to trickle the last of their water into the teen's mouth, but Blood's jaw was clamped so tightly in his sleep that neither Clay nor Ayala could pry his mouth open without fear of breaking his jaw. After the first few times Blood awoke, Clay and Ayala accepted the Harraka's yells as they had the noises of the river and the birds.

Eventually, Ayala felt her mind and soul fade away, and her life became only the repetitious back-and-forth of the oar.

That night, she slept deeply and without dreams. The morning of their second full day on the river, she awoke to find her arms and upper back filled with leaden weights; moving them shot ripping pain throughout the muscles, and even thinking about moving them caused pain.

Clay rowed the first two hours, and then Ayala took over again, gritting her teeth against the burn that now existed where her arms used to be. Every laborious breath burned her cracked lips, and she no longer possessed the strength to even acknowledge the mosquitoes that bit her constantly. Clay didn't even bother to slap them away, instead letting them feast on his blood as if they were ignored guests.

They had no food nor water left: all they had was the blanket. The blanket lay draped over Blood's lower half, as much to keep the mosquitoes away from his reopened wounds as to hide it from sight. A ghastly smell was developing around the wound, and Ayala didn't even want to think about what it'd look like once the bandages were peeled off.

The foliage was sparser, and one could even see a way into the land—tall landmasses that jutted from the water, forming a wall of rocky mountainside. The trees there were not so tall nor so large, and the growth along the floor was not so vibrant nor aggressive. The river had pooled into a lake, broad enough to fit all the houses on Clay's street from one bank to the other, and its water was an opaque green that gave no hints as to what lay below the surface. Land masses had started to develop in coves on the edge of the lake. Most of them were fairly small and housed miniature hills that could be peaked within a few minutes. But there was one hill that rose higher than all others. It resembled a small mountain, and its shadows covered the land nearby.

"I think I see something," said Clay. "Up there, on the cliffside."

In the far-off distance, atop the small mountain, the cream-colored silhouette of a chapel came into view, overlooking the edge of the mountain. The sun was behind it, and along the edges of the building's form, sunbeams split the sky.

Within minutes, they reached the shore. The three of them hopped into the water and dragged the canoe safely onto a bed of sediment that lay just at the edge of the lake.

Ayala did her best to contain her wincing whispers, but she knew Clay heard them. At least Blood didn't. Blood's leg was stiff and was much the same as she last saw it hours ago—dirty, bloody, and warm to the touch.

"Think it's safe?" asked Clay, his eyes tracing the path that led up the hill to the chapel doors. Ayala was glad to hear his voice. She hadn't realized how much she had missed it.

"There's only one way to know for sure," she replied, grabbing the bag that had their blanket and trash stuffed inside. Clay and Ayala stumbled out of the boat and up the hill, the half-conscious body of Blood propped between them.

XIII

CATO

Gree—" she cut herself off, willing her voice to be louder and stronger. "Greetings, sir. I am Sergeant Cato Nemoida of—"

"I know what you are." The man hadn't moved from behind the pale horse, his features still hidden from Cato. His voice wasn't as she'd expected—deep, yes, but soft like a summer breeze. "Why are you here?"

Cato's nerves bundled in her throat. She adjusted her grip on the briefcase. She had to make sure it was him.

"You're Knight-Commander Samael Tashunka of The Cynical Order?"

The man sighed, patted the big horse on the neck, and stepped back. He moved toward a tool rack further back in the stables, his back to her and the brush in hand. "What of it?"

Cato swallowed, licking her lips. Tools rattled on the rack and against each other as Samael, unhurried, tidied and reorganized.

Horses neighed in the corral, seeming to grow more discomfited by the moment, and though a soft wind carried the sounds of swaying grass, birds, and insects, Cato felt a tension in her chest, as if someone were wringing her spine.

"Sir, you're needed for an operation. Sir." Cato winced; she hadn't sandwiched a sentence with 'sir' since her days in boot camp.

Samael turned around, stepping forward with purpose and coming into the light. The stallion huffed and shook its head, stomping its foot on the wooden stable floor. Cato fixed her gaze on the stallion's eye, reminding herself to not make eye contact with the older man. In her periphery, she noted his leathery brown skin and his clamped fists. She realized that he was shorter than her by almost a whole head.

"I'm retired," Samael said, his eyes locked on her face. The weight of his gaze was almost unbearable. Cato squinted, doubling her efforts to stay locked on to the stallion's dark eye.

When he says he's retired, tell him that it's an important mission for him, Cato's superior had advised, his voice modulated, his face swaddled in shadow.

"Sir, it's an important mission. For you," Cato said, finding comfort in the rehearsed lines. She dared to add her own words, "Important enough to bring you out of your deserved retirement."

Cato hated the way the stallion held her gaze, how it seemed to look through her. She always had an affinity for horses, could always tell how they felt. The stallion's face seemed pinched, and it pawed constantly at the floor. It vocalized every few seconds, its neighs reverberating through the stable, echoing the muffled neighs of the horses outside. To Cato, it was clear as day: This stallion wanted her gone, and in its eye loomed an unspoken threat.

"No mission's that important," said Samael, his low timbre edged with irritation.

The stallion tossed its head. Out of the corner of her eye, Cato saw Samael shaking his.

He placed a hand on the stallion's neck, and it calmed somewhat. "No. I was promised this. I'm not leaving it."

When he mentions a promise, tell him that it must be broken for his family to be repaired. That this is as much for him as it is for the Empire. It was a cryptic and vague direction, and Cato's superior wouldn't expand on it.

Still, she was impressed at how well her superior had predicted this conversation so far. Impressed and worried.

She swallowed again, fighting the urge to look away from the stallion's eye. She feared that if she looked away, she would enter *his* eyes. "The promise must be broken for your family to be repaired. This mission's as much for you as it is for the Empire."

Silence coated the air, and Cato saw his gnarled hand stroking the stallion's mane. The scarred knuckles traveled back and forth. The stallion tilted its head, its eye now narrowed at Cato.

"Who's speaking through you?" Samael asked, notes of curiosity laced through his voice.

Her superior hadn't predicted this question. "Someone important." She decided to tell the whole truth, in the hopes it would win him over. "I don't know, sir. Like I said, this is an important mission . . . a need-to-know basis. Even I don't know many details."

After you mention his family, take the box from the suitcase and hand it to him.

"But I do have this for you, sir," Cato said, finally breaking contact with the stallion's eye. She shoved her gaze to the dark wood floor, squatting and placing the briefcase on the ground. Cato could feel Samael's eyes on her as she opened the briefcase and retrieved the small box, its wood a similar shade to the stable floors. She stood and, keeping her eyes downcast, approached the deadliest man in recent history.

She held the box out to him and was surprised by how gently he took it. She stared at the floor, studying the dried mud on Samael's worn moccasins as he slid open the container. The stallion pawed the ground again, its bare hoof clicking against the wooden floor as Samael unfolded a piece of paper—one that must've been in the box itself. Cato noticed that the horse's hoof had been recently trimmed, and she saw the glistening of some not-yet-dried dressing on the horse's hoof, which remained unshoed.

Samael grunted, and it reminded Cato of how her father would grunt when he was about to punish her for the latest trouble she had cooked up.

And when her father made that grunt, it meant one thing: *Look me in the eye for what I'm about to say.*

And while Cato didn't think that the grunts of her father and the legendary hero of the Assyrian Empire meant the same thing, she couldn't stop herself from looking at his face.

At his eyes, which peeked at her from over the letter.

His eyes were beautiful and terrible to behold—they were the night sky, absent light or white. Darkness covered every visible part of his eyeballs, and for every part of darkness except the void of his pupils, ghostly stars swirled—tiny moon-silver specks floating across the black expanse where his iris and whites should have been.

Her breath was stolen, and the sounds of the world faded to a muffled background. On the edge of her hearing, Cato suddenly heard screams—no, throes, like that of a man caught in a slow and agonizing death, layered over itself countless times. Time collapsed into some infinitesimal speck; a second stretched and grew heavy, and Cato felt as if she were trapped in a web. Within his eyes were an infinity of damnation, a hell itself, filled with the souls of those he's claimed—they cry, scream, suffer, and rage, their pain a clamorous whisper in her mind—all coalesced in the fathomless black of a soft-spoken man's eyes. At the edges of her vision appeared silhouetted forms, littering the stable and grasping with light-cloaked hands, begging her to save them from their eternal fate.

He turned his gaze back to the letter. The screams disappeared, and Cato's breath returned.

What was that? Cato thought. *What did that to him?* Her hands had grown clammy, and she wiped sweat from her brow, even though it was a temperate and breezy day.

She watched his face, curious and terrified and needing to have more answers about why the night sky lives in his eyes. As he read, his expression grew sourer—his brow furrowed and his eyes widened, his jaw growing tauter.

Cato dared another glance at his downturned eyes; those infernal screams appeared again, though they seemed much further away this time and were quiet enough that she did not feel afraid. Her breath wasn't stolen when she looked at his periphery either. It was little consolation—whatever effect his eyes had, she only needed to look at him for it to affect her. He didn't have to look at her, and that unnerved her.

It made her feel like his eyes were alive and separate from him.

She took a few steps back, keeping her gaze away from his. Though she was certain her gait was silent, Samael still glanced at her, as if he heard her move.

It bothered her. And then she remembered the years of experience—real, wartime experience—that he had on her. She recalled that he created the Rangers and was the first teacher of many of the methods they used to travel silently and smoothly—that he was the progenitor of all that she could take pride in herself for.

It still bothered her.

He finished reading the letter and then looked at the opened box. Cato craned her head, seeing the items placed in the modeled paper inserts of that box: a syringe and a vial of garnet-hued liquid, the same color as the crystals on her face.

She'd never seen medicine or drugs that looked like that. If that vial could even be classified as one of those.

Samael was scowling at the vial. As he shook his head, the neighing surrounding the stables grew louder, and Cato heard the muffled sounds of horses galloping from outside.

The stallion next to Samael was strangely calm though—almost sad, really. It lowered its head, brushing Samael's shoulder affectionately. The old man reached for its mane and began stroking it again, his eyes unfocused.

Samael muttered lowly. It took a moment for Cato to piece together what he had said—something about dogs and leashes.

"It'll be the two of us, then," he said, his tone bitter.

"Yes, sir," Cato said, feeling no small wave of relief come over her. It looks like he's accepted the mission and, more importantly, like he won't be killing her. She'd been worried about the latter.

"So what do you know?" he asked, still petting the stallion. He was now staring at the vial in the box, shifting it as if to see how it caught the light.

"Well, sir, that we're to retrieve an object—though I haven't yet been told what that object is. All I know is that it's in the possession of a Quaestor residing in an integrated town near the eastern edge of the Empire, a place called Ruka. We're to retrieve the object through any means necessary, even if we have to harm Assyrian officials to do so. I was told that . . ." she hesitated, hating the allowance this next order gave, ". . . even the Quaestor himself is expendable, should it allow for the object's acquisition."

136

Samael shook his head, looking up at Cato. She focused on the stallion's eye again, shying her gaze in time to avoid his. "Secrets and skullduggery . . . is this what my Rangers have become?"

She didn't know how to answer that. While she knew that she bore no responsibility over a Ranger's duties in the Cynicals and that she was the best Ranger she could be, she still felt shame.

He spoke after a moment. "The object's a rare crystal, different from the others. It's kept in the Quaestor's vault. I'll know it when I see it." He sighed then and looked to the pale stallion. "We'll set out tomorrow. I'll spend today packing and preparing, and I'll have to shoe Solstice."

Solstice must have been the pale stallion, for the horse nudged Samael again when the name was spoken.

Cato was quick with shoeing horses and found the activity meditative in its own way. "I could shoe him for you," she offered. "Give you more time to prepare or spend with your wife."

He looked at her again, as if weighing her. "No. No one touches Solstice but me." He pointed to the stable closest to the door. "That there's your room for the night. It's unattended. Judging by the look of you, you have everything you need to set out except for a horse. Spend the day getting to know the horses here and see which one chooses you."

Cato had never heard of a horse choosing its rider before, but then again, she'd heard strange things about the Kota and their horses.

"What if one doesn't choose me?" she asked.

"Then you're not worth riding with," Samael said. "Now get going. We don't have much time, and my horses are picky about their riders."

"Yes, sir," Cato said. She rendered a salute, dropping it after he didn't return it. As she made to leave, she lingered in the open barn doors, looking back to see Samael gathering the tools to shoe Solstice.

"Sir?"

Samael grunted.

"For what it's worth, I'm real honored to get to travel with you—you've been a hero of mine for—"

"Shut up," he growled. In the dimness of the stables, the starlike specks in his eyes shone, stealing her breath and buffeting her with those terrible screams. Then he looked away, and she was released.

"We ride at dawn," he said, his voice steadier and softer.

"Yes, sir," Cato said.

She didn't notice how loud her footsteps were when she rushed out. She was too focused on how her hands trembled.

XIV

AYALA

The bluff protruded from the lake, its summit mighty, higher than any other in view, its surface emerging from the waters like the throne of God. Trees were stationed all along its protruding slope, bending in the wind as if caught in a throng of worship. They obscured much of the path ahead, but Ayala could always see the suspended tip of a steeple that hung just over the edge of the hill's large slope.

They had only made it a few steps from the shore when Blood stirred, grunting as his head lolled. Clay and Ayala paused, their breathing already heavy and skin slick with sweat—Clay turned to his right and Ayala her left, both watching Blood. Some semblance of life arose from Blood's body, and with another grunt his eyelids flitted open.

"You back with us?" Ayala asked.

As if slowly realizing where and whom he was, Blood shoved Clay and Ayala away, stumbling out of their grasps and almost falling to the ground. He recovered at the last moment, righted himself, and then faced the two kids. He looked at Ayala, then to Clay, and back to Ayala, his eyes growing clearer with each passing moment. He nodded then to Ayala.

"Gonna start screaming again?" Ayala said, a small smirk tilting her mouth.

Blood's brow furrowed. "Screaming?"

"You scream in your sleep," Clay said softly, his voice weighed with fatigue.

Something near to embarrassment crawled across Blood's features; he shied his gaze and balled his fists, color rising in his cheeks. He turned away from Clay and Ayala, looking up the hill and to the chapel spire. "Let's go," he said. He took one step forward and fell to his knees, his bad leg crumpling beneath his weight.

Ayala snickered. Clay tapped her arm softly, and she cut it short, a little pleased that he was back to reminding her to be her better self.

"Wait there," Clay said to Blood, dashing back to the boat.

"Don't think he's got much of a choice," Ayala muttered, smiling lightly.

If Clay or Blood heard her, they didn't let her know.

Clay returned with the remaining oar from the boat, offering it to Blood, who had been struggling back to his feet.

"Not the best crutch, but . . ." Clay said as Blood took the oar. "Lean on me as we walk." Clay stepped closer to Blood, offering his shoulder for the taller man to prop himself on.

Blood paused a moment, his brow furrowed with pain and maybe something else. "No, I don't like to be touched. I can make it on my own."

Ayala walked up from behind, holding back the urge to slap him upside the head. "No you can't, you idiot—we just saw you try to—" she lowered her voice in a crude mockery of Blood's "—'make it on your own.' Just shut up and accept the help—and thank him too. Clay didn't have to do this for you." That said, she walked past the two boys, beginning the slow, taxing hike up to the chapel.

She heard Blood mutter something beneath his breath, followed shortly by Clay saying, "Don't worry about it."

She glanced back and saw him leaning on Clay's shoulder, uncomfortable as if he were wearing shoes two sizes too small. Even leaning on Clay, he looked like he was placing as much weight on the oar as he could; even then, it was clear to her that he needed Clay's help to move. His leg may as well have been dead weight. It still wasn't misting as it had earlier.

Both Clay and Blood adopted a slow, lethargic plod, and Blood looked as if his body was moving, but his soul was elsewhere.

Ayala thought it might be better if she followed them, just in case one stumbled down the hill. She waited until they passed and trudged in their wake.

Using the dull end of the canoe oar, Blood steadied himself up the steady incline of the hill. It clicked against the concrete footpath, scraping at some points and raking at others. Once, Blood's stick caught on a jagged piece of concrete. His oar chipped, causing him to lose his balance. Clay caught him, holding him long enough for Blood to reposition the oar.

"Thanks," Blood said, the word thick and viscous, as if it had no place coming from his mouth.

"Yeah," Clay grunted.

It took about an hour to get over the main crest of the foothill. Looking over its sloping hills, Ayala could again see the face of the water. Its murky green was now a clearer, more elegant jade. She saw the silhouettes of all manner of creatures that swam underneath. Schools of fish and the infamous snapmaw, a scaly four-jawed reptile that darted to and fro just underneath the surface of the water. Suddenly, she was thankful to be standing on land once again.

Ahead of her, she could see the chapel in full view. It was a modest structure: ivory with accents of blue and looking as if it could house a parish of maybe forty. Its steeple was long and magnificent, extending toward the sky like a hand reaching for the sun. Its stone walls may have been white once, but age and weather had taken their toll, marking the building a mottled cream and rust. Its belfry lacked a bell and the roof had seen better days—there were many areas where the shingles had abandoned their duty, and it was safe to assume that many leaks sprung on a rainy day.

The chapel lay mostly alone atop the summit. It was at the edge of a clearing surrounded by a field of mostly yellow glass, with faded patches of emerald green that signaled Fall had settled in full. Its rich, grassy plain danced playfully in the afternoon breeze.

There was also a functional water wheel attached to the chapel itself, spinning lazily in the mid-afternoon humidity as if it were yearning to take a long nap. As she approached, she saw that its trickling water spilled over into a small aquarium, with tiny fish swimming about peacefully, content and lacking for nothing. Steam billowed from various pipes which peeked out from the wall by the waterwheel, hissing out clouds regularly.

Various pieces of scrap metal and machinery littered the chapel grounds, some rusted and ancient and others still bearing a dull gleam. It wasn't uncommon to see metal carcasses littering the landscape—remnants of wars before Ayala's time. The Wraithwood was littered with metal, and so Ayala didn't think much of it.

Most interesting to her were the words etched over the doorpost. While the wood around them had been decaying and festering with rot, she could read the words clearly: "*Calvariae Hill Chapel.*"

"Listen up," said Blood, his words forced through heavy breaths. "We don't know what lies beyond this door. Remember that almost everyone we meet will want to kill us or turn us over to the Empire. We keep our eyes peeled for any—and everything." He looked to them for confirmation. "If you have to run, leave me behind."

Ayala nodded immediately. Clay paused, as if wanting to say something, and then seemed to think better of it and nodded too.

"Alright," he said. Blood huffed three sharp breaths and untangled himself from Clay's arm. Limping and hopping awkwardly but smoothly enough, he went to the chapel's stairs. Taking the oar in his left hand, he stepped on the flat edge of it, breaking it off and leaving a jagged end in its place. He gripped the stick firmly with both hands, heavily favoring his good leg but standing on his own. Ayala wondered where he was drawing this strength from. They must've built kids differently in the Harrakas.

"One," he counted.

Ayala felt the familiar sensation of her heart's quickening pace.

"Two."

Her legs got weak. Running from danger was one thing. Running toward it was another. She braced herself for what may lie beyond the door.

"Wait!" Clay whispered, his voice sharp.

"What?" said Blood.

"Do you hear that? Listen."

They all craned their heads forward to the door. Behind it, the faintest lilts of music passed through its wooden struts. The piano started out softly at first, with an arpeggio of notes that richly flowed, like they were climbing the hillside and coming back down.

A tapestry of chords and keys were woven together, with steady pacing, as if telling a story that was equally beautiful and heartbreaking. Occasionally, it would swell and frantically rush to a rich crescendo, only to drag out its notes for a long stretch and go back to its familiar, soft tune.

"It's . . . beautiful," said Ayala, then she caught herself. She hadn't meant to say that out loud.

Blood looked at her, then back to the door. He rested his hand against it, then gently pushed until its broad, wooden doors inched open.

Blood skulked forward with trepidation, oar firmly in hand like a bat.

Ayala followed, her eyes wide with wonder. The room was made of a deep, dark wood, layered with a stain that had a ruddy brown tint to it. Beams, fashioned of the same wood, leaned against the walls, evenly spaced and sturdy.

She inspected the strange shape and arrangement of the seats, if they could even be called seats. They were long and box-like benches, but they came up to support the back like a chair and were so polished she could see her reflection in them. She thought it strange that guests would be sandwiched together next to everyone else, but it was also new and fascinating. She plopped down on the wooden seat, feeling its uncompromising density beneath her, uncomfortable as it was, swinging her feet and taking in the sights. Unlike its withering outside appearance, the inside of the chapel was in pristine condition, as if it were frozen in time, like an exhibit in a museum. It was almost like whoever lived here found holiness in polishing even the smallest of niches and sin in losing an inch of its beauty.

No artificial *lumin* light polluted the dim cathedral. Its only light came from the stained-glass windows. It was illuminated by an aurora of natural light as it scattered through the panes of pious figures. The result was a kaleidoscope of porous colors: reds like a ruby, garnet greens, truffle blues, and ambers that resembled the sweet, oozing honey from one of Ayala's fondest childhood memories—all coming together to highlight a path between the pews, its central aisle.

At the end of the aisle, on the altar, covered in shadow, was a single grand piano.

Blood approached it cautiously, walking up the short altar steps, and making his way over to it. Slowly, he walked, making sure not to drop his guard, watching for a sneak attack. He finally reached the piano and searched behind it.

After a moment of waiting, he finally called to them. "There's no one here."

"What do you mean?" Clay asked.

"I mean," he said, "there's nobody playing the piano."

"But that's impossible," replied Ayala.

"Come see for yourself."

When Ayala had reached the stage, her own two eyes confirmed that his words were true. There was no one on the piano bench, but its keys depressed and hopped with all of the fine delicacy and precision one would expect of an expert pianist.

"I don't get it. Is it magic?" she asked. That was the new buzz-word. Everything from now on was magic.

"Technology?" Blood contributed, still unsure himself.

If the guy who literally seemed to use magic and was made of magic didn't think it was magic, well . . . Ayala grew even more unsettled. She wanted to get out of this place and back to a world that made sense.

"I've never seen technology that can do that. You?"

Blood shook his head.

"Wait," Ayala said. "Where's Clay?"

Frantically, they looked up from the altar, scanning their surroundings. Suddenly, the dark stain and dim lights seemed less friendly and inviting. They were back-to-back, watching any signs of a potential threat.

"Clay?" Ayala called.

No response.

"CLAY!"

Still no answer.

"Shh. We don't know who knows we are here, and we don't want to give away our presence. Just stay calm."

"'Stay calm,'" she mocked. "Like there's much to stay calm about—where do you think he went?"

Blood sighed, breathing out slowly in what looked like an attempt to 'stay calm.' "I don't know. Maybe he wondered off somewhere. Let's keep exploring, but stay quiet."

Ayala and Blood checked every sequestered door and broom closet in the cathedral. They checked above on the balcony, where there was extra seating. They looked in the priest's quarters. All to no avail.

Finally, they arrived at the last door.

"This is the last one," he said.

"No . . . really?" she said, voice dripping with sarcasm. She was itching to find Clay and get out of here.

Blood shot her a glare, some choice words likely on the tip of his tongue, but he stayed silent.

Blood and Ayala stood side by side. This time, it was Ayala's hand that reached first for the door. She twisted it open slowly, careful not to let it creak too loudly.

She stepped through.

There was a dark, cavern corridor, with steps leading downward to unknown depths. Her eyes searched for light, finding naught but a pin-needle of orange light, further ahead and much further below.

They walked, keeping their hands carefully flush against the cold, rocky wall. The orange glow grew brighter the further down they went. As they descended, the piano's music grew fainter, and a new arrangement of sounds filled the air: a sound of hobbling, a *bop, bop, bop* beating against a hollowed piece of scrap metal; the inhale and exhale of a great fan, so loud that the cave itself sounded like a living, breathing thing; the bubbling of hot liquids, rising to ungodly temperatures; the sizzle of hot coals and the chill of metal being placed into cool water. And above it all floated the complex arrangement still playing on the piano, the notes now muffled and indistinct.

It became increasingly hot as they continued their descent. Ayala wiped globules of sweat from her eyes.

Great. More sweat. Where the hell did Clay go?

The light grew brighter as they descended further into the depths.

Finally, they had reached the bottom.

And there, crouched behind a rock, was Clay.

He turned and saw them. He put one finger to his lips and motioned for them to join him behind the rock.

She wanted to throttle Clay for just slipping away like that. She wanted to hug him because he wasn't in danger at all. . . . he was just being an idiot. She did neither.

Swiftly, the two of them—as best as Blood was able—hurried behind the boulder and out of sight.

"Clay!" Ayala said in exasperated whispers. She hit his arm a little harder than she meant to, but he didn't even wince; he was that transfixed on what was below. "Don't just slip away like that—say a word or something. What were you thinking?"

147

"I found that door and it led me down here. I figured you guys would find me eventually."

"Okay, well we did, now let's go," Ayala said. "This place is creepy. The piano was playing itself!"

"Oh, you don't know the half. Look there."

He pointed her beyond the boulder, to the source of all the noise. It was a workshop alright, but one unlike any they had ever imagined. Shelves were filled to the brim with glass bottles filled with multicolored liquids—some dull and thick, others glowing softly and bubbling constantly. Bookshelves were crammed end to end with old tomes organized haphazardly. Incomprehensibly complex diagrams were nailed to the walls without rhyme or reason. There were racks of iron tools, prongs hanging from the mantel. A steaming furnace formed the centerpiece of the room, so large that all three teenagers could swim in it; the furnace coated the room in a rich orange light that pulsed and vibrated, and shadows moved repetitively against the walls as pistons moved back and forth and levers moved up and down. Ayala had seen workshops and pictures of factories before, yet the technology and machinery in those seemed rudimentary to the contents of this room; where the machines of the Empire were clunky and awkward, belching steam and smoke as they jerked back and forth, the machines here were smooth and graceful, moving fluidly back and forth in a rhythm that was almost entrancing. Ayala could make no heads nor tails of what the machines were making, and she could scarcely even imagine their purpose, for the feeling of awe within her had caught her breath and stilled her mind.

Like the piano, and quite wondrously, it was all operating by itself, as if a guild of invisible ghosts were smithing hunks of metal, cooling molten iron, forming gears and cogs and shafts and all manner of machinery from molds—yet there were no floating hammers, tongs, or tools; everything looked mechanical and autonomous. It was some great self-actualizing cycle of life unto itself.

"Whoa," she breathed.

"I know," Clay replied. "And look over there."

He was referring to a desk nestled away in the farthest corner of the cavern. There were copious notes scattered about, covering every inch of the desk. They were filled with drawings in black ink and strange diagrams. And in the midst of all that chaos was a man, hunched over, absorbed with his work. It sounded like he was muttering to himself.

"I think we should get out of here," Blood added. "Follow me and move very quietly."

He was tiptoeing backward when he heard the *clunk* of the large, metallic object he bumped into. He turned around, his eyes wide with horror.

"Hello there," it said.

XV

AYALA

They were silent.

The sounds of the workshop filled the room. Into the silence erupted the intermittent hiss of the bellows, inhaling and exhaling in their own circadian rhythm, keeping time with Ayala's own breath.

From the dryness of her mouth, she was pretty confident it had been open for a while. From the silence of her companions, she figured they were in much the same way.

"Oh, dear. They aren't moving," it said, clasping its hands together in an overtly dramatic fashion. "Hon . . . are they dead?" Its voice was a facsimile of a woman's, overly bright and cheery and punctuated with whirs, all filtered through a vibratory noise.

"They're not dead," said a grumpy voice from behind them; his voice, though hoarse and slightly slurred, was powerful and resonating. "Just surprised. It'll wear off."

"Oh, thank heavens," it said, wiping its hand in some mimicry of a person wiping sweat from their forehead. "I was afraid I had killed you. Humans are so frail, after all."

Ayala's face hid nothing. Her eyebrows were stark and distorted, eyes wide and deformed. She looked the . . . thing up and down, trying to get a good read on what she was looking at. She didn't come up with a good answer.

The intonations in its voice were laid with dramaticism, as though it had binge-watched old tv shows about what it meant to be a woman and took them to heart. If it even had a heart. Ayala was still working this all out.

The initial shock had finally passed, and Ayala was able to really examine what was in front her for the first time, though it didn't do her much good. She could see that it was dressed in a thin but modest dress that went all the way down to its ankles. The dress was adorned with yellow and black stripes over a layer of white. A white belt adorned its midline in the form of a bow. The sinews ebbed and flowed over the curvature of her body frame. Even still, the dress did nothing to hide its chrome arms, which still had wires poking from sockets just outside the cuff of what should have been a human shoulder.

And none of this compares to its face, which was a far stranger overture. It reminded Ayala of one of those porcelain dolls that used to sit at the front of the stores in downtown Ruka. Ayala was too poor to ever buy one, but she always remembered how awful their makeup was. It seems the tradition was not lost on whatever this was. Its cheeks were covered in pink blush, a modest amount but still ill-fitting, creating a bizarre contrast that was hard to unsee. Its lips wore red lipstick, although its lips never moved. Only its eyes and eyebrows were animated: the rest of the face was still, frozen in time.

"Um . . ." Ayala said, gradually finding her voice ". . . what are you?" She was never good at beating around the bush.

"Oh, well let's see . . . how to describe it . . ." it said, getting lost in its own thoughts. Could it even think? It sure looked like a robot, but robots didn't exist—sure, stories were full of them, but the tech of the day wasn't close to creating one.

"Marva," called a voice from across the room, "enough of this. Bring them here."

Blood stepped forward, wavering on his own two feet and holding the oar defensively, ready to strike or defend as needed. His brow was set, and the strength of his eye belied the sweat on his brow. "We're not . . . " he paused, and his head lolled, and he bravely passed out.

"Oh my," Marva said, covering its mouth with two blocky hands.

"Blood!" Clay rushed to the Harraka's side, kneeling and checking him over.

Ayala looked at the strange robot-thing. "He does this," she said, not the least concerned about Blood's health. "I think it's kind of dramatic, but . . ." she trailed off, shrugging at the glare Clay shot her. She even felt a little bad—the guy was really worried about Blood; she could see it in his eyes.

"Oh, I understand!" Marva said, far cheerier than was proper. "It's a game!"

"Marva!" called the grumpy man from below again. He was now spun around in his chair, and from here Ayala spotted a mass of grey-white hair atop a stout and well-built frame. His thick beard split apart as he called, "Bring them down here, now. Let me see the boy."

"Okay, hon!" Marva said. With ease, she scooped up Blood and descended the stairs that led to the workshop, her stride light and bouncing in a way that reminded Ayala of a bunny, if bunnies were made of metal and could easily lift an almost-grown man.

"Hey, Clay," Ayala whispered, cocking her head back to the workshop's entrance. "Let's split—I got a bad feeling about this guy and his creepy doll."

Clay looked at her, his eyes wide and brow set, and he shook his head. "And just leave Blood?"

"He literally told us to leave him behind!"

Clay kept shaking his head, the orange light from the forge glistening back and forth on his sweaty cheekbones. "We're not gonna leave him behind. And anyways . . ." he looked toward the workshop, where Marva had just reached the old man. Blood was lain atop the man's desk, recently cleared of papers and tools that Ayala couldn't make out from here. ". . . I think we can trust them," Clay said, sounding more confident than Ayala would have expected. He looked back at her, and the confidence in his gaze settled her nerves. "Call it a gut feeling."

Ayala's head floated back and forth for a moment, as if caught between a nod and a shake. Then she nodded at Clay. She didn't trust this place or these people, but she trusted Clay.

Worse comes to worst, they can always run.

As the two teenagers walked down the workshop steps, the noises surrounding them grew louder, lending a claustrophobic feeling to the otherwise spacious workshop; it reminded Ayala of insect orchestras on a summer night, but instead of buzzes and chirps, the air was filled with a song of metal and flame. It was discordant, but there was a strange melody in its repetition—she couldn't decide if the noises set her at ease or flared her nerves.

". . . miracle that he's still kicking," said the old man to the robot, his voice the soothing sound of a person who's eaten nothing but cigarettes and whiskey for the past two decades. He was standing next to the desk, studying Blood and his wounds with fingers dangling from his beard, which looked as if it had been kept in the same plaits for days. Between his mess of tangled shoulder-length hair and the beard were a pair of small dark eyes, nestled beneath eyebrows that seemed too delicate and thin for him. Dirt and soot caked the crow's feet and wrinkles that crowded his skin, and cheekbones that seemed too sharp peeked out of his face. He wore a worn gray jumpsuit that held up well, given its apparent age. Tools, pens, and doodads of all kinds peeked out of its many pockets and pouches, and the whole suit was just as covered in soot and oil as his face.

As Clay and Ayala approached, the man looked to them, his eyes widening with surprise. "By the forge, Marva, look at them! You should've brought them here as soon as you saw them—you kids look like you've been buried alive twice and dug yourself out of the grave."

"Wow, thanks," Ayala deadpanned. But now that her adrenaline was waning, she could feel the weakness coursing throughout her body, and the dull pinprick aches of her arms and back caused her to look at Blood. No wonder he collapsed—hell, it was impressive that he woke back up in the first place.

"Is this not how human children look?" Marva asked the man, her head cocked in a way that annoyed Ayala. For a robot, she was a ditz.

"We're not children," Clay said. "I'm thirteen and she's fifteen."

"Oh, teenagers!" Marva said, as if she'd just discovered a wonder of the world.

The old man had his back turned to Blood again, and he was fiddling with a pouch filled with tools of some sort. They looked medical to Ayala, but they also looked nothing like the forceps and syringes she had seen before—these were sleeker and pale, their

155

shapes smooth and alien, and they looked far too clean for someone like the old man to be using. "When's the last time you kids ate?" he barked, not turning back from Blood. He was trimming away the Harraka's grimy bandages now, all but peeling them off of the boy's tattered pants and skin.

Ayala and Clay looked at each other, both trying to remember when they last ate a proper meal.

"Paused too long." The man grunted, sounding rather displeased. "Marva, for flame's sake, go get them some food. Kids ain't supposed to look like that."

"You got it, hon!" Marva said, launching the man a thumbs-up that looked wrong; it only had two digits and a thumb. To call them fingers felt wrong, for they were blocky pieces of metal connected by hinges. They looked like their creator put no effort at all into making them fingerlike.

"And Blood? Will he be okay?" Clay asked, peeking around both Marva and the man to get a better look at him.

"Get them out of here, Marva," the man said, his voice gravelly and grave. "I gotta concentrate."

Ayala tapped Clay's shoulder, throwing her hand in a carefree gesture as she said, "Ah, I'm sure he'll be fine. He's weird, remember?"

She wasn't quite ready to talk about Blood's mist thing around these people, but she noticed Clay recognize what she was alluding to. He nodded.

"Come along then, kiddos; let's fill those stomachs with some food," Marva said, ushering the two away from the man, his desk, and the aloof Harraka.

"We're not kids," Clay muttered.

"Oh that's right! You're little teenagers; I won't forget again!" The cheer in Marva's voice was starting to grate on Ayala.

* * * * *

Marva may have been an annoying tin can of bubbliness and cheer, but she was a great cook. Truthfully, right then and there, on her third serving, Ayala decided that she could stomach Marva's artificial exuberance forever, so long as she could also stomach this divine broth. Ayala couldn't even tell what was in it or what it was made of, but it was one of the best meals she'd ever had: creamy, earthy, rich, filling and fulfilling, and with chunks of what might've been the tenderest meat she's ever had—seriously, it just fell apart in the mouth. Ayala was so lost in the delight of her first two bowls that Clay and Marva's conversation faded into syllables and noises. It wasn't until her third that she came back to the present.

They were situated in a room behind the nave, in what must've once been a priest's combined living area and kitchen. Like the rest of the chapel they'd seen, it was spotless and clean, and Ayala felt absolutely wrong inhabiting such a pristine space, even if she weren't coated in the rust of travel and escape, she would feel wrong. In Ruka, Ghoulas weren't allowed in places this clean. At first, her nerves were alight, but the broth helped calm her down.

The room had since been retrofitted in a similar style to the items in the workshop; sleek and tidy appliances of all shapes and sizes were spaced evenly on the counters, and Ayala couldn't make sense of them. There was no sink in the kitchen: instead, there was a rectangular trough filled with running water that flowed out from the wall and bent at two 90-degree angles, flowing back out through the wall. The water was cool and refreshing, and Ayala vaguely remembered Marva mentioning that it was water from the nearby river, filtered of all impurities.

Maybe that was why the broth was so good; back in Ruka, they boiled the water to cleanse it, and it always left a metallic aftertaste that lingered longer than the sense of being full. She guessed that they had some kind of filtration here, the kind that Assyrian houses had.

"Would you two like some tea? I see you were quite hungry, and Nemo has mentioned that tea aids digestion and soothes the spirit." Marva had been floating between the kitchen and its modest table, where the kids sat, since they arrived, cooking more broth as needed and cleaning some specks of dust that only she must have noticed.

Clay looked at Ayala, silently asking if she wanted tea. Truthfully, Ayala didn't like tea at all, but the broth was so good that she was willing to take a chance. She nodded, and Clay said, "Yes, please. Is Nemo the man in the workshop?" Clay asked, looking more at ease than Ayala's seen him in days.

"That's my hon!" Marva leaned forward, dangling her hand out as if sharing a secret. "He may come across as a grumpy man, but he's got a heart of gold in him, just you believe me." She made her way back to the kitchen, retrieving sachets from cupboards, pulling a lever on one machine, turning a wheel on another.

"And what are you?" Ayala asked, propping her chin on her hands, elbows on the table.

"Ah, yes! I've been thinking on that question since you've first asked it, and I believe I have an accurate answer." Marva faced them, its hands together in front of her waist as if she were giving a presentation in class. "I am a construct created by Nemo. I tend to the chapel and run its technology remotely; while the items in the chapel are not autonomous, I sure am! My duties involve keeping the building clean and the gears turning so that Nemo can focus on his work between the chores that I cannot help with."

Its response just left Ayala with more questions, and once again, she had the surreal feeling that this wasn't a real place. The piano notes floating through the air sure didn't help, considering that no one was on the bench.

"So . . . you're the one playing the piano?" Ayala asked.

"Yes!"

"Why?"

"Nemo has said that artistic expression is the apex of humanism, and that to understand various art forms is the best way to understand humanity as a whole," Marva said. "To that end, I have been studying and replicating various famous compositions from your history, among other forms of art, such as painting and literature."

"You want to understand humans?" Clay asked, sounding as if he couldn't believe why someone would ever want to. Ayala resonated with that.

"Of course!" Marva said, its artificial voice rising as if it were excited. Could a robot—or construct, as it called itself—be excited? "I find humans fascinating creatures, more worthy of study than any other living being on this world." The construct walked over to the table with a steaming mug in each hand, setting them down before Clay and Ayala. Its scent was minty and refreshing, and the warmth that crowded the sterile white mug was comforting.

"Enjoy!" Marva said.

"Thank you, Marva," Clay said. He nudged Ayala under the table with his foot.

"Yeah," she said, catching on. "Thanks."

"It's my pleasure!" said the construct, its eyebrows rising. "It's such a pleasure to meet you two, as well as your strange friend! I've never met teenage humans before." It placed a blocky finger on its chin, cocking its head as if in thought. "Actually, I've never met any humans before." It perked up again, and where before Ayala found its exaggerated mannerisms annoying, they were starting to grow endearing. "So, this is quite the auspicious occasion," Marva chirped. "Anyhow, drink up!"

They did, and so Ayala discovered the first tea that she's ever enjoyed.

They sat in silence for a few moments then, simply enjoying the tea and the piano. It almost felt wrong to stay so still and to exist in a place so serene after the chaos of the past few days. Ayala felt her mind wander to those events—to Blood in the woods, Lena in the house, running into Billy and—she cut that train of thought short. She didn't want to think of those things: not now, not ever.

She sipped the tea, took a deep breath, and felt a calm emptiness flow through her.

Footsteps clambered down the hall, uneven and heavy. In the doorway to the kitchen appeared Nemo, and Ayala realized that he was a rather short man; standing, she'd have almost a full head and a half on him. Despite his stature, he carried himself with an assured confidence, and, even without speaking, the man had a presence that seemed to fill a room. Clay, Ayala, and Marva all looked to the man; his face was impassive, his dark eyes revealing nothing.

"Is he okay?" Clay asked, as if scared to hear the answer.

Nemo's beard tilted—a smirk. He stepped to the side and from around the corner limped Blood. A crutch was nestled under his arm and bluish mist rolled steadily from beneath his fresh white bandages.

"Blood!" Clay all but leapt out of his chair and approached the teenager, bombarding him with questions about his pain and well-being. Ayala watched the exchange, sipping her tea and wondering if Clay would act the same if she were in Blood's position.

Blood waited patiently as Clay spoke, and there was an odd confusion in his gaze as he watched the boy. Once Clay finished, Blood almost smiled and said, "I am fine." That said, he limped to the table, taking a seat as Nemo entered the room.

"They sure build Harrakas tougher than I remember," Nemo said nonchalantly, moving to the kitchen and preparing a cup of something.

Marva banged her hands together in a facsimile of a clap. "A Harraka! Fascinating!"

"You know?" Clay asked, watching the back of Nemo's head closely.

Nemo opened a cabinet, taking a bottle of whiskey and pouring it into a mug. "Don't take a rocket scientist to figure it out." He set the mug beneath one of the strange appliances, turned two cog-like wheels on its face, and then pulled a lever, which locked in the downmost position. As black coffee funneled into the mug, Nemo turned around and floated his gaze across the three kids, settling on Marva's unanimated eyes. "Does take one to figure out how you three got past the perimeter defenses," he said, raising his eyebrows at the robot.

"Sorry, hon," Marva said, ever sounding a little abashed. "I turned them off when I saw them coming up the hill—we never get guests, after all, and besides an ineffectual oar, they weren't carrying any weapons. Additionally, their behavior aligned more with needing aid than seeking harm."

"You saw us coming?" Blood asked. There was less tension in his tone than normal, as if Nemo had given him some painkillers.

"From the moment your dinghy slipped onto shore, dear," Marva said.

"Well," Nemo started, taking the fourth and final seat around the kitchen table. Marva stood nearby, watching the exchange and standing uncannily still. "You're all here now, and just in time." He sipped the whiskey-coffee and nodded to Blood. "You didn't have much time left, son. Likely wouldn't have made it if it weren't for that healing ability you got."

Ayala watched the mist rolling up from Blood's lap, curling around the edge of the table and disappearing as it reached for the ceiling.

"Now then," Nemo said, shifting in his seat, "I suppose introductions are in order. I'm Nemo. That's Marva."

He looked at Clay.

"I'm Clay. Thank you for helping us."

Nemo waved his hand, brushing the gratitude away.

"Ayala."

"Jax," Blood said.

Both Clay and Ayala looked at Blood.

"Your name is Jax?" Ayala asked.

Blood—Jax nodded.

"Why didn't you tell us? We've just been calling you Blood this whole time," Clay said.

Jax shrugged. "You never asked."

Nemo chuckled—it was a brief snort-like sound that seemed more sardonic than joyful. "Blood's a stupid name anyhow."

Ayala glared at the old man. "Who asked you?"

Once again, Marva's hands clacked together. "Oh, how wonderful—humans interacting!"

"It gonna blow a gasket?" Ayala asked Nemo.

"There are no gaskets involved in my construction!" Marva said with an odd amount of pride.

"'She,' not 'it,'" Nemo corrected.

Weird, but alright, Ayala thought.

Nemo shifted again, leaning back in his chair, one arm draped across its back and the other gripping the mug on the table. "Now, given how graciously we've received you and overlooked your trespassing, how about you tell us how you found us. And why you're here."

Ayala and Jax bristled. Clay looked to the both of them and said, "It's alright; it's fair. He deserves to know."

"By all means, then," Ayala said, taking her mug and sipping the still-warm tea. She sure wasn't going to tell this tale. She didn't even want to be in the room as it was being told—maybe she could hide in the restroom until it was over.

Then she looked at Clay and decided that she shouldn't run from this. As bad as its retelling would be for her, it'd be worse for him, and maybe having his best friend nearby will help it digest.

Clay hesitated long enough that Nemo prompted, "Well?"

Then Jax leaned forward and started speaking. His tone was level and his diction clear as he spoke. For those parts that he was unconscious for, Clay spoke up. Ayala stayed silent the whole time, fiddling with her mug.

Nemo was silent for some time after the tale's conclusion, his fingers running along his greasy plaited beard.

"I just . . ." Clay started, the emotions of the story plain on his features. Ayala hoped that he didn't feel that burning sensation again—when Jax spoke about the explosion, she saw him tense as if every muscle in his body locked up, but Clay had kept a neutral expression throughout. "I don't understand why that all had to happen," he said.

"Oh, hon," Marva said, her warbling voice dripping with sympathy.

"Then you're an idiot," Nemo said.

"Hey!" Ayala sat up, her hands jumping into fists.

"Hon!" Marva admonished.

Nemo didn't flinch or bristle. He leaned forward, holding Clay's gaze. "You're a Ghoula. You all are. I know how the Empire works, and there's no chance that any of you were confused about your place in their society. You stepped out of your lane, saving him,"

Nemo said, nodding toward Jax. "You did what you weren't sup-posed to do, and you say that you're not sure why it happened?" He cocked his head, looking at Clay with a slanted brow and a quirked mouth. "You know why it happened. You all do. And guess what?" He slapped the table. "It happened, and now you got to live with it—got to live past it. There's only one way left for you—forward. Now tell me, Clay and Ayala," Nemo said, his voice softening, "why'd you save him?"

Clay didn't hesitate. "Because it was the right thing to do."

"Yeah, what he said," Ayala added.

Nemo leaned back in his chair, looking rather pleased with that answer. "Good. Good. See, Marva," said the old man, waving his hand towards the teenagers, "this is what human goodness looks like; remember that."

"You got it!"

"Now," Nemo said, "you kids are going to need a place to stay as Jax's leg heals up. At the rate he's recovering, shouldn't be more than a week or two. You'll stay here with us."

"We will?" Ayala asked, not liking how he made the decision for them.

"You will. You said it yourself; you're being hunted by the most powerful Empire in the world, and you're trying to find its greatest enemy. You set out from here without being rested and ready, and you're good as dead," Nemo said.

"He's right," Jax said.

Nemo nodded. "We'll feed you, get you cleaned up, get you beds in a room—whatever you three need. But it won't be free; all three of you will be expected to help out with chores."

Clay nodded, relief in his features. "We'll do whatever you need us to. Right?" he asked, looking at Ayala.

She bristled. "Yeah. Sure."

"Good," Nemo said. He pointed at Jax. "And that 'something' you stole? We'll talk about that later on, and you won't be getting out of it. Consider that information payment for the medical attention."

Jax was silent a moment, his lips pressed together. Then he nodded.

"Oh, how fun!" Marva exclaimed. "Guests!"

Nemo chuckled again, looking at the robot with a great deal of fondness in his gaze.

"Uh, Nemo?" Clay ventured.

"Yeah?"

"Why help us?"

Nemo paused, weighing the question. He took a sip of his coffee-whiskey, which was somehow still steaming and warm. And half-full. "Not every good deed needs an explanation, you know."

XVI

CLAY

It had been forty-eight hours since they arrived on Nemo's doorstep.

Somehow, it felt much longer than that. Time had become this warped, distorted thing since arriving at Nemo's front door. Nothing was as it seemed. Things with Nemo and Marva had progressed quickly. Honestly, Clay felt like he had known them for his entire life. He found amusement in the way they bickered back and forth, but they never argued or fought. It reminded him a lot of the drunk uncle and nagging aunt he never had. Jax and Ayala were still at each other's throats—well, more like Ayala was at Jax's. Luckily there was plenty of space for them all to fan out on their own and finally catch their breaths.

On the other hand, it felt like no time had passed at all. For Clay, the pain of losing his mom was fresh with every morning. A dull throbbing reminded him that it wasn't a dream. . . . it was all real. Something hurt, deep within his chest—like someone had shifted his heart two inches to the left. And he didn't know how long that feeling would last.

As if he were feeling it through a thick blanket, Clay noticed a pulsing writhing within him—some far-off emotion that seemed to exist on an unreachable horizon. A thick fog lay between him and it, and he didn't know what this distant feeling meant or was—only that it existed within him—and that it held some kind of truth he hadn't yet uncovered.

There was a gentle current over the water. It lapped over smoothly, like silk, and its ripples were like mild disturbances in the grander sullen vista. Clay stood at the edge of the shore, watching as the amber sun hovered, hanging low, its golden flame setting fire to the typically jade waters.

Clay breathed in the cold autumn wind. It should have bitten into his skin like a million daggers, but he felt nothing. Everything was far away, blurred in the distance like the sun, hovering just out of reach.

Clay picked up a smooth stone. He rubbed his thumb over its stratified surface. His arm arced back, and he chucked it quickly over the water.

It sunk immediately.

"You call that a throw?" said a familiar voice behind him.

Clay didn't even turn to look. He went on to pick up the next smooth rock he saw.

Ayala approached him, stopping by his side.

"Mind if I join you?" she asked.

Clay shrugged his shoulders and passed her the stone. "Sure."

"Watch this," she said. She chucked it at the water, and it skipped once before sinking. Smiling, she looked to Clay. "Not bad, huh?"

"Beginner's luck," Clay said, smiling lightly to let her know he joked.

He saw the spark of the challenge in her eye, and she offered him a flat stone. "Then you try."

They skipped stones across the pond for a time. Neither could get a single rock to skip off the water—not even once. They just plopped and sunk, but no matter their inefficacy and no matter the silence that sat between them, they continued.

It felt good to just do nothing with Ayala again. Something as mindless as skipping stones across some random pond threaded nostalgia throughout Clay's being.

The fog within him seemed to lessen, and that elusive feeling grew a little clearer. It pulsed and frothed, like an ocean in a box.

"I had the nightmare again," Ayala said as she picked up another rock.

"The same one?" Clay asked. For years—ever since he'd known her, really—Ayala's been haunted by a recurring nightmare. It never changed, and it always featured her alone, scared for her life, running through Ruka only to find every house empty—all the lights out, everyone gone. She'd often sneak off to Clay's house in the dead of night, slipping through his window just to sleep where she felt comfortable; Clay and Lena were always there for her in a way her parents never were.

"Yeah, it came back," said Ayala, a forced casualness to her tone. "Last night." She paused, mulling something over for a moment, and then she looked at Clay. She had that worried look about her again.

It was always jarring to see Ayala afraid. She always carried this cavalier way about her, as if nothing fazed her and she was untouchable, but Clay was one of the few people who knew better.

And then she smiled. Chuckled. "There was one night I had it and Lena thought a robber was in the house with how I was screaming. She busted into the room, a bat in her hand and ready to kill whoever looked outta place—and you know, I woke up to the door being kicked open and your mom with a bat in her hands, and that's not the best way to come out of a nightmare, yeah?"

Clay chuckled, picturing it perfectly. "Yeah." He bent over to pick up another grey stone, studying it mindlessly to see if it was flat enough to skip off the water. It wasn't. He threw it, and it sank.

"She didn't even know I had snuck in," Ayala said, chucking a rock. It sank immediately. "But as soon as she saw me, the look on her face was gone—she almost deflated, like the fight just left her all at once. She didn't say a word. Just put that bat down and hugged me tight until I stopped crying and fell asleep."

Clay didn't remember this—hadn't even heard about it until now. "When was this?"

"Earlier this year, when you were on a field trip to wherever it is that fancy school sends you on field trips," Ayala said, smiling as she picked up another rock. "She never told you about it?"

"No, never."

Ayala chuckled. "Good."

"Good?"

She side-eyed him. "I really didn't want you to know about it."

Clay shrugged, brow furrowed. "It's not like it's embarrassing or anything." He bent and picked up another rock. "It's kind of sweet."

"Eww."

The two of them chuckled.

Ayala hesitated, as if searching for the right words, and then she shook her head and threw her rock. It skipped across the water twice before sinking.

He expected her to cheer or gloat or rub it in his face, but Ayala just stood, watching the pond ripple in the three spots the stone landed, the tiny waves rolling under and over one another where they met.

"How you doing, man?" she said to him at last.

"I don't really know," he said.

She did not press, and they were silent for some time. Her question kept running through Clay's mind until he landed on something that more closely resembled an answer.

"I . . . I think I'm angry. I think I have been for a long time."

Ayala's tried to contain her facial expressions, but Clay saw her eyes widen for a split second. Clay was usually the one calming Ayala down, so hearing this must've been a shock. But today, he couldn't ignore the venom in his veins, the fire swimming in his gut.

Still looking at the pond, Ayala said to him, with her brow furrowed and fists clenched, "Angry, huh?" She sighed and seemed to deflate. "Yeah. Me too."

"Yeah," Clay pondered, his voice low. He studied the rock in his hand, rolling it back and forth, noticing how the sunlight burned across its smooth parts and edged its jagged ridges.

"At what?"

Clay shrugged. "I don't know."

Again, silence stretched between them, and with each passing moment and each rock thrown into the water, Clay grew closer to knowing.

"I'm tired of . . ." he paused, knowing the feeling but failing to find the right words to capture it. He threw a rock, which sank without skipping, and then discovered the words. "Tired of feeling like I can't do a damn thing." He looked at Ayala. "I'm sick of feeling powerless. Like some forgotten thing which can't affect anything." He looked back to the water, picked up a rock, and threw it. He didn't know if it skipped or sank. "I'm weak as they come, Ay. I can't do a damn thing."

"That ain't right, Clay," she said, shaking her head. Her voice wavered somewhere between sympathy and anger—at what, he wasn't sure. "You saved Blood. You've . . ." she trailed off and threw a rock. "You're not weak, man."

"I am," Clay said, his voice hushed. "I feel like I am." He caught Ayala's gaze again. "You know, I bet that if we just left Blood in the Wraithwood and went home, everything would be okay. Everything would be normal."

Again, Ayala shook her head. "I wouldn't be friends with you if you were the kind of person who'd do that. You've got an open heart, Clay, and—"

"And that's the problem!" Clay hopped to his feet, gesturing as he spoke. "If I didn't have that 'open heart,' things would be okay. Mom would be alive, and we wouldn't be here running for our lives and . . ." he trailed off, having no more words to share. He was a kid with a rock. He had no power. No control. He was just some dumb good-for-nothing Ghoula. A sewer rat.

Ayala's voice was husked with emotion, and she seemed close to tears. She kicked a rock into the pond, wincing as if she hit her toe the wrong way. "I get it. I mean, look at where we are. Look at what we've been through." Ayala was pacing back and forth across the water's edge, kicking rocks here and there into the pond. That choked emotion in her throat had fled; in its place now was an edge to her tone, and as she spoke it grew sharper. "We never even had a choice. It's like everything that will ever happen in our lives is decided before we are even born—where we live, the jobs we have . . . how we die . . . gods, it makes me want to scream."

"Yeah," Clay said, just now noticing that his grip around the rock had grown so tight that its jagged edges cut into his palm. "I'm angry, and I want to . . ."

He didn't know what he wanted to do. He just knew that he was angry.

He never had the privilege of anger before. Anger was a commodity spent by those on the top and those with nothing left, not the people trapped in the middle like he was. His whole life, Clay had to swallow his anger; he couldn't act on it or even verbalize it, because that'd ruin all that mom had built for him. She worked hard for him, and he did his best to respect that. And at the end of the day, it wasn't even anger that caused everything to happen—it was kindness.

"Ayala?"

"Yeah?"

"We did a good thing, right?"

XVII

JAX

Jax was taught that pain was good. He knew that blood was coin to be spent in purchase of the future.

He had liked that name for him: Blood. He wore it better than he's ever worn Jax.

Jax, who was never enough for those around him.

Jax: a failure and a disappointment.

Blood felt . . . like an insult he liked to wear.

"Mr. Jax!" Marva's voice brought him back to the here and now. "Should you be moving around with your leg like that? Much less carrying such heavy things." She had her hands on her hips, shaking her head as if she were a tutting mother.

Jax looked at the iron ingots he carried; they were heavy, and he liked that. It made him feel useful, and the pain that shattered his leg with every other step was good fuel. "Nemo asked for them," he said.

Marva stomped her foot—actually stomped her foot. "Oh, that man," she seethed. "He should know better than to ask you for that. You should be healing, Mr. Jax, resting and tending to that nasty wound of yours. Not running errands for Nemo."

Jax felt his lips quirk. Marva was absolutely ridiculous, and he found that he rather liked her. He couldn't pin down why, but there was something refreshing about her passionate naivete.

They were in the back of the chapel, where the air was stuffier and filled with muffled noises, the piano playing from the nave and the metallic breaths of the workshop below.

"I volunteered," Jax said.

"Now why would you do that? You know that you should rest, Mr. Jax."

"Just Jax." He shifted his weight; his wound ached, and his leg stiffened when still for too long. He wanted to get moving. "Could you open the door?" Both his hands were on the tray he held, stacked in a pyramid of ingots.

"Oh, I sure will," Marva said. "I'm going to give that man a piece of my mind." She opened the door and turned back to him. "I can take those off your hands; you could use the rest, I'm sure."

"I don't mind," Jax said. "I'll follow you down."

"You sure, hon?"

"Yeah."

Marva quirked her head. "Now why would you make it harder on yourself? I imagine that it can't be comfortable." There was genuine curiosity in her voice, and Jax again found himself wondering how Nemo built this creature.

Words that weren't his sprung from his lips. "Comfortable is complacent. Stagnant water breeds disease; the rushing river stays pure."

"Hm. Okay!" Marva started down the stairs, and Jax followed. It was slow going—he could only step down with his good leg, and the balance the descent demanded of him was satisfactory. He lost himself in the movement and the pain, and then he was at the bottom of the stairs.

Tomorrow, he would try to reach the bottom faster.

He followed Marva through the workshop, limping steadily. Nemo was at his desk, hunched over and focused on reading and writing.

"Oh, you," Marva seethed again, stomping over to Nemo. She stood next to him, hands on hips, and said, "You've got some nerve, you do, making this poor boy do manual labor not even three days after he's almost died."

"Got the metal," Jax said, placing it down on a nearby workbench.

"Thanks, boy," Nemo said, not looking up from his desk. He gestured, waving aside Marva's words. "I'm sure it doesn't bother Jax here." Now, he looked at Jax. "Does it, boy?"

Jax wasn't bothered. "How long until it's ready?" Jax asked.

"Until what's ready?" Marva asked, her voice still tilted with reproachment. Impressive.

Nemo, still looking at his desk, gestured in Jax's direction. "A shortsword for 'im. Should be ready within the week." Now, he looked up and at Jax, his beard tilted with a grin. "And don't worry about the quality; I guarantee you that my blades are made quicker and better than anything the Harrakas can cook up." He watched Jax, as if studying him for a reaction.

Jax nodded, glad to hear that it would be ready so soon. He limped away, leaving the old man and the robot to bicker beneath the workshop noise.

✴   ✴   ✴   ✴   ✴

Staying still . . . it felt wrong. Resting and relaxing felt like a step backwards. But there was too little to do during the day. Nemo had promised chores and such, but between the three of them, it turned out to be no more than a few hours of work a day. He longed to move and to train, but after five days here, his leg was still too stiff. The muscles had been shredded, and it would take time for him to regain his strength. For five days now, his wounds have been misting constantly, and he viewed the world through a soft blue haze. Today, though, the mist was thinner.

"Hey, Blood." It was the girl. She was wandering the outskirts of the forest, gathering leaves and acorns and other useless things as she often did. His route to the pigpen passed by her, and as ever, she seemed unable to resist an interaction. She was unlike the boy, and Jax puzzled over their friendship. He puzzled over the boy, to whom kindness was as breathing. He—Clay—seemed to have an open heart.

She had that taunting grin on her face again, the one she so often wore when she looked at him. "Guess you like pain, huh?"

He quirked a brow at her.

She gestured to the buckets of slop he carried in both hands. Both were filled to the brim.

"That much weight on your leg, throwing up mist like it is?" She shook her head. "You're insane, man."

Jax had nothing to say. He kept walking toward the pigpen. She scoffed and turned away, returning to her dalliances.

Tomorrow, he would resume his training.

* * * * *

It felt good to move. To sweat. To be surrounded by mist, and to ache throughout the body. It assuaged the pain in his leg, which had subsided to a dull ache that throbbed with his heart some hours ago.

The motions were simple. The basics. The Harrakas taught this regimen to children. It seemed an apt place to begin his rehabilitation. With each kick and strike, his leg ejected mist until he had created his own fog. The mist's thickness felt like proof of his progress: proof that he was worthy of this life, at least for today.

As Jax moved, punched, kicked, stretched, and posed, he planned. They would be able to depart from this place soon. Once he was able to finish the first tier of training—the routines and patterns the Harrakas taught to their young—they would move on and continue their journey to find the Harrakas.

The thought of returning home settled within Jax's lungs; as if the thought had claws and hooks, it pulled his throat tight and kept his lungs tense.

No matter. Jax had a life debt to pay. He would pay it.

Though, Jax did not know where the Harrakas were. His people—"his people," as if he hadn't considered himself separate from the Harrakas for some time now—were nomadic. They did not stay in one place long, and they did not leave even ghosts of their presence when they moved on. It's been many moons since Jax had been with them, and Uxiah will have moved the Harrakas three times over by now.

So where to go from here? They masked their trail well—

The faces of those Assyrian children flashed in his mind: his kick was too high and he planted his foot too narrowly, stumbling and regaining his balance shortly after.

He did what he had to do to keep their tracks hidden. To ensure that no one knew where he took the boy and the girl.

Uxiah would have been proud of his actions. If Uxiah was proud, Jax should be happy. Such were the simple truths of a Harraka's life.

Jax shook his head, grunted, and planted his feet, steadying his stance and facing the trunk again. He studied the tree before him: where the bark bent and cracked from his punches and kicks; the dew that stuck to the leaves and branches, created from the diffuse mist unfurling from Jax's leg; those areas where he's stripped the bark from the tree with his hits, the underbark's paleness like skin.

He nodded. The tree before him gave him his direction, and he sent gratitude to The Source for guiding him.

Ilaali lumay: The Mother Trees. Conduits for The Source. Great trees with roots so deep that they brush the spine of the world, where a person can interface with The Source and travel its channels. Harraka shamans, the Sangomawo, can even transport people and things from one *ilaa* to another. From an *ilaa lum*, Jax could search through The Source to find the Harrakas. His people can hide their tracks in the physical world, but The Source is as much a historian as it is a provider.

But Jax had no clue where the nearest *ilaa lum* was. The trees were only cultivated outside of the borders of the Empire and in those rare places where Uruk traditions survive, even if in bastardized form.

Jax conjured a map in his mind's eye, recalling his tedious geography lessons from his childhood and briefings.

To the east, in the flowered marshy lowlands, was an ancient city, built by Uruk exiles: Thiva. Nowadays, it was a place where Assyrian corporations exploited Ghoulas in the name of progress and profit, but it was also a place where some old ways were kept alive. Harrakas often spoke of a group of shamans who lived on the outskirts of Thiva, dedicated to preserving what little of the Uruk culture survived the wars against Assyr.

Such a shaman would know where the nearest Mother Tree is.

Footsteps coaxed him from his reverie. They were plodding and unsure, and the right leg had slightly more weight placed on it than the left. Clay approached. Jax stopped the ritual movements and peered through the thick fog. Yes, it was Clay. The boy approached.

It unnerved Jax. He thought that he made it clear that he'd rather be left alone: he hunted for his own food in the area, ate by himself, made conscious efforts to not bother anyone else. Yet the boy often sought him out. Jax could not understand why, and with his confusion came the strangeness of unfamiliarity.

"Jax?" The boy's tone wavered somewhere between uncertainty and courage, like a bird about to leap from its nest.

Jax limped out from the thickest parts of the fog, reveling in the ache of his legs. Though his wound throbbed, his leg felt better, looser, stronger. The mist was working miracles. Though its healing factor was more than welcome, the mist concerned him greatly. He did not know where it came from or why it billowed from his wounds. There were no answers to be found from it, though, and so he tried his best to not think of it.

He met the boy's gaze and nodded, waiting for more words. He had the indistinct impression that Clay would repeat the sentiments of Marva and the girl: that Jax was doing too much too soon. They did not understand that there was no such thing.

"I want to train with you." Clay spoke confidently, and Jax saw vestiges of the same boy who faced down his bullies while running for his life. That was good. If he was to be accepted by the Harrakas, Clay would have to draw strength from his tragedies.

He would face more in the future.

Jax shifted; though he recognized these truths, the notion of training Clay sat uncomfortably in his chest. The boy had shown himself to possess a good heart. Jax's lessons were not for those with a good heart.

"I warn you; it's not an easy path." Once again, words that were not his own escaped his lips.

"I don't care," Clay said. "I want to get stronger. I need to be . . ." he trailed off. Jax waited patiently for him to find his words. Clay seemed to find them—he squared his gaze with Jax. "I'll do whatever it takes."

"You'll be broken," Jax said, some small part of him hoping that Clay would give up here. Is this how Uxiah felt?

No.

Clay shrugged. "Eggs and omelets, right?"

Jax had no clue what that meant. He assumed it was an affirmation, judging by the boy's posture and brow.

"Alright then," Jax said. "Let's begin."

XVIII

AYALA

Ayala had never done chores in her life—not a single one. There wasn't much to do for things already ruined, like her house and her parents. Neither asked nor expected anything of her.

What surprised Ayala was how good it felt to do chores—to have her presence felt, and to see the effects of her labor. To work towards the maintenance of something. Seeing her impact gave her some fulfillment, even if it was something as simple as feeding pigs.

And this chapel—this odd little place with a weird old dude and an actual speaking robot with a personality—was good. It was peaceful, a place where the rest of the world didn't seem to hold influence.

And the view . . . oh, Ayala could stare at the view from here for hours.

The chapel itself was no grand structure, just a room with a tower attached, really. Yet it stood atop a hill, and the country here was open, bounding, and spotted with herds of pines and broad-leafed maples, colored with Autumn's touch. Mountains rose in the distant west, and the land flattened into marshes and rivers to the east.

Throughout the day, insects and birds—those who hadn't yet migrated south—called and sang, filling every moment with this peaceable feeling. The machinery scattered around and within the chapel hummed, banged, and scraped with clockwork repetition; while at first it bothered Ayala, the noises of metal and steam were now like her own heartbeat. And it hadn't even been a week since their arrival.

She just finished her last chore of the day—fueling one of the many generators scattered around the chapel. Nemo had explained why he needed so many generators, but Ayala had zoned out, staring at the patterns of the chapel's stained glass. She knew that he wanted her to fuel up the generators every other day; she didn't care to know more than that.

She made her way across the sloping hill, floating her gaze across the landscape and feeling a breeziness in her chest. Ayala wandered, searching for something to kill the rest of the time in the day. Clay was training with Jax again. They'd started it yesterday and she could see the aquamarine fog gathered at the foot of the hill, their silhouettes moving back and forth in it. If it was anything like yesterday's session, Clay would be too half-dead to want to do anything with her.

It left her feeling a little out of place. She wasn't quite sure what she should do or where she should go.

She stopped in her tracks, realizing that she'd spent most of her life waiting around for Clay—for him to get out of school, to get back home, to come back from a field trip, to unlock his window in the dead of night.

"Huh," she said to herself. She looked at the chapel, simply marveling at its pale simplicity.

She wanted to ask Marva about something.

She made her way to the chapel, trying to ignore the fog below. She had no clue why Clay and Jax would want to go through all that trouble when they finally had a chance to rest.

The chapel's doors were open like the gates to a city. It was that time of autumn where the air was perfect throughout the day, and the bugs grew fewer as the nights grew longer. From the chapel floated piano notes, and Ayala was nodding her head almost immediately. Marva wasn't playing what she had the past few days—slow peaceful tunes that made Ayala restless or sleepy; this was something fresher and more dynamic. The notes wavered all over the place, each haphazardly connected to the last, though there was a definite rhythm to the piece itself that Ayala liked. As she passed beneath the chapel's shadow, she couldn't help but feel that something was missing from the arrangement.

Marva was standing at the far end of the nave, her hands folded together in front of her. She was looking at a music book, splayed on the piano's stand; as ever, the piano played by itself, and the music book even flipped its own pages, aided by a small mechanical lever.

"I like this tune, Marva!" Ayala called, her voice playing around the stained glass and tall ceiling.

"Thank you, Ms. Ayala," Marva chirped.

When Ayala reached a comfortable distance from the robot, she asked, "Get tired of the snoozers?"

Marva cocked her head. "I am afraid I don't know what that means."

"Snoozers." Ayala closed her eyes, knocked her head back, and snored. "The music that puts you to sleep—you done with it?"

"Oh! I see. 'Snoozers.' How quaint." Marva brought her hand to her "mouth" and chuckled. "Yes, I've decided to move on to a newer form of music." She looked at the piano keys, bouncing seemingly at random. "The form I was playing before relies on tight compositions played flawlessly to a rhythm. Performing songs from that genre was almost mathematical in nature, yet this one is more experimental. Though there's sheet music to this song, its performer never played it the same way twice."

"So the sheet music's more of a guide than a . . . something else more concrete," Ayala said.

"Indeed. Though . . ." Marva's voice trailed off, her tone despondent. "I struggle with injecting notes outside of the music. Without those, it feels . . ."

"Flatter? Two-dimensional?" Ayala offered.

"Yes!" Marva said, as if pleased to find the appropriate words for her dilemma. "My preliminary hypothesis is that such pieces require an interaction from something I refer to as 'the human spirit.' Traits such as ingenuity, spontaneity, and creativity are hallmarks of this music genre. I am afraid I lack these traits."

Ayala clapped Marva's shoulder, surprised at how dense and sturdy this robot was; for something built like a housewife, she sure stood like a brick wall. "I'm sure you'll figure it out. Anyways, I have a question for you."

"Yes?"

"You mentioned that you paint?"

✳ ✳ ✳ ✳ ✳

In Ayala's house, there was a singular object of value: a painting. Amidst the rotting wood, stale trash, bugs, and mold, it hung from the main room wall, always slanted. Her grandmother had painted it, and it was the only thing Ayala knew about any of her family outside of her parents. Black and white, it was a peaceful painting of a beach, silhouetted figures across the sands and palm trees crowding the borders. Little v-shaped birds flew over the water, and two figures cuddled on a bluff in the foreground. And there, nestled in the corner of the painting, were the initials 'AVG.' Ayala always imagined that she was named after her grandmother, and she'd always felt more connected to those three little letters than to her own parents.

And she had to admit that Marva was a better painter than AVG.

"Marva, these are crazy," Ayala said, bent over with her eyes squinting at the canvas. Her studio was nestled in a small room off the workshop, and they could hear the rhythmic sounds of Nemo's work through the wall. Only four paintings hung from the walls of the workshop: One was of the chapel, viewed from the bottom of the hill; one was of Nemo, his expression focused and his beard folded in with his lips; one was the distant mountains; one was of a hammer and a chisel, resting on a workshop table. They were all incredibly lifelike and detailed; the texture of each object was perfectly matched to life, and it looked like Marva had painted every single strand of Nemo's hair.

A fifth canvas rested in the center of the workshop, propped on an easel. Around it lay a number of palettes. Each palette was clean but for perfectly round globs of paint spread along its edges, each equidistant from each other. It looked as if six different painters had prepared their paints, just to forget about their palettes.

"What's up with that?" Ayala asked, gesturing to the blank canvas.

"Ah," Marva said, her modulated voice bearing the same despondency of earlier. "My latest attempts." She pointed stiffly to each of the four finished paintings. "These are all recreations of life. Copies of things I have seen."

"Well, they're really good copies," Ayala said.

"Thank you! I do not wish to make copies," Marva said. "Painting what I can recall perfectly is imitation, not creation. It is not what humans would consider 'art.'"

"Oh? And what would humans consider art?" Ayala asked.

"Creation," Marvas said. "Something new and unique. I believe that I am incapable of this. As with the piano, I believe that the act of creation requires a human spirit. Six times, I have stood before that canvas for three hours each, trying to paint something I have never seen before. I find that I cannot."

"Huh." Ayala looked at the studio, imagining Marva standing and having a creative crisis. She stepped closer to the canvas. "Maybe you just gotta feel it. Not try so hard, you know?"

"I do not comprehend," Marva said.

Ayala moved her head back and forth, trying to find the right words for it. "I'm not really sure if it's something that I can explain. Maybe it's best if I show you."

"Oh, please!" Marva said, gesturing to the easel. "I've never had the pleasure of watching a human paint before."

"Nemo doesn't paint?" Ayala asked. It didn't surprise her, but she found it odd for a man to build a robot with hobbies he didn't have.

"That man has a mind of metal and gears," Marva said, waving her hand.

"And bourbon and beers," Ayala said under her breath, chuckling to herself. She went to the canvas, picked up the palette with the freshest paint, grabbed the first brush she saw, and felt intimidated.

Something about standing here, paintbrush in one hand, paints in the other, standing before this blank white canvas felt wrong.

To Ayala, the world of art was one of the few places Ghoulas had the privilege of being seen—truly seen. It was a rare interstice of beauty and reality, and she'd seen art transcend the divisions between even the worst of enemies; not even the arbitrary boundaries throughout Assyria could hold up against it. Be it "low-brow" mediums like poetry or graffiti, or vibrant frescos on the roof of a mausoleum, the Ghoula spirit always found a way to endure the cruelest of realities and carve its mark of beauty on the world.

Art—painting, especially—enraptured her since she was a young child. Unbeknownst to anyone, not even Clay, Ayala had long wished that she could create like those other Ghoulas do. To add even one beautiful thing to this cruel world.

But how could she give what she does not have?

Ayala grabbed that feeling within her. She squeezed it. She choked it.

She dipped her brush into the darkest glob of paint and swiped it across the canvas.

And then she stood there, staring at the single black curve on the wide white canvas. Teardrops fell down from the curve, leaving dark paths in their wake.

This felt right.

XIX

CLAY

Oh, by Cyrus . . ." Clay huffed, his breaths like needles across his lungs. His hands were on his knees and sweat rolled off his face and into his eyes. Just like the day before, training with Jax felt like the worst mistake of his life; he had transcended bodily aches—he felt it in his bones and in his soul now.

"Don't bend over like that," Jax said. He was, of course, barely breathing hard—even with a blown-up leg, he was smoking Clay. Jax's hands were clasped behind his head and he paced back and forth. "Do what I'm doing."

Clay tried, straightening his torso and clasping his hands around his head, trying his hardest to get his breathing back in order. This stance was far less comfortable.

"Pace around, too," Jax mentored. "Keep your body moving."

"Why?"

Jax's voice stayed low and calm, and his breaths were weighted but even. "Don't breathe as well when you're bent over. Stopping movement altogether can shock the body. That's why you threw up yesterday—you stopped moving as soon as we were done, and your body didn't like that."

"Man, my body doesn't like any of this."

To Clay's surprise, Jax chuckled. It may have been the first joyful sound he'd ever heard from the morose teen.

Clay planted one foot in front of the other, almost falling into each step as he waddled around, breathing like an asthmatic goose.

This sucked.

Today was like the day before: exercises and movements that didn't make much sense to Clay. He assumed that it was mostly conditioning—they sure did a lot of sprinting, push-ups, squats, and all kinds of calisthenics that Clay didn't have names for. But then there were stranger movements that felt almost ritualistic, where they'd stomp with purpose and wave their hands around in wide circular patterns. They seemed silly to Clay, but Jax treated the motions with such respect that Clay followed his example without asking a question. Mostly, Clay was glad for the chance to catch his breath—they'd almost always follow up a bout of conditioning with one of these ritualistic sessions.

"We'll stretch when you catch your breath," Jax said. Man, the guy was barely even sweating.

Clay breathed out sharply. He had to get to Jax's level. "So, is this like . . . your normal training?" Clay pushed out.

"No. These are the exercises we perform with children after their seventh winter."

Clay studied Jax's expression, hoping that he heard him wrong. Or that it was a joke. "That's a joke, right? Please say that's a joke."

Jax's smile fit him like a stranger. "No."

Clay groaned and fell back to the ground. "Cool! There are seven-year-olds who can do this better than me."

"Yes," Jax said. He sat next to Clay, crossing his legs and propping his elbows on his knees. "You should sit up."

Groaning again, Clay wiggled up.

"Now for Agbasã," Jax said, standing with the ease of a dancer.

"Agbasã," Clay repeated, flopping around until he too was standing. "The slow movements, yeah?"

"Yes. Let us begin." Jax entered the first motion, his body rigid and stable.

Clay followed, teetering and wobbling. Many of the poses required a sense of balance that Clay had never developed in his life. He fell down frequently, and Clay was grateful that Jax never mentioned it or made fun of him for it. Once he settled into the first pose, Clay asked, "What does Agbasã mean?"

"Bridge," Jax replied.

"Bridge to what?"

"The Source."

"The what?"

"The Source."

"What's the Source?"

Jax flowed into the second pose, and Clay clumsily repeated the movements.

"The metaphysical world layered beneath ours," Jax said. "A spiritual tether connecting the past, present, and future." Once again, his tone had a rehearsed feeling to it. Kinda like when Clay would recite the Pledge to Assyria at the beginning of each school day.

At least he didn't have to do *that* anymore.

Jax continued. "From the Source, we derive our sense of being. Without it, we would have no identity, no substance. No ingenuity nor creativity. We would not know who we are or where we belong." Jax shifted into the third pose of Agbasã. "One could say that it is where our soul comes from."

"So," Clay grunted, settling into the third pose, "why are we Agbasã-ing with it?"

Jax grinned and said, "A connection with the Source must be maintained, just as the warrior must constantly sharpen their blade. The Assyrian way of life ignores and blocks this connection; through their idolatry, oppression, and distractions, the Empire keeps its people complacent and ignorant. Connecting to the Source requires an attunement of the body and spirit; through opening and maintaining a connection, we gain power that lies outside of this world."

"Like the mist from your leg?" Clay asked, looking around at the bluish fog surrounding them. He just realized that it was almost the same color as the sunlight that filters through one of the stained-glass windows in the chapel.

"I think so."

"Can I get mist on my leg?"

"No," Jax said. He looked down at his leg, and for some reason his face grew tight. "I've never seen this mist before. I don't know where it comes from."

"Seriously?" Clay asked, now regarding Jax's leg as well.

Jax nodded. "No Harraka I know has a gift like this, and I did nothing to earn this one."

"Any idea what it is?"

Jax shook his head.

"Weird."

"Yeah." Jax nodded, and though he appeared serene in tone and countenance, Clay could feel worry roiling somewhere deeper within the warrior.

"So, what kind of powers *do* Harrakas get?" Clay asked, thinking back to the burning sensation he experienced throughout their escape. It had been a few days since he had an attack, though he still had no answer for it. He didn't want anyone other than Ayala to know about it, for now at least.

"All kinds," Jax answered. "We're all different from each other. Our souls are unique. I am not you; you are not me. Our connection to the Source—and the powers that it may grant us—is unique."

"Cool," Clay said.

They shifted into the fourth pose. Clay noticed how similar it was to a fighting stance he had seen in a *Revolt* comic.

"Wait, 'may grant us'? So, not everyone gets stuff like your mist?" Clay asked.

Jax shook his head. "Anyone can connect to the Source. Only select bloodlines and lineages receive powers from it. Even from those bloodlines, only a select few are chosen."

"Any chance I'm one of those bloodlines?" Clay asked.

"Maybe." Jax studied Clay for a moment. "The Assyrians label you Ghoula. They label me Harraka. Both are untrue terms."

"What do you mean?"

"I am Uruk. The Harrakas are Uruks." Jax inhaled and exhaled. "I believe you and Ayala are Uruks as well. Your eyes are the color of the sunset, and this is a hallmark of Uruk lineage."

Clay regarded Jax's indigo irises. "But yours aren't."

Jax brought a hand near to his face, resting a finger on his cheekbone for a moment before returning to the proper pose. "They are not." Jax's mouth quirked, as if he were chewing something sour. His gaze grew a touch more distant for a moment, and then he seemed to return to the present.

"Uruk." Clay tossed the new word around in his mouth, and he felt as if it should have weighed more.

"The Uruks first discovered the Source," Jax said. "Of all the peoples of the world, the Uruks are the most connected to the Source. Our blood is strong and powerful, and Assyrians fears us for this."

"Is that why they tell us we're Ghoulas?" Clay asked, the thought of it all giving rise to an anger within him. "Why they keep us down?"

"Yes."

They finished Agbasā and stretched, and Clay pondered the Source and Uruks. His entire life, he had only ever known that he was a Ghoula, a caste of people who had no past nor future that existed outside of Assyria's yoke. But he wasn't a Ghoula. He was an *Uruk*. With that single four-letter word, there came a connection to a culture, a past, and a future. A culture that had been totally erased from the Empire's lands; a past and a future that they had stolen from him.

Clay wanted it back.

When they finished, he said, "I'm gonna limp up to the chapel and find some food. I'll see you later." Clay held out his fist to Jax.

"Is this a declaration of war?" Jax asked, regarding Clay's fist and seeming to be completely serious.

Clay laughed. "Nah, man. Bump my knuckles with yours. It's how friends greet each other and say bye."

Jax's brow furrowed. He looked at Clay. He looked at Clay's knuckles. Then he nodded, balled his hand into a fist, and punched Clay's knuckles so hard that Clay felt vibrations in his bones.

"Okay that's . . ." Clay eked out through gritted teeth as he nursed his hand ". . . a good start, I guess. Go lighter next time, yeah? Just meant to be a little skin-to-skin—no force involved."

"Oh . . . you alright?"

"Yeah, fine." Clay forced a smile through the pain.

"I have to say," Jax said, his words slow and uncertain, "that . . . it's nice to . . ."

Clay had a distinct feeling that he knew what Jax was trying to say. There were little things about Jax's mannerisms—his reticence, his social reclusiveness, the way he seems to take on everything by himself without asking for help, even the way that he looks through people instead of at them—they all gave Clay the impression that Jax has been alone for most of his life.

And so, he ventured to finish Jax's sentence for him. "Have someone to train with and watch die every day?"

Jax smiled. "Yeah."

With no small degree of bravery, Clay put his other fist out towards Jax. "Yeah, it's nice."

This time, Jax bumped Clay's knuckles correctly.

✻ ✻ ✻ ✻ ✻

Ayala entered the kitchen around the time Clay was finishing his meal. Her arms were splattered with paint up to her elbows, mostly dark purples and pastel oranges. They chatted for a bit—him about training with Jax and her about painting with Marva. Clay didn't even know that she liked painting. He promised her that he'd come down to the studio tomorrow to see what she'd been up to. As for today, he was wiped. Take a bath, go to bed. those were all the plans he had left that day.

His plans were ruined by Nemo.

When Clay exited the kitchen, he saw Nemo in the chapel nave, sitting in the third row of pews. It was the first time Clay had seen Nemo outside of his workshop, not counting the day they arrived. The man looked like he had finally washed; his hair and beard weren't so greasy, and his skin was relatively free of soot and grime.

The smell was better, too. He wore a fresh green jumpsuit that looked sturdy and well-tailored, if not used often.

Nemo caught Clay's eye and, with a glass of what looked and smelled like bourbon in hand, waved him over. "Come on over, Clay. Sit a spell."

Exhausted as he was, Clay didn't particularly want to, but he figured that he should indulge the man who's been so generous towards them.

He sat next to Nemo on the pew, and for a moment the two of them just sat and listened to the piano. Marva had switched its songs to play more enigmatic music, which brightened the atmosphere of the chapel. Where the last genre had induced a calm peaceable mood, this one was lively at times and somber at others.

"Want a lick?" Nemo asked, a grin on his face as he offered the glass of bourbon.

"I'm thirteen!" Clay said.

From the kitchen, Ayala called, "Wimp!"

"Hey! You eavesdropping?" Clay called back.

"No."

Clay could hear the smile on her face. He chuckled and settled into his seat. For a pew made of wood, it wasn't that uncomfortable.

Nemo lowered the glass from his lips, smiling as well. "You settling in all right?" he asked, the words gravelly and rasped, though laced with genuine concern.

"Yeah," Clay said. "It's nice here."

"That it is." Nemo sipped again. Clay felt, for the first time since meeting the eccentric old man, that Nemo was relaxed. "I've been thinking about your situation," Nemo said. "Don't worry—I ain't kicking you out. Just have some thoughts to share, some questions to ask."

"Okay," Clay said. Some part of him shifted to unease, but the larger part recognized Nemo's energy: it was soft and calm, and it dulled his unease.

"What happened to you kids and your mother . . . it ain't right. It ain't fair." Nemo shifted in his seat, meeting Clay's eye; Clay was surprised at how resolute the man's gaze was. "That's this world in a thimble, son: It ain't right; it ain't fair. Evil gets rewarded; good gets punished. It's all a crock of—" Nemo's curse was interrupted by a harsh out-of-key note from the piano. He chuckled, sipped, and then continued, "I say this to ask what you and yours'd like to do. What your plans are. I first reckoned that you'd be here for a few weeks at best, but with how hard your Harraka friend's been pushing himself and how fast he's been healing, I think the three of you would be ready to head out soon, were you so inclined." He looked at Clay, waiting for the boy's response.

"You're asking me? Not Jax?" Clay asked.

"That's right. Sure, Fog-boy's the one leading you to the Harrakas, but I have a feeling that boy's gonna pay attention to your wishes, Clay. Call it an old man's intuition. Ayala will, too. Your opinion and decisions mean a lot to both of your friends. The power to choose a path for all of you might lie with you, at the end of the day." Nemo leaned forward, elbows on knees, and he looked at the piano as he spoke. "That choice is coming soon, and I just wanted to let you know—Marva likes having you three here. I don't mind as much as I thought I would—you're all decent with the chores, and you don't complain much." He looked at Clay. "You, Jax, and Ayala can stay here as long as you'd like. We aren't close to much, but this chapel and this hill? It's closer to right and fair than the world is. It's a peaceful life."

Nemo clapped Clay on the shoulder, reminding the boy just how sore his muscles were. "Think about it, son. Don't need an answer right now or anytime soon. Just let me know when you know."

"Okay," Clay said. "I will."

XX

CLAY

Clay didn't wait one second—after entering his room, he immediately collapsed face-first onto his cot.

"Ahh, that's the stuff," he said, kicking his shoes off and melting into the modest comforter.

He lay there a few minutes, trying to settle his mind. He found that the pain from yesterday had compounded onto the soreness of today, creating an altogether slothful mess. He discovered an intimate awareness of body parts and joints he didn't know existed, from the notches of fire burning beneath his shoulder blades down to his calf muscles and even the middle of the soles of his feet—not the even whole foot, just the middle.

He tried closing his eyes. For minutes, he sat there in the pitch blackness. He tried to clear his mind, but his hazel eyes were restless under the dark canopy of his eyelids. The darkness had amplified his accelerated heartbeat, which was still soaring, thumping loudly in his ears.

"This isn't working," he begrudgingly sighed.

He rolled over onto his back and consigned himself to what looked to be another bout of insomnia.

Add sleep to the list of things left behind in Ruka. He thought he would be better once they arrived at Nemo's; after all, he had his own quarters, a fancy cot . . . but no. Instead, he often found himself staring at the ceiling trying to clear his mind from the crippling loneliness that inevitably set in.

He was beginning to hate the nighttime.

Clay sat up from his bed and swung his feet over the edge of the cot. No sense staring at ceilings all night. That'd just be sad.

Maybe Nemo had some good books. Something about how to make objects levitate and do chores or how to grow a ten-inch beard.

He stood up in the dark, summoning all the strength left in his legs. There was only a small window frame in his tiny quarter. Outside was a moonless night. His hands were stretched out right in front of him and he couldn't see a lick. After bumping into every cornered piece of furniture in the room, Clay found his bag. He fumbled around, finding the matches by touch only, and lit the candles in the room. Wavering amber light flickered and swayed on the walls and ceilings, and he stared at his own shadow for a moment.

Almost like a different reflection, Clay thought, looking at his shifting shadow. Maybe there are two kinds: the face we stare at in the mirror and the shadow we leave on the wall.

Clay wasn't quite sure what that all meant—if it meant anything. It was a nice thought to have, though.

The room now lit, he scrounged up the action figures he had. They had left a lot behind in Ruka, and Clay's hand-me-down figure of the hero Lonesome, whose wide-brim plastic hat had been chipped for years, was likely a pile of ashes now.

Truth be told, the figures before him were a lot nicer than those he used to have. A few days into their stay at the chapel, Clay finally felt safe enough to ask Nemo for some figures like he used to have. To his surprise, the old man knew about Lonesome and even owned a few copies of Revolt. By that night, Nemo had made top-of-the-line figures for Clay—Marva delivered them, of course. At the time, Clay half-thought that Nemo was bound to the workshop, given how he never left it.

Clay looked at the assortment of figures before him. They were glossy like new things were, and Clay noticed that Nemo had even redesigned some of the classic *Revolt* characters. Clay liked Nemo's touches.

Clay had performed this ritual countless times throughout his childhood. But now—staring at these too-good-for-him figures, sitting in a room that wasn't his, existing in a place that wasn't his home—something about this felt both right and wrong.

He shrugged and grabbed Lonesome.

✳ ✳ ✳ ✳ ✳

The poor girl was blindfolded, her heels flush with the cliffside. Sweat matted her hair to her forehead. It was a small mercy she couldn't see. The barrels of two guns were staring right at her.

"Stay back or we'll kill her, I swear to God!" called a tremoring voice, shouting into the air as if calling out to a ghost.

The eyes of the ringleader and his minions were looking for an invisible enemy, knowing he could be anywhere. That was the scariest part. . . .

The ringleader cowered at the flank, his eyes panning back and forth across the landscape; beads of paranoid sweat clung to his cheeks.

He was looking in the wrong direction.

Lonesome leapt up from the nearby brush.

Before the two goons could even swing their guns at the renegade, they were disarmed and unconscious. Lonesome's shadow draped over their bodies.

The ringleader raised his hands. "Alright, you got me. I surrender."

Lonesome didn't give him a chance. He dashed forward, his hands magnetizing to the outlaw's neck.

Lonesome squeezed . . . and squeezed.

Even as the man's face bloated and grew purple, he squeezed.

And as the man bit through his own tongue, he squeezed.

Pop!

The head flew off its neck with a satisfying noise. Clay watched as the decapitated ringleader's head rolled across the floor.

He jumped when it stopped by a pair of metal feet.

"Marva!" Clay said, startled to find the uncanny robot lingering in his doorway. She held a silvery tray, piled with folded clothes and bearing a steaming mug.

Marva looked from the head on the floor to Clay. "Hello," Marva said. She cocked her head, and her eyebrows pinched together. "Are you alright, Clay? I called your name twice, but you appeared to not hear me."

Clay blinked. Marva waited patiently; he wondered if she heard how fast his heart was beating. He looked at the figure's head on the floor, imagining how angry mama would be if she knew he popped the head off a new toy.

Would've been, Clay thought. *She* would've been *angry.*

"Oh, dear," said Marva with modulated tones of warmth and sadness. "Clay, is everything alright?"

He looked at Marva. He shook his head, surprised at how quickly tears leapt into his eyes when he spoke. "I don't. . . . I don't think I'm okay, Marva."

"Oh, hon." Marva set the tray down on the bed and picked up the steaming mug, bringing it to Clay's desk. "Here, I brought you some hot cocoa."

Clay, surprising himself, chuckled a bit. *Hot cocoa? Like I'm seven years old?*

"Is that okay?" Marva asked.

"Yeah," Clay said, sniffling and smiling softly. He took the mug. The scent of roasted chocolate accompanied its soothing warmth. Clay took a moment to regain his breath, which had spiraled out of control. The first sip, while hot, was flavorful. "Thank you," Clay said, scooting his chair so that he could properly face Marva. She stood a touch awkwardly, her blocky hands folded in front of her. Marva wasn't even alive, but there was something about her that was calming. Maybe it was the way she didn't have expectations of anyone. Maybe it was how her patience was endless. Maybe it was just because she was a degree removed from a human, and that made her presence kinder to tolerate.

Whatever it was, Clay was thankful that she was here.

"I have heard that it is polite to inquire about a person's willingness to speak of what ails them," Marva said. "Would you like to talk about what ails you, Clay?"

Clay's thumb rocked back and forth across the mug's handle, his nail swaying like a pendulum. "Well . . . my mom is dead. My house and my things are blown up. I'm wanted by the most powerful nation in the world." Clay blew air out of his nose and leaned back. "Just normal thirteen-year-old problems, yeah?"

Marva quirked her head again. "Sarcasm, yes?"

"Yeah," he said. "The last part, anyhow."

Marva's head straightened again, and her eyebrows shifted, painting her face in a facsimile of sympathy. "I am sorry, Clay, for all that you have had to contend with."

"Why are you sorry?" Clay scoffed. "It's not like you're the one who killed my mom and blew up my life."

"That may be." Marva stepped toward the bed. "May I sit on your bed, Clay?"

"Go ahead."

Marva did so. Her hands folded onto her lap and her torso was unnaturally straight, like she's spent years in etiquette classes. "To quote Nemo," she said, playing a recording of Nemo's exact words, "'I'm not saying sorry because I had something to do with it. I'm apologizing for the world. I'm saying that I'm sorry that this world ain't right or fair or kind. I'm telling you that I'm sorry that I didn't do more to keep it from getting this way.'"

Clay sat there for a moment, mulling over the recording. "Who did he say that to?"

"I am not sure," Marva said. "Many recordings of Nemo have existed in my databanks, even before I gained a degree of sapience. Whenever I've asked about them, he has deflected my answer with humor or grown sullen. I have learned not to ask. While many of the recordings impart knowledge and experiences that are useful for me, others appear to be more niche or even nonsensical, as if I am only hearing Nemo's half of a conversation."

"Huh." Clay wasn't sure what to say, but he was distracted from his own inner turmoil, at least.

"I have found another recording that may provide comfort," Marva said. "Would you like to hear it?"

"Yeah, go for it."

"'People who face normal problems stay normal. People who face great problems grow to be great. Life is tough, and it'll bite you. But without those tough parts, the good don't hold as much meaning. Don't be afraid to face big things—it means that you'll leave a big mark on the world.'"

Clay absorbed this recording, his introspection dueling with his curiosity about Nemo. The Nemo voicing these snippets didn't slur nearly as much, and his voice wasn't quite so gravelly. In both recordings, he also sounded emotional, impassioned in a way that Clay hasn't seen him.

"I think that helps a little," Clay said, sipping more cocoa.

"Can I ask what your emotions feel like to you?" Marva said. "I apologize if that is an impolite request; I'm simply so curious."

"About emotions?"

"About humanity and all its wonders. Emotions remain elusive to me, however; throughout history, humans have made illogical and unwise decisions based on emotion. I fail to comprehend why."

"Because it feels right, I guess," Clay said. "People do lots of things for lots of reasons. I guess we're all just acting to get emotions we want or to get rid of emotions we don't want." Word by word, Clay calmed. The anger within him abated, and he felt a little concerned about how easily he had slipped into that fury.

"To me," Clay started, his words slow and hesitant, "well, I was angry. I am angry. It feels like fire building in my lungs. Makes me want to just . . . destroy something to get rid of that feeling."

"Fascinating," Marva exclaimed, as if she had discovered a new element. "I am sorry that I could not offer more comfort than another's words. There are no codes or formulas for interacting with humans, especially concerning emotional matters. It grows quite confusing."

"It's okay, Marva." Clay looked at the smoke swirling from his mug, smiling at the marshmallows bobbing around in the thick drink. He felt tired now, and his eyelids grew heavier. Somehow, he just knew that once Marva left, he'd fall asleep without any problems. "You're nicer than most humans I've known. I hope humanity doesn't rub off on you."

XXI

CLAY

They had been at the chapel for just over a week, and Nemo had asked everyone to gather in the common room. It felt like a random request, but Clay sensed a purpose behind it. Jax had healed at a miraculous rate, given that he'd been on death's door not too long ago, and considering his last chat with Nemo, Clay had a feeling that the old man didn't want to hang out and play cards.

Clay, Ayala, Jax, and Marva were all settled around the kitchen table. The teenagers sat, and Marva stood nearby, her blocky hands folded in front of her.

They chatted and sipped on tea, and laughter often flowed between Clay, Marva, and Ayala. Though Jax remained mostly silent, Clay was glad to see the stoic man crack a smile here and there, even if Jax's smile looked more like a snout full of fangs than a mouth full of teeth.

They quieted when Nemo entered, all eyes upon him.

"What's up? Why'd you want us here," Ayala asked.

Nemo made his way to the kitchen. "You gotta work on your small talk, Ayala."

"You gotta work on your smell, Nemo," Ayala retorted.

Nemo chuckled along with Clay. The old inventor poured himself a glass of bourbon or whiskey or whatever it was that looked brown and smelled sharp. With his back still turned to the others, his hands busy with a bottle and a glass, Nemo said, "I figure it's time for Jax to give us some answers." He turned around, glass in hand, and leaned against the counter. He took a sip, closed his eyes contentedly, and exhaled softly.

Clay glanced at Jax; the Harraka had tensed up. Jax slid his hands from the table and placed them in his lap, and Clay wondered if he did that to hide fists.

Interacting with Jax felt like poking a sleeping bear with a stick most of the time.

"Don't worry, Jax," Nemo said, his beard tilted with a sardonic grin. "I'm no spy—ain't someone who's looking to sell your secrets. I just want to know what brought you three here, and I think that everyone in this room has a right to know as well."

Jax was silent, slow breaths passing through his lips. All eyes were on him. He stayed stolid and still.

Nemo went to the table, lowering himself into the last chair and grunting with the effort. He leaned forward in his seat, looking closely at Jax. "I need to know what you've done—what you've stolen—so that I can know if I can help you. I need you to trust me, Jax. I know that's no cheap currency for your people, but I've given you space, medicine, food, and shelter: it's currency that's been earned, wouldn't you say?"

Jax's jaw tensed and relaxed, tensed and relaxed. He nodded. "It's better if you see it first."

Nemo gestured, open-palmed. "By all means."

"I will be back," Jax said, pushing back from the table and standing. Without much ado, he left the room, turning right and heading for the dorms.

Nemo looked at Marva. "Follow him, would you? Just so we know if he slips through the window."

"You think he'd run?" Clay asked as Marva stepped—quite silently—out of the room.

Nemo shook his head and sipped his drink. He placed it back on the table. "Force of habit. You save a lot of trouble if you plan for the worst-case scenario off the bat."

"Smartest thing you've said since we've met," Ayala muttered, aiming a teasing grin at Nemo.

"Gee, thanks," Nemo said. He looked to the room's entrance. Both Clay and Ayala twisted in their seats, and Clay was surprised to see both Jax and Marva reentering the room; he was put off by how unnaturally quiet both of them were.

In Jax's hands was a bundle of dark blue cloth, swaddled in many layers over a spherical object. Though it could have easily fit in Jax's palm, he carried it with both hands, holding it closely and firmly, as if to safeguard it and to honor it.

With the object's arrival came silence and weight; its presence filled the room without so much as a whisper, and Clay found that he could not tear his eyes from the bundle of cloth. There was something magnetic about it, something that pulled attention as naturally as gravity grounded him.

He looked around the room, seeing if the others felt the same thing. Nemo and Jax appeared too: Nemo's eyes were glued on the thing, and he was fiddling with his glass, rolling its edge back and forth on the table. Ayala and Marva seemed oblivious to the effect;

Ayala folded her arms on the table, back hunched, and Marva's eyebrows—the only part of her face that moved—were neutral.

Jax laid the object on the table and, gingerly, as if the cloth were made of thin glass, folded back the object's blue shawl, revealing a crystalline object. It was perfectly spherical and colored a deep crimson, its surface glossy and dark. It looked like an abyss filled with blood.

"Cool rock, but I don't see the big deal," Ayala said, leaning closer and squinting at the orb. "So what's special about this guy?" She now rested her head on her arm, which lay flat on the table. She flicked the orb.

"Don't do that," Jax said.

"Yeah, don't pop a vein—not gonna do it again," Ayala said, shaking the pain off her finger.

"Do you recognize this?" Jax asked Nemo. He looked upon the old man with intent, his eyebrows drawn in.

Nemo nodded. He stretched a hand towards the orb, hesitated, and then, as if thinking better of a bad choice, withdrew his hand and sipped more of his drink. "Do you not?" Nemo asked.

Jax shook his head. "I was given the description and location. Nothing more."

"Well, son," Nemo said, shifting in his chair, "I'm no historian on crystals, but . . ."

Crystals? Like the ones that power cars and lights in Assyrian neighborhoods? Clay thought. Most of the crystals he'd seen were small hewn gemstones, not perfectly round orbs like this one.

". . . if'n I were a betting man, I'd say that were *the* crystal," Nemo finished. "The Crystal of Cyrus." He spoke those last three words in a hushed whisper, and the man seemed overcome by awe.

"The what?" Ayala asked.

Clay was glad she asked first. He must have heard Nemo wrong.

"Crystal of Cyrus," Nemo said, using the exact tone and inflection as when he said it before.

"*The* Crystal of Cyrus?" Clay said, joining the mass of gaping mouths and awestruck eyes.

"Hello? Is anybody going to explain what the heck that is?" Ayala interjected amongst the doe-eyed men, clearly annoyed.

Nemo cleared his throat, "Well, if I have my legends in order, this here was the personal implement of the founder of the Assyrian Empire. It single-handedly laid the path for conquest. Other nations didn't stand a chance. 'Most holy of holy relics of the Empire's history, lost to time and myth and thought to have been laid to rest with Cyrus.'"

"Ahh," Ayala said with a facsimile of surprise. "*The* Crystal of Cyrus."

"It actually exists?" Jax asked, doubt plain on his face.

"Yes," Nemo said.

Jax leaned forward, placing his hands on the table. He kept his gaze on Nemo. "Are you sure?"

"Well, I've got a book in the basement with a drawing of it." Nemo scratched his beard. "I do know this for sure: there isn't a crystal like this one on the continent," Nemo answered. "Most focusing crystals you'll find—the kinds that power Assyrian machinery and such—are artificial. Far as I know, this here is the only real focusing crystal left available. Thing like this could power the capital of Assyr by itself. Could also destroy the capital."

Nemo's expression softened, and he looked at each teenager with sympathy. "This here's the reason for a lot of troubles worldwide."

"Why do you think it was just sitting in Quaestor Gratus's vault, unused?" Jax asked.

A flash of recognition passed over Nemo's face. "Gratus? Ilvius Gratus?"

Clay shook his head. Due to Lena's job, he had some knowledge about the Quaestor who presides over Ruka and its neighboring villages. "Quaestor Ilvius died a while ago. His son, Arius Gratus, is the Quaestor now." He cocked his head, looking at Nemo. "You knew Ilvius Gratus?"

Nemo huffed, his arms now crossed. "Well enough to know that he was an idiot and a hoarder. Wouldn't be surprised if he or his son found this crystal and their first thoughts were to shove it in some vault to rot, just so they could look at it and stroke their egos ever so often."

Jax nodded, and Clay thought he saw something near to discomfort flash across his features. "It was in a vault."

"And how'd you know it'd be there?" Nemo asked, gaze leveled on Jax.

The Harraka was silent for a moment, as if weighing his words. "A spy. It's easy to infiltrate households like Quaestor Gratus's."

"This spy still kicking around?" Nemo asked, worry plain in his expression.

Jax shook his head. "Our spy was a groundskeeper. He . . . died when I retrieved the crystal."

"Good," Nemo said, more to himself than the others. "One less thing to connect you all to this business."

Was it groundskeeper Reggie? Clay wondered. Mama had often spoken of Reggie—he was one of the few parts of her workday that could bring her to smile. Clay had never met him, but he always appreciated Reggie for that. He hoped Reggie wasn't dead.

Nemo leaned forward, crossing his arms on the table. "Now why, Jax, do the Harrakas want this crystal?"

Jax shifted. "I'm not sure, really. It's powerful, though, and if the Assyrians want it, then that's reason enough for us to take it."

"You stole somethin' like this without knowing why?" Clay asked.

"It's common. The less our warriors know, the less they can reveal if they're captured."

A sour look crossed Nemo's face, but he nodded. "It's not a bad doctrine, really."

Jax nodded slightly, agreeing.

Nemo shifted and took in a breath. "Now that that's cleared up as much as it can be, I got an offer for you all. A big decision—either the first of many or the last you'll ever have to make."

"Ooh, dramatic," Ayala murmured, her head still lain on her arms.

"Appropriately so, this time," Nemo said, his tone grave. "I'm offering the three of you a permanent place here. We've got the room for you, and you're all decent."

"Hey, I'm decent," Ayala said, perking up a bit and looking at Clay with mock joy.

Clay chuckled.

"If I may interject," Marva said. Clay had forgotten she was there. "'Decent' is high praise from Nemo. In all my time knowing him, the highest compliment he's ever paid to another human being is 'tolerable while sauced.'"

Clay and Ayala snickered. Ayala looked at Nemo and said, "What a charmer you are."

"Ha ha," Nemo deadpanned. "Now, Jax, I have people who can get this crystal to the Harrakas. Means that you can stay too, should you want to."

"You have people?" Jax asked.

"Old contacts. They'll get the rock where it needs to go."

"How can I trust you?" Jax asked, tenser than he was before. If that was even possible. Sore as he was, just looking at how tight Jax's shoulders were made Clay's ache.

Nemo shrugged. "I'm not sure if you can. My old contacts? They don't leave trails, so I wouldn't be able to get you a certificate of authenticity or anything of the sort."

Jax's features betrayed nothing, and none of the tension left him.

"So, what do you say?" Nemo asked.

Ayala rested her head on her arm again, looking at Clay with a cheek smushed into an eye. "Up to you, man. I'm good with whatever. Harrakas or robots . . . both sound neat."

"You're rather flippant about this," Jax said, his arms now crossed.

Ayala didn't even shift to look at him. "What can I say? I'm the easygoing sort."

Clay laughed and Ayala smiled, knowing that lie for what it was.

"What about you?" Clay asked, looking to Jax.

Jax pondered the Crystal of Cyrus for some time, his mouth slightly open to let out slow exhales.

Ayala drummed her fingers on the table, growing bored.

Clay gently placed his hand over Ayala's and the drumming stopped.

"I owe you a life debt," Jax said, looking at Clay and Ayala. He now spoke hesitantly. "If Nemo speaks truly, then I can complete my mission to retrieve the crystal and stay here." He held Clay's gaze. "I . . ."

Clay had a vague idea of what Jax was thinking. "Do you *want* to stay here?"

He was silent for a few beats, as if he had never considered what he *wanted* to do before. He blinked a few times, and then looked around the table, as if suddenly aware that everyone was watching him, waiting for an answer. Again, he spoke hesitantly, though with more confidence than before. "We are still in the Empire. We will be at risk every moment we are within its borders. The Harrakas are safer, and I trust myself to deliver the crystal more than anyone else."

"Well," Nemo said, shifting forward a bit, "this place has good defenses, and in all my years of living here, the Empire hasn't bothered me a bit. So, you'd be safe."

"The Empire will be looking for us," Jax said, gesturing to Clay and Ayala. "The risk would be greater." To Clay, Jax almost sounded like he was trying to convince himself.

Nemo nodded. "Can't fault that logic."

"You never answered the question, Mr. Jax," Marva pointed out. "Do you want to stay here?"

Another moment of silence filled the space between people. "I don't know. I do know that I think it's safer to leave; no matter the defenses here, they can't equal the protection offered by the Harrakas outside of Assyrian borders." Jax looked to Clay. "What do you say?"

"Well, Clay?" Nemo prodded, looking at the boy with an annoying *I told you so* expression. It disappeared quickly though, replaced by genuine curiosity.

"I think . . ." Clay started, trailing off. He glanced at everyone, and briefly looked around the kitchen. And then he found his words. "Well, firstly, thank you for the offer. Everything you've done for us and offer to do for us has been more generous than we deserve. So thank you." Clay twisted in his chair, looking at Marva. "Both of you."

"You're welcome, hon!"

Clay turned back, looking to a smiling Nemo. "But we won't make a difference here. We won't have an impact if we stay here."

Clay caught both Ayala and Jax's gazes. "We owe it to mom to make an impact."

Jax nodded. Ayala stretched her fist across the table, bumping knuckles with Clay.

"Then you've made your decision?" Nemo asked.

Clay nodded. "We'll move on to find the Harrakas."

Nemo clapped his hands together. "Fantastic. I imagine the first place you go will be Thiva. I'd bet my last bottle that you—" Nemo nodded at Jax "—don't have the foggiest idea where the Harrakas are. But the shamans at Thiva might, right?"

"You know much," Jax said.

Nemo spread his hands. "My blessing and my curse."

Jax shook his head. "But I don't wish to seek the shamans so they can tell me where my people are: I wish to seek them so they can point me to an *ilaa lum*."

"Huh?" Ayala grunted.

"A Sacred Tree," Nemo answered. "They're old parts of this world, trees connected to The Source, which is kind of another world layered atop to ours. The place where you'd think "magic" comes from. Think of an *ilaa lum* as a radio tower, but older and nonsensical, blended with a teleporter."

"Oh, yeah, that clears it up," Ayala muttered into the crook of her arm.

"So," Nemo said, clapping his hands together once, "we're off to Thiva."

"Sorry, 'we'?" Ayala asked, lifting her head from the table and looking at Nemo.

"Oh, did I not mention?" Nemo said, his beard tilted with his smile. "Marva and I will be coming with you lot."

"You will?" Clay asked.

"We will?" Marva asked.

"Yep," Nemo said. "Think about it: three teenage kids cutting across the country by their lonesome, right after news breaks out of Ruka that two teenage Ghoulas and a Harraka have gone missing? You'll stick out like a sore thumb on a polydactyl hand."

"But three teenagers, a drunk old man, and a robot won't raise suspicion?" Ayala deadpanned.

"Oh, we'll raise suspicion," Nemo said. He pointed at Jax. "But we cover up his tattoos—and Marva—and we won't look like anything but the weird family of some eccentric, devilishly handsome genius."

"Oh, really?" Ayala looked around the room. "Where is this 'devilishly handsome genius'?"

"But, hon," Marva interjected, stepping forward, "I can't leave the chapel. You designed it yourself so that I was bound to these grounds."

Nemo nodded. "That's what I've spent the last few days fixing. A few hours in the shop, and you'll have all the power you need to be self-sufficient. It'll cost the chapel and the workshop, but I doubt we'd be coming back here anyways." He met the somewhat doubtful expressions of the three teens. "Trust me when I say you'll need me to get where you're going. None of you are legal adults, you all look like Ghoulas, and one of you isn't even Assyrian. There are checkpoints between here and the Harrakas, and you're not getting past those without someone like me."

"An adult or an Assyrian?" Ayala asked.

"Someone who looks like an Assyrian and who has the paperwork to verify that he's Assyrian," Nemo corrected. "I don't hold myself with the Empire or their people. But to answer your question: both."

"Why do you want to join us?" Clay asked.

Nemo shrugged. "Well, Marva here'd love to see the world."

"Indeed!" Marva said.

"As for me, well . . ." Nemo rubbed the back of his neck. "I'm curious about these Harrakas. Besides, I have a car," Nemo said, raising his eyebrows.

"Oh, I'm for it," Ayala said, perking up a bit. "There's no way I'm walking out of the Empire when I can sit."

Clay, a smile on his face, nodded. "Alright. We'd love to have you along."

"Oh, how exciting!" Marva said, clapping her hands together and making an awful clanking noise.

"Alright then," Nemo said, nodding. "Start preparing your things. When do you want to head out?"

Clay looked to Jax.

"Tomorrow," said the Harraka.

"Then tomorrow," Nemo said, "we're off to Thiva."

XXII

CATO

Traveling with Samael was nothing short of a humbling experience.

Even though their destination was miles and miles from Samael's homestead, he demanded they ride the entire way on horseback. It harkened back to the early days of the Cynical Order when Samael was Knight-Commander. He had made it doctrine for rangers to travel by horseback wherever they could, to better entrench the lay of the land in the mind: its rises, its falls, its landmarks, its hidden places, its open places, its pathways, its roadblocks, and its obstacles. Cynical Rangers bore many similarities to the rangers of Assyr's military. They were scouts first and the vanguard second—at the forefront of every military movement, guiding armies and logistical channels through untamed and wild lands.

Cato was a good ranger—no, not just a good ranger—she was prodigious. She grew up in the far countryside, forging paths through the woods, setting snares, hunting game and shooting varmints to keep them from crops, and she even helped her parents distract and confuse bandits and raiders, fighting when needed. She was born tough, and she grew up tough, and she excelled as a Cynical Initiate; she overcame the pointed looks and sneers her "siblings" in the order aimed her way, all because she had crystals around her eyes—at first, her fellow Assyrians only treated her marginally better than the Ghoula initiates. Once she was past Initiate, those sneers faded to memory—she had earned her place, and she had become part of the Order. She had found her family.

As much to spite them as to prove that she belonged, even when she no longer had to, she excelled. Cynical Cato Nemoida became the order's youngest Ranger ever at the age of seventeen, and by the age of nineteen, she had killed four Gwandanian terrorists single-handedly, preventing an assassination in doing so.

She knew she was great.

At least, she thought she knew before meeting Samael.

From the first moment he rode his horse, Cato realized how stiffly and wastefully she rode her own. Horsemanship didn't come naturally to a poor farmer's daughter, but she had worked hard at it—she rode until her thighs chafed and her hands were burned by the reins, and she practiced until she had total mastery of her steed.

Samael did not have mastery of his horse; he had a brotherhood. Riding Solstice was as natural for him as breathing. Without even a saddle or a harness, Samael guided the horse with barely any movement at all; even touches and prods seemed unnecessary, for Solstice seemed to move as soon as Samael was ready, like their minds were shared.

For days on end, Samael only spoke to correct Cato's flaws and shortcomings, ignoring any other attempts at conversation. The air between them was filled with phrases like "Don't pull so hard on the reins," "Check behind you more often," "Change your socks,"

"Bend your knees when you dismount so it doesn't sound like a tree falling each time," "You shouldn't be this tired on only four hours of sleep," and so on.

Though, as much as he corrected her and ignored her attempts to connect, he never spoke down to her because of her *squamae*. For Cato, that made him a man worth following.

✳ ✳ ✳ ✳ ✳

Cato studied the Knight-Commander as they traveled, hoping to learn from his ways. He was the one to pen the lifestyle she lived, after all.

She saw him sway side to side in his saddle, shoulders lax and gaze wandering the branches, bathed in the golden light of early dawn. When he thought she wasn't looking, he let down his guard. Sadness would creep into his posture, and in rare moments, he seemed as if he were somewhere else entirely. He never broached a conversation; the only time he spoke was to correct her, and the shame which would flood her afterwards always clamped her throat shut.

She was grateful for the guidance, but she couldn't stand being reminded that she was worse than someone else. She used both feelings as fuel to grow better to be the kind of person who could impress Knight-Commander Samael Tashunka.

He looked relaxed right now. It was a nice day, and they were still in one of the safer regions of the Empire. Cato straightened in her saddle, summoning the courage to ask him a question.

"Knight-Commander, sir, why are you teaching me so much?"

"So I'm not killed because of your mistake."

✳ ✳ ✳ ✳ ✳

Cato listened, trying not to think about how the Knight-Commander's low tones complemented the crackle of the campfire. He told her of the horse who had chosen her, a gray Nokota by the name of

Chetan—one of the smallest horses Samael owned, and as a foal, he was a runt with spunk. She watched as he rubbed red paint across Chetan's coat in symbols of luck and surefootedness. "All a ranger needs for travel," she said, feeling warmth blossom within when the Knight-Commander nodded approvingly. She learned the symbols, and every day since, she would paint Chetan, who remained a runt with spunk even when fully grown. She ignored the little voice in her head that found it odd to copy a Ghoula tradition.

"How long have you been raising horses, sir?" Cato asked, leaning forward and prodding the fire with a stick. It hissed and sparks leapt into the air, and once again, Cato resisted the urge to look Samael in the eye. The more she traveled with him, the easier it had become to bear the weight of his gaze, but it was still unpleasant.

"Since I retired," he said. He was sat on a log by the fire, elbows on his knees. He stretched his head back and forth, working his neck. And then he settled his gaze on Solstice, who was grazing nearby. The firelight shimmered along his coat. "I've ridden many horses to their deaths. Killed plenty more." He looked at Cato and she averted her gaze a moment too late; her breathing grew thinner and her hands grew clammy, but soon the sensations passed. Catching his eyes was growing more familiar and tolerable.

"Once I didn't have to cause horses' deaths anymore, well . . ." Samael trailed off, thinking for a moment. "Guess I wanted to bring more into the world. Give them good lives."

Cato regarded Solstice. The pale stallion was well-built, and she could see his muscles shifting beneath his coat with each movement. As she looked closer, she could see some age in the horse's features and a number of scars along its flanks. "Do you still have any horses from back then? From the war?"

"Solstice is the only one left. He's getting old; this'll likely be his last adventure."

Solstice tossed his head and huffed, as if to say, *Like hell it will be*.

Samael turned and smiled at the horse, and Cato was struck by how Samael's smile made him appear both older and younger, like she got a glimpse of the man he used to be beneath his cracked-leather features. She imagined that he looked much older than he was. He turned back to the fire.

"I had three horses after the war ended. Two stallions and a mare . . . they all had seen battle. One died of old age. The other of a broken leg." His voice held the careful distance of one who accepted grief a long time ago.

"What's it like? Battle?" Cato imagined it was glorious; there could be no greater test of oneself than in war.

Samael mulled a moment. "Terrifying."

She hadn't expected that. "Really? You're scared of fighting?"

Samael shook his head. "Not fighting. Battles. Nothing in the world more chaotic and nonsensical than a battle. It gets loud and messy quick, and if you don't give your fear its proper space, then you'll slip up and die."

"Is that what happened to Uxiah?" Cato asked.

He looked at her. She averted her eyes in time, though she still felt the weight of his attention. "I mean, I've heard the stories, same as everyone else," she said, excitement growing within her. "About how you used Uxiah's pride against him—coaxed him into a duel and showed him who the better warrior really was. Showed him that Assyr's got the best of the best."

Samael shook his head and sighed. "Stories're wrong, then. It was the other way around. He coaxed me into a duel—used my overconfidence to get me alone. And it wasn't skill that saw me the victor—it was luck. He tripped on a rock." He shook his head again, his lips now hidden behind clasped hands. "A dumb rock."

That night, Cato noticed how fitfully he fell asleep, tossing and turning for hours before settling into an uneasy slumber. Yet, he never wore his fatigue for a moment.

✻ ✻ ✻ ✻ ✻

She watched as he would drop weathered reins, allowing his horse to guide them both to a nearby creek. Both the horse and its rider seemed old and wise, with majesty and time as allies. As Solstice drank and rested, Samael foraged.

She questioned him every time he picked an herb: What is it? What's it called? Why'd you pick it? What else can you use it for? and so on. Before long, Samael began answering the questions before they were let loose.

✻ ✻ ✻ ✻ ✻

Cato knew her history. She knew her geography.

She could hardly keep the smile from her face as the two rangers rode through Samael's old stomping grounds. The eastern reaches of the Assyrian Empire still held the memories of warfare tightly. Cato saw it in the scars that marked its trees, the areas where there was no birdsong nor tracks, in the silent metal carcasses that littered roadsides, their rusted bones now home to spiders and ants.

Most of all, she saw it in Samael, in the weight that settled over his shoulders and in the tension that kept his back straight. In the way his eyes narrowed and his frown deepened, she saw the choking memories of the war he waged here against the Harrakas.

"Keep your head on a swivel," Samael ordered. "These lands are too dangerous for you to stare at every dead machine we pass."

"Apologies, Knight-Commander," Cato said, feeling somewhat aggravated that she hadn't been following one of the ranger's cardinal rules of travel: eyes open, ears wide. She straightened in her saddle, scanning her gaze back and forth across the crowded woodland and the thicket that hugged the flanks of these dirt paths. The east was still an untamed land, and Cato wondered how long it would be before Imperial roads and highways replaced these footpaths.

"Pardon, sir, but what makes you say that this region's dangerous?" she asked. "Harrakas haven't been seen in decades, especially in these parts."

"Wherever there aren't patrols, there are bandits, Ranger," he said. "And the Harrakas may be gone, but their memory isn't. Between bandits, punks who want to be Harrakas, and Ghoulas who want to kill you just because they saw your uniform, this is one of the deadliest regions in the Empire. If anything, this region was safer when the Harrakas were here." He looked around at the woods flanking them, as if he expected someone to jump out right then and there. "They kept banditry under control, and the people liked them." He looked back at Cato, emphasizing his next point. "We can't claim either of those things."

Cato shrugged. "I can handle bandits."

Samael sighed, shook his head, and said, "That's what all young rangers think. Then they fail to catch the light in the bush nearby, and they're bleeding out on the ground and dead in a minute. Don't disappoint me, Sergeant."

She swallowed and nodded, though he wasn't looking at her anymore. "I won't, sir."

As she scanned the landscape on their flanks and behind her, for she trailed behind Samael and he covered the front, she took in the region. It was a dense woodland with thick trunks every which way, their feet crowded by thickets, bramble, heath, and brush. Animals, both kind and unkind, scurried through tall grasses. The paths here were narrow and snaking; they sloped around and over the hilly terrain, which limited sight in almost all directions. Though it was late autumn, the heat beneath the leaves was thick and cloying, and she imagined that disease flourished in this humidity.

"It couldn't have been easy, campaigning through these paths," she said, imagining Samael leading a column of Assyrian troops through these same paths, wary for the ambush that could come at any moment. Back then, he was a Legatus of Assyr. The Cynical Order hadn't even been formed yet, and he was still forging his legend. Once Uxiah lay dead by his hand and the war was over, he used his newfound clout to establish the Cynicals alongside a number of other influential Assyrians.

Silence stretched for some time, long enough that Cato didn't think Samael heard her. She was surprised when he responded.

"It wasn't."

✳   ✳   ✳   ✳   ✳

Firelight flickered across Samael's features, drawn in concentration as he tended his saber. It was a simple implement, far simpler than the one which built his legend: Mar, the blade that drank souls.

Cato was maintaining her own weapons: two revolvers, a lever-action rifle, and a long survival knife with a serrated edge on one side.

She glanced from Samael to his blade, and then back to him. "Where's Mar, if you don't mind my asking, Knight-Commander?"

"Retired."

His tone brokered no further questions. Though it took considerable effort, she did not press the matter. Truthfully, she was disappointed that she wouldn't see the legendary weapon.

She had a feeling that he wouldn't want to talk that night. He seemed a little more withdrawn than normal, and so she focused on her own weapons. Cato lost herself in the meditative movements of disassembling and cleaning her guns from the rust of travel, oiling their mechanisms and polishing the steel to gleam.

She almost jumped when Samael's voice broke the silence between them.

"Those standard issue nowadays for rangers?"

She looked at him, confused, and he nodded to the guns around her.

She nodded, quirking her mouth as she regarded her own fire-arms. "Most Rangers only carry one revolver, but some have two. They're mostly for self-defense or for when things get loud. The rifle's suppressed; good for long-range . . ." she paused, finding a better way to say *assassinations* ". . . quiet engagements. The knife's for utility and killing."

Samael studied the firearms from across the campfire, his mouth set in a way that implied displeasure. "What else has changed with the Cynicals?"

"A lot, sir." She shook her head. "I grew up with stories of the Order in your day, back when it actually *did* something—you know, finding rebel cells and filling in the cracks that the peacekeepers and military couldn't cover. Now, don't get me wrong, there're Cynicals that still do that—like me and a lot of the other Rangers—but it ain't the focus of the Order anymore."

He raised a brow, prompting her to explain further.

She sneered. "Nowadays, it's a lot more *political*. Got diplomats and ambassadors and politicians now who're more focused on changing policies than saving lives. There's a bit of a split in the Order, really. Got the Old Guard who had served under you, who want to keep up what you'd focused on when you were in charge, and then there's the New Guard who are a lot more concerned with . . . well, trying to make Assyr the way they want it to be, I guess. There's a bit of contention, but we all still get along, more or less."

"And which are you, Sergeant?" Samael asked, weighing Cato with those terrible eyes.

"Old Guard all the way, sir."

He nodded approvingly, and Cato felt a warmth blossom in her chest.

She studied him as they approached Ruka. Both he and Solstice seemed made of stone as they heard the signs of a Ghoula crackdown: whimpers of mercy from the town square, pained guttural screams, angry Assyrian voices. The Knight-Commander rode without pause or hesitation. He rode like an Assyrian.

Ghoulas were locked in stockades along roads and paths; their heads drooped, and not a single one looked up at Cato and Samael as they passed. Their loss. They'd likely never see a duo of their like again. As they rode through the town, performing their preliminary survey of the site, Cato saw two peacekeepers corner a boy—no older than thirteen—outside of a school. They asked him questions, leering at him with batons in hand. The boy, obviously scared, started blubbering answers. As she and Samael rounded the bend, just before that trio passed out of sight, one of the peacekeepers grabbed the boy by his stained shirt and raised the baton high.

Ruka's peacekeepers were harsh, almost brutal. She didn't think much of it. Her father had always told her to not judge the way other ranchers handled their livestock.

After they passed through Ruka, they headed for Quaestor Arius Gratus' mansion.

She had been studying Samael so intently and so constantly throughout the journey that it was second nature to tense when he tensed, to follow his gaze when it snapped to an object.

Something had happened at the Quaestor's mansion in Ruka. The garden hadn't been trimmed in over a week; craggly branches peeked out of hedges, and the grass was too tall.

There were no Ghoula servants on the grounds—only Assyrian guards. A construction crew buzzed around the mansion's far side, and the noises of drills, hammers, and crystal-powered machines accompanied workmen's calls and orders.

Anxiety bloomed within Cato. Something was wrong here, and she had a feeling that it was connected to the peacekeepers' brutality back in Ruka.

"Your handler mention anything about construction?" Samael asked, nodding his head at the workers. He sported a wide-brimmed hat, tilted low over his eyes so that they were shrouded in shadow. It made it easier to look at him without getting caught by his eyes, though they still glimmered beneath the shade.

"No, nothing. I think something's happened here—should we find the Quaestor?"

"No," said the Knight-Commander. "Never start an investigation by talking to a politician; you might as well just shoot yourself in the foot now." He fixed his gaze on a person who lingered by the front door of the mansion, a man with a pot belly shoved into a khaki guard uniform. His flat-topped hat marked him as an officer, maybe even the captain of the Quaestor's guard. He looked less than impressive, to be kind about it. "Let's go see what he has to say," Samael said, spurring Solstice onwards. He looked to Cato. By now, his gaze was almost bearable, and if she focused, she could prevent the feeling of time dilating and even keep her breathing steady. "Best if the Quaestor doesn't know we're here, if we can help it."

"Better to keep the politicians away from the important things?" Cato asked, smirking.

"Something like that." She couldn't see his mouth, as he had turned forward again, but she thought she heard a smile in his tone.

She studied Samael's face when he questioned the Quaestor's Guard Captain, a jowly pale man, whose cheeks were blood-flushed from alcoholism. As Samael's scowl deepened every time the Guard Captain said, "No offense, sir, but you know how they are," Cato's own concern mounted.

After the third repetition of that phrase, Samael leveled his eyes on the man, and Cato watched, as a curious child would watch a bird eat a worm. The Guard Captain's pupils dilated, and his face flushed even redder, and sweat squeezed through his pores, and the Knight-Commander said his piece.

"They aren't my people, so I don't 'know how they are.' I'm Ghoula of the Kota, not Ghoula of whoever these poor bastards used to belong to."

The Guard Captain blubbered his apology, trying to mask the fear behind his eyes.

"My apologies . . ." the Guard Captain said, wiping the sweat from his eyes ". . . I've been worried about my son—they found him after the night of the explosion, by the edge of the Wraith-wood. Someone beat him and his friends so badly that they've all been in the hospital, practically comatose, and it's been weighing on me bad. I just *know* that those Ghoula brats have something to do with it, but I can't do anything about it and it's tearing me up inside, sir."

As Samael crossed his arms, he seemed to grow broader, and the Captain shriveled even more. "Explosion? Ghoula brats?"

The Captain nodded. "Ever since the Quaestor's vault was broken into, it's been one calamity after another. You know how . . ." he paused, weighing his words ". . . Ghoulas in these parts get riled up easily. Don't take much for knives and bombs to come out. We think the Ghoula in charge of the house's the one to break into the vault. A woman by the name of Lena."

"You let a Ghoula run the house? No wonder you're having problems. Where is she?" Cato asked, worrying over the disapproving glance Samael sent her way.

The Captain smiled, glad that Cato was speaking his language. "That's what I said when they promoted her to Manager! I knew it'd be nothing but trouble. Anyways, she blew herself up," the Captain said, making an explosion gesture with his hands. "Her shack's leveled. It's not uncommon for Ghoulas to do stupid things when they're caught red-handed, but I tell ya—fifteen years I've been serving as part of the Quaestor's retinue, and I ain't even seen something like this. We found traces of her bones in the wreckage, but not her kid's." He stepped forward, anger narrowing his eyes. "That kid of hers is in the same class as mine, and he's been causing trouble for my Billy ever since he joined the school. If you ask me, I think she was caught before she could skip town with what she thieved. Tried to blow up her house as a distraction and ditch with her kid, but I guess they got caught up in the explosion. Strange thing is that the dogs found three different scents leading away from the house, and our records only show the woman and her kid living at that address. Shouldn't have been more people there past curfew, especially on the night of a theft. We tried searching the area, and some of my men even went into the Wraithwood, where them scents led." He shook his head and sighed, wiping the sweat from his forehead. "We still haven't found them. Just up and went missing entirely."

The Knight-Commander shifted his weight. "What'd the woman steal?"

The Captain shrugged. "Don't know. Only the Quaestor is allowed in the vault. Only he knows what's missing, and he won't tell anyone what it is, but it sure was important." He rubbed the back of his neck. "Truth be told, the whole thing just left everyone with more questions than answers. The Quaestor set out for Purpose two days ago, aiming to find some trackers to catch that kid." The Captain rubbed his chin, and as he looked over them, Cato could feel all two of his brain cells making a spark. "Don't suppose you two're them? Got here really fast, if you are."

Samael and Cato shared a look, and Cato found his gaze tolerable. She wasn't sure if she had built a resistance to it or if it was something he was doing.

"Just tell us where this woman's house was," Samael said. "We'll take it from there."

The Guard Captain gave them directions, mentioning that he'd offer to show them the scene of the crime and the vault itself, but all hints of the mess were cleaned up already, and he wasn't allowed to show anyone the vault without the Quaestor present. With nothing else left for them at the mansion, the two Rangers mounted up and headed for the house manager's former home. Once they were out of earshot of the people on the grounds, Samael glanced at Cato.

"Sergeant."

"Yes, Knight-Commander?"

"Next time I'm questioning someone, keep your mouth shut."

"Yes, Knight-Commander."

The woman's shack was rubble and dust. Blackened wood pillars peeked out from scorched appliances and piles of ash. It was situated on the outskirts of the town, just over a small hill from the Assyrian town center. Black tape, patterned with a stark yellow line, fenced the area around the shack—a warning to keep away scavengers and looters.

"Surprised they bothered with the tape, considering how hard they're cracking down on Ghoulas here," Cato said.

Again, Samael sent her a disapproving look. She felt like she said something wrong, but she couldn't imagine what it could be.

The Knight-Commander told her to stay out of the way and to keep an eye out. She watched, silently, as he picked his way across the shack's carcass. She chuckled when, with blatant disregard, he picked a bone from the rubble and tossed it aside. With a bow-legged slant to his gait, he stepped across the rubble, his eyes narrowed and focused on discovering the secrets it held.

"Find anything?" she asked. She was just too curious to keep quiet.

He straightened his back, arms akimbo. He looked at the rubble around his feet for a moment, then said, "Explosion looks intentional, and I found a bone with what looks like a recent knife wound on it. Evidence matches up with the Guard's story."

"But . . .?" she prompted, hearing that dubious note in his voice.

"An explosion like this . . ." he gestured around at the obliterated house—not a single wall still stood ". . . you gotta prepare for that. If she had time to prepare, she had time to run, so why didn't she?"

Cato shrugged. "Maybe she wanted to die."

Samael shook his head, not even dignifying that idea with a response. "I'm going to keep searching through this; Sergeant, scan the nearby grounds for tracks, rubble—anything out of the ordinary."

"Aye, Knight-Commander."

She prowled the area around the house, going slowly and keeping an eye out for anything out of the ordinary. For the most part, the grounds around the house were trampled—the Guard had mentioned an Inquest, and she assumed that a number of amateurs tromped around the scene, obscuring any footprints of worth with their own clumsy steps. Knowing that she wouldn't learn a thing near the house, she cast a wider net and began circling farther away. After almost half an hour of diligently staring at the earth, she found something.

"Got tracks here!" she called, kneeling and studying it closer. The grass was trampled, and beneath it were a number of footprints; she counted three different sets of imprints and even a spot where it looked like someone fell.

A shadow appeared above her; she looked up to see Samael looming over her, once again surprised at how she hadn't heard him approach. The man seemed unnatural at times. Well, most of the time, really.

He nodded and kneeled. "Good find, Sergeant."

That warmth, growing more familiar by the day, filled her chest; she latched onto the feeling, greedy for it, and then reminded herself that their job wasn't done yet.

"The house doesn't have much. No sign of the crystal. A few hints at a fight before the explosion." He rubbed his chin briefly, studying the ground. "These tracks are just about all we have to go on right now. Catch me up, Sergeant."

She relayed her findings as he studied the scene himself, parting grass to get a better look at the prints.

Samael bent over and picked something up. "Dried blood," he muttered, holding a trampled leaf. On its underside, where it was shielded from the weather, was the matte stain of blood. "So, at least one of them was wounded."

"The guard mentioned that the dogs picked up some scents, right? More than there should've been," Cato said.

"Looks like we've found them," Samael said. He looked up to the edge of the forest ahead. "They go into those woods."

Cato followed his gaze and studied the dense forest ahead. The shadows loomed too dark for midday beneath those eaves, and the woods had already shed most of their leaves. It was too early in the season for a forest to be mostly bare, especially in this kind of heat and especially since other areas in the region still had multicolored leaves. "Got a bad feeling about that place," she said lowly.

Samael nodded. "Good intuition. I remember those woods. Lot of blood spilled there. Lot of death."

"What happened there?" Cato asked.

"Ambush." Samael got a little more comfortable, shifting so that he had a knee and a fist on the ground. "It was earlier in the war. The Hars couldn't match our technology or our numbers, but they were masters of guerilla warfare. Hit-and-runs, ambushes, diversions—they excelled with these. I was leading an armored division through this region, and we had to cut through those woods—they'd blocked off other serviceable roads, funneled us through these woods, where we couldn't maneuver. We were careful; we camped for the night and had operatives plant mines all throughout those woods to ward off any ambushes, or at least give us some warning." He glanced at Cato. "They didn't detonate a single mine. Both Azarriah—head of the Harrakas back then—and Uxiah were leading different war parties. They pincered us."

"What happened next?"

"They struck our tanks and trucks first," Samael said. "Took them out almost immediately."

"They had anti-armor?" Cato asked. "I thought they didn't even have guns back then—thought that only Assyr had stuff like that."

"No. No guns. The Hars had some kind of magic—it was different each time we encountered it. Well, each Har's powers were different from the other's, I should say. That day, we faced lightning and rust; within minutes, I saw a tank rusted out to the point where its crew couldn't escape the cabin without cutting themselves on corroded metal." His mouth corkscrewed. "Half of them died from disease later on." He shook his head and stood. "We're burning daylight. Let's follow these tracks."

"Yes, Knight-Commander."

She followed him as he walked towards the nearby forest, watching and waiting when he would go to his knees to study a track. She studied them as well, though she never quite saw as much as he did.

As they went along, questions mounted; it was obvious that whoever left these tracks were amateurs, and yet there were odd breaks in the tracks and even false ones laid that, once discovered, seemed to disappear entirely.

"What in the hells is going on?" Cato asked, the second time she saw a footprint all but disappear, as if it were a dispelled mirage.

"Wraith magic," Samael muttered, concern throughout his tone.

"Huh?"

Samael stood, and she noticed that he grasped the hilt of the saber slung at his hip. He looked around, eyes narrowed and tensed. "Whoever left these tracks, the wraiths in these woods were helping them." He looked at Cato, catching her confused look, and explained, "Battles often leave wraiths. Taint the land—change it. Lot of sudden deaths in a battle, lot of unresolved emotions. Means that a lot of warriors never pass on to the next world. Their spirits become trapped in an area. Wraiths. Harraka wraiths in particular are nasty; some of them can use that same magic they had in life. I'm sure that's what's screwing with us. With *me*, really." He glanced to her, and she thought she saw a strange expression beneath the shadow of his hat. He sighed.

"So . . ." Cato looked around, even more unnerved by the deepness of the shadows and the giant webs which curtained between trees. She resisted the urge to pull her revolvers from her holsters, and though she also had her knife on her, she wished that she hadn't left her rifle back with her horse. "What you're saying is that we're in the home of a bunch of dead people who hate us."

"Yep. But it's daytime, so they can't do a thing to us."

That offered some relief. Cato looked back to the ground, where the footprint used to be. "So, will this be a problem? The wraith magic?"

"Nuisance, more like," Samael said. "I know how to work past it. Come on. Let's find the trail again."

Into the forest, he tracked. Through winding paths and past broken branches, he tracked. It was a long, slow, process, and Cato was awed at the patience and focus the Knight-Commander maintained, even when doubling back or after losing the trail.

He led them to a tiny clearing, surrounded by large knotty roots and hugged by rocks. To Cato, it looked unbothered . . . a dead end. Yet, as she stepped forward, Samael thrust his arm out, keeping her from disturbing the sunlit soil.

"Step back."

She did as ordered and watched. He dug around in his bandolier bag, retrieving a cloudy white crystal, hewn like an obelisk. The size of half a finger, he held one end with his index and the other with his thumb. He closed one eye and brought the crystal to the other, and from his lips ushered foreign arcane words.

Tales were spun about the Knight-Commander's magics and rituals. Such overtly Ghoula rites were taboo to perform or even speak of, but the Knight-Commander's mastery of heretical magic was far too useful to ban. As could be expected from Assyrian scholars and historians, no mention was made of the details of

Samael's rituals, and where mention of it could be avoided, it was. And so, Cato felt like she was witnessing a secret, and witnessing her progenitor perform such magic evoked both awe and discomfort.

The air about the clearing shimmered and seemed to lift, and no longer did the sunlit soil seem undisturbed. Cato saw dark patches—dried blood—laid over dirt that was kicked up and slid over. A confrontation happened here. Samael ambled through the clearing, eyes scanning the ground, and peered through into a tiny cave, nestled beneath a thicket of roots.

"We have our trail." He gestured to the footsteps that led northeast. They followed them further away from Ruka, alongside a creek until they broke free of the woods and found a river. It was wide, murky, and flowed into the east. The mud by the riverbank preserved their elusive marks' footsteps well, and they could even see where the trio pushed a boat into the water.

"They even had a boat stashed," Cato said. "You think this was planned?"

Samael licked his lips and thought for a moment. "It looks like it. Between the premeditated explosion at the house, the wraiths, and now this boat, well . . ."

"Think we're dealing with professionals?" Cato asked.

Samael shrugged. "Maybe."

"Any clue who?"

Samael shook his head. "Nope. But it doesn't matter. They'll be dead soon enough anyways."

XXIII

AYALA

A cramp in her neck jolted Ayala's awake, and her head jostled from the back driver-side window in Nemo's car.

How long was I out? she asked herself, wiping the crusted slobber from the crooks of her mouth.

She didn't even remember falling asleep. All she knew was that her legs desperately needed to stretch and her butt was starting to ache.

She looked to her right.

Clay and Blood were out cold.

When Nemo had shown them that his "car" was really an antiquated automobile looking to be on its last legs, with a cramped backseat to boot, she knew somebody was going to have to get stuck with the crap seat and knew it might as well not be her.

"Dibs on the window!" she and Clay exclaimed, so in-sync it was hard to tell who had said it first.

"Ha!" Ayala had said to Blood, smug grin on her face. "Looks like you've got the middle."

He was slow catching on, but the look on his face when he figured out . . . priceless.

How she got this tall mythical warrior-whatever to ride middle-seat, she'll never know. Say what you will about Ayala, but she finds her wins in the little things.

Nemo's car sucked. Like all other cars on the outskirts of the Empire, it was an old jalopy gasping for life, coated in rust and rattling with more moving parts than was intended by the factory. The hand-crank windows required some serious elbow grease to open, which was a necessity as the car had no air conditioning—Ayala wasn't even sure that air conditioning had been invented when this car was produced. The seats smelled like Nemo poured whiskey on them for fun, and the backseat was so cramped that even Ayala and Clay, who were yet to be full-grown, had their knees pushed against the back of the front seats. To top it all off, the only music Nemo had was an old one-track filled with muzak—the kind you hear in elevators or malls. Not that Ayala would know, really—her only exposure to elevators and malls were through corny black-and-white sitcoms that would play on Clay's little TV. It's funny, she never much liked those sitcoms, but now she missed them.

The boys' heads were drooping, Clay's into the windows and Blood's deeper and deeper into his lap. Clay had passed out early on, his head slumped against the window, and Ayala had a sinking feeling that he was only pretending to be asleep. He'd been doing that a lot since they left Ruka.

Blood's head began to tilt towards Ayala, and she was faced with the uncomfortable realization that he might actually fall asleep on her. Her initial reaction was vehement, of course; that is, until she looked at him. All of the gruff anger and brooding he normally carried had all but disappeared. Framed between his braids, his face carried an almost cherubic quality to it. It was the most at peace she had ever seen him.

She felt her abrasive demeanor dropping toward the man-child. *I guess it wouldn't be so bad to pretend I didn't notice, just this once.*

Ayala kept her eyes glued to the window; she and Clay had never been this far from their clustered batch of villages. She had never seen a landscape so wide that the sky clung to the edge of the world. It had always been cramped trees and brush, and seeing so much land and sky was unnerving at first, then fascinating.

It made her want to sprout wings and fly.

They passed great arches of rock and stone which trapezed across the horizon. In the vast distance were large objects that seemed to be mountains, but their shape was jagged and deformed, like a flame frozen in place.

They passed rolling hills of moonlit-hued grass, swaying gently in the wind as they reflected like silver coins in the sunlight.

They passed open moors speckled with spindly trees, giant flowers growing along their length instead of leaves. Bees as large as her fist bumbled between the trees, coated head to toe in pollen.

They passed a great lake, its far end walled by a fantastic cliff. Thin waterfalls snaked their way down its gray-red face, softly trickling in among giant lily pads and frog-like creatures.

There was so much *world* beyond the forest, so many different places and wonders. It was inspiring, beautiful, terrifying, humbling.

A soft smile found its way onto her face.

She'd never made it this far out of Ruka before. Sure, she had run away before, gone for days on end without a bed or a decent meal, but never once did she make it past Ribota, the neighboring village to Ruka. Everything around there was much the same, give or take a corn field or two. But out here . . . Ayala was still struggling to put words to it. It felt like she'd been hidden her whole life, and now the world was finally opening up to her. A chuckle escaped her mouth before she could catch it.

"Oh, dear Marva, she's gone off the deep end," said a grumpy voice from the front seat, the words passing through a smile. "The laughing means we're too late."

Embarrassed, Ayala noticed her cheeks becoming warm. She did not offer a retort.

Behind the wheel, Nemo hummed along to the bad muzak, tapping his hands along the rubber and saying little. Marva must've been on some tour guide setting—she constantly pointed out things they passed and regions they were entering with the joy of someone who couldn't feel or smell the inside of the car.

They had been driving for a few days now. Maybe once or twice a day, they would have to pass through an Assyrian checkpoint; the anxiety would spike in the car, and Ayala worried that Blood would attack the peacekeepers in every moment. But Nemo was able to pull out a surprising amount of charm, and his papers always got them through without a problem. Ayala wasn't sure if his credentials were real or if they were forgeries. Regardless, Nemo made this journey much, much nicer than it would have been otherwise. It felt more like a road trip with a dysfunctional family than running for their lives.

Blood shifted on her shoulder, still asleep.

Ayala unglued her eyes from the window. Unbidden, they fell upon Blood's backpack.

There had been a feeling of sorts—no, more so a calling—building in the back of her mind over the past few days. It reached its zenith now, when she had nothing to do and nowhere to go; she felt as if she had no choice but to open his bag and pull out the crystal.

Blood. It still felt wrong to call him Jax. "Jax" felt like too kind of a name compared to Blood, compared to what he caused.

Well, some things were better left unthought of.

As she grasped the cloth that shrouded the crystal, that "calling" feeling faded. It didn't disappear, not quite, but it was no longer so demanding.

It felt as if the object demanded a certain kind of reverence. Like it was haughty. Arrogant. Ayala opened the lid slowly, studying the crystal closely for the first time.

It was an impossibly smooth thing, colored a red so deep that it was almost black. It was so small that it could nestle in the palm of her hand, yet there was a certain thrumming vibration about it, a faint feeling of static electricity that prickled the skin when you were near. Ayala moved her face closer, and she could almost feel the hairs on her eyebrows standing on end. Through the stone flowed thin rivulets of indigo dust, as if the crystal had its own veins. As if it were alive.

The dust shifted direction, and Ayala felt a strange pressure in her mind—no pain like with a headache, though strange enough to be foreign. The dust within the stones began forming shapes— telling stories! Each moment showed something different, forming a kaleidoscopic tapestry of tales. Though it was little more than dust swirling and forming shapes, Ayala felt as if she were seeing more than just dust—as if she were looking at memories the crystals had, shown only to her. She floated her gaze across the crystal, taking in the tiny vignettes.

Two figures, a great man missing his hand, a strong woman by his side, bandaging his still-bleeding stump while chiding him. Vestiges of battle raged around them.

A great marble hall, impossibly large, filled with rows upon rows of people in red robes. Every single person held a candle, showing only the jaws and mouths of their hooded faces. They all faced a dais at the far end of the hall, upon which was an ornate black coffin.

The pressure grew in Ayala's mind.

Pain leapt from her wrist. She tore her gaze away from the crystal; Blood's face was close to hers, his hand clamped around her wrist.

"Give it to me." His voice was low, little more than a whisper, though the look in his eyes told her that he was on the verge of lashing out. She knew that look. She wore it often.

"Alright, geez, man." She shook off his grip and offered the crystal to him. "I was just curious."

Blood swiped the orb from her hands, swaddling it again and shoving it back into his pack. He glanced at her from the corner of his eye. "They take fingers for breaching another person's privacy in the Harrakas. Don't do that again." His tone had no hint of intimidation—he spoke as if he were reciting facts.

Ayala didn't respond, but she believed him. She crossed her arms and looked out the window.

A few moments passed, and she could still feel Blood's stifling tension filling the car. She glanced to the front seat and saw Nemo's eyes looking at her in the rear-view mirror.

✳ ✳ ✳ ✳ ✳

Thiva arose from the edge of the horizon.

It lay at the edge of the water, its city the prized tip of the peninsula, its waters beautiful and pristine. The city itself was a weave of rivers and canals, which served as the roads and paths between buildings—boats, gondolas, and canoes took the place of cars and bikes here, while foot traffic stayed to the walkways that skirted buildings and the bridges that leaned over the water.

From a distance, it almost looked like the city was floating.

Its port remained active, receiving as many as five large boats at a time at its sapphiric harbors. Ayala saw men sitting on the edge of their river homes with fishing poles and wondered what it was like to fish. Maybe she and Clay could fish when they get to the Harrakas.

People were speckled across every visible part of the city, walking or fishing or selling wares. Both Clay and Ayala were glued to the windows as they neared the city—it was the most beautiful thing either of the village kids had ever seen, and it stole their breath.

"Thiva is an ancestral city of the former Uruk population," said Marva in her best tour-guide inflection. "Some historians believe that it was one of the first settlements following the Uruk migration west from the continent of Ma'Gia."

"Exile," corrected Blood, sounding almost bored. "Not migration." He did not wear wonderment as Clay and Ayala did; his arms were crossed and he slouched in his seat, his bag guarded by both his legs.

"It's not Assyrian?" asked Clay.

"Not entirely," said Marva. "It was originally created as a small, self-sustaining settlement by separatists during the Imperial Colonial Wars. Eventually it became an asylum for all peoples, regardless of race or creed. You may be shocked to see so many ethnicities living in such close proximity to one another. Even after its recapture, Thiva's distance from the heart of the Empire has allowed for its famously ubiquitous culture."

"How do you know all this?" asked Clay.

"Nemo programmed me with the knowledge," said Marva, nodding to Nemo. The old man looked like he was chewing on some thoughts and was—or acted like he was—oblivious to the conversation in the car.

"Got secrets, old man?" teased Ayala.

"More than you, that's for sure," said Nemo, a scratchy chuckle following his words.

After passing through yet another checkpoint, they found parking by one of the many docks—Thiva was a city fragmented across islands and tributaries, with fewer roads than streams. They would have no luck driving into the city—it was either walking, swimming, or floating from here.

Nemo placed a hand on Marva's angled knee. "You're gonna stay with the car while we're here, Marva."

"Oh," said Marva, clearly disappointed.

"You're just the only one I can trust to keep it safe," said Nemo.

Marva's bluish eyes turned to the window. "I was hoping to see the city."

"We'll come back when we can."

Marva's head swiveled back to Nemo. "You promise?"

"Yeah."

Ayala felt like she was intruding on something; she opened the door and was greeted by the salty fish-scent in the air. Clay followed suit, then Jax, and then Nemo. Marva stayed in the car.

"Where are you going?" Jax asked.

"I've got my own contacts in Thiva. I'm going to see if any of them are still kicking around," Nemo said. "Gonna go catch up on news in places that don't allow three minors, or Ghoula-looking kids, or Harrakas."

"Point taken," Clay said.

Nemo straightened and sobered. "I'm serious—keep a low profile. In fact, Jax," he said, looking at Blood, "it's best if you don't enter the city at all. I'll search through my contacts for the shaman. For now, it's probably best if you help Marva find a place to keep the car and stay out of sight."

"I can handle myself," Blood said dismissively. "I know my way around Thiva."

Nemo shrugged, then slapped the trunk of the jalopy good-naturedly. "Alright, I'm off! I'm not your parent and I won't pretend to be." He pointed at the three teens like a gunslinger, his hand the gun and his eyes squinted—even had the stance. "But don't you kids do anything I wouldn't do."

Ayala looked at Clay. "I think that means we can do everything."

"Maybe not shower," Clay deadpanned.

Nemo placed one splayed hand against his stained t-shirt. "Thought we were tighter than that, Clay."

So you're just leaving us be?" he asked Nemo.

"That seems irresponsible, man," Ayala said.

Nemo nodded his head. "Well, it'd be more irresponsible to bring you where I'm going, and my gut tells me that you won't stay put if I tell you to. Don't worry. So long as you keep your head down, no one will think of the two of you as anything more than two Ghoula kids on the street. Just don't get into trouble." He looked to Blood. "What are you going to do?"

"I'll be in the old city. I remember there being a temple somewhere around there. Could lead me to a shaman."

"Don't spend too long in one place in Thiva," Nemo told them. "In fact, just don't spend too long in Thiva. See the sights, spend a few hours wandering, and then come back here. Alright?"

"Okay," Clay said.

Ayala nodded, her gaze still on Thiva's buildings and shadows. She was eager to get there.

"Alright then." Nemo walked away, waving in a fake, good-natured manner. "I'll see you later—try to be back before dark, yeah?"

Ayala smirked, glad to see Clay mirroring her. "We'll see, grandpa."

XXIV

CLAY

The first thing that Clay and Ayala did upon entering Thiva was join a gondola ride. There were a number of Ghoulas crammed into the long, thin boat, and they slipped aboard quietly and unnoticed. While the adults around them bore their own unique stench, they were kind, and Clay even struck up a conversation with a few of them as the gondolier guided them through Thiva. As they floated along, the city showed itself as a study in contrast.

To the north was New Thiva, where bright buildings with fresh paint lined cobbled streets. Business and busyness filled the air of New Thiva, accompanying the sounds of construction and machinery. Automated boats—not brand new but newer than any Clay and Ayala had ever seen—glided through the veins of New Thiva. Some were even the newer models, powered by crystals instead of gasoline, and they glided throughout the canals with barely a noise.

And then there was Old Thiva to the south, where the buildings sported their age. Once-colorful paint loomed faded and splotchy, and many shacks stood where buildings have long since fallen into disrepair. It was a far marshier area, with more tributaries than paths, and many Ghoulas of all kinds rowed in weathered dinghies and canoes between here and there. It was far quieter in Old Thiva, where people listed about aimlessly or seemed still as corpses, a bottle in hand or a smoking pipe cradled to their chest.

It was to Old Thiva that the gondola traveled, bringing a number of Ghoulas home after a long day of hard work.

Clay and Ayala stepped off the boat and onto the marshy grass. Despite the oddness of the ride, there was a peace upon Clay. *A city on water.* Thiva, though gilded, was nothing short of magnificent. He had never been in such a populated area before; had never seen buildings so grand as those in New Thiva.

Here, though, the grass grew tall and flanked tributaries and rivers. Many ramshackle houses, their foundations nothing more than wooden stilts which rose from the water, sat on the banks of the waterways. Each had a dock, and each dock had at least one rowboat or dinghy. The houses, though modest, stood with pride: each sported a bright color, and some had different colors on the walls than on the roof. Rowboats trafficked across tributaries, so many that on some waterways, sunlight shone on more wood than water. Ghoulas paddled their boats by their neighbors, laughing and speaking as they passed each other by. Some families latched their boats together with woven grass, anchoring them side by side so that they could walk from boat to boat, eating and spending time beneath the sun.

Clay had never seen Ghoulas that were so familial. In Ruka, Ghoula houses were spread along the outskirts. There were no neighborhoods. But here, there was a community.

Yet, he also saw things which disturbed him. Here and there throughout the neighborhood, in the shadows beneath docks, lying down in boats floating aimlessly with the current, and even close to where they disembarked were human zombies, living corpses who barely moved except to huff smoke, snort crushed leaves, or even inject some strange liquid into their arms—from what he could see, they were all using the same drug but in different forms. Some of them twitched and convulsed; some were still as corpses; others reached for the sky, tears on their faces and desperation eking out from their throats. The people of the neighborhood paid them no mind, as if the strung-out humans were part of the scenery and not people suffering addiction.

It made Clay sick. Many of these Ghoulas had sunken eyes and golden irises; many of them belonged to the same people he did. Families laughed among each other while a man overdosed not two dozen paces away, utterly apathetic to his suffering.

Clay looked at Ayala and saw that she was looking at that same man.

"That could've been my parents," she said. "Could be them now." She shook her head and kicked a nearby rock.

A breeze whispered across the land, and the grasses waved and bowed. With it came voices lilted in song. Clay looked to his right, whence the voices came, and saw a grove of trees, their roots hidden beneath khaki-colored water.

"Let's go check that out," Ayala said, her voice tight, as if she were eager to get away from this neighborhood.

"Took the words from my mouth."

The trees were evenly spaced throughout the grove, as if planted by men. Thin dirt paths trailed between and around them. It felt like a park to Clay, and it was larger than he had first assumed. Almost deceptively so—from the shore, it seemed a grove, but once they stood beneath the shadows of leaves and branches, the place felt almost endless. The song was near enough now that, when the breeze brought the noise to them, words could be made out, though it was a language that neither Clay nor Ayala recognized.

The two teenagers shared a bewildered and surprised look, but neither spoke. When the breeze fell, the sound faded. Something about the grove caused silence to cast a spell, and both Clay and Ayala felt that it would be wrong to break it.

They walked the narrow paths, finding their way toward the song. It was sung by a procession of people, and though there was little harmony shared between the disparate voices, there was much beauty and soul in their tones.

To their right was a man, standing by a tree and listening to the procession along with them. He was tall and thin, his skin wrinkled and pulled tight across his bones. He held himself like the trees of the grove: tall and proud. Thick dreadlocks formed a mane around his features, spilling across his shoulders and down his back. He wore a simple, poor tunic that fell to his knees, secured at the waist by a belt. Leather sandals well past their youth wrapped around his gnarled feet. Wrinkles weighed his dark face, the crows' feet particularly prominent. His features were serene, and his hands were wrapped around a wooden walking stick. Though his eyes were closed lightly, as if he were sleeping, he turned and looked directly at Clay—no, *into* Clay, as if he saw more with his eyes closed than he ever would if they were open.

Clay and Ayala halted. He felt tension roll off of his best friend; he glanced to her, and saw that Ayala was ready to run.

"Do not fear, children," said the man. His voice was smooth and soft, though it carried powerfully and clearly across the distance. "Though tread carefully, for the ground you walk is paved with many graves."

"Man," Ayala said, "you cannot follow up 'do not fear' with that."

The man laughed, throwing his head back. To Clay, it sounded like the laughter of a good man, the kind who knew where to enjoy life when possible.

"Very true!" said the man once his laughter waned. "I assure you that there is no ill intent behind my words; I simply do not wish the shame of disrespect added to the burdens you already hold."

Ayala was still tense, her brow furrowed. She turned her head slightly, looking at the man with shadowed eyes. "Why are you talking like you know us?"

"Ah," said the man, "I do not know you, but I know of you—but I am being rude, am I not?" He placed his hand on his chest and bowed his head. "I am Afed, a caretaker of these parts and others. It is a pleasure to meet the two of you."

"Nice to meet you too," Clay said, taking a step forward. "So, is this some kind of Ghoula parade?" Clay asked with genuine curiosity.

Afed's sadness seemed to deepen further. "No, my child. There are Ukkadians, Lokkans and Imu'ate, Kota, and even Assyrians. But there are no Ghoulas here."

Clay took this in stride, doing his best to follow the strange man's meaning.

A second's pause seemed too long for the man. "And, if I might add," he continued, "this is no parade. It is a funeral." The breeze picked up, and the sound of the song flowed over them; it did not sound like a dirge or a lament. It sounded almost joyful.

Even without opening his eyes, Afed seemed to notice the look of genuine shock on their faces.

"You're kidding," Ayala said, though the words could've easily come from Clay's own mouth. Never before had he heard such raucous sounds coming from Ghoulas, especially not in public. He'd only been to a handful of funerals himself, and one thing he knew was that funerals were supposed to be sad, events where everyone wore long faces, even if you didn't know the person that well. There was no smiling or gleeful singing or dancing of any kind.

At least, so he thought.

"Look around you, can't you see that this is a cemetery?" he said, with a facetious tone behind his words and a sly smirk wrinkling his aged face. He stepped off the trail and into the murky mangrove water. His legs moved smoothly through the calf-high pool, coaxing barely a sound from the water, and ripples echoed outwards as he moved. He rested his hand on the trunk of the nearest tree and bowed his head. "Every tree here is a grave." He turned his head to Clay and Ayala, his eyes still closed serenely. "When Assyr conquered these lands, our people lost much. Many cemeteries now lie buried beneath structures of stone and greed, and too many of our ancestors will never feel the warmth of the sun again." Afed lifted his hand from the tree and squared his body towards the kids, folding his hands before him as he had before. "The resting places of the dead hold many truths of the world, whether it's a battlefield or a mangrove." He gestured behind him, to where the voices rose and fell in the distance. "If you will excuse me, I have another matter to attend to. I would most certainly enjoy your company at these proceedings. Who knows—you may even find whatever else it is you seek." He lowered his hand and bowed to Clay and Ayala, his lips tilted in a tranquil smile. "The choice is yours." With that, he glided through the water and back onto the trail, not once opening his eyes, and he began walking towards the crowd in the distance.

Clay stepped forward, intent to follow him, and was stopped short by Ayala's grip on his arm.

Doubt and concern shone like embers in her eyes Ayala leaned in close and whispered, "When Nemo told us to go have fun, I don't think he meant 'go watch a funeral.'"

Clay did not hesitate before he nodded. "This is our chance to learn who we are. Who we *really* are, Ay." He looked at Afed, who was still walking away with even, measured steps, his gait slow and assured. "Plus, I don't think this guy means any harm. Yeah, he's weird, but I get good energy from him." He met Ayala's gaze again. "Trust me, Ay. You know I have good instincts with people."

Hesitantly, she nodded, releasing his arm. She stepped ahead first, and Clay followed. He noticed that Ayala kept herself between Afed and him, and a warmth lit his chest. He was glad Ayala was here.

In silence, they followed Afed, who did not acknowledge their presence on the trek. He walked slowly enough for Ayala to get antsy; Clay could feel her impulse to pass the man and get to the voices ahead, and he was somewhat surprised when she never did.

The voices flowed like rivers through the mangrove, weaving around trunks and echoing off the water, and with each step, they grew stronger.

The trail led them to a clearing, and through the leaves, trunks, and branches, Clay saw a throng of people in bright clothing colored amber and saffron. He had never seen such garb worn by Ghoulas: layered robes, lovingly crafted and arranged loosely, adorned with bracelets and necklaces of wooden beads and polished blue stone. Their arms were interlinked with each other, and they swayed and sung and bobbed and smiled, and many wore tears beneath their eyes. They were not even in the clearing yet, and the energy surrounding these people was almost overwhelming to Clay—there was a power to their togetherness and song, and Clay felt like an outsider and an intruder.

Before entering the clearing, Afed paused and looked back to the two teenagers. He smiled and bowed his head, and said to them, "Do not fear. This is your people; this is your family." He turned back and entered the clearing.

His words soothed Clay's anxiety, and together with Ayala, he followed Afed into the glade.

The song dwindled to silence. Every person gathered looked at Afed, and it seemed that everyone was happy to receive the wizened man. With a silent respect and reverence which Clay had never seen given to a Ghoula, they watched as Afed strode to the center of the clearing, where the earth horseshoed around a small bay of water. On the shore, in the center of the horseshoe, was a body swaddled head to toe in amber-and-saffron cloth. Around the body were a number of unlit candles, each one propped up in a shallow wooden bowl, and in each bowl was a match and a piece of charcoal. The deceased's head was lying on the earth; their feet floated on the water. Afed approached the body, went to his knees, and placed his lips upon the body's forehead. He whispered words to the deceased, and though they were too foreign and too soft for Clay to understand, he felt the power behind them—a weight in his chest, a tightness in his throat. The clearing and the crowd were saturated with sorrow and grief, which until now had been held in secret places within their hearts. But here, they could find catharsis and closure. Without a word of explanation, Clay felt that he understood where they were and what they were doing.

Afed stood and faced the crowd. With hands clasped and smile wide, he said, "Sawubona."

All together, the crowd replied, "Shiboka."

"Thank you all for coming," said Afed. Though his eyes remained shut, he looked at individuals in the crowd. "The years have not been kind to our people, and with each generation we seem to lose more of our ancestry, whether you are Uruk," he paused, nodding to Clay, "Kota," he nodded to a woman whose hair was pleated in two over-the-shoulder braids, "Ukkadi," he nodded to a man with high cheekbones and wideset eyes, "or Assyrian," and he nodded to a woman with violet eyes and platinum hair.

Clay was at first surprised to see an Assyrian among so many Ghoulas, but when he saw the Ukkadi man from earlier lace his fingers with her, he understood: Assyrians who loved Ghoulas were ostracized, and many fled to the outskirts of the Empire. Places like Thiva were popular with caste-breaking couples like them.

"For generations, our culture and identities have been erased and repressed, and many of us have known nothing more of ourselves than the word 'Ghoula.' But the spirit of a people cannot be killed so long as one person remembers their language, their traditions, their rituals. We may have assumed the names, gestures and pagan gods of those who oppress us—of the Empire and their ways—but we have held onto our own souls. In this, we resist; in this, we overcome; in this, we maintain our long outwaiting until the time comes for us to thrive once again. In honoring the death of a great woman, Kalina, according to the traditions of our ancestors, we keep the spirit of our peoples alive. Kalina was a bright soul, and even once sickly, she still fed her neighbors and filled the air with the scent of that scrumptious catfish curry." He smiled as if he could smell that curry, and that act coaxed sadness from within Clay; he wished that he had gotten to try Kalina's catfish curry. "Yet," Afed continued, "even as the end came, Kalina was joyous and loved to share smiles. I recall her saying to me that she looked forward to joining her ancestors in the land of bounty. Let her grace serve as an example to us all."

Afed tilted his head upwards. Sunlight dappled his hair and face, and Clay felt like the sun's radiance shone through this man. He took a deep breath and, in a language long forgotten by many of its children, began to sing. His voice was deep and strong, and he sung the first lyric in a slow and reverent manner, as though he were wailing.

A tambourine joined in the diaphony of singing. Clay looked at Ayala and saw that she stood as transfixed as the others in the clearing; there was no hint of mockery or boredom in her features, and for this Clay was glad. After all, this was a song they both knew well: "I've Seen Beyond de Troubles," mama's favorite lullaby. He'd always catch her singing it to herself when she thought no one was listening. The only remnant of their erased culture that she and he could claim to know. Though most of the words were utterly alien to Clay, he knew their meaning by heart:

Hold on child you need to—
Hold on
Through all my trials I had to—
Hold on
When you get down you better—
Hold on
Hold on child because the Lord has been
Good
When you feel as if you've had enough,
the mountain's high, and the valley's rough
With my own eyes, I've seen what lies
Beyond de troubles child
Don't you give up now
You better hold on
Hear me now, you better—
Hold on
On the other side of the mountain high
Glory's shining bright
If you can hold on

Afed paused for some time after the first lyric. He scanned the crowd. His gaze was intense, and though his eyes were cloudy and dim, they saw every individual present; when Afed faced Clay, he felt as if he were standing upon the edge of a cliff, staring out at a world that has long since been ruined and dead. Yet, there was also a warmth in Afed that was comforting, assuring, as if he were silently saying, *It may seem bad, but it will be okay.*

And then, once he had lingered in a private moment with all those gathered, Afed smiled, clapped, and swayed. All those present clapped along with him, shifting from foot to foot and clapping with their whole bodies. Many began intoning, their hums harmonized beneath their claps. When Afed began singing again, his voice was joined by the crowd's.

And Clay could not resist; he sang and clapped. For a moment, Ayala simply watched; then, when she met Clay's eye, she too broke into song.

The past and the future melted away, and all that remained were the feelings of the soil beneath Clay's feet, the joy in the song that hugged him and echoed throughout the mangrove, the simple pleasure of singing and dancing without worry or fear. Strangers danced with Clay and Ayala, their smiles wide and voices strong, and the two newcomers were treated as if they had always been there.

Time seemed to slip away, and for the first time in his life, Clay felt truly free.

When the song ended, his cheeks were wet with tears, and though he could not tell whether it was from happiness or sadness, he felt ten pounds lighter. Throughout the clearing, people embraced and hugged, and Clay and Ayala were no exception.

Ayala sobbed when embraced, and it seemed like some dam within her had broken.

The last person to hug them had been Lena.

For almost an hour, they continued in this way. Many songs were sung, and though Clay and Ayala did not understand all of them, they clapped and danced along until their hands stung and their legs were sore. It began to rain at one point—a deluge which seemed to join them in song and dance. No one minded the rain; if anything, the chill it brought was welcome.

Once the collective energy dwindled, Afed took his position by the body again. Without a word, the crowd regathered their attention on the wizened man. Clay and Ayala, slicked with sweat and breathing heavily, their hands intertwined, watched and waited.

They had exited the gondola in the late afternoon, and now dusk had fallen along with a light rain.

"A fine celebration of a life well lived!" Afed said. "Our sister will travel home with joy and peace, knowing that her life has inspired such happiness. Now, let us invoke our ancestors to show her the way, and to ensure that her spirit will not be lost on her journey home."

The crowd moved toward the body, and each person took a candle. They began marking the bowl with the charcoal: Some wrote names, some symbols, and some designed patterns.

Afed approached Clay and Ayala. Though he had sung and danced with as much vigor as everyone else, he did not sweat nor seem out of breath in the slightest. "When we set our fallen adrift in the water, they are accompanied by the spirits of our ancestors and loved ones, so that they do not journey alone." He gestured to the others. "Upon each candle, we summon the essence of a loved one, a distant ancestor, or a good person who is no longer with us. Then, we light the candle and send them away with our sister." Afed shifted his gaze between the children. "Would you like to light a candle?"

Clay and Ayala shared a look.

"Yes, please."

Afed smiled and retrieved for them two candles. As he returned, he said, "You may write anything upon the bowl, be it a name, a letter, or a pattern. It is the action and intent that matter most, not the content." With that, he nodded and handed them the candle, stepping away then to speak to others gathered.

When Afed and three others lifted the deceased and lowered her gently into the water, the candles were lit. All gathered watched in peaceable silence as their fallen sister drifted away, accompanied by a crowd of floating candles.

Upon two of them, marked in rubbed charcoal, was the letter 'L.'

As he watched the body float away, he couldn't help but to think of the futility of it. It wouldn't reach Mohi'ri. Clay knew it. Everyone here knew it. They were grasping for a pipe dream.

But Clay couldn't deny that it was a beautiful ritual.

Still, a blight of sadness panged in Clay's heart as he finished the inscription. He felt the strange sensation of being incomplete, like he ate a meal and was only half full.

He recalled, back at Nemo's chapel, the feeling of wanting the culture that Assyr had stolen from him, the identity that had been erased. But now, after getting exactly that, he couldn't help but feel hollow. Is this all that's left: a celebration of the end of a life? Where are their festivals? Their celebrations? How much has been taken that will never be seen again?

How can a people recover from what happened to them? From what happened to *him*?

They watched until both the body and the candles were out of sight.

"Farewell, sister. May your journey be filled with comfort and ease."

With Afed's final words, the ceremony closed. As chatter between people filled the clearing, Afed approached Clay and Ayala.

"Thank you for joining us, Clay and Ayala," Afed said.

"You know," Ayala began, "somehow it doesn't surprise me that you know our names."

"Yeah," Clay agreed.

Afed smiled. He looked at Clay. "I know that you feel more than you should, Clay. I have felt the echoes of your pain through The Source, and I am glad that it has brought you here."

"Uh, we drove here," Ayala said, her face scrunched.

"The Source guides us all," Afed said, "whether by car, boat, or the paths we walk."

"Sorry," Ayala said, hands raised, "but I have no clue what you're talking about. 'The Source'?"

Clay looked at Ayala. "Nemo explained it to us before we left."

"You think I listen to him?"

"Good point."

Afed laughed. "Would you listen to me, then?"

Ayala shrugged and nodded. "More than Nemo, probably."

"Then, if you would honor me, Clay and Ayala, I would love to show you what you seek," he said.

"How do you know what we seek?" Clay asked.

"Ah, I do not." Afed raised his finger, like a teacher about to elaborate on a lesson. "But we all seek answers, and The Source can guide you to them."

Clay looked at Ayala, checking how she felt about it. She shrugged again. "Sure, why not? If we were gonna get scammed, it would've happened by now."

For Ayala, that was a vote of confidence and trust. Clay looked to Afed. "Lead the way."

XXV

JAX

Under the black of his hood, Jax became an ethereal membrane, a translucent void dancing across every street corner in dusk-laden Thiva. He was everywhere and nowhere; no one seemed to notice him wherever he went.

He spent the first part of his day walking through the cobbled streets of New Thiva Square. A million busy steps clacked against its stone façade. He watched from the walls, the corners and park benches splayed around its perimeter as though he were affixed to them—like they'd been made with him in mind. His indigo irises glided over the enclave of high cheekbones, bleached hair, and amethystine eyes. Their carefree gaits held no regard for the trove of history they trampled upon with each step.

He could still remember how it looked all those years ago.

While there used to be dilapidated awnings and a rundown corner store on nearly every block, the old city had character. There was a charm to the way they did their best with what little they had. They'd scrounged the sparce resources they could find and built a magnificent city on the water from nothing. It was the kind of city that would be holding its head up high if it could. It was the kind of city that made you want to lift your head high too.

But now . . .

Where those faded signs and awnings once stood, Jax could see workers crowding the sidewalks with fresh buckets of paint in hand. They interrupted the once-sacred silence of Thiva with their constant chiseling and drilling, installing of sewage canals. Others reviewed schematics for the building that would stand in place of the old antique store Jax had once shopped in as a young boy. There were scaffolds lining the outside of nearly every building along the square—tell-tale signs of a city deeply steeped in gentrification.

It made Jax's blood boil just thinking about it. He made sure to count as he watched each deed, adding it to the growing tally of their sins. He promised himself that he would never forget.

But he wouldn't find a Sangoma here. Best to keep moving.

It was beginning to rain.

Even before the first droplet of rain made its way down the bridge of Jax's nose, he could sense the oncoming drizzle. He felt the damp moisture of the air, saw its imprint on the stucco walls and the looming clouds, and of course caught that earthy smell that always seemed to linger just before a good storm.

While others began to pack up their belongings, running for cover, Jax allowed the cool rain to seep through his hoodie. Soon, what started as a light drizzle became an outright downpour, soaking the garments he wore underneath, its chill drenching him to the bone. But he was unbothered. He considered rain an old friend of his and was comforted by its presence among the unfamiliarity of this strange new Thiva.

Kamarinth—his earliest and fondest hometown—was an arid environment with very little moisture. Very nearly a desert, some Harrakas had settled there after the end of the Shadow War, living on the outskirts of civilization. They built their homes under the shade of mountains or alongside their slopes to block out the heat. Homes that emulated the rocky terrain of the range and blended in nearly perfectly so as to be naked to the untrained eye. What they lacked in resources, they made up in community. The hard times had forced them to be more than a band of vengeful warriors; it forced them to be a family, a community dedicated to survival. Even with little water and food, they learned to endure. No one ever went hungry. Times were good amidst the struggle.

And when it rained, oh, those days were the best.

While the adults ran around, setting up buckets to store up pools of possibly the only water for Gods-know-how-many days, the children would dance in the rain. When Jax thought of the few good times he'd ever known, his mind often led him back to Kamarinth.

Today's rain felt like fresh water for a parched soul.

It became difficult to see far into the horizon. Down the cobbled streets, men and women were running with newspapers in hand, covering sopping heads in a desperate bid to outrun the storm.

Jax lingered a bit longer in the rain, not at all minding the heft of his jacket as it filled with water. The streets were thinning out and soon he wouldn't have to worry much about anyone paying him too much attention. Jax had only been to Thiva once before, on a supply run with Uxiah many years ago. Back at the height of Harraka power and influence, when Uxiah's father, Azariah, was still their leader, places like Thiva were invaluable to the Harrakas.

Uxiah often called it "one of the last free cities left on this accursed continent." Even in the Harraka's decline, free cities like it remained the best places to resupply, recruit, and regroup, but only Thiva held the unique distinction of being considered a bastion of what remained of their people, and one of the few places left where Harrakas and Uruks could live free.

He continued his march around the city, following the canals and rivers to the heart of the city, to a much older part of Thiva, not yet crawling with the infestation of Assyrian commerce. It would be the best place to look for a temple, he thought. He was right, but not in the way he expected.

His journey took him back to a district referred to as "Fellowship Avenue." This was a historic district, known as the first establishment, where outlaw Uruks on the run decided to lay down their roots and create a settlement away from the politics of the mainland. He remembered its crowded streets as he and Uxiah watched the festival parade that overtook the city that day. Everywhere the eye could see, there were awesome statues and beautiful graffiti coloring the walls of each storefront lining the avenue.

And he remembered how different Uxiah was then. Not worried about hiding, and in no hurry to leave. It was as if the whole town were filled with great friends and trusted brethren. He even caught him flashing *a smile*. It was short-lived of course—only for a few seconds—but Jax knew what he saw, and he would never forget it. Together they took in the smell of salty ocean spray that spilled over from the ports and coated the air like a thin veil of sand. It was sweet like sugar and carried by the canals surrounding them.

Now the place was a gutter. A lack of proper sewage outlets and maintenance caused wastewater to pool along the fringes of its streets, causing the inner city to reek with the casual but malignant combination of feces, vomit, and ocean spray.

Jax couldn't help but notice the congestion of homelessness around him, even worse than the stories alluded to. Most of them were either drunk or wasting away on Luna. They lingered in front of what looked to be a small, dilapidated building. He saw the tree bristling through its roof and knew that this was once the chapel of these parts.

It didn't take long to realize that was no longer the case.

Inside, large vines grew along the walls. A number of living skeletons lingered, huddled closely around the once-vibrant *ilaa lum*. What should've been a sacred artifact was now a dry, decaying grey husk. The homeless pined over its bark, digging what was left of their distressed nailbeds into the tree, pulling its bark away and picking apart its cork for a taste of its luminescent sap. Some were picking pieces of bark and cork to roll into thin papers, others grinding it down into bowls, and others were licking the translucent substance, turning their tongues a radiant blue.

Jax couldn't believe his eyes. He had come to Thiva by way of this very *ilaa lum*, back when he visited with Uxiah. As a child, it was one of his fondest memories. *Riding the lightning* was how he had thought of traveling from one *ilaa lum* to another almost instantaneously, and that trip was the first time he had used that Harraka method of travel. And now, looking upon the abused tree before him, he wondered if it could even be used in such a manner anymore.

White flame churned in Jax's gut. He was disgusted.

One woman was hunched over, back against the rundown temple's cold, stone walls. From the look of her, she wasn't high, but he nearly wished she was. Her arms knit together in a bid to keep warm. It wasn't just that she was cold that bothered him: It was the look in her eyes. He had never seen eyes so distant, so lifeless before. Well, not on anything still alive.

This woman was Uruk, as her golden irises indicated, but it didn't matter. Uruk, Ukkadi, Lokan . . . Assyrian—Thiva played no favorites with the downtrodden.

Even as he left that chapel, the look in her eyes haunted him. He went to the corner of the street, unsure of where to go, still trying to process how Thiva had gotten this bad. Worse still, he couldn't shake the feeling that things were only this way because the Harrakas had abandoned them, that in some way, this was his fault. Guilt's winding, black tendrils enshrouded his sunken heart, penetrating the fortress that usually protected him from such dangerous feelings. Never before had the shame of the Harraka's defeat been so roughly forced down his throat.

He was so disturbed he didn't even notice the woman approaching him until she was already walking beside him.

"Hey handsome," she said. Her voice carried the native creole accent often heard in these parts.

Jax didn't pay any attention to her. He was still staring ahead at nothing, his hands balled into fists.

"You from around here, bubba?" she asked.

"No."

"Okay . . ." she said, clearly trying to keep the conversation going. "Look like you've seen a ghost." She paused, waiting for his response. When she didn't get one, she continued. "Look at you, all wet. I can get you out this rain, make you nice an' warm?"

Jax rolled his eyes, already tired of this interaction. He peeked out of the corner of his eye towards her: trashy wig, ill-fitting clothes, two-inch dress, and fishnet stockings; but he didn't have to look at her to know what her angle was—he'd heard prostitution had become a thriving business in Thiva in recent years.

"Don't care," he said. "Leave me alone." Now he began to walk again, away from the street corner.

"Hey, hang on . . ." she said, grabbing the sleeve of his jacket.

Jax could hardly control his reaction. His eyes expanded, beading out of his skull, nostrils flaring. He whirled his arm, removing her grip and pushing her to the ground.

"DON'T TOUCH ME!" he bellowed; his eyes glazed over in white-hot rage.

The woman flew onto her back. The wig that previously draped her face fell onto the ground. Only then did he get his first good look at her face.

She was only a child. Probably around his age.

"Ouch," she said, holding her elbow where it sprouted blood.

His burning anger abated as he saw what he had done. He hated losing control so easily, though his regret never seemed to prevent it from happening again. "I-I-I . . ." he started but had the hardest time getting the words out of his mouth. "You're a kid . . .?"

The girl looked at him, and then across the street. He followed her eyes. There, in a window on the second floor, was a man staring down at him, infuriated. He said words to an unseen associate and then moved away from the window.

"Oh no," the girl said, getting back to her feet. Jax assisted her up as she wobbled in heels too big for her. "Look, you've gotta go. You're gonna get me in trouble!"

"Are those the guys that are making you do this?" he asked. She didn't answer him, doing her best to avoid his piercing stare.

"Look at me."

She did.

"Is. That. Them?"

The girl nodded reluctantly.

Jax felt that white flame arouse itself in the base of his stomach once again, rising upward to his chest, filling his lungs. His face twitched, nose crinkling uncontrollably, his eyes blind with rage once again. He knew that he *should* keep walking, stay out of sight. There was no place for emotion on a mission, especially with all the heat he'd drawn recently. But he couldn't fight the feeling that something had . . . changed within him. Maybe it was Clay and all his talk about Lonesome. All he knew was he wasn't the guy who could walk past something like this. Not anymore.

"Hey what are you doing? I told you to go!" she said, but her voice had already begun to fade to merely an echo in a faraway place. . . .

He drew his breath in. *In . . . then out. In . . . then out.* Each breath fanning the flame, coaxing the heat until it filled his lungs and burned his nostrils. He closed his eyes.

He heard the approaching clatter of footsteps against the cobbled stone. It sounded like four—no, five men, all carrying a variety of weapons. He heard the ringing of their lead pipes against the various jewels and rings lining their fingers. There was a hollow weapon too, possibly a metal bat, and then of course the casual *thwip!* that let him know a knife was involved as well. He considered drawing his blade, nestled beneath his jacket against the small of his back, but after weighing the approaching men, he decided that he wouldn't need it. They seemed the kind to prefer intimidation and numbers to actual skill.

The girl was holding onto his sleeve. He could feel her shaking.
Is this what it means to be a hero?
Dang it, Clay.

"Don't be afraid," Jax said to the girl in his usual whisper. He removed his sleeve from her hand. The men were finally upon them, flanking him and the girl on nearly every side. Throughout the chaotic grumblings of their foreign curses and jeers, he waited for the first victim to reveal themself. He'd make that one an example. He didn't have to wait long.

The first attacker stepped up, pipe in hand.

Jax nearly felt sorry for him for what he was about to do.

His eyes flared open as he lurched forward, intercepting his arc mid-swing and trapping the man's arm, leaving him open to a flurry of headbutts and devastating punches. Each blow created a small crater in the man's face, and Jax kept punching until he was down on the ground, face oozing blood into the puddles of rainwater.

He looked up from the bloody pulp to his next victims, and a devilish smile crept to his face. He enjoyed seeing their horror, and he hated himself for enjoying it.

As the other goons stepped back, reevaluating their opponent and encircling Jax so that he was surrounded, Jax puzzled over that self-hatred he felt. He was doing what he had trained to do: protect himself. He was doing what he was meant to do: attack evil people.

Three of the goons charged at once, one in front of Jax and two behind.

Jax sidestepped the one in front of him, whipping his right leg high and catching the goon with his shin; clotheslined by his own momentum, the man fell hard onto his back, cracking his skull against the uneven pavement.

He pivoted, facing the other two—one made the mistake of looking at his fallen friend, and Jax pounced. He closed the distance and launched a sharp kick at the man's sternum; he heard a sharp inhale as the man desperately gasped for air.

He planted his foot and went low, spinning and sweeping the last standing goon's legs from underneath him. The man fell to the ground hard.

Jax caught the lead pipe as it flew from the man's hands. Fluidly, not once breaking his momentum, Jax rattled off three successive strikes. His pipe cracked three skulls.

And he realized, as he looked at the way the goon's eyes rolled into the back of their heads and tongues lolled, that these weren't the people he should be fighting. They were bad, but they weren't his enemy; they were his people.

There were two men left. Jax could smell their sweat, and their eyes were wide with anger and fear.

He glanced to the girl from earlier and saw terror plastered on her features.

She's scared.

Scared.

Jax was a Harraka, yet he was spreading fear, not hope.

Am I really helping her?

What else was he supposed to do? Here he was, attacked by men with weapons who couldn't even touch him, and yet he felt utterly powerless.

One of those left seemed to gather his courage. He charged, his knife gripped by both hands and held low.

Jax met him in kind, catching him by his forearm and punching him in the nose. He disarmed him, feeling the man's wrist crack in his hands as he flipped him onto the ground.

He squared up to the last goon, a man with a bat. The man looked from Jax to the writhing people on the ground who used to resemble humans.

And he dropped his bat and ran.

Jax exhaled and took in his surroundings and realized that the girl was still staring at him, her eyes wide and filled with tears. He approached her, an arm outstretched to help her to her feet, but she scrambled backwards. Whimpering, she struggled to her feet and ran from him, not even picking up her wig as she fled.

He recoiled, bringing his hands back to his sides. What had he done wrong? Why did it feel like he could never do anything right?

Whispers and murmurs filled the air around him. He looked around and saw that a crowd was gathering. Horror was painted on many of their faces, and they pointed at him and those half-dead men on the ground. They looked at him like he was a monster.

He looked down at himself and, for the first time, noticed how his arms were covered in welts and blood. He felt a warmth sprinkled across his cheeks and neck, and he guessed that it was the blood of one of the men on the ground.

Am I a monster?

He wasn't trying to be—didn't *want* these people—these Ghoulas—to look at him like this. He was trying to help. To save a girl from men who used her, but . . .

But he failed again. He didn't bring that girl comfort. Just fear. Terror.

Isn't that what monsters do?

A tightness entered the back of his throat, and he felt with every fiber of his being that he had to get out of there, away from these people and the way they looked at him and the proof surrounding his feet that he was nothing more than a weapon to be aimed at something—that he was meant to destroy, not to save.

And so he ran. The crowd parted, and some even ran away from him.

He ran, and as he flew through the crowded alleyways and dirty streets of Old Thiva, a strange thought entered his mind: *Would Clay and Ayala be proud of what I've done?*

He had never cared about such things before.

XXVI

AYALA

Afed had led them through old, barely visible paths from the funeral. They wound through the wilderness, where the light rain pattered against the leaves of trees and bushes: a soft ceaseless drumbeat which was utterly calming.

Not long into their walk, Clay and Afed began talking about . . . well, she didn't really know what. Things and stuff. Whatever it was, they slowed down enough while conversing that Ayala quickly grew restless. Promising to not go too far ahead, she broke away from them, eager to find out what kinds of things she could forage in this region.

As she walked, she noticed that the leaves were already deep in their autumn coloration, and she grew sadder. She hated the winter months, where she had to huddle indoors to ward off the cold, trapped with her parents when she couldn't be at Clay's.

Well, it was different now, wasn't it?

Still, autumn meant less things to find in the wild—less flowers to pick, berries to eat, insects and birds to watch. Less, but still some.

More than a touch greedy to appreciate it while it lasted, she soon lost track of how much distance they covered and how much time had passed when walking through these strange old paths, sure to never leave earshot of Clay and the old blind man.

And so, when she was shaken from her reverie by the sounds of strangely familiar grunts, she stopped short, taken aback at how this situation rhymed with when they found Blood in the woods that day.

She snapped out of it and jogged ahead, rounding the bend, and was surprised to find Blood on his knees, drenched from head to toe and scrubbing his jacket with a terrifying intensity. He was by the shore of a great lake, its surface covered with giant lily pads and big pink flowers, and he did not notice her at first.

She stood and watched him for a moment, wondering how he had gotten here and where he had come from. His face was twisted like he was in some terrible pain, and there was a tension wracking his body.

It was the most bare and vulnerable he had ever looked to her.

"Blood, you good?" she called, maintaining a careful distance. "Someone break up with you or something?"

He startled and stood, facing her and whipping his hand to the grip of the sword strapped against his waist. And then he saw that it was her, and he took his hand from his sword. The torment in his features disappeared entirely.

She didn't like that he could just do that. It was creepy.

"What?" he snarled, looking confused by what she had said.

"What's up with you, man? Why are you drenched?"

"It rained."

"Not enough to soak you to the bone, unless you were standing in the open for it all." She quirked her head, feeling tension between her brow. It had rained kinda hard during the funeral, but it just drizzled afterwards. Even now, it was more of a mist than a proper storm. "What're you doing here?"

He looked to the water nearby, droplets still dripping from his hair and onto his face. He shrugged on his jacket, making it clear that he would not answer her.

Whatever. She'd come to expect no less from him. Still, she sighed with frustration.

Afed and Clay came tramping through the brush behind Ayala.

"Jax?" Clay sounded as surprised as Ayala had felt when she first saw the guy.

"A friend of yours, I assume?" Afed said. His smile was easy, and it crinkled his face in a friendly manner. He seemed oblivious to the tension which lingered between her and Blood. Something about Afed's smile and tone calmed Ayala, and she felt her earlier frustration bleeding away.

"It does not surprise me," said Afed, "to see a child of the Harrakas drawn to such a place. After all," he leaned forward, a whimsical glint in his eye, "it is where I was bringing Clay and Ayala."

Blood tensed again, widening his stance as if ready to fight.

Man, Ayala thought that she was wound tight at times, but the more she saw of Blood, the better she felt about herself. It *cannot* be easy being him.

"How do you know that?" Blood hissed, his hand inching to the blade on his back.

Afed tilted his head and, with incredible calm, said, "I would make a poor Sangoma if I did not recognize one who fights for our people, would I not?"

As quickly as he had wiped his face clean earlier, Blood's posture changed. He bowed his head. "Sorry. I . . . I didn't know." He looked at Afed. "Forgive me."

"Do not worry, child," Afed said, his tone soothing. "Your path has not been easy, I am sure." He placed his hand against his chest. "I am Afed, a Sangoma of Thiva."

Blood mirrored Afed's action. "I am . . ." he glanced at Ayala for some odd reason ". . . Ajax. It's an honor, Sangoma. What brings you here?" He posed the question to the three of them.

Wait, his real name isn't even Jax? To herself, Ayala chuckled and flopped her hands. She was just going to call him Blood anyways.

"Ah, I ran into Clay and Ayala here as we departed a dear member of our community. I am now leading them there," Afed said, pointing to a rise across the nearby lake, "a place where answers and guidance are held for those that need it."

"So, that's the place?" Ayala said, doubt in her voice and features as she squinted at the foliage-crowded mountain. It could hardly even be called a mountain—the thing paled in comparison to the mountains by Nemo's place. All it looked like was a place to get scratched by thorns and stung by insects, and there were too many trees for it to offer a nice view of the landscape. "It don't look like much—much less like it's got 'what we seek,' or whatever you said earlier."

"You don't believe a Sangoma?" Blood said, stepping forward and sounding as if Ayala had broken some rule. She didn't even know what that was.

Afed cautioned a hand towards Blood. "It is fine, child. Skepticism is no flaw, especially in the face of the unknown. One cannot expect to possess blind faith in that which they have not seen or felt, and that," he said, facing Ayala, "is exactly why I wish to take you to my home—to open your eyes and heart to the truths which lie around and inside us."

Ayala pursed her lips and raised her eyebrows, holding Jax's gaze for a moment, seeing if he was going to try anything, and then she shrugged. "Alright, sure." Blood bristled at her tone, and she smirked; there was some strange satisfaction to getting under his skin.

Afed smiled. "It is better experienced than explained. I require your trust for now, and I know that is no small thing to ask."

"If Jax trusts you," Clay said, tapping Blood's arm with the back of his hand, "I trust you."

Afed cast a strange look upon Blood. He said nothing, though, and then faced the hill in the distance. "It is not so far as it looks," he said, "nor is the lake so deep."

Afed stepped off the trail and into the lake; his movements were fluid, and he barely rippled the water's stillness.

The three teenagers followed the wizened man, and all together, they waded through the water.

Lily pads and lotuses brushed Ayala's calves. The breeze carried birdsong and amphibious croaks. Insects buzzed and darted through the air. A thin rain, barely perceptible but for how it caressed one's skin, fell over the land in translucent silver sheets. It lifted the sweat and heat from Ayala, and she grew to feel some measure of peace on their journey through the lake. The land around Thiva was beautiful. As they walked, she picked a few of the flowers from the lake, rubbing their petals and studying how they were layered. She wanted to paint this lake, these flowers, the mangrove trees—even that ugly rise they were heading for. There was a natural and unde-niable beauty to this region, and she couldn't believe how much *world* existed outside of Ruka and its looming forest. There weren't many flowers and beautiful things there, though she still missed the purplish berries which grew along the edges of the woodland.

Maybe there were berries at Afed's home. She looked at the back of his head; his dreads bounced along his shoulders as he walked, like he had a bounce to his step even when wading through a lake. "So, you live in a forest?"

Afed did not look back at Ayala when he answered. "I live *with* the forest, Ayala." He glanced back, that note of whimsy still twinkling in his eye. "But, to offer an answer closer to what you seek, I do not scratch a living off bark, berries, and rocks." He looked around then, as if to ensure no one was eavesdropping. "I live among the memories of my ancestors, tending to what little they have left behind."

"Ruins?" Clay asked.

"Can it be considered a ruin if warm bodies roam its halls? Or is it then a home?"

"Why not both?" Ayala posed. "Living in a ruin would be neat."

"Yeah, nothing like wondering when the roof's gonna cave in," Clay deadpanned.

"Oh, do not worry about that," Afed said. They seemed to be about halfway to the ruins. "After the first few months and funerals, we did not have to wear helmets anymore."

Clay blanched.

Afed smiled back at him. "I jest, Clay. It is quite safe: I assure you."

Even at the foot of the hill, Ayala could see no hint nor sign of ruins. The vegetation seemed to grow unnaturally close and thick here.

Maybe it's some Sangogo magic—or whatever Blood had called Afed. She frowned at the thought, feeling some strange and foreign tension in her chest. The old man was weird, but he was kind and warm. She made a point to listen to what Blood referred to Afed as, so that she could properly remember the title.

She expected Afed to stand before the barrier of bark, branches, shrubs, leaves, and vines and offer some grand pronouncement: an arms-splayed display of power and importance.

Afed lifted a big leaf.

He held it aside, revealing a narrow break in the foliage. Blood stepped forward and gently took the leaf from the Sangoma, holding it aloft so that the others could pass. First passed Afed, then Clay, and then Ayala. Once through, he followed, setting the camouflaging leaf back in its proper place.

The path was so cramped that both shoulders were brushed by twigs and leaves. The four Uruks snaked and wound their way upwards, following a route which only Afed seemed to sense. The vegetation was claustrophobic, and they took so many turns that Ayala quickly lost her sense of direction. She didn't mind. Here, it almost felt like the rest of the world didn't exist. All she had to do was follow Clay, and with that simplicity came a sense of freedom. She scanned the nearby brush and foliage, keeping a lookout for anything pickable. She wanted to stop and search more thoroughly—even go into the woods and rummage around—but Blood was behind her, and she had the feeling that he wouldn't appreciate it if she stopped.

Without any apparent rhyme or reason, the path opened into a large clearing. Ayala stopped short, realizing that they had reached Afed's home, and thus the breath was stolen from her.

They stood near the peak of this mountain, on the outskirts of a wide and open clearing, ringed by thick, tall vegetation. Before her lay ruins worn by weather and time, and people dressed like Afed roamed among the ancient stones. Even frozen in dilapidation, Ayala knew that this was one of the few relics of a time long past.

Throughout the clearing were buildings of mossy stone; maybe once they possessed the color of fertile red soil, but now the stones were faded and pale with lichen. Some stood apart from the others, squared and squat, while other structures formed pieces of a whole. Stairs rose before them, leading to a trio of tall buildings, obelisk-like in shape yet large enough to host a crowd. Carved on their outer walls were the faces of his ancestors, and though time has worn the details of their faces smooth and chipped away at their façades, Ayala felt as though they were watching her. Their brows were as their features: harsh. Their gazes seemed timeless and perceptive, and Ayala would not have guessed that stone could hold such weight.

From these three center buildings horseshoed a greater structure, where rust-orange stone rooms were connected by bridges and columns. Grand as the ruins were, they stood eclipsed by the trees and brush which rose around the clearing, and even they stood in the shadow of the far mountain peak—a spur which sloped from behind the centermost three buildings like a horn. Streams and waterfalls fell from the horn, trickling and traveling to the largest structure of all the ruins: the centermost building at the farthest end of the clearing. Statues of men and humanistic animals stood guard along the corners and roofs of buildings, and few of these have survived time's touch. In every structure and statue, Ayala could see where they had cut and fashioned stone blocks, and she marveled at the foresight they had to make such a temple; in its day, it must have been a glorious sight. The vegetation on the temple grounds was well-kempt and tidy; many flowers lined old, cobbled paths, and every tree which grew on the grounds seemed meticulously placed. Most striking of all was a great bone-white tree which rose from near the center. It stood tall upon ruins themselves, and its roots dripped over windows, columns, and archways like an ivory lattice.

"Wow," Clay whispered. His eyes were as wide as his smile.

"We have done what we can to maintain this place," said Afed, pride and grief blended in his voice. "Without the resources our ancestors possessed, however, we can only hope to slow time and nature from their inevitable conclusion."

Other men passed them by, and each greeted Afed and the others as if they lived here. Only Afed's eyes were closed; the other denizens of the ruins each had their eyes open and filled with peace.

"Sawubona," they would say.

"Shiboka," Afed would reply.

"What do those words mean?" Clay asked, after the third such salutation, when they reached the top of the stairs and approached the centermost buildings.

Afed glanced back. "To greet a fellow with 'sawubona' is to say, 'I see you.' To reply with 'shiboka' is to say that 'it is good to be seen.' In these days, few things are more valuable than to be truly known." He paused, and the others stopped with him. Afed splayed his palms, gesturing to the buildings which flanked them. "We are here. We are visible. We stand where our ancestors stood. We exist where they existed, and so we honor and remember them. So long as one person remembers and sees, a people will not perish."

Clay and Jax nodded. Ayala looked around at the buildings, feeling as though she were traveling the woods, picking berries and roots.

The moment passed, for Afed turned back and made for the centermost structure, where waterfalls flowed from the mountain's peak and into the building.

The air was filled with birdsong, the trickle of water, and the rustle of leaves, and though they were buffeted by noise, it was orchestral and soothing, as if the sounds guarded them against the world beyond these ruins.

Afed stopped again before the entrance of the centermost building. He faced the teenagers and asked, "Are you ready, my children? Answers and guidance will not come to those whose minds and hearts are guarded." As he spoke, he looked between Ayala and Jax, passing over Clay entirely.

"Yes. I'm ready," Clay said without hesitation.

Jax swallowed. "I am ready."

Why do I feel nervous? Ayala thought. "Yeah." Her voice was low and weak, but she stepped forward first, her hands balled into fists.

Afed smiled, turned, and entered the temple.

They followed.

The trickle of flowing water resonated from within the dark building. As she passed through the arched stone entrance—the intricate and multifaceted designs and etchings upon it long worn smooth and uneven by time—the water grew even louder and smoother.

And then her eyes adjusted, and she stood with mouth agape.

The building itself had no roof and was bared to the sky. From the open ceiling flowed sunlight and water, guided along two opposing troughs which funneled the clear liquid into the center of the building. From there, the water fell and flowed through the building and the earth; each stream curled around the other in a perfect helix, bridged by streams of water which—impossibly— flowed in perfect horizontal bridges between both curling streams. This flowing double helix, set sparkling by the sunlight cast upon it, fell down into the building itself, which yawned deep into the earth. Daylight was slipping into night, and so the sky was filled with oranges, pinks, and reds, and in the amber hue which saturated the air, the waterfall glimmered and sparkled. The four Uruks stood upon the topmost landing of a great spiral staircase that hugged the wall of the structure, looping around the helical waterfall.

It felt wrong to speak in such a place. Maybe Clay and Blood felt it too, for the group was silent as they descended the stairs. Protected from the winds of centuries, the stairs were relatively well-kempt compared to those outside, though it was still rare to see a step without cracks, chips, or flaws. A thick stone railing guarded the left side of the staircase, keeping them from both falling down and from seeing the bottom.

It was not until they reached the lowermost floor, where the crash of water upon a pool resounded, that they could see the temple's treasure. The three teenagers, hesitant, looked upon the innermost chamber from near the temple wall, as if to step further would be to trespass. The helical waterfall fell into a pool of water set in the floor, arranged in concentric circles, flowing around and orbiting a small tree, which rose from the exact center of the chamber. No taller than Ayala's hips, the tree was a rich brown color, its bark braided and gnarled, its leaves the deepest emerald-green Ayala had seen. Beneath the water-refracted sunlight which spiraled around it, the tree shone as if made of gemstones.

Afed took a few steps toward the tree and then faced the teenagers. "Welcome to my home," he said, bowing his head deferentially.

"What is this place?" Clay asked, his voice hushed by wonderment.

"A Source Node, Clay," answered Afed. "And that is the seedling of an *Ilaa Lum*, one of the last treasures from our homeland." He pointed to two Sangomawo, bowed in reverence on the other side of the tree, muttering to themselves words Ayala couldn't make out. "Uruks from all over the Empire used to make pilgrimages to places like this, praying for guidance and answers."

"Guidance from a tree?" Ayala was shocked when this remark did not come from her mouth but from Clay's.

"Indeed. I admit it sounds strange when put like that. But perhaps you would be less skeptical if you knew the history of the trees?" He paused a beat, as if thinking of where to start a long tale. "I suppose it'd be best to start at the beginning: The Source."

"Alright, hang on," Ayala said, raising her hands. "I'm getting tired of being confused. What's the Source? Why is this place a node for it?" She squinted and leaned her head forward a bit, as if trying to peer through a translucent veil. "How do we know you're not just making this all up?"

Blood curled his fingers into fists, taking deep breaths.

"Ay, Nemo told us about The Source," Clay said, as if the conversation had occurred this morning.

Ayala scoffed. "Yeah, you said that earlier, but I still don't know what it is."

Clay sighed and nodded. She didn't like the notes of disappointment in his features. He motioned to Jax. "Jax taught me about it, and yeah, it sounds like some weird new-age scam to open your mind and to your inner power, but it's not. It's real. I mean, can't you feel it, standing here, surrounded by all this?" He motioned to the waterfall and the tree, to the sky and sunlight far, far above. "Whatever The Source is, it's real. You can't tell me that you don't feel it here." Clay pressed a finger to Ayala's sternum, studying her face.

Color rose in her cheeks, and Ayala was silent for a moment. And then she licked her lips pensively, nodded, and smirked, hoping that it would mask the heat in her face. "So, what you're telling me is that you have no clue what it is either?"

"Not in the slightest," Clay said, laughter coloring his speech.

"Have you connected with The Source before, Clay?" Afed asked.

The boy shook his head, seeming disappointed in himself. "I've tried, and Jax has taught me some Agbasã. Sometimes, I feel like something's happening, but it's a tip-of-the-tongue feeling and nothing really does."

Blood shifted and spoke, looking at Clay with intensity. "For many, it takes years of continuous practice until the first connection is made with The Source. Even in the Harrakas, many children don't connect until their late adolescence. It's good that you feel something so early in your practice."

Afed nodded approvingly. "Well said, Jax." He looked at Ayala. "Imagine The Source as a force of nature, such as time or gravity. It pervades our world, an invisible presence which we cannot see but we can feel . . ." he stopped himself midway, bit his lip briefly then snapped his fingers. "Ah, it is better if I show you!"

The blind man walked to the outermost rim of the circles, reaching out above of it. "These rivers have been forgotten and lost to time," he said to them. "Yet, their memory and essence remain here, and there still lingers the memories of what they contain." In a language Ayala couldn't understand, he began to speak to the water. Nothing happened at first, but then, slowly, ebbs of water rose to meet his hand: first droplets, then sheets of water, until globs of condensed water hovered above his hand.

Their eyes widened in wonderment.

"In the beginning, it is said that as the Elder God, M'ynhyvch, crafted the universe, he took a part of himself and laid the foundations of the universe with it." As he spoke, the water, creating moving images and statues in step with his words. "This 'part' was the first of all created life, but it is more than a living being—it is at both times his Breath and his dominion over creation. That force—that energy— still exists today, transcending space and time, moving throughout the universe, according to that divine mandate, that mysterious Will, creating order out of chaos, life from death, weaving together past and future. *That* is what we refer to as *The Source*."

Clay and Ayala both let out an enlightened, "Ahhh."

The water shifted into a large orb, filled with bumps and plains. The image zoomed in, until they were looking at a lonely tree in the middle of a savanna. "That Will eventually led to the creation of life on this planet, from that of the sea, to those of the forests, and finally to you and me. The Elder created the Source and the Source created life. But when it came to us, the Source did the unimaginable and breathed a part of its original essence into us, creating an inextricable connection between the two and a new lifeform on a scale never seen before: human life.

"The Source—and by extension, M'ynhyvch—gifts us our souls and our sparks, and it is what separates us from creatures based only on instinct and reaction."

Something clicked behind Ayala's eyes; they sparked, and she perked up a bit, remembering one of Marva's favorite phrases. "It gives us the human spirit."

"Precisely," said Afed, pleased. "Through it, we gain the ability to think for ourselves: to plan, to create, to laugh and love and grieve. And so much more."

He paused for a beat, then continued, "Tell me, Ayala, have you ever created before?"

"Created?"

"Have you written a word, drawn a picture, fashioned a piece of something from where there was nothing?" Afed said.

Ayala shrugged, paused, and then nodded. "Yeah, I've dabbled with painting."

"Then you have created something from nothing. You have poured your essence into a part of this world which stands apart from us."

"So, inanimate objects can't connect to The Source?" Ayala asked.

Afed shook his head. "One needs life, sapience, and a soul to connect."

"Ooooh," Ayala said, as if a question that has long been without answers finally found one. She tapped Clay's arm. "That's why Marva can't riff on the piano, man. No soul."

Clay repeated Ayala's, "Ooooh."

"Wait," said Clay after the wonder had passed. "So how does this all connect to the tree?"

"Ah yes, the tree. To understand that, I must tell you a much sadder tale. That of Mohi'ri."

The name didn't ring any bells for Ayala, but by the way Clay cocked his head to the side, she wondered if he had heard it before. Blood nodded knowingly, and it annoyed her how nothing ever surprised him.

"Never heard of him," Ayala offered.

"Ugh," exasperated Blood, rubbing his forehead.

"Please Jax, allow Ayala the privilege of curiosity. It is, after all, a valiant endeavor to seek the truth."

"Sorry, Sangoma."

"Now," Afed continued, turning to Ayala, "you must understand that Mohi'ri is not a person. It is the beginning of all living things on this planet and the homeland of the first people, the Uruk. The stories say it was a den of peace and wonder, a land of bounty, a place where each can say to their neighbor, 'Take of my vine, eat of figs, live with me in harmony.'" He turned to the tree. "It is a land filled with many precious crystals and resources, present from the spark of the universe. For millennia, these primordial objects have soaked Mohi'ri's soil in Source energy, eventually resulting in the *ilaali lumay*: trees born of the Source that soak in latent Source potential and expel it into the surrounding land, enriching the soil with boundless power and providing sustenance to all its creatures.

"Now, no one knows how the Uruks came to be in these lands. People have their theories, of course, but none truly know. Whatever the case, there seems to be no way back. Truly, it is said the exile of the Uruks has been a hardship from which we have never fully recovered. But for whatever hope we may have lost . . ." he said, reaching his hand into a pouch behind his hip ". . . still, we have brought some with us."

He brought forth a closed fist, then opened it, revealing small kernels of seeds. "The trees," said Clay.

"The trees. For centuries, Sangomawo of my order have migrated from place to place, looking for a way to bring back the Trees and, with them, the presence of the Source again. But we have faced many hardships. The land in Assyria is not kind to our seedlings. Worse still is our own people; their hearts are filled with sacrilege; they've desecrated any successful attempts to plant new trees. They have lost sight of who they are, scraping and burning its sap for the sake of indulgence. They have become the biggest threat to our mission," Afed said, a sorrowful regret coloring his baritone voice.

Ayala looked to the floor. A veil of shame wrapped itself around her like an undersized coat, but she did her best not to draw attention.

"After centuries of abuse, our trees have stopped growing altogether. Many believe it is what we are owed, that the Elder has finally turned his eye from the Uruk. But my people continued our ways. And after one hundred years, light shines on the Uruks once more." He waved his hand to the sprout in the center of the room. "Providence. We are not forgotten."

A tear collected itself in the corner of Afed's eye before gently streaming down his cheek. "Wow," said Ayala. Every word Afed spoke nestled into Ayala's chest, like the bundle of joy she imagined that seeing a newborn created. There was pride and hope behind his speech. And she also saw why they went to such great lengths to protect it.

"So," Blood began, "why are you showing us all of this? You've gone through such great lengths to keep it hidden. Why risk showing us?"

"Ah, I wondered the same thing myself. But I am obedient to the Source. I move as it instructs, and it has led you all here. Who am I to question?"

Blood nodded pensively, like he was shocked by this man's blind faith.

"That reminds me," began Afed. "I didn't just bring you here for a history lesson. There is more to be done. Though this place lacks the power of yore, it still holds some. There is a small cistern beside the tree. Should you wash yourself in it, the source may show you something."

"What kind of 'something'?" Ayala asked.

"It differs," said Afed. "But whatever form it may take, you will exit this place with more than you entered. The Source is kind in a place such as this, and more readily guides us here than elsewhere.

"Come," Afed said, beckoning them to follow, "let us approach."

They followed Afed to the outermost ring of flowing water—Clay with restrained eagerness, Ayala with feigned nonchalance, Jax with guised hesitation.

"The ritual is a private event," said Afed, looking between the three. "I shall accompany only one of you to the center, where you shall wash. You will see things, and I shall help you decipher their meanings. The others are welcome to stay here and listen, but what the water reveals should only be witnessed by the person who washes in it and myself. Is that all clear?"

The three teenagers nodded.

Afed smiled. "Now, who would like to wash first?"

Jax stepped forward, bowing his head to the Sangoma.

Afed nodded and gently placed his hand on Jax's back, guiding him along the circumventive routes to the center of the room.

Ayala and Clay watched the two snake their way around the long troughs of water. A fine mist lingered in the center of the chamber, kicked up by the helical waterfall, and so Jax and Afed were half-silhouetted, their features obscured and strange.

Ayala, growing antsy, looked at Clay, but he was so transfixed by the chamber that she didn't speak to him. This was about the happiest she'd seen him since . . .

A weight dropped in her chest. She sat on the ground, knees pulled into her chest. Afed and Blood were at the center now; Blood's silhouette was kneeled by the tree, and she guessed that he was washing now. Low rumbling tones came from the center of the room, and it seemed like their voices were diffused by the mist as well; no matter how intently she listened, Ayala could not grab a single word of Blood and Afed's conversation. It continued for some time, though, long enough that Clay sat beside Ayala. Together, the two watched the silhouettes of Afed and Blood in silence, bobbing their gazes around the chamber throughout.

Ayala stared upward at the waterfall, marveling over the sparkling sunlight shimmering along its curves and angles. "I'm not sure if I really get all that about The Source," she said, her voice whisper-soft, "but that waterfall's definitely unreal."

"Unreal?" Clay asked, mirroring her tone.

"Like . . . there's no way this thing can exist, right? But it does."

"Yeah. It sure does." His tone was almost worshipful.

"Are you feeling something here?" she asked.

He looked at her, brows drawn in. "How do you mean?"

"Like with the fire feeling." She struggled to find the right words. "I don't know—I guess I'm asking if you're feeling that intense stuff you've felt before, but here instead."

Clay blinked and nodded. "Yeah, but . . . it's not bad like the fire. I feel calm here. Really calm. Loose. Like it's safe here. Do you feel it?"

Ayala shook her head, wondering if there was something wrong with her. "I don't feel a thing."

Footsteps brought them from their conversation. Ayala looked up and saw Afed ahead of Blood. Blood's hands and forearms were still slick with water, and his head was lowered. Ayala tilted her head and saw that his features were drawn and troubled, and he seemed many years older than he was. This time, though, she felt a little sympathy for the boy, and she made no mention of it.

If washing his hands by a tree could make Blood look like that, then Ayala really wanted to see what it was about. She felt scared—scared of finding out what she seeks—and eager—eager to feel what Clay and Blood were feeling here. Before they were close, Ayala stood and stepped forward, declaring, "I want to go next."

Afed smiled and nodded. "Very well, then." He half-turned and gestured for her to follow.

She made a point not to look at Blood as he passed her by—to offer him some privacy after whatever he experienced.

He seemed too . . . vulnerable to acknowledge. And that was a feeling she knew very well.

Afed led the way, and as they stepped into the boundaries of the mist, her breathing grew shallow and her chest grew tight.

The Sangoma paused and looked back to Ayala. His mien was kind, and his smile was gentle. "You are safe here, Ayala."

"I know," she blustered. His expression was kind and patient, and she almost told him of the inexplicable tension in her chest: like a tangle of knotted yarn, sitting in her lungs and making it difficult to breathe.

She shook her head and began walking again. Afed waited until they were adjacent, and they walked side-by-side. She preferred to have him next to her than in front of her, though she could not pinpoint why. Somewhere in the back of her mind, a little voice wondered, *Why am I afraid?* The voice was eclipsed by the knot in her chest.

Afed leaned forward with his stride, catching Ayala's eye. "Deep breaths, Ayala. There is no shame in feeling fear—"

"I'm not afraid." The words fell from her lips without thought, and she hated how her voice trembled.

Afed's smile did not waver. He nodded, as if he understood, and did not press the matter further. At first, his blind acceptance needled her—like he saw through her completely, like he knew she was a liar and a coward. Yet, with each successive step, the feeling ebbed away, and she began to think that maybe Afed was like Clay and simply accepted her as she was.

She tried his advice, and as they walked along the unnecessarily long and winding route to the little Source tree, she breathed in deeply, slowly, and exhaled measured breaths. The knot in her chest loosened, and she noticed how cool the mist felt—refreshing, like a soft spring drizzle. There was a fresh smell in the air, like she was surrounded by nature. The two other Sangomawo in the chamber ushered low intonations; they chanted in some soft and lyrical language, and it soothed Ayala. Somewhat.

Truthfully, by the time they reached the tree, she was still uneasy. Though, more at ease than she would have expected.

The tree itself rose from the center of a pool and was situated on a mound of rich red soil. Its roots dipped and wound around the soil before burrowing beneath, and Ayala wondered how deeply this little tree reached. From this close, she could not deny that there was something special about this tree: Its trunk was braided around itself, its bark curved and twisting; the leaves were so vibrantly green that they seemed almost like gemstones, and sunlight glimmered along its crown. The air felt fresher and easier to breathe by the tree, and a calm energy rushed through Ayala with every deep breath she took.

Afed waited patiently for her to absorb the moment. He did not move nor speak through the long moments where Ayala centered herself.

She looked at him once she felt better; once the knot in her chest was smaller and weighed less. "So, what, I just wash my hands by the tree?"

Afed nodded. "The water will react. Should you wish, I can offer insight and help explain its movements."

She nodded. "I would like that."

"Very well, then. Do not think too much about what happens; simply listen to your heart and follow your feelings."

Ayala swallowed the lump in her throat. "I'll try."

She stepped to the edge of the water. Though the pool had water flowing into and around it, it was mirror-still, and she could see her reflection wavering in the pool. She went to her knees, took a deep breath, and reached her hands towards the surface of the pool.

The water shifted and recoiled from her hands, as if it didn't want her to touch it.

She, in turn, recoiled too, leaning back on her knees and feeling a sharp pain blossom in her chest. She swallowed, feeling like she might cry, and looked up at Afed.

"It doesn't want me," she said, her voice so soft that she could barely make sense of her own words.

Sympathy tilted Afed's brow, and he smiled. "Do not give up." He looked to the tree. "It is a test. The water is not afraid of you. It is not repulsed by you."

"But it doesn't want me. You saw it run away like I've got some disease or something."

Why am I so close to crying? she thought.

Afed shook his head in a tender manner. "It is a test," he repeated. "The water wants to know that you truly desire to connect with The Source."

"I do."

"Then show it," Afed said, as if it were the simplest thing in the world to do. "Show the water that you are willing to go after it. Show it that you are worthy of its attention."

Ayala nodded and, before she could sit and think about it for a moment longer, she bent over and pushed her hands towards the pool. Once again, the calm water receded from her, as if her hands were repulsing magnets; she hesitated, swallowed, and then pushed further.

The water did not flow away further; it waited for her, and as soon as her fingers broke the tension of the water, it rushed to meet her. It was warm and felt fresh, and with its greeting blossomed warmth in her chest. The knot that had been sitting in her lungs seemed to evaporate all at once. She looked back at Afed, smiling and feeling, for what may have been the first time in her life, proud of herself.

He, too, seemed proud. He gestured, and said, "Please, wash. The water will show you things."

XXVII

AYALA

Ayala was falling.

She couldn't remember how she wound up so high, or where she had fallen from. All she knew was the ground was rapidly rising to meet her.

Her descent stopped shortly after colliding face-to-face with solid ground. It felt as if she were hit with a sledgehammer and all of the air had evacuated her body. She gasped, turning onto her side, searching for her next breath. Finally, her breath returned, and she lay on her back. The earth was cool and soft, and she noticed that she was lying flat in a black patch of dirt, like the kernels of a coffee jar.

"Ugh," she groaned. Her body ached all over, but all the essentials seemed to still be working. As she focused on recovering her breath, she looked up at the night sky, at the large celestial boulder of silver, iridescently hovering far above her. It seemed more distant than usual, as if retreating to some far-off place, taking its light with it. She wondered at this for a bit, thinking of where it was going, then asking herself where it had come from. She'd never thought to ask that before.

This line of questioning was interrupted by an irritation in her belly, the kind she gets when she feels something is desperately, desperately wrong but she can't put her finger on it. Ayala sat up, taking in her surroundings for the first time. She felt a sense of familiarity here: the gentle flow of the creek at the edge of her awareness; those long oak logs stretching high into the black sky; and that hollow white oak, the one Clay used to hide in when they were kids.

I'm in Ruka, she surmised slowly. But the ache in her stomach didn't go away. It was drawing her, gnawing at her until she turned her attention to a break in the forest, a tunnel of darkness emanating a ferocity that made the hairs on her skin stand. She remembered this feeling. *It* was back for her.

She wasted little time. Holding her hand around her aching ribs, she lifted herself off the ground, turning and running away. She weaved through tangled vines and tree branches, but her feet felt as though they were encased in cement. Still, she pushed through and finally reached the edge of the forest. She could finally see the thin strip of land known as Ruka.

She lifted her leaden legs and made for the first house she saw. No matter how fast she ran, the presence felt as though it were right behind her. "Help!" she called. "Help!" She continued running, barely able to bring herself to an amiable stop. She crashed into the door and to her surprise the door came crashing down. The lights were all out and no one was home.

No, she told herself. *It's happening again.*

Ayala pushed on forward, from the next house to the next house to the next. Every home had the same result: The lights were out, and no one was home. But in the distance overlooking the town, beyond the standard row of houses and cottages, she found a familiar lean-to. It had no windows save for one, and its walls were made of a material so flimsy one could be forgiven for thinking that it'd crash down at a moment's notice. But it wouldn't. It had survived many years of abuse and mistreatment, and it was here to stay.

It was home.

She climbed the small hill leading to the shack and approached the small window. She put her face to it, peering inside. There they were. Her mother and father were hunched over in front of the small television screen, their faces illuminated by blue light.

Ayala smiled softly. It was good to see a familiar face. She knocked on the window.

"Mom, dad. It's me. I know I've been gone for a while . . ." she said. "Please let me in."

After a few successive knocks, she was surprised when her father finally looked over to the window, confused. "Oh, look, Artemis, Ayeesha's back. Oh, and she's smiling." They both smiled and waved at the girl. Their eyes were largely glazed over and drooping. It was hard to know if he even really recognized her.

"It's been so crazy. I'm sorry I ran away," she said, tears filling her eyes. "I'm sorry. But I need you to let me in."

"Hey now," her mother called back to her, a loopy smile contouring her face, eyes crossed. "Y . . . You should be in school! You're not supposed to be here. Go be useful somewhere. Go back. . . . go. . . ." her words drifted off as Ayala's father passed her a dirty pipe, blue tendrils of smoke rising from its chamber. The life returned back to her eyes as she eked, licking her lips and clapping her hands. She giddily took a hit from the steaming pipe, losing interest in whatever she had been previously saying. Ayala's heart turned to mush, falling deep into her intestines. She shook her head, tears falling down the crest of her cheeks. But the hair rose on the back of her neck once again, and she knew she had to leave. There was only one place left to run. She turned away from the shack and continued on her way.

✳ ✳ ✳ ✳ ✳

Clay's house was cold and desolate, not filled with the vibrant burning candles Lena liked to leave scattered around the home during the night. There was an emptiness, a hollow feeling as she stepped into the small cottage, the floorboards creaking beneath her feet.

"Clay?" she called into the darkness. No one answered.

No, he has to be here. He has *to!*

"CLAY!" She called again. She ran through the halls, the kitchen where a small flame burned over the stove's eye. She ran up the short flight of wooden stairs. There was but a singular hallway before her. One she knew very well.

A bolt of electricity raised the hairs on her arm. *It* had found her. *It* was near again.

She moved with a new haste, opening each door, one by one, calling her best friend's name. Each room was empty, and Ayala tried her best not to give way to panic, but her lungs began to tighten against her will, and her breaths grew more and more terse. Finally, the only room left was the one at the end of the hall.

Lena's room.

As she approached slowly, wooden beams creaking beneath her boots, she heard the faintest sobbing.

"Clay?" she said, placing her ear against the door. She knocked. "Clay, it's Ay. I need to you to open the door."

"Go away!" he shouted back at her. His sobbing continued.

She tried the stubborn door handle, but it wouldn't give. The tingle surged throughout her body once more, this time fiercer. *It's getting closer.*

"Go away!" he shouted again. "I won't let you use me again."

"What're you talking about Clay?"

"Do you even care about me? Huh?" A sledgehammer seemed favorable compared to this.

"Face it, Ay," her sobbing friend continued, "You're just using me because you're too afraid to be alone. You *need* me. Without me, you're just another wasted Uruk, too broken for anyone to love."

The presence was nearly upon her now. She could feel it, brushing against her neck. She held her head against the door, unable to look back at the presence as its aura crawled up her spine. She tried the doorknob again, twisting and turning, and banging against the door.

"Well, guess what? I don't need *you* anymore!"

"Clay, CLAY! Open this door. Please . . . Please open this door." And for the second time that night, she sobbed.

In her despair, a calm and familiar baritone voice intervened. "You must face it."

"What?" she asked, seemingly to nobody. But she knew somebody was listening.

"My child, I see your pain, hear your longing. For so long, you have been fighting," the voice continued, "Fighting every battle, except the one that matters."

"I can't do it. I just can't," she said as she choked down sobs. "I'll just wait for it to go away like it always does. You'll see. It'll go away if I just stay still."

"That is only hibernation, child, not resolution. The torment will lie ever-present."

Ayala fists slowly unclenched as she lost the strength to continue her pounding. She allowed her hands to drop by her sides.

"Do not be fooled into thinking you are the only one fighting," the voice began once more. "If loneliness were a dream, everyone would be sleeping.

"The road to healing carries many travelers. It is true that the path ahead is difficult, yet longer still is the road we delay. Take your step, Ayala."

Ayala focused her breathing, doing her best to ignore the adrenaline laying waste to her senses. She pulled her head from the door. Her left foot took a backward step, into the murky air of the *presence*. She pivoted, now fully facing the spell of darkness looming in the hallway.

The darkness hovered as if it were sentient: looming, watching, and waiting to see how she'd react. She figured it was on her to make the first move.

"Come get me, you rat bastard," she said to it. "Do your worst!"

The shadow recoiled, girding itself, then launched forward onto Ayala.

✼ ✼ ✼ ✼ ✼

Ayala's reflection shone back to her in the crystalline water. Ripples formed in the water where tears fell off her cinnamon skin.

Still staring at her reflection, she reached up to touch her moist cheeks, and watched in awe as her reflection did the same. She couldn't remember the last time she had cried like this, but the moisture on her cheeks confirmed this was not an illusion.

"Well done, Ayala," came Afed's voice behind her.

She startled and leapt to her feet, using her shirt to abrasively wipe the tears from her cheeks.

"Sorry, erm, I'm not normally like this," she said to him, still wiping her eyes.

"Apologize not for tears shed in light of one's true self. Tragedy is to live never knowing oneself at all," he said with a proud smile. "Even a blind man can see you've got a warrior's spirit. Now that you are ready, I am eager to see the battles that lie ahead of you. Whatever they may be, I believe you have the strength to endure them, should you choose to."

A warm feeling came over Ayala's body, mending the balls and knots that had occupied the space before. She smiled. "Thanks, Afed."

"It is my pleasure," he replied in his typical courteous manner. "Now, let us see what your fellows are up to. There is still one whose touch the Source seeks."

XXVIII

CLAY

Clay and Jax sat in silence throughout Ayala's experience. Something told him that Jax had a lot to think about; the Harraka's gaze was drawn inward, and his jaw kept flexing and relaxing, flexing and relaxing. Clay tried to see what was happening by the tree, but as with Jax's ordeal, he could neither see nor hear Ayala and Afed clearly.

And so, he leaned back on his hands and looked at the chamber idly, basking in the peace of this place.

When Ayala and Afed returned, they carried a heavy silence. Ayala seemed distraught, and she wouldn't meet Clay's gaze—was that shame? Fear?

He didn't like it. Ayala never felt so apprehensive around him before.

What happened at the tree?

"Are you ready, Clay?" Afed asked.

Clay watched Ayala walk past him, her gaze still averted. What-ever happened, it looked like she needed time to process it. He wouldn't push her—not yet.

He faced Afed and nodded. The Sangoma beckoned, and Clay followed him into the mist. All the while, the two other Sangomawo in the chamber were still chanting; along with the incessant noise of the water, the chamber felt cushioned. Like a place out of time.

They entered the mist, and though the noise grew, it was never uncomfortably loud. He glanced back, searching for Ayala and Jax through the mist, but the light was too diffused for him to see beyond.

"Do not worry, Clay," Afed said. "True growth is never easy, and they have much to ponder." He glanced back, smiling at the boy. "They will be fine."

"How do you know?" Clay asked.

"Faith, my child."

As they neared the center of the circle, Clay felt the jitters of excitement. He shook his hands and flexed his fingers, trying not to vibrate. "What can I expect?" he asked Afed.

"The water may test you. It may accept you. It all depends on what you seek inside. Once you touch it, you may see a vision or images reflected in the water's surface."

"So it's not an exact science?"

"Just as life is not," Afed concluded.

The ambiguity of it all made him uneasy. He thought back to his time in school, which seemed far simpler by comparison; sure, it was far from perfect or even good, but it was straightforward. Be here by this time. Study for this test. Get good grades. By comparison, everything now felt disjointed and unpredictable and unstable. As exciting as everything had become, he missed the old familiar rou-tines. He missed his mom.

They reached the tree. Clay quirked his head, surprised at how small and vulnerable the tree looked; from afar, it almost had more presence. Regardless, it was beautiful.

"Whenever you're ready," Afed said, "approach the pool and wash your hands. Do not be afraid if the water shifts when you approach; it is part of the process."

"Okay." Clay shook his hands again, flexing his fingers, and approached the central pool. He didn't feel quite nervous—eager and curious, more like.

He knelt by the pool and splayed his hands, inching them towards the austere silvery water. He dipped his hands into the water, up to his wrists.

Absolutely nothing happened. The water didn't even feel special.

He looked back to Afed, and Clay grew worried when he saw the concern laced through Afed's features.

Before a word could pass from his lips, the water leapt up—it did not splash nor flow; no, it *leapt* and surrounded Clay, forming a whitewater barrier of churning water between him and Afed. In each direction he looked, Clay only saw water: up, down, left, right. He stood, and though the movement was sudden, the noise clamoring, he did not feel fear. More so curiosity.

"Clay!" Afed called.

"I'm here," he responded. "I'm okay." The water swirled and twisted clockwise, as if Clay were caught in the center of a cyclone.

He heard splashing from the other side of the barrier, and then a wince. "I cannot get to you," Afed said, some pain laced through his voice.

Now *that* made Clay a little scared. If the tree was willing to harm its caretaker for whatever reason, then he had no reason to believe that the water wouldn't harm him.

He inched as near to the center of the cyclone as possible, keeping a wary eye on the water. From the direction of the tree appeared a break in the water's rhythm, as if something—or someone—were breaking through the surf from the other side.

He took a step back, careful to not edge too close to the water-wall. The disruption took shape, revealing a figure which stood over a head taller than Clay.

It stepped through the water, and before him was his mother.

She looked as he remembered her. She wore simple clothes, the kind she would wear around the house. Her face, worn and weathered by labor and time, still had those stubborn remnants of beauty, the kind which a person could not ignore when she smiled. There was joy in her eyes.

And, though she passed through the water, she was dry. This was how Clay knew this wasn't his mother—at least, not her flesh and blood. He had felt her pass; he had felt it again, and again, and again.

Yet, nonetheless, his heart climbed into his throat, and he flubbed his words; he could not summon the breath at first, though with his second attempt came the whisper-soft word: "Mama?"

Emotion welled up in Lena's eyes and at the corners of her mouth, and though Clay knew this wasn't entirely his mother, he could not deny that it was, at least in some small part, her. She nodded, and went to a knee, and spread her arms. "It's me, baby."

His legs needed no persuasion; in a moment, he was in his mother's arms, overwhelmed by her scent. He hadn't realized before this moment that he had forgotten her scent, her strength, the feeling that nothing could hurt him when he was in her arms.

"It's really you," he breathed into her shoulder.

"Yes, baby," she said. "Well, it is and isn't me." She untangled from their embrace but kept both hands on his shoulders. "I'm here in spirit."

"How?"

"I'm not really sure how, but . . ." She glanced to the water surrounding them, and then met his gaze with pride in her eye. She squeezed his shoulders, smiling wider. "It's sure good to see you again. I am here for a reason; I have things to show you. Things to tell you about."

"And then you'll go?" His voice quivered.

Lena nodded. "I ain't meant to stay here, baby, no matter how much I want to. I've passed. The only reason I can be here is because of you." She pressed a finger against his sternum. "Because of the strength within you."

"What do you mean?" Clay asked.

Lena squatted so that she was at Clay's eye level. "Clay, I raised you. I know you—I know the goodness that lives in you."

He quirked his head, unsure where she was going with this.

Lena smiled, her eyes sad. "You've inherited a messed-up world, baby, and you're still young. Life'll try to twist you up into something unrecognizable." She squeezed his shoulder. "You gotta try your best to not let the world harden your heart. You're a good person, and I'm not just saying that as your mama."

Clay shook his head. "But I'm . . . I'm not. You're gone because of me."

A flash of what seemed like anger passed through Lena's features, and a warmth entered Clay's chest; it was the exact anger which used to peek through when he didn't believe he could do something or that he wasn't enough.

"That's what I'm talking about, Clay," she said, the anger replaced with a determined look. "You better not, for one moment, believe that you did something wrong by saving that boy. Okay?"

He nodded. "Okay."

She nodded too, satisfied that he had listened. Then, she stood, facing the wall of water which surrounded them.

She gestured, and the water shifted; the whitewater streaks in the wall faded, and the water seemed to grow clear and still, though the wall appeared as strong as ever. In its reflection wavered images of a place both alien and beautiful. Clay had never seen a landscape so golden, not outside fiction. But he could not shake the gut feeling that this place was *real*. "Mohi'ri," Lena said. Her eyes shone with the reflection, and her smile was easy and thoughtless.

To the right was a cityscape unlike any other. Not built by competition but by cooperation. Pyramidal towers, fashioned of warm-toned stone, reached for the sky. Surrounding the pyramidal skyscrapers were orderly city blocks of smaller buildings, each structure different from its neighbor: some roofs were elegantly curved, some stabbed for the sky like obelisks, and some were flat; some were small and rectangular, their shapes sturdy and strong, while others bore elegant struts and flying buttresses; some had stained glass while others had no windows at all.

"Our ancestral homeland and the dream of our people. Of Uruks everywhere." She looked at Clay.

A gentle breeze rustled golden grass, shaking it with a calm *shh-hhhh*. A gust of wind swept around Clay and Lena, creating a gentle cyclone that lifted her hair and kissed her skin.

"A long, long time ago, our ancestors were . . ."

Lena's voice faded. She still spoke, but Clay wasn't listening; he just couldn't tear his eyes from her, and he was soon lost in memory and thought. It felt surreal. There she was. His mom. Just as he remembered her.

She stood before him because of The Source. In a way, she was still alive. Still with him, watching over him.

In a way, he hasn't lost her. She's just . . . further away.

If The Source could manifest her spirit like this, then maybe it could do it elsewhere too.

He wasn't sure how much time had passed; with glazed eyes, he had watched the images in the water shift, looking but not seeing, hearing but not listening. He guessed that she was showing him this because she wanted him to go there—to Mohi'ri. "The home once-promised and long-forgotten," she called it.

He only returned to the moment when his mom turned towards him and squatted, so that they were closer to eye level with each other.

"I'm proud of you, baby," she said, "and I miss you very, very much. You and Ayala both."

Clay choked up and nodded.

"I'm going to go now," she said, spreading her arms, "but not before I get a hug."

He smiled, nodded again, and embraced his mother.

And when he pulled away, she was no longer with him.

The water surrounding Clay fell and flowed back into the pool around the tree. It seemed as if no time at all had passed in the chamber; everything was as it was before he placed his hands in the pool.

"Clay!" Afed rushed towards him, taking a knee and studying him closely. "Are you okay?"

Clay nodded, coughed his throat clear, and said, "Yeah, yeah. I'm fine, Afed."

"In all my long years, I have never seen something like that before," Afed said, his voice caught between wonderment and incredulity. "You must have a very unique connection with The Source."

Clay shrugged. He didn't know.

He didn't much care either. All that filled his mind and heart was how he missed his mother. It seemed cruel to see her again for just a little bit.

"I could not breach the water," Afed said. "But I heard a voice from within. Whom did you speak to? What did you see?"

Clay felt too consumed by grief to give the Sangoma a full answer; he spoke of a woman and of a place shown to him, but he did not mention names, nor his connection to that woman. He did not want to talk about it. Not now. Not while her loss was so fresh.

XXIX

JAX

Thank you, Sangoma, for all that you have done," Jax said, knelt in deference.

"And thank you for indulging an old man," said the Sangoma in good nature.

Clay and the girl thanked the Sangoma as well. The group had left the temple ruins in silence; many thoughts pinned their tongues to their teeth, and Afed did not speak either.

Night had fallen. The moon was full, and so it was nonproblematic to travel. All was cast in soft silver light, and insect noise lent a sense of comfort and life to the air.

They traveled back to the shore, winding through the incomprehensible forest paths once again. This time, Jax had not felt the choking unease of before, when he had realized that he had lost his sense of direction. He was too lost in his inner world to notice such things.

Afed revealed a hidden rowboat, nestled amongst a tangle of brush and vines. He provided them the directions to get back to Thiva and described where to leave the rowboat so that he could retrieve it later.

"I have only one request," said Afed as the three Uruks entered the rowboat. "Do not share the location of this place. I have given each of you my trust, and I beg you to not forsake it."

"I swear," Jax said.

Clay and the girl promised as well, and with that, they were off.

Through lily pads, lotus flowers, and reeds, Jax rowed. Once again, he found himself guiding his charges down a river, and he thought back to the last time he had done so. He glanced at Clay and then the girl and reflected on how they have grown beyond strangers to him. It was a foreign feeling; he cared for their safety, yes, but he felt something different from camaraderie with them. Though it brought him an indistinct unease, he was glad to be with them now.

"So . . ." Clay began, tone tentative and voice low, "what did you guys see?"

"Water," said the girl, smirking. "And a tree."

Clay, in the playful fashion which passed so easily between him and the girl, slapped her arm with the back of his hand. "You know that's not what I meant." Though a smile flowed alongside his words, his eyes seemed weighted and troubled.

The girl flashed a skin-deep smile and then settled into serious-ness. She clasped her hands together and leaned forward; one of her legs was pumping up and down, shaking her shoulder and the right side of her body with it. She glanced to Jax and then looked at Clay, and she said, "I saw the dream again."

"The one where no one is—"

"Anywhere, yeah," she interrupted Clay. "But it was . . . different this time."

"Different?" Clay asked.

"Yeah. You were in it. My parents, too. Said some stuff that, uh . . ." she looked at Jax and trailed off to silence, and her mouth corked to the right. She shook her head, as if to signal that she was finished talking about it.

Clay placed a hand on his friend's arm. "I'm sorry, Ay. For whatever I said—doesn't seem like it was nice."

She shook her head and sat up straight, almost flinching from his touch. "No, no. Clay, it wasn't really you—just. . . .I don't really know," she said, shrugging. "An idea of you, maybe."

Clay nodded as if he understood. Jax made no sound nor expression; he rowed and watched, mulling over what he had seen and the thoughts it left him with.

"I think . . ." Clay spoke slowly, as if the words were heavy in his throat ". . . I saw mom."

"You saw Lena?" Ayala asked.

Clay nodded. "She showed me things. A place called Mohi'ri."

Jax perked up at the mention of the land.

"Then she left," he said. "It wasn't really her, but it also was. Like, her spirit or something. Whichever part of her went to The Source, I think."

Ayala shifted. "Did she . . . did Lena mention me?"

"Yeah. She said that she misses you a lot."

Ayala swallowed, nodded, and bowed her head. She swiped at her eyes a few times. Jax looked away, floating his gaze across the landscape.

"Hey, Jax?"

He looked at Clay, flicking his brow to let him know that he was listening.

"I have a stupid question."

"Okay."

Clay weighed his words, doubt heavy in his eyes. "Do you think people live on, you know, after they die?"

"We can't know for sure, but I know some Harrakas who believe they do. Say they can feel the spirit of their loved ones, guiding them onto the end. I've never felt it before."

"Hmm," Clay said, twisting his mouth, pausing before asking what seemed to be another uncomfortable question. "Has anyone ever come back from the dead before?" Jax thought for a moment, rummaging through all that he knew of The Source. But he was no expert. "I don't know. That's a question for a Sangoma, not me."

Clay nodded and looked away.

Jax rowed on. Silence stuck to the air between them. He could feel Clay's gaze lingering upon him a few times, though the boy did not say a word; Jax did not doubt that he was curious about his own experience with *Ilaa Lum*.

Jax sighed. If he did not speak of it now, then he may never speak of it again. There were few places more private than here—few times more appropriate than now.

"I feel compelled to tell you something."

At his words, both Clay and the girl perked up. They leaned forward and gave him their attention, letting him know that they were listening. He was softly surprised that the girl was so attentive; for some odd reason, it gave him the courage to continue.

"One of my earliest memories is of Uxiah," he said, noting the ache in his arms as he pulled the oars. "He is the leader of the Harrakas and has been since the days of Azarriah and the Shadow War. When I was young, we hiked up a hill near an Assyrian city." He was silent for a moment, searching his memories. "I do not remember its name. Uxiah took me to the edge of the hill. From there, we could see the city. I had never seen something so beautiful before; I grew up among tents and sparring grounds. I . . . remember him pointing to the city. 'See those people on that hill over there?'" he said, deepening his voice slightly. "'Your only goal in life is to kill as many of them as you can. And anyone like them.'"

Jax swallowed and found that he could not look Clay nor the girl in their eyes. He kept his gaze to the rich wood of the boat. It was easier to speak without acknowledging them. "Ever since, I've killed people. So many that I've lost count."

"Did they deserve it?" Ayala asked.

Jax blinked rapidly and swallowed. "Some did, I think. Many didn't. I don't really know. My life has been . . . colored by blood. Almost every important memory I've had since that day on the hill has blood in it. That name . . ." he said, glancing up at Ayala and Clay and then casting his eyes back to the wood between his feet ". . . *Blood* . . . it felt like the most natural name I've ever held. Like the only name I've truly earned—the only thing I deserve to be called.

"Uxiah is a strong leader, an anchor for many Harrakas. We look to him for guidance, and he has led us with unwavering conviction." Jax swallowed again and stayed silent for two strokes of the oars. He looked further down so that he could not see them at all. "I have lived my life attempting to meet the expectations placed upon me. Uxiah's expectations. The expectations of everyone I have ever known. I never knew a life outside of that until . . ." He glanced at Clay and Ayala, hoping that his gaze could convey his meaning. Clay nodded; he understood. Jax shied his gaze again. "I lived according to those expectations, never questioning them, barely thinking for myself. I was told who to be, and I tried to be that person. I *was* that person."

"Was?" Clay's voice was soft and sympathetic, and hearing such a tone elicited a sharp self-loathing from Jax.

Jax swallowed and nodded. "Until a mission went . . . until I failed. It was my first time being entrusted to lead others. I failed, and they died, and I lived, if barely." He felt his throat clamping up, and so he spoke before it could. "I left my team behind just so I could live. I should have died with them." He chuckled briefly and wryly, with no humor at all. "I thought I *had* died until I awoke in the care of an Assyrian monk. A man of peace."

"An Assyrian monk saved a Harraka?" asked the girl, her voice laden with disbelief.

Jax nodded. "For six months, I lived with him. He nursed me back to health and caused me to question everything I had been led to believe."

"He was your enemy, and he saved you," Clay said, his voice soft.

"Yes," Jax whispered. "After six months, I ran away. I heard a tip about the crystal, and I decided to finish the mission I was sent on. The mission I initially failed. I couldn't live with the shame of that failure, and so I resolved to finish the mission, and then. . .then I would feel as if I could leave the Harrakas behind."

"You didn't want to stay with the monk?" Clay asked.

"I did," Jax said. "I was too much a coward to stay." He shook his head and swallowed, trying to ignore the all-too-familiar shame frothing within him. "I cannot escape Uxiah. All I can hope for is to beg for forgiveness and to be allowed to live my own life.

"I speak of this because I have been selfish." Jax could no longer keep his voice level; the passion of his shame affected his inflection. "I was too blind to realize this until—until the vision I had. When I washed by the tree, I was shown a choice: abandon the Harrakas and forge my own path, or return to them." Even speaking of leaving the Harrakas filled his chest with a tight feeling, and he could feel a weight settle over his shoulders. He swallowed and pushed past it. "To speak the truth, the time I have spent with . . ."

he paused, debating on whether or not to include the girl ". . . with both of you has been important to me. Very much so. You have shown me a kind of bond I have never experienced before. It is something more pure and good than I have ever seen or felt." He now looked up at Clay and Ayala, resolved to see them for what he said next. "There is a goodness in both of you. That's why you must stay away from me and the Harrakas. I do not wish to taint that goodness. I do not wish to ruin what little there is left of it in this world. My journey leads to Uxiah; I must confront him or I will not be able to live with myself. But I wish for the two of you to stay away; you do not deserve me or the Harrakas."

He fell silent and unfocused his gaze, having spoken his piece. To his surprise, silence was broken after just a moment.

"Jax," Clay said, "we're not going anywhere without you."

Jax blinked and looked at Clay.

Clay motioned, gesturing between Jax, Ayala, and himself. "We're all each other have, man. Good or bad or whatever, this is us. But I'm sorry you had to go through what you did, with Uxiah and your past and all that. That's a tough life."

"Yeah," Ayala said, "considering it all, you're kinda well-adjusted, really."

Clay tilted his head, almost smiling. "Well, I'm not sure I would have put it that way, but Jax . . . well, Ayala and I aren't the only ones in this boat with goodness in their hearts. I've seen it in you, even with all the distance you've tried to strike from us."

Jax shook his head. "I've stayed away because I'm not—I know what I am, and I don't want—"

"Hey Jax—shut up," Ayala said. "We're sticking together."

"We want to go with you to the Harrakas," Clay said. "We *want* to. And we'll have your back when you meet Uxiah again, alright?"

Jax nodded, blinking rapidly to stem tears from falling. "Okay," he said, and that was that.

"I have one more thing, too," Jax said. Now that they were coming along with him all the way, they should know this. "My vision also showed me where we can find the Harrakas." Clay and Ayala perked up. "It's good news," Jax said. "They are not far from here."

✻ ✻ ✻ ✻ ✻

"Where in the name of all that's kind in this world have you three been?!" Nemo yelled, his words slurred together and borderline incomprehensible. "I told you to get back before dark!"

"Is he drunk?" Clay asked.

"Oh yeah," Ayala answered.

They had docked the boat and made their way back to where the car was hidden, shortly after night fell.

"And why is Jax with you two? You three didn't head off together." Nemo hopped off the hood of the car—where a bottle of liquor sat—and stumbled closer to the three approaching kids.

"Are you drunk?" Clay asked once they were within an indoors-voice range.

Nemo scoffed. "How else was I gonna pass the time, waiting and worrying for you lot?"

"Aw, you worried about us?" Ayala deadpanned.

"Oh, shut up and tell me what kept you all past sunset," Nemo said. His earlier bluster seemed to fade, and he leaned against the car again.

"Uh, let's see, while you were getting drunk," Ayala said, holding her hand out and counting off her fingers with each statement, "Clay and I went sightseeing and found the shaman Jax was looking for, we met up with Jax, we went to a place, and we learned where the Harrakas were." She smiled then with faux cheer.

"Alright, great, thanks," Nemo grumbled, looking then to Clay. "Mind telling me what really happened?"

Clay smiled and shrugged. "She's not wrong, Nemo."

Nemo looked to Jax.

Jax shrugged and half-nodded.

Nemo folded his lips inwards and banged the hood of the car, shaking his head as he said, "I spend all day chasing old friends, don't get a single piece of useful information except for the rising prices of sheep, and you three stumble right into what we need." He looked at Marva, who had been standing by the car and watching the exchange raptly this entire time. "What kind of luck is that?"

"I have no idea!" she said with too much cheer.

"When do we leave?" Jax asked, eager to move on and not wanting to spend more time watching this charade.

"Ah," Nemo grunted, thinking for a moment, "let me nap off this buzz and we'll head out. Where are we heading?"

"East," Jax said, "to a place called Sacred Trees."

XXX

CLAY

They left Thiva in the dead of night. Clouds blotted out the moon and stars; the world outside the windows of Nemo's car seemed drenched in lightless ink. From Thiva eastwards, there were no proper roads nor highways, and so they bumped and vibrated over dirt roads and gravel paths.

Jax was yet again in the middle seat, as if he had claimed it for his own; Clay was to his right, Ayala to his left. Only Nemo and Marva spoke; she provided directions through the fathomless night, and he grumbled and mumbled beneath his breath, his eyes squinted and posture close to the wheel to better see the path ahead.

Clay leaned his head against the window and searched the world outside, but it was so dark that he only saw half-formed shapes in the darkness.

The fatigue of the day caught up with him. Lulled by the rumbling seat and the white noise of the car, he drifted off to a dreamless sleep.

✳   ✳   ✳   ✳   ✳

He awoke to what sounded like a gunshot.

Clay bolted up in his seat.

"Son of a—"

"Nemo!" Marva interrupted. "There are children here."

Jax and Ayala were awake too, and both peered over the front seats. Clay angled there as well. Through the windshield, Clay saw black smoke billowing from beneath the hood of the car. Nemo's jalopy slowed, its normal staccato rumble fading to a purr. Nemo banged the dashboard, flicked switches by the wheel, and pushed the accelerator to the floor, but nothing seemed to have any effect. And then the car's voice died entirely, and everything seemed terribly still. They rolled to a stop.

Clay wondered how long he had been asleep. The night was brighter, and it seemed as if they had traveled beyond the cloud cover. Stars and celestial nimbuses painted the sky here, and moonlight reflected off the trees and hills which surrounded them. They seemed to be in a more temperate clime, the kind where grass grew in all the places where branches and leaves did not.

"Hey Nemo, something's wrong with your car," Ayala deadpanned, pointing to the smoking hood as if it wasn't obvious.

"Thanks, professor," he said.

"Didn't you say that 'This beauty's as reliable as they come'?" she needled, a smile breaking out.

"Oh, go shove your head in a bucket," Nemo grumbled, opening the door and stepping out into the night.

Ayala caught Clay's eye. "I forgot my bucket; did you bring yours?"

Clay was grateful for her jokes; they helped ease his nerves. He shook his head. "Nah, I think I left it in my locker."

"Dang." She looked to Jax. "How about you? Any bucket?"

"Why would I have a bucket?"

Nemo popped the hood of the car and was blasted by black smoke. He fanned his hand in front of his face, coughing and backing away until the smoke thinned. He approached, rolling up his sleeves, and began digging through the engine.

Marva rolled down her window. "How does it look, hon?"

Some choice words and grumbles joined the sound of crickets, and then Nemo called, "She's hurt but not dead." He stepped around to Marva's open window, crossed his arms on the sill, and peered into the car. "It's dark out and I'm tired, Marv. Let's just camp here for the night, and I'll fix 'er up in the morning."

✳ ✳ ✳ ✳ ✳

As Clay, Ayala, Nemo, and Marva unpacked the car, Jax searched for a place to make camp. He found a secluded copse of maple trees, nestled between two hills, and before long they were all gathered around a campfire, sitting on bedrolls Nemo had brought from the chapel. Jax had weaved leaves through a net and strung it above the campfire: "This will keep anyone from seeing the smoke from our fire," he said. Clay thought it was neat, if not overcautious; as far as he could tell, they were in the middle of absolutely nowhere. He searched the horizon for any sign of civilization and found nothing.

"Where are we?" he asked as he settled on his crinkly sleeping bag.

"Far, far east," Nemo answered. He was snacking on dried nuts, his phrases paused between his snacking. "Basically at the edge of the Empire."

"Uruks once roamed these lands," Jax said. He was staring into the fire, one knee propped up, one arm hung loosely over it.

"Do they still?" Clay asked.

Jax shook his head. "After the Shadow War, the Empire claimed ownership of these lands. It became illegal for our people to roam as they once did. We had to settle in cities or villages, and so many were forced west, where such places exist."

Nemo grunted. "All this land's so freshly gained that the Empire hasn't done anything with it."

"So they just want it to have it?" Ayala asked.

"Yep."

She shook her head, picked up a rock from the dirt, and threw it into the distance. "Why? What's the point?"

"So we can't have it," Jax said. Though he appeared impassive, Clay could sense sadness and maybe anger in his eyes.

"Well, it's a beautiful area!" Marva pitched in. She stood by the campfire, her hands clasped politely before her. Her eyes glowed dimly in the night, and the thin flames reflected throughout her metallic body.

"More the shame," Nemo said.

Crickets filled the air around them, blanketing the world with a pleasant white noise. The temperature was almost perfect, and the air felt crisp and fresh. A breeze would whisper through the leaves on occasion, tickling Clay's skin.

"Why do they do that?" Clay wondered.

"Why does who do what?" Nemo asked.

"The Empire. Why do they want to control everything? Everyone?"

Nemo chewed a nut, swallowed, and said, "Power. Ambition. Fear. Take your pick. There're as many reasons as there are people."

"I just don't get it," Clay said, shaking his head and gnawing on the inside of his cheek. "Why take when you already have enough?"

"Well . . ." Nemo said, "that's just human nature."

"It shouldn't be," Clay said.

"But it is."

✳ ✳ ✳ ✳ ✳

Marva looked to Clay, her eyebrows tilted in a comically quizzical slant. "Why should it not be human nature to take more than one needs, Clay?"

Clay shook his head and thought for a moment, organizing his words. "Because it never stops, and then there are people left with nothing for no good reason." He looked at Jax and found that the Harraka had been watching and listening to him. "That's why we need people like the Harrakas," Clay said. "Those who fight for people without anything."

Nemo scoffed, and all eyes turned to the old engineer. "Don't kid yourself, Clay. The Harrakas are just like anyone else; as soon as they get some real power, they'll hoard it and keep anyone else from flourishing. Like I said, it's human nature." Nemo popped another snack into his mouth and, while chewing, looked to Jax and said, "No offense, kid."

Jax waved his hand, showing that none was taken.

"You sure have a lot of opinions for a hermit," Ayala said, eyeballing Nemo.

"Well, sure I do. Hermits have plenty of time to think about things, you know."

"Were you always a hermit?" Clay asked, realizing now that he didn't know much about Nemo. Didn't know anything, really. Though, he had never felt the need to ask; he always had the vague feeling that Nemo didn't like to speak of his past, and he never felt comfortable enough with the man to ask after it until now.

Nemo's beard twitched. He scratched his chin and shook his head. "No. Not always." His voice was somber and soft.

He sighed and glanced at each of the wide-eyed children looking at him. "Let's just say I used to be someone most people would consider important. And then I left it behind." Nemo raised a hand, cutting off any incoming questions. "Don't ask about it. I'm not proud of what I've done or what I've caused, and you'll understand if I'd rather not revisit that time of my life."

"It's okay," Clay said. "We don't need to know." He shot Ayala a meaningful look, asking her silently to not press the matter further. She pressed her lips together, and he could see her resist rolling her eyes.

"Well," Ayala said, leaning back on her hands, "can you at least tell us what you were doing in a chapel? You don't really strike me as the religious sort."

"Oh, I don't now, huh?" Nemo asked, offering a good-natured smile. He shrugged. "The place was empty, isolated, and big enough for me to do what I wanted. Plenty of land, a nice view, easily defensible. Why wouldn't I pick it out?" His face shifted, and some of the lightness fled from his eyes. "Dang, now I'm missing it."

"So, you just holed up there because it was convenient?" Ayala asked.

"The river also offers a great power source!" Marva added, eager to add to the conversation, or so it would seem.

Nemo nodded. "That water wheel made it even more convenient. Even alone, didn't take long for me to get comfortable."

"Was Marva with you then?" Clay asked.

Some more of the light faded from Nemo's eyes. He grew a touch more withdrawn, and in a lower voice said, "No. No, I lived there for some time before I . . . built Marva here."

Marva cocked a hip. "I am seven years, four months, and forty-three days old!"

"You're the youngest one here, huh?" Clay asked, more than a little tickled about it. He didn't like being the youngest in a group, even if it was only a robot who was younger.

"Yes!"

He couldn't help but smile at how happy she sounded about it.

An easy silence settled between them. The fire was kind, and though the night was cloudy, the moon peeked upon the land often. There was a mindless enjoyment to watching the others' faces in the shifting lights.

Nemo's features were somewhat drawn when he thought Clay wasn't looking, but when the old man caught Clay's eye, he'd offer a warm smile that twisted his tangled beard.

Marva looked as at peace as she could, considering that only her eyebrows could move. She kept looking around at the fire and the trees and the sky, marveling at the world around her like some newborn pup.

Ayala, oddly enough, wouldn't meet Clay's gaze. He tried to catch her eye a few times, but she'd always look away, like she couldn't bear to look at him for some reason. He wondered if her time at Afed's temple was still bothering her.

He wondered if it was still bothering him.

Jax, for his part, kept scanning their surroundings as if it was a habit. Even now, maybe the most relaxed Clay had seen him, he still held a tension to him, as if it was a part of his DNA. Maybe all Harrakas had that energy about them.

"So, Jax," Clay said, wrapping his arms around his knees, "what's it like in the Harrakas?"

He was silent for a moment, and were it not for the way he fixed his gaze on the fire and quirked his lips, Clay might've thought that he hadn't heard him.

"There's never a lack of work to be done," Jax said. "Everyone pulls their own weight and contributes. There's no space for laziness. Especially after the Shadow War, we—they need everyone who can contribute to contribute their most."

Jax made it sound very serious, and it must have been; after all, the Harrakas were fighting for freedom. He felt a dim excitement building in his chest. All his life, he had dreamt of escaping to the Harrakas and fighting people like Billy, saving people like Paul. And now, he got to do that; he got to live that once-silly dream.

"Is there space for fun? Relaxation?" Nemo asked, some worry in his tone.

Jax nodded. "There's some time in the day to unwind. We don't work all the time; if we did, we would be too fatigued to do anything well. There are feasts and celebrations for special occasions, but they don't happen much." He looked at Clay, who could not help but to notice how dull the light in Jax's eyes was, even though he faced the campfire. "I was raised as a warrior. Most of my time was spent training and hunting."

"Did you like it?" Nemo asked.

Jax shrugged. "It was what I was supposed to do. So I did it."

Clay nodded. "Everyone pulls their own weight."

"Yeah," Jax said, his voice breathier than normal. He stared into the fire for a moment before looking at Clay and Ayala. "What was it like? Going to school?"

"Well, Ay wouldn't know," Clay said.

"Hey!" she said, pushing him lightheartedly.

"Am I wrong?"

She smiled, looking at the fire. "Nah."

"You didn't go to school?" Nemo asked.

"As much as I could help it," Ayala said.

"Why not?" Jax asked.

Ayala shook her head, crossing her legs and leaning forward. "They didn't care about teaching us. The teachers, that is. And the other kids cared more about their stupid hierarchies and cliques than learning anything, so the teachers didn't even try. And man, the fights . . . it seemed like a fight broke out every day. It was a waste of time."

"Is that where you learned to fight?" Jax asked.

Ayala nodded. "Yeah. A school like that, you gotta know how to defend yourself. Once I stopped going, though, I stayed sharp beating up whoever messed with Clay."

"You went to different schools?" Nemo said.

Clay and Ayala nodded. "He went to a fancier school that had both Ghoulas and Assyrians. They cared more there," Ayala said.

"Well, with some things, yeah," Clay said. "But they didn't care if we were hurt or struggling—the teachers didn't help us like they did Assyrian kids." He tightened his arms around his legs. "And they sure didn't protect us from those kids." He took a deep breath, remembering briefly how Billy had looked after Jax had pummeled him that night. He looked up at Jax, and wondered what the Harraka was thinking. "To answer your question, though, school sucked. Nothing but lessons and tests and homework and learning a bunch of things that don't matter."

Jax nodded. He looked like he was genuinely trying to picture it. "What did you do for fun?" he asked.

Clay met Ayala's gaze and the two friends shared a smile. "We'd wander the woods. Go exploring where there was no one else. Watch bad shows on the TV." Clay shrugged. "Normal stuff, more or less."

"How fascinating!" Marva exclaimed.

"You know, Marva, I think you would've loved school," Ayala said, looking up at the automaton with a lopsided grin.

"I think so too!"

Clay looked at Jax and saw that his eyes were shifting back and forth, like he was processing something. His arms were looped around his legs, and his thumb kept flicking back and forth over his index finger.

"You worried about seeing them again?" Clay ventured. "The Harrakas?"

To Clay's surprise, Jax didn't grow tenser or withdrawn. He just nodded.

"Still want to leave them?" Clay asked.

"You want to leave the Harrakas?" Nemo said, leaning forward and looking at Jax.

Jax's lips pressed tight. "I think so, but . . ." he glanced around to Clay, Ayala, Nemo, and Marva. He sighed. He shrugged. "We'll see."

"Far as I know, people don't just 'leave' the Harrakas," Nemo said.

Jax nodded. "I'm hoping that with the crystal returned . . ." he trailed off, shaking his head as if to say that he was done speaking of this. "We should rest," Jax said. He was still peering into the fire. "If we set out at dawn, we should reach Sacred Trees in the early afternoon."

Hushed bids of deep sleeps and good nights passed between the crew. Crinkling sleeping bags joined the dying crackles of the camp-fire as everyone settled in to rest.

Though the air was cool and calm, and the noise around them was soothing and peaceful, Clay could not keep his eyes closed. His thoughts wandered to his time with Afed, and he could not still the torrent of contemplation which ran through his mind. He kept revisiting his moments with his mom in the temple, and he still had the sense that it wasn't quite real. It was hard to believe—almost *impossible* to believe.

But he knew it happened. He knew that she had been here, in this world with him again, if only for a fleeting moment.

No matter how tightly he squeezed his eyes or how many deep breaths he took, he could not stop replaying that time in his head. He was greedy for it, and he was upset that he could not stay there forever. He couldn't stop thinking that it was terribly cruel to see her like that again, only to know that she remained forever out of reach.

"Hey, Clay," Ayala whispered.

He opened his eyes and saw her form, squatted by his sleeping bag.

"I can't sleep," she said, her voice still soft and breezy.

"Me either," he murmured.

She dangled something in her hand. Clay shifted up to his elbow, squinting to see what she held for him to see. The fire was mostly dead by now, and beneath the trees, light was scarce. It looked like a bottle.

"I swiped this from Nemo," she said, and he could hear the smile in her voice. "This feels like as good a time as any for our first drink, yeah?"

He smiled too. It was a promise they had made each other long ago: that they would share their first sip of alcohol together. Living with Lena, though, actually doing such a thing was impossible.

He nodded and, quietly as he could, slipped out of his sleeping bag. Once out, he looked around the campfire. Nemo was bundled beneath his sleeping bag, curled around a bottle of liquor. Marva was powered off and "sleeping," though she was still standing and so her silhouette looked creepy in the dead of the night. Jax was sleeping ramrod straight on top of his sleeping bag; it didn't look like he even untied the opening to think of crawling inside. Everyone looked dead asleep, and Clay was softly surprised that

Jax was too—it *had* been a long and very emotional day. For all of them.

"Let's go," he whispered to Ayala, and together they prowled away from the campsite.

Once far enough away, they began walking casually, silently. The trees of this region grouped together like one strung-out herd traveling around hills and great rocky outcroppings. They kept to the trees; though they were in the middle of nowhere, Clay did not want to tempt fate by traveling along the crests of the hills, tempting as the view might be. Ayala, though disappointed, understood.

"Hey, let me see that bottle," Clay said, holding his hand out. Ayala gave it to him, and he was surprised at how mundane it felt. The bottle was thin and rectangular, shaped like a flask.

Clay held it up to the light, peering at the dark thick liquid rolling around inside. "You said you got this from Nemo?"

"Yep."

"Sure he won't miss it?" Clay asked. Nemo was fond of his sauce, and Clay was worried that he would be upset if he learned that they had pilfered his stash.

Ayala scoffed. "Nah, man—he had about a dozen of those in the trunk of the car. He mentioned that we'd probably be better off leaving them behind, replacing them with more important stuff like food."

"Wow. Considering that, he's been holding up pretty well."

"Pfff. Right?" Ayala walked with her hands in her pockets, head tilted up to the stars. "Remember that pond by Ruka? The one in the Wraithwood, surrounded by all the berry bushes."

"I remember you pushing me into it when we first found it," Clay said, smiling nonetheless.

"Man, you *stunk* that day—I was doing you a favor," Ayala said, laughter in her words.

"Hey! It wasn't my fault: someone stole my spare clothes and it was fitness day."

"Fault or not, you still stunk." Ayala looked to the ground beneath their feet, coated in a carpet of thick low grass. She looked at Clay through the corner of her eye. "That's where we made the promise, yeah? To have our first drink together."

"Really?"

"Yeah."

Clay had forgotten about that.

"I want to do it by the water," she declared.

"Is there even water near here?" Clay asked, looking around as if he could see through the trees surrounding them.

Ayala nodded. "Before I came to get you, I climbed one of those big rocks. Got a look at the landscape. Don't get that look on your face—I was careful."

"No, it's not that; I'm just surprised that you did that much before getting me," Clay said. "Sometimes it scares me—how quietly you can move."

Ayala's voice adopted a wistful tilt. "I've had a lot of practice. Anyways, we're almost to the river."

"Oh, it's a river?"

Ayala nodded, smiling like she was revisiting a good memory. "A pretty one, too. You can see the moonlight in the water, swaying back and forth like . . . like . . ."

"Like grass?" Clay offered.

"That's a bad comparison, man."

"At least I had one!"

They laughed and settled into a peaceable silence. For a time, they walked, their companions the breeze and the orchestra of insects.

"Should be just through here," Ayala said, nodding to the dense group of trees ahead. Clay trusted her sense of direction; she was always good at navigating the wilderness. Growing up, she had always been the one to lead them through the strange and wild places around Ruka. He smiled, grateful for the pang of nostalgia this moment evoked.

They passed the trees and before them lay a river. It was not grand nor terribly impressive, but it held its own charm, and Ayala was right—moonlight shimmered in a thin line, trailing across the soft current. Past the river was a scattering of spiring stones, so tall that they seemed unnatural among the landscape of rolling hills. Dark clouds inched across the sky, solitary and large, only seen by the starlight they obscured.

"Yeah, this'll do," Clay said, his voice hushed with wonder. The beauty here was soft and gentle, and he was fond of the sights before him. He took a step forward, only to be stopped by Ayala's arm, barring his way. He looked at her and saw that her eyes were narrowed and locked on something to their left.

He looked and saw, on the bank of the river, a man, well-built and rather short. He was knelt by the water and appeared to be washing a jacket. The moonlight shimmered along the edges of his brimmed hat and in his pale hair, its black streaked with white from age. He wore traveler's garb, sturdy and dirty, though his shoes appeared to be simple leather moccasins.

Ayala spoke in a low, terse tone: "Maybe we should—"

"Come on out from the shadows," called the man, his voice strong yet soft; though it lacked the gravelly effect many men came to hold when they aged, there was an undeniable authority to his tone, as if he had spent many years issuing orders. He tilted his head in their direction, though not enough for them to see his face clearly. "You have nothing to fear. If I wanted to kill you, you'd already be dead."

XXXI

SAMAEL

It had been a bad day. A long day.

Bandits never knew how to leave well enough alone. In these lands, they wore desperation as if it would keep them warm through the winter. And desperate men fought like cornered animals.

Not that it made much difference for him. But it threw Cato off guard, to see men who acted more like beasts than humans. She'd be dead if it weren't for him. He had forgotten the pain of a wound: the sick-warm feeling of blood trailing across chilled skin.

Beneath the moonlight, he looked at the bandages wrapped around his forearm. It was a shallow thing, made by an ugly blade, and it would heal with barely a scar.

Samael grimaced. He hated the needling way a wound kept talking after it was made, and he knew that the pain from this one wouldn't shut up for days. He already had Cato; he didn't need more noise in his life.

Some voice in the back of his mind wondered if he was too harsh on the girl. She *was* good, just unrefined—steel ingot destined to be a blade. The voice left as quick as it had come . . . no point in wondering about someone he would never see again, once this was all over.

He leaned back and sighed, looking across the landscape: the river, moonlight reflected like glass in a dream along its surface; the rolling hills across the bank, painted silver beneath starlight; the great spires of rock which loomed stark-black against the horizon.

Not much longer now.

It had been a tiresome, tedious hunt.

He sighed again, leaning over and grabbing his jacket. The blood was almost scrubbed clean. He lifted it from the river, wrung it out, and submerged it again, scrubbing at the last bit of blood clinging stubbornly to the sleeve.

To Samael, the sounds of the wild were as natural as the rhythm of his breath. Just as he'd notice a break in the rhythm of his breath, he noticed the break in the rhythm of nature; and there it was: leaves rustling when the wind came low. His ears perked, and he made a conscious effort to appear as if he were still washing his jacket. He tilted his head to the right, though, so that he could peek from his periphery at the source of the sound. It had come from a nearby thicket; the slope of the hill was such that no one could shoot him from the thicket I, and he would be hidden from sight until they broke free of the brush.

He stifled a curse; he had left his blade back at camp. He meant to only wash here and head back, and they hadn't seen another human for weeks before today.

Not that he needed his blade.

Sword or not, he had sported and shed enough blood for the day.

And so, he pretended to busy himself with his jacket until the woods rustled again, and again, and again until two figures, shining blue beneath the moonlight, stepped out from the thicket.

He quirked his ears and tilted his head, catching the words the wind brought him.

"Yeah, this'll do." The voice of a child—no, older than a child, but only just. There was wonder in that tone, and a kind of innocence of pleasure which reminded Samael of his own youth.

And then a beat of silence; cloth rustled; something in the air shifted. Samael recognized the silent energy which seemed to fill a space at a moment's notice: the moment a wolf bares its fangs; a cat hisses; a sword is loosed from its scabbard.

They had seen him, and they were defensive—good, that meant they were scared. He could take the upper hand.

The other one spoke—a girl, maybe a little older than the boy. Her words were hushed and warded, and Samael could not make them out.

He cut her off before she could finish a sentence. "Come on out from the shadows." He waited a beat; they didn't run. Good. "You have nothing to fear. If I wanted to kill you, you'd already be dead."

Not many people earned the right to make a statement like that. Samael knew, with no sense of ego nor pride, that he had.

He shifted so that he could look at them more clearly and vice versa. Just as he thought: They were kids. Most of their features were shrouded by the night, and moonlight shone bluish-silver along the tops of their heads, their cheeks, and their shoulders. They were young, and they seemed scared.

Samael watched them, disguising his tension to disarm them.

This near the edge of the Empire, it was common for children to run away, especially if they were Ghoulas. There was the faint promise of wild hope beyond the border—a place unknown, where a Ghoula might find a better life. Orphans, unwanted children, and all kinds of unhappy kids escaped to these regions, blinded by the kind of youthful idealism which saw them die hungry and far from civilization.

He hoped these were children like that, and not the ones who were missing from Ruka.

They stepped, tentative like newborn foals, towards him. Moonlight glimpsed their features as they stepped down the slope. Samael looked back at the river, and he saw that all traces of blood had been scrubbed from his jacket arm. He must have been so focused on the strangers' approach that he finished the job without noticing.

What if they *were* the kids from Ruka?

He gestured, beckoning them like some friendly traveler. Whispers passed between the two, and they began to walk with a little more comfort than before. The boy held a bottle of what looked like liquor; he gripped it tight.

If they were the kids . . .

He sighed and glanced back at the jacket. His arm still prickled with pain, and he realized—not for the first time on this trip—how tired he felt. It wasn't from a lack of vigor or stamina: He led an active life, even in retirement. The simple truth was that he had no passion for this work anymore.

"Hey, mister." It was the boy. They were close enough to speak comfortably, but they kept a careful distance from the man. Though a cloud had since rolled over the moon, he could see them better now. The girl had tension from head to toe, and she kept glancing around, like she expected some monster to come from nowhere. The boy, though, wore curiosity and friendliness like clothing.

"Didn't think we'd see another Ghoula all the way out here," the boy continued.

"Well, that makes two of us," Samael said, leaning back. The moon was to his back, and he guessed that his features were cast in shadow. He wondered if it was too dark for them to see his eyes. And if they knew what his eyes represented.

He gestured to the bottle in the boy's hand. "I'm guessing that isn't yours."

The boy shifted the bottle behind his leg, obscuring it from view.

"It's our uncle's," said the girl. She was a practiced liar; if she kept the tightness from her tone, Samael might have believed her.

He shifted again, trying to see their features more clearly. They matched the descriptions of the kids from Ruka, more or less. A tall, thin girl, around fifteen years of age with a messy throw of hair, and a shorter boy, broad-shouldered and on the stockier side, with loose curls shorn close to his head.

The boy rubbed the back of his neck. "Truth be told, we snuck out here to have our first taste of it," he said, wiggling the bottle of liquor.

Samael wore a smile and kept his tone easygoing. "So your uncle doesn't know?"

"No, sir."

"And just how old are you two?"

A beat of silence, and the two shared a glance.

"Fourteen," said the boy.

"Seventeen," said the girl.

Maybe those were lies, too. Truthfully, Samael didn't have the energy to pick those words apart just then. He held his hand out towards the boy. "Give it here." Though his words were soft, they brokered no discussion.

"Want a sip of your own?" the boy asked, handing the bottle over. The boy was either a good liar or he was just a genuinely good-natured sort. The kind of person who would trust a stranger in lands like these.

Samael tilted the bottle—more a pocket-sized flask, really—back and forth, catching the moonlight so that he could read the label. It wasn't a brand he recognized. He shook his head and offered the bottle back. "I've known too many people who've been killed by this stuff." When the boy grabbed the bottle, Samael held it tight, making sure that the boy was looking him in the face before saying, "Do me a favor, though, huh? Don't take more than a sip or two—either of you. This region's filled with dangerous people, and you best keep your wits about you."

The boy nodded, and Samael released the liquor. He gestured to the riverbank. "Come and sit for a spell, if you've a mind to. Might as well take your first sips here. No guarantee that other parts of the river are safe."

"Can we trust you?" the girl asked.

Samael spread his hands, making sure to keep his head tilted down, hoping that the shadow beneath his hat kept his eyes shrouded. "I don't have any weapons."

The boy and the girl shared another look. Beneath the cloudy night, he couldn't see their expressions well, but when the boy tilted his head, the girl shrugged and some of the tension bled from her. They settled on the grass; the boy was closer, and the girl farther, but both sat far enough from Samael to jump up and run, should they have to.

"Has anyone told you, mister, that you look like Lonesome?" the boy asked.

"Who?"

"Oh, he's a character from a comic series." The boy sounded almost genuinely disappointed that Samael didn't know about the character.

"Oh? Which series?" Samael said, finding that the amiable lope to his tone came without effort. It was a soft surprise.

The boy smiled. "*Revolt*. Do you know it?"

Revolt? It *did* sound familiar. He thought for a moment, some small voice in the back of his mind telling him to stop talking about comics and start interrogating these children.

He snapped his fingers. "I do." He remembered picking up a box set of *Revolt* comics in a shop not too long ago. "My daughter likes comics, you see. She asked for that series by name." Seeing the excitement building in the boy's eyes, he held his hands out. "But I've never read a page of it, so I can't say I know it too well."

The boy nodded, understanding. "Well, you look like my favorite character. I'd show you what he looks like—I've got an action figure of him—but I don't have it with me."

The girl looked at him, a quizzical expression on her face.

"Oh, yeah," the boy said, pausing a moment as if to find the right words. Then, he said to her, "Our uncle got me another one. A few of them, actually."

"Oh, I haven't seen you use them."

Something seemed to pass behind the boy's eye, and it seemed to Samael like his light dimmed.

"I haven't much felt like it lately," said the boy.

The girl nodded. She seemed to be more relaxed than at first, as if speaking of comics lowered her guard, at least somewhat. She looked at Samael. "Been a tough few weeks, lately," she said by way of explanation.

Samael nodded. "That it has." He grinned and shifted. "Want some unsolicited advice from an old man?"

"Sure," said the boy, some of his earlier energy restored.

"It won't get much easier from here on out. Older you get, more problems seem to pop up. So, you just gotta get stronger. Just got to keep on going through it."

"Until what?" asked the boy.

He was surprised to chuckle; it came so naturally that he didn't even notice it at first. "Until nothing. That's life—it keeps going and it never gets easier, and you just gotta keep getting stronger to keep up with it."

"Well, that sucks," the boy said.

And, miraculously, Samael laughed. "Yep. You can wish all you want that world were a bit kinder, or you can accept it and adapt to it."

Samael learned that lesson long ago, maybe when he was about the age of these kids. It led him down a lot of paths in life, and some small part of him wondered if that outlook was responsible for the evil he's caused.

He looked back to the river, mulling for a moment. What was he doing? He should be interrogating these two, vetting them to see if they were the fugitives. But his shoulders felt heavy, and if he were being honest with himself, it was nice to have an interaction with someone who didn't know who he was.

Maybe he would be selfish, just for one night.

"So, what do you do?" the girl asked. There was still a little tension in her tone, and he could feel her gaze piercing the darkness between them.

"I raise horses," Samael said, bringing his legs in and crossing them. He rested his forearms on his knees and looked across the river. "They'd love it here. Lot of open ground to run free."

The boy grunted. Samael looked over and saw him fiddling with the liquor. Noticing the man's gaze, the boy looked up, and even in the low light, Samael could see a sheepish smile. "I can't open this dang thing," the boy said.

"Give it here. They have special caps on them," Samael said. "That way, kids who steal them from their uncle have a hard time actually opening the things."

The boy chuckled softly as he handed the bottle over.

Nostalgia wracked Samael. It felt like it'd been too long since he'd heard a child laugh. He unlatched the cap of the liquor and handed it back to the boy, who looked at it as if it were some mysterious treasure.

The girl leaned forward, also ogling the bottle. "If you're not going first, then give it here," she said.

The boy looked at her for a second and then tipped the bottle against his lips.

He spat it back out, coughing and choking. "Oh, that's vile!"

"Oh, come on, it can't be that bad," the girl said.

The boy, tongue out and groaning like he was on his deathbed, said, "It's like eating fire." He held the bottle out for his friend.

"That's a better analogy than your earlier one," she said.

"Oh, shut up and try it. You'll see."

With something between courage and foolishness, she tipped the bottle and took a swig. Silence passed, and in what Samael could see beneath the dim light, she wore a brave face as she swallowed.

"Well?" asked the boy.

The girl exhaled, started shaking her head, and upended the bottle, pouring the liquor on the grass. "I don't know how N—our uncle does it; that's the worst thing I've ever tasted."

The boy looked at Samael and asked, "Does it taste better after puberty?"

Samael shrugged. "I wouldn't know."

"You've never drunk liquor?" he asked, as if he had never heard of an abstinent adult.

Samael shook his head. "I promised my father I never would." A promise made before his eighteenth year, just after his grandmother's funeral. She, like so many other Kota, had drunk herself to death. The last time he had seen her, her skin had yellowed, as if she was pickling from the inside out.

The girl groaned. "Easy promise to keep."

Samael nodded.

"What are you doing here?" asked the girl.

He fished his jacket from the bank and started to wring it dry. "Just trying to get back to my family."

"They live all the way out here?" the girl asked, rightfully doubtful.

Samael shook his head. "No, they—my wife and my daughter, that is—live in the Imperial Heartlands. Quite far from here."

"So you haven't seen them for a while," the boy said. The sympathy in his voice was too raw to be feigned.

"That I haven't."

"Do you miss them?" the boy asked.

The words came without thought. "More than I thought I could." Samael looked at the boy and the girl. "You both are older than my daughter, but you remind me of her—especially you," he said, nodding at the boy. "She's got a good heart."

The boy nodded. Though Samael could not see him well, he felt grief from a person too young to have it. "I miss my mom. She, uh . . . well, she died not too long ago."

"I'm sorry to hear that," Samael said, his voice whisper-thin.

"Thanks," the boy said.

Samael almost apologized again, but he bit his tongue.

"So . . ." the girl prodded, "if you miss your family so much, why are you all the way out here?"

"I've been on a journey, you could say."

"A journey?"

Samael nodded. "Well, maybe 'obligation' is a better word for it." He sighed, finding that he could not look at the children anymore. "It's funny. I used to like this kinda thing. Used to find a sense of purpose in traveling and acting with meaning."

"But now?" asked the boy.

Samael cocked his head. "Well, now I'm just tired of it. I've had my fill."

"So, why are you still doing it?" the girl asked, sitting up a bit more.

"Ain't that the question," Samael murmured, a wry smile tilting his lips. He shook his head. "Because I have to. Because not doing it would be worse."

"Is that because you're a Ghoula?" the boy asked.

Samael shrugged. He honestly hadn't thought much about that part of it all. But the boy had a point: He doubted that an Assyrian who had done what he had done would be in this situation. No, they'd just give an Assyrian the medicine without any catches.

He sighed again. "Yeah, probably." He looked at the boy and the girl again, and that small voice from earlier grew louder, meaner. It started gnawing at the back of his mind, asking why he was making nice—why he wasn't doing the damn thing he was supposed to be doing.

He guessed that meant it was time.

"But there is one silver lining to it," he said, affecting his voice to be lower, allowing it to rumble. He looked at them straight-on. The shift in tone had the intended effect; he saw the girl tense up a bit and a soft confusion entered the boy's features. "In fact, I'm glad that I stumbled into the two of you."

"And why's that?" the girl asked, her voice tight.

A cloud shifted, and moonlight fell across the landscape again. Samael didn't tilt his head this time, and he kept his face raised. Light revealed the boy and the girl, and he could not deny that the boy matched the description of the dead woman's son. "I have a feeling that my journey's almost over, now."

They tensed, and he knew then that they had seen his eyes. He pretended to focus on drying his jacket. In the beat of silence following his answer, he saw, from the corner of his eye, the girl tap the boy with no small amount of urgency.

"Well, I hope you get to where you're going, sir," the boy said, more uneasy than before.

Samael nodded and said no more.

The two children departed, and he watched their silvered silhouettes recede into the distance. They walked quickly along the riverbank until they were out of sight.

The night fell terribly silent.

Samael sighed. If those were the fugitives from Ruka, then they could use one last night to just be kids.

XXXII

JAX

"Say that again."

The moment they began their description, a buzzing filled Jax's ears, and he did not hear past the first few words. His heart hammered against his ribcage, as if it too wished to run far, far away.

Clay shirked from Jax's tone, and Ayala did not hide her confusion nor her judgment at his apparent overreaction.

Clay spoke. "It's like he had the night sky in his eyes—they were just dark and dotted with little white lights. But . . . the night sky is pretty; his eyes were just cold."

"Did he tell you his name?" Jax asked, stepping forward. He knew that he spoke with an urgency neither Clay nor Ayala had heard from him, and he saw that it scared them.

They *needed* to be scared.

Jax glanced to Nemo, who was biting his fingernails and watching raptly. The two made eye contact, and they both recognized who this could be—the danger they could be in. Marva was standing by Nemo's side, her eyebrows tilted in a facsimile of confusion.

"No," Clay answered. He opened his mouth to say more, but Nemo cut him off.

"Then describe him to us. Don't leave out a thing."

"On the older side, but not like Nemo," Ayala said. "More like a forty-something who's lived a hard life, or a fifty-something, you know."

"On the shorter side," Clay continued. "Well-built, though." He brought his hands to his head and trailed them down, along his shoulders. "He had long hair that fell."

"Did he have a sword?" Jax asked. "A strange one, made of black and red metal, almost marbled?"

Clay and Ayala exchanged looks, and Clay shook his head. "No, he was unarmed. Even made a point of showing it. Hey, Jax, what's going on? This guy had creepy eyes, yeah, but he never tried to hurt us."

"Then you got lucky," Nemo said, his voice grave. He looked to Marva. "Marva, tell them what you know about Samael of the Kota." Clay's expression shifted immediately—his jaw popped open, and his eyes went wide. So, he must've known that name and the terror it demanded. Nemo caught Jax's eye. "If it's him, then we need to move; no time to fix up the car. We need to get packing. Now."

"Wait, we're leaving the car behind?" Ayala asked, visibly distraught.

"That we are," Nemo said, his tone brokering no argument. "Trust me, Ayala, we do *not* want to stay in the same place for any period of time."

She looked confused. "This guy's that nasty?"

Nemo grimaced. "You know what they call him—what his own damn people call him?" He didn't wait for an answer. "The Reaper. So yeah, he's that nasty.'"

Clay nodded, already sweating. He swallowed thickly.

"Yeah," Jax said, knowing the Harrakas to have the same name for him. He caught Nemo's eye. "We need to leave whatever we can behind."

The man nodded. "Essentials only."

Together, Jax and Nemo hurried around the camp, gathering light packs which they could travel quickly with. As they bustled about, Marva told Clay and Ayala about Samael. As she did, terror seemed to grip Clay tighter and tighter. After the first few sentences, he was gripping his hair tightly, eyes wide, and shaking his head.

Jax wished that he could do the same.

The robot, however, did not do the tales justice; she *couldn't* do the tales justice. Jax grew up with stories from veterans—brave men and women, whose scars were many and proud—and he could still see the fear that inched into their eyes when stories of the Reaper passed around the campfire—the way their voices would hush, as if to speak his name loudly would summon him.

Marva spoke of his deeds, both brilliant and infamous. She spoke of his accomplishments on the battlefield and of his strategic brilliance. And then she mentioned Azariah and Uxiah, and Jax had to lend his voice to the lesson.

"Azariah was my grandfather," he told Clay and Ayala while shoving packets of dried food into a knapsack. "He was the best of the Harrakas, practically invincible, and Samael treacherously assassinated him."

"Dang, Jax, I'm sorry," Clay offered.

Jax did not know why Clay apologized, and he did not have time to wonder. "He is the worst of our enemies, a man who steals warriors' souls and dooms them to an eternity of torment."

With that, Jax began to see the appropriate fear from Clay and Ayala.

Clay rubbed the back of his neck and looked as if he was about to say something. Jax paused what he was doing, and so did Nemo, and both watched the boy and waited.

"I'm sorry we snuck off," Clay said. "I didn't think—"

"Hey," Nemo interrupted, "you couldn't have known, Clay. Sure, it was idiotic, but it all worked out—and if anything, for the better. Now we know Samael's here, and we can bet he's chasing us. It was a mistake, sure, but now we're warned, and now we can be ready. Don't blame yourself, alright?"

Clay nodded, though he looked no more at ease. Ayala seemed to feed off of Clay's energy, and she looked as fearful as Jax had ever seen her.

"Marva, stay close to me and keep your arm charged," Nemo said to the robot. "You know what I mean."

"You got it, hon!" Once again, her tone was too cheerful.

"You ready to go?" Nemo asked Jax. He, too, looked flustered, and his eyes kept darting to the trees which surrounded them, as if he expected Samael to manifest at any moment.

Jax tossed one pack to Clay, and then another to Ayala. He hoisted his own onto his shoulders and nodded to Nemo. He then addressed the group at large. "We move fast, and we don't stop; eat on the run."

He half-expected a complaint from Ayala. She only nodded, wide-eyed, and, for some reason, that worried him most.

❋ ❋ ❋ ❋ ❋

They jogged the whole way to Sacred Trees, stopping only when they absolutely had to. The terrain was kind for such travel, and Jax had packed Clay's and Ayala's packs light enough that it should not hinder them. Most of their supplies were in his own pack.

They did not move as quickly as Jax would have liked, but he did not wish to push the others too much; if they came across Samael, they would need reserves to escape or—if it came to it—to fight. It was apparent that neither Nemo, Clay, nor Ayala made a habit of running long distances. Still, no one complained; no one said a word, in fact, on the entire trek.

It was good that they didn't. Jax felt wired, as if an indescribable amount of energy were coursing through him. Every distant movement caused a crescendo with his adrenaline, and every shifting shadow felt like it was about to strike. If someone spoke, he did not trust that he wouldn't lash out at them before he could control himself.

He did not want to hurt any of them, even Ayala.

Wherever he could, Jax led them through groves and brush. They never surmounted a hill but kept to the valleys, and every time Jax could see the horizon, his nerves spiked.

Samael of the Kota was chasing them.

He knew the crystal was important; he knew that he could not return to the Harrakas without it.

He never would have guessed that it was so important as to bring the Reaper from retirement.

The Harrakas had many older warriors who were smarter than him, stronger than him, even some who were quicker than him. And every single one of them fell asleep with gratitude in their hearts that they never met Samael of the Kota in battle.

Only Uxiah had faced such a menace and survived the Reaper. Flashes of his childhood darted through Jax's mind.

"Your footwork is sloppy; the Reaper would have killed you three times over by now," a trainer had said, his brow drawn and voice sharp. *"You must be better than the worst of your foes."*

"He is a demon incarnate," a warrior had said, her eyes lost in flickering firelight, her skin slicked from heat and drink. *"Even when calm, his speed is terrifying; his strength is uncanny. He is brilliant. Perceptive. Your first mistake will be your last if you fight him."* She had taken a drink then, as if to chase away a memory. *"He is good at forcing others into mistakes."*

Jax inhaled sharply, then exhaled sharply. He could not afford the distractions of the past; he could not afford the fear which they brought.

Around noon, when everyone but Marva was slicked with sweat, the landscape began to shift. The trees thinned until they were memories; the air grew drier; the hills flattened and smoothed until there were no more valleys to hide in. The only feature which stayed constant was the spires of stone. Even in the sunlight, they seemed cast in shadows—such was the darkness of the rock. As they traveled, the stones grew sparser yet taller, until their tips could be peeked even over the horizon.

Once again, he was leading a group to what seemed like a certain death. Jax tightened his fists. Pain flared where his nails dug into his palms. He breathed in and out with measured breaths, willing away the doubt and the fear and all which would distract him from his highest potential. He would not fail Clay, nor Ayala, nor Nemo, nor Marva. Even should they die, he was determined to do all that he possibly could.

Another memory flashed through his mind.

"Wait!" she yelled through blood and spit, even as the fire ate her whole. "Take me with you—don't leave me here!"

She was pinned beneath a fallen beam, and behind her the rest of his team was trapped, fighting, dying. The whole building seemed like it'd collapse at any moment; he couldn't save her. He couldn't save any of them.

Or so he told himself.

And then he ran.

Jax promised himself that whatever may come, whatever may happen, he would have no regrets once it was over.

✽ ✽ ✽ ✽ ✽

When afternoon came, the grass thinned as well, and an arid landscape loomed on the horizon. Even still, an almost unnatural mist settled over the land. A stroke of luck—it would obscure them as they traveled.

Throughout the day, they kept a leisurely pace—at least, for Jax it was leisurely. Beads of sweat didn't roll down his face as with the others, and he never began to breathe heavily. For Jax, it was barely a jog. Yet, his heartbeat never stopped sprinting.

✽ ✽ ✽ ✽ ✽

These days, Sacred Trees was a misnomer. Long ago, in a time Jax could scarcely even imagine, this region sported dozens of *ilaali lumay*. Supported by so many of the wondrous trees, this region had been truly unique; Sangomawo often spoke of the Sacred Trees of yore, where the land was fertile, the plants and trees verdant and lush, and the animals were unique and beautiful. Many compared Sacred Trees to stories of Mohi'ri, and in those days, the Uruk people could be found all over this region.

In the Shadow Wars, Samael campaigned through this region. He burned every single *ilaa lum,* except for one. It stood as a reminder that this region—now arid, sandy, and uninhabitable to all but the most resilient forms of life—used to be a paradise.

The mist had since thickened to a fog, and it provided some relief from the dry and scratchy air . . . the overbearing weight the sun had in this region. Without sunlight, though, the air grew more frigid.

With the fog came a problem. Jax slowed his pace until he stood still, and after a moment, he heard the laboring breaths of the others behind him—hm, maybe he had been pushing them too hard.

"What's going on?" Clay rushed the words through heaving breaths. "Are we there?"

"No," Jax said, squinting through the fog. It pressed around them on all sides.

"Are you lost?" Ayala asked. She wasn't breathing quite as heavily as the others, but she was still winded.

Jax stifled the urge to sigh—his nerves were high, and it took effort to stay calm. "It's nearby. With this fog, we need to go slow, or we can miss it."

"What's nearby?" Ayala asked.

"The last of the Sacred Trees," Jax answered. He then started walking, squinting through the fog and hoping to see it soon.

The others followed. He heard Ayala whisper to Clay, "That didn't tell me anything." Clay did not answer.

"Stay quiet unless you have something useful to say," Jax hissed at Ayala, the words slipping out without thought. Her lips tightened and she eyed him down, but she stayed quiet.

They wandered the mist, stepping tentatively and catching their breath. For some time, they wandered, and with each passing moment, Jax's worry grew stronger. If he was leading them in the wrong direction and this fog stayed constant, then they might find themselves truly and completely lost. Were it not for the threat of the Reaper, he would stay put and wait the fog out—doing so would make them easier targets, though, and he did not wish to tempt fate.

When the fog ahead and to their right appeared thinner, Jax quickened his pace. By then, everyone had caught their breath, and the nerves between them felt electric and tangible. The fog thinned more and more with each step, and then, through the fog ahead, appeared a dark shape. Jax slowed, fearing for a moment that they had stumbled upon one of the great stone obelisks which dotted the landscape. He took a few steps, not daring to hope, and then his pace quickened; no stone obelisk had a silhouette like that.

They broke through the fog, and Jax noted with some surprise that the immediate area around the *ilaa lum* had no fog at all, as if the ancient tree formed a barrier against the mist.

Jax looked upon the tree with equal parts relief and lament. Just as he had grown up with tales of Samael, he grew up with tales of Sacred Trees, and to see that all which remained of such a place was this wounded, lonesome tree saddened him deeply. The *ilaa lum* before him stood tall and large: it towered over them, and to look upon its crown, Jax had to tilt his head to the sky. It may have been as tall as the stone spires they had seen. With a trunk wider than four horses' lengths and a crown so large it could be considered its own canopy, it should have been an impressive sight. Yet, only a handful of stubborn leaves grew along branches. The scars of an inferno marked most of the tree's bark: blackened and gnarled but for a few patches saved from the flames. Even those areas did not look healthy. Some old charms and trinkets, carved of wood and inscribed with runes of luck and protection, still dangled from some limbs, those which weren't blackened and dead. An *ilaa lum* this size should have scattered the fog for miles around, but its scars were so many that it could only manage a few dozen yards.

Not for the first time, Jax felt that it should not be this way. An anger filled his chest and hands—this should not be the world they inherited—not him, not Clay, not Ayala.

He understood why those who caused this deserved to die.

"Wow."

Jax looked back and saw both Clay and Ayala with their mouths hanging open, their heads craned upwards.

"Is this what Afed's tree would look like, once it's fully grown?" Clay asked.

"Yes." Jax kept his voice low and soft, so that his anger did not come through. He did not wish to sully this moment for his friend.

"It's beautiful," Ayala said.

"It's not what it should be," Jax said, running his gaze along the tree's blackened flesh. "It barely survived the Shadow War. It's weak. Almost powerless."

"That makes it no less beautiful," Ayala said, a resolute note in her tone which Jax did not expect.

"Yeah, yeah, that's all very touching," Nemo butted in, looking around at the fog which surrounded them. "Jax, where are the Harrakas? Your vision showed them here, right?"

Shame filled Jax; he had been so caught by the sight of the *ilaa lum* that he lost sight of their purpose. It was not a mistake a leader should make.

He thought back to his vision at the temple. He had seen a number of Harrakas gathered around this very tree, armed and wild. Yet, there had been no fog in the vision. They were the only living beings here, and Jax had not sensed any kind of life aside from the *ilaa lum*.

He spoke the truth. "I don't know."

Jax turned back to the tree. The *ilaali lumay* were not only beacons of the Source and shepherds of nature, but they were also used by the Harrakas to travel great distances. The Sangomawo could also use them to communicate across the Source itself.

Maybe in his vision, the Harrakas had come because Jax told them to.

He did not have time to think of a better idea. He approached the trunk, took a deep breath, and entered the first pose of Agbasā. He took another deep breath—and another, and another.

He exited the pose, unable to still his nerves and slow his heartbeat.

"What's wrong, Jax?" Clay asked.

Jax shook his head, feeling the tension from his knit brow, forcing himself to speak above the shame which clamped his throat. "I can't get calm."

"Is it because of Samael?"

Jax looked back at Clay. He nodded.

"For what it's worth," Clay said, "I'm scared, too. But we trust you, man. You were able to get the crystal by yourself, right? You'll figure it out. I know you will."

Jax nodded. He faced the trunk again, filled with renewed purpose.

He entered the first pose of Agbasa. He took a deep breath—and another, and another. The tension in his shoulders slackened. His heartbeat calmed.

He shifted to the second pose, and he felt the connection to The Source open.

A new and foreign sound ripped Jax's concentration away. He felt the connection collapse, and he tensed up.

Horse hooves upon cracked ground, crunching from the other side of the *ilaa lum*.

They all stilled, their gazes transfixed on the sound which was slowly making its way around from the far side of the tree.

Jax backed up, rolling his feet so that he didn't make a sound.

And then, from around the left side of the tree, he appeared.

His horse was pale and large, his garb simple and rusted by travel. His back was straight, and a saber and a dagger hung from his hips. His hair, long and straight, framed a grim countenance. From this angle, Jax could see beneath his hat; Jax saw those terrible eyes, and he broke into a cold sweat—time seemed to dilate, and for a moment he thought he saw figures looming in the fog—he ripped his gaze away, and those silhouettes disappeared entirely.

Were those the souls of slain Harrakas?

Samael of the Kota looked to each and every person gathered, and then he spoke. "This is your one chance. Don't waste it."

Clay stepped forward. "Please, just let us go. We're good people. We just want to get somewhere safe, where we can live our lives."

"So do I." With slow, practiced ease, Samael unsheathed his saber. Relief flooded Jax when he saw that the blade was made of steel, not black-and-red meteorite. For whatever reason, Samael had left his infamous blade behind.

"Don't throw away your lives," said the Reaper. Though his posture was strong, he sounded tired. "I know you have the crystal. I know that you know who I am. I don't need to tell you what will happen if you don't give it up."

"I thought you were retired, Sammy," Nemo called, his voice with a taunting edge.

Samael looked past Jax and narrowed his eyes.

He heard Nemo shudder behind him.

The Reaper grunted. "So, this is where you ran off to." His gaze flicked somewhere else. "I see you're still breaking new ground."

"Hello! I am—"

"Stay quiet," Nemo hissed, cutting Marva off.

For some reason, the Reaper's mouth popped open and he even looked surprised. "You used *her* voice? By Cyrus, Nemo, what—"

He was interrupted by a sound unlike anything Jax had heard; it was similar to the noises of Nemo's workshop, but far quicker and with many more hisses. He dared a glance back, wondering if they had been flanked, and saw Nemo next to Marva, moving with incredible speed. There was an odd hissing noise, and Nemo detached Marva's arm. In only a moment, he was holding a long rifle which made a soft humming noise. Jax had never seen its like before. It still looked like Marva's arm, though where the hand used to be, there was now a flared opening.

Nemo pointed the rifle at Samael, and Jax faced the Reaper again.

Of all the things Jax expected to hear just then, it was not the noise of the same concussion mine which had blown his leg to pieces.

A strange projectile passed by Jax: It was a purplish mirage, seen only by the way it faintly colored and rippled the air as it traveled right towards the legs of Samael's steed.

The concussive blast punched the ground next to the horse, spraying dirt and rocks into the air. It made an awful sound and, pushed by the shockwave, fell on its side, bringing Samael down with it.

This was his chance.

In one fluid movement, Jax sprinted forward and unsheathed his shortsword. He had always been fast, and the Source had gifted him with a speed that bordered on unnatural; by the time Samael hit the ground, Jax was within range.

The Reaper had quick reflexes; as his horse fell, he leapt from the saddle and was tumbling back to his feet.

Jax did not strike as Samael rolled; he waited for the right moment. In this fight, his first mistake would be his last. He would be cautious, and he would be smart. That was the only way to survive.

Jax aimed a thrust, and though he waited for only half a second for the right moment, it was agonizing; every fiber of his body screamed to strike wildly.

To his side, he heard hooves scrambling on the dirt; in his periphery, Samael's horse bolting into the fog.

Samael planted his free hand on the ground, and as he pushed himself to his feet, there was a hair-thin moment where his guard was down and his footing was unsteady.

Jax stabbed; he felt the give of flesh on the other end of the blade—a glancing strike along Samael's shoulder, but a strike nonetheless.

He stepped forward, getting within Samael's guard.

Jax needed to stay close and aggressive. Where Samael's longer blade held the advantage in reach and power, Jax's shorter blade was faster and more maneuverable; so long as he stayed close and quick, he could control the rhythm of the fight.

As Samael regained his footing, Jax delivered a backhand slash, twisted, and flowed into a forward cut; he paid attention to his footwork through the sequence, and he knew it was impeccable.

Yet, it was not enough. Even while regaining his footing, Samael's speed was preternatural; he twisted away from both the backhand slash and the cut—both strikes grazed the Reaper's clothes, but they did not pierce flesh.

Now standing upright, Jax noticed that he was taller than Samael. Good. That meant that he had an innate advantage with his—

Pain flared in his throat, and it grew difficult to breathe; he hadn't seen Samael's fist until the man pulled it back. With that same preternatural quickness, Samael had jabbed Jax in the throat.

The Harraka retreated, taking large steps back and fighting his own body, which struggled to breathe and wanted to collapse. He couldn't believe the power of the man's strike—Samael's footing was off, and even still, he had delivered a jab which almost collapsed Jax's windpipe.

He tried his best to adopt a defensive posture, but he could barely breathe, and he knew he was unsteady and weak.

Yet, Samael did not press his advantage. He simply stood, looking past Jax.

"Get out of the way!" Nemo called from behind; of course, Jax was in his line of fire. The Harraka sidestepped and leapt to his right, hoping that he had struck enough distance to offer Nemo a clear shot—even a simple movement like that winded Jax. He needed time to catch his breath again; it felt like there was a stone lodged in his throat.

"Cato!" Samael barked.

A gunshot rang out, and then a scream filled the air: Nemo's scream.

"Hon!" Marva called.

Jax did not dare take his eyes off the Reaper, no matter what happened behind him.

Samael rushed forward.

Jax braced, knowing that his stance was weak and that he was powerless to strengthen it.

But Samael sprinted past Jax, barely paying the Harraka any heed.

Jax whirled and took in the scene.

Nemo bled from his right shoulder from a bullet wound—nonlethal, but almost crippling in a fight. Marva watched from a distance, her remaining hand against her mouth. Behind both of them were Clay and Ayala, and behind them was a newcomer: a Cynical, tall and young. Even in the dim and scattered light beneath the tree, the crystals pocking her cheekbones and eyes glistened like fresh blood. She stood right behind Clay and Ayala, who had both flinched from the revolver she held; its barrel still smoked, and based on how both Uruks cupped their ears, Jax assumed that she had fired the gun right next to their heads.

Where did the Cynical come from? Had she been trailing them through the fog—no, if she was, then Jax would have sensed her.

Right?

No. There could be no other explanation for how she flanked them, for how she appeared so suddenly. Jax had failed those who followed him. Again.

Samael was going for Nemo. He moved fast—faster than any human who wasn't connected to The Source should.

Nemo, despite the bullet in his shoulder and the pain it must've caused, hoisted his rifle and trained it on Samael. The barrel quaked, and Jax knew that the engineer's arm was weak.

Nemo shot another concussive blast at Samael, aiming for the man's feet.

Samael leapt out of the way, and once again, the blast kicked up a cloud of dust and rocks. Though Samael dodged wide, he could not quite escape the shockwave—he stumbled from the impact but planted his foot and spun, using the blast's momentum to propel him forward.

Nemo's rifle charged again. Jax wagered he had one more shot before Samael was upon him. His instincts were telling him to chase after Samael; Jax was quicker, and he might catch him in time. But Jax stayed put; he was just now catching his breath again, and if he charged after Samael, he would keep himself vulnerable. He could afford no risks.

Still, Jax felt like a hostage in his own body.

Beyond Nemo and Samael, the Cynical drew another revolver from a holster. She aimed one gun each at Clay and Ayala, who were just now recovering from being deafened.

"Hey, kiddos," she said. "Best stay put, if you know what's—"

With a speed and ferocity that surprised Jax, Ayala batted the gun out of her face and punched the Cynical square in the nose. Clay seized the moment and charged her, tackling her around the hips—but the Cynical sunk shifted her hips and stayed upright.

Jax could breathe a touch easier now, but he was still nowhere near where he needed to be.

Nemo aimed again, and Jax focused his attention there. In his periphery, he saw Clay and Ayala brawling with the Cynical—for some reason, she wasn't using her guns. So, they wanted to take them alive. Jax grimaced. Such a fate would likely be worse than death.

Nemo shot, and Samael dodged again, leaping farther than last time, and even then, the shockwave stumbled his rhythm. He regained it fast, though, and then he was upon Nemo.

A single slash—blood splattered against the sand; the rifle fell; two fingers went flying through the air and fell to the earth. Blood pooled beneath them.

Nemo went to his knees, his good hand clamped against his bleeding one.

"Hon!" Marva rushed to Nemo; Samael intercepted her. He kicked her in the chest, knocking her to the ground as if she weighed nothing. A staccato rattling noise came from Marva's chassis, as if something was knocked loose.

Jax could almost take a deep breath now.

He glanced to Clay and Ayala. The Cynical had shaken Clay loose and holstered both revolvers; in a sequence of well-placed jabs, elbows, and kicks, she beat both Ayala and Clay to the ground, where they writhed in pain. The Cynical, with blood running from both nostrils, kicked Ayala in the stomach; Ayala groaned and curled up, wrapping both arms around her head to ward off any further blows. The Cynical drew her guns again, aiming one each at the Uruks. "If I see you so much as twitch, it'll be the last thing you ever do." Her voice was harsh and angry. "Orders be damned."

Nemo glanced back and saw that Clay and Ayala had been taken hostage. "Don't move; just stay down, all of you!"

Samael punched Nemo near the eye; the engineer crumpled to the ground. Jax wasn't sure if he was knocked out, but he was sure that Nemo's orbital was broken.

He knew firsthand how hard that monster could punch.

The female Cynical looked at Jax and, as if seeing him for the first time, raised her eyebrows. Samael, his back still turned to Jax, ordered, "Keep an eye on the others."

"Yes, Knight-Commander."

As Samael turned to face Jax, the Harraka found that he could almost breathe normally again. It would have to do. He took as deep a breath as he could, attempting to steady his nerves.

When he spoke, his head was tilted low so that his eyes were hidden behind the brim of his hat. "You have some skill. You know that it won't save you."

Jax swallowed and tightened his grip on his sword, trying his best to stop the tip from shaking. "Let's find out."

Insultingly enough, Samael sighed. "Alright then."

The Reaper leveled his gaze on Jax, and the Harraka made the mistake of meeting those terrible eyes.

It felt like he did not hold contact for more than a second, and yet Jax once again broke out into a cold sweat; his sense of time warped, and by the time he regained his faculties, Samael was running in a wide arc to Jax's right. He kept his sword by his opposite hip and low, telegraphing a quick and wide slash in the future. The man disappeared into the fog; at first, Jax could still track his silhouette, and once that faded, only those cold dark eyes loomed through the mist. Those, too, faded entirely.

The sun dipped low in the sky, and as twilight settled into dusk, the air grew colder and darker.

Jax braced, scanning the fog which surrounded his right flank, making sure to never keep his eyes fixated on a single point. He quirked his ears, trying to hear Samael's footsteps, but the man may as well have been a ghost. He needed to be cautious—wait for Samael to strike, dodge, and counterattack. He would not risk blocking or even parrying; as powerful as Samael had shown himself to be, Jax did not have confidence that his shortsword would hold up to clashes, even though it had been forged by Nemo.

There! To his right: a flash of those eyes, peering through the mist and into his soul.

He could not meet Samael's eyes. If he peered into that abyss, he would die. So, Jax closed his eyes, disregarding them so that he could more intently listen to his surroundings.

He heard Nemo crawling across the hard-packed dirt.

Clay whispering to Ayala, who was groaning in pain.

Marva's machinery whirring and clanking arrhythmically.

The young Cynical shifting her weight from one foot to the other, the dirt crunching beneath her boots.

Footsteps, feather-light and almost imperceptible, rapid and to his right.

Jax turned in that direction, knowing that his back was to the young Cynical; he did not like that he was flanked. Should the Cynical wish, she could shoot him in the back and he would be none the wiser. But if he turned, Samael would cut him down.

He opened his eyes, looking first at the ground in front of him and raising them until he could see the Reaper's moccasins.

By the Source, he was close. Jax lifted his eyes a little more. As Samael ran, Jax trained himself to watch the man's shoulders and hips—it was old and trusty advice, for the shoulders and hips could not lie.

Jax widened his stance, preparing to duck and riposte; with the momentum Samael had, he would not risk dodging backwards or to the side.

The distance closed.

Samael swung for Jax's neck; the man was fast, but Jax was faster, if only just.

He ducked so low he propped his free hand on the ground; the blade sailed so close to the top of his head that he felt wind rustle his hair.

But he had his opening; he was close, and he had the advantage, so long as he stayed aggressive. Pushing off with his hand, he stepped forward and thrusted at Samael's midsection.

Only to feel the jarring vibrato of steel on steel; Samael, somehow, moved his blade just in time and, holding it reverse-grip, parried Jax's blade, knocking the younger warrior off balance.

Samael slashed.

From chest to shoulder, Jax felt pain, and then a sickly warmth. He rolled away, attempting to strike distance.

Samael stepped and kicked, catching Jax in the gut and knocking him back mid-roll. The breath, once again, was torn from Jax—he pushed through, rolling as he landed and leaping to his feet, forcing a sharp inhale as he regained his footing.

Samael did not relent; he advanced, dancing through a sequence of slashes, chops, thrusts, feints, and strikes. Jax kept his eye on the man's shoulders and hips, and he read every single beat perfectly; but he was not fast enough to dodge; he was not strong enough to block; he was not skilled enough to parry.

Jax's earliest memories involved conditioning his mind, his body. Ever since he was able to, he held a weapon; for as long as he could remember, he had never gone a month without training to fight. To kill.

All that was only enough to keep Jax an inch from death; he had no time to think, and only his instincts kept him alive. He blocked when he could, and even then too high, at the foible—the bones in his arms shook, and the blade grew scored and chipped. He dodged when he could, but he could not step wide enough to dodge Samael's sally without losing his balance; he could not move quickly enough to avoid the attacks. He tried to parry the Reaper's blade only once, and he almost lost his fingers.

All the stories about Samael of the Kota were understatements.

No story could capture this man's prowess.

Jax dodged a slower backhanded slash—finally—and stepped in close, seizing what may be his last chance.

Only to be greeted by the pommel of Samael's blade, which slammed into his nose. Jax knew off the cuff that it was broken. Behind the fatigue which crowded his mind, a small voice wondered how he had fallen for such an obvious trap.

His energy faded; his flesh wept blood.

And Jax fell.

He had been sliced so much that his body had gone numb. He did not know if he would die from these wounds; there were too many, and he was too overwhelmed to even judge such things.

Samael regained his footing and stood tall. "You've been trained." His voice was low and cold. With the tip of his sword, he shifted a tear in Jax's shirt, revealing the tattoos around his collarbones. The Reaper grimaced. "I thought your movements were familiar. You're a Harraka, aren't you?"

With an uncanny excitement, the Cynical behind Jax said, "A Harraka? Really?"

Samael did not answer her.

A peculiar feeling settled over Jax; it did not come from his injuries. The hairs along his arms and on the back of his neck rose. The air felt thicker, but only slightly so.

It was an old, familiar feeling, long forgotten and more than welcome.

He just had to survive a few moments longer.

"Yeah," Jax said. It took some effort to speak, but he did not sound weak. He did not sound defeated.

Samael tipped his saber, pointing it towards Jax's throat. "Who trained you?"

Jax found the courage to glance at the *ilaa lum*, and he had to exert conscious effort to not betray the relief he felt, for its leaves were standing upright, as if magnetized to the sky.

Jax tightened his grip on his shortsword; he would have only a split second chance, and he would make the most of it.

He saw Samael's hair begin to rise as well, lifted by a crescendo of static electricity; the man's sword wavered as he looked around, confused by the tangible crackle which filled the air around them.

And then lightning struck.

All the world became blindingly white, and thunder set Jax's ears ringing.

He was fast—in this moment, as fast as lightning.

Jax aimed for the man's spine. He felt the give of flesh on the other end of the blade.

Jax's vision was filled with dark spots; he had not dared close his eyes for that crucial moment, and his ears rung. Yet, he focused, and his vision cleared just enough.

Even blinded and deafened, Samael twisted at the last moment; Jax's blade was sunk almost to the hilt through Samael's left flank.

Samael stepped back, and Jax's shortsword slipped out of his torso; a flick of his wrist, and he knocked Jax's blade from his hand. Then, oddly, he turned his attention from Jax and took another step back, clamping his wound with his free hand, tilting into a defensive posture, with his saber pointed low and forward.

The ground rumbled near Jax; he looked to his left, and though his vision was still spotty, he saw a huge boot next to him.

A new shadow loomed over Jax. He looked up, and his vision cleared even more. Standing next to him was a beast of a man; he must have been over two heads taller than Samael and was almost twice as wide. A mane of dreadlocks fell over his shoulders and down his back, and he was shirtless, his arms clad in leathers, furs, and jewels. In his left hand, he held an axe so large that only a man built like him could wield it. Jax focused his vision on the man's face, and though dark spots flitted in and out of sight, he saw that the man wore a wicked grin, leveled at Samael.

Jax whipped his head around, looking at the clearing; were he healthy, he might have possessed the urge to cheer.

The Harrakas had arrived.

They had come with the lightning: an old way of traveling between *ilaali lumay*. Jax could scarcely believe that this old, damaged tree could facilitate the transport of so many people; there were at least two dozen Harrakas gathered throughout the clearing. Like the brute by Jax, they wore leathers, furs, and many sported the same kinds of tattoos which marked Jax's skin. Unlike Jax, their tattoos traveled across their bodies, and they had many more braids and dreads than him, for these were experienced and veteran warriors, ones who have earned such markings.

Though his teeth were gritted against the pain of his wound, Samael stood upright and lifted his free hand from his torso, placing it on the grip of his sword. He shifted his stance and stood as if he wasn't bleeding through a hole in his gut; his eyes hardened, and Jax had the feeling that Samael hadn't been taking him seriously at all. "So, you're not dead," Samael said, his gaze leveled on the man by Jax.

The man spoke through a wolfish smile. "Surprised?" He held Samael's gaze with no fear nor effect.

The air grew thicker and colder, so cold that Jax could see his own breath. Silence and tension filled the air; it felt as if the whole world was waiting for Samael or the giant to make the first move. A thin snowfall floated from the sky—Jax glanced upwards and saw dark clouds roiling around the canopy of the *ilaa lum*. He wondered briefly if it was only snowing within its radius.

And then the first snowflake touched the earth.

Gunshots split the air; Jax heard the thin whistle and snap of bullets flying overhead. The Harraka brute ducked, shielding his face behind the flat of his axe blade. Jax shielded his head with his arms and curled up, making himself as small a target as possible.

Two sharp whistles pierced the air near the end of the volley; one came from Samael, and Jax guessed that the other came from his Cynical companion.

The earth rumbled again, and the sound of galloping horses approached.

"Get them!" called the Harraka by Jax.

He looked up from the ground and saw Samael pulling himself into the saddle of his horse, grunting with the effort and the pain. The other Cynical was already mounted; her horse must have been waiting in the fog.

The Harrakas all moved at once, chasing after the two Cynicals. Bowstrings thrummed; arrows hissed through the air; men and women moved with incredible speed, chasing after Samael and the Cynical.

Their enemies shifted, weaved, and ducked in their saddles—the Cynical caught an arrow in her shoulderblade, and Samael's horse took one in the flank.

The Cynical escaped first, disappearing into the fog.

Two Harrakas were quick enough to position themselves between Samael and the opaque fog; one had a spear, and the other a two-handed club, its head a dense ball of polished wood.

Samael drew his dagger, flipped it so that he gripped the point between his finger and thumb, and flicked it into the neck of the spear-wielding Harraka. The movement was so quick that Jax would have missed it if he wasn't focusing.

The Harraka with the club stepped out of the horse's path and swung wide and high, aiming to catch Samael in the chest and knock him from the steed.

Samael threw himself to the left side of the horse, hanging low off the saddle, only his right arm and leg keeping him attached; the club missed, and so did three arrows, which passed harmlessly into the fog.

Throughout the sequence, Samael's steed did not break its stride. Once past the last club-wielding Harraka, the Reaper disappeared into the fog.

A Harraka knelt by the man who had the dagger jutting from his neck, shook her head, and then joined the others in chasing after Samael and the Cynical.

Just as the first warriors disappeared into the fog, the Harraka with the giant axe barked, "Do not chase after them!"

Immediately, the Harrakas ceased the pursuit. They funneled back into the clearing. Jax looked around, his vision almost wholly back now, and saw with no small relief that Nemo, Clay, and Ayala were alive and okay. Relatively. Marva looked as if she was still functional, though she was clearly damaged; her movements were stuttering, and the light in one of her eyes was dimmer than normal. Clay and Ayala sported bloody lips and noses, and they would be wearing bruises for the next few days. Nemo was in worse shape; his eye was already swollen shut, and he clamped the stubs where his fingers were tightly. His skin was pallid and clammy. Even then, he met Jax's eyes and forced a smile and a nod, as if to say, *Good work, boy.*

Jax exhaled and felt the tension leave his shoulders.

They had done it.

They had survived the Reaper.

It seemed that the Harrakas had brought Sangomawo with them; where the warriors sported leathers and weapons, the Sangomawo wore simple red-and-yellow robes. There were three of them, and they began tending to Clay, Ayala, and Nemo.

The giant Harraka with the equally large axe approached Jax. He squatted before the boy, the pommel of his axe resting on the ground, the head of it leaned against the man's shoulder. He was so large that he cast Jax in shadow.

The man's features were strong and blocky. His cheeks were gaunt, his jaw strong, and most of his wrinkles were concentrated above his nose, between the eyebrows. He looked Jax over, studying his wounds with an impassive expression. And, when Uxiah finally made eye contact with the boy, he simply nodded.

Jax nodded back. "Hello, father."

ENDNOTES

i.   Ombada: ahm-bah-duh
ii. Uxiah: uhks-EYE-uh
iii. Samael: sah-MAY-ul
iv. Ayala: EYE-all-uh
v.   Crystalli Squamae; "Crystal Scales": A condition afflicting more and more newborns with each successive generation. A side effect of exposure to the crystal-powered machinery common in Assyr's heartland, it is a condition marked by small crystalline growths on a person's skin. Though there are no recorded cases of Crystalli Squamae where the growths affect a person's ability to function, many superstitions revolve around the condition, and many see it as a bad omen, leading many upper-class families to buy expensive surgeries to hide the condition.
vi. The highest-ranking member of The Cynical Order, the Knight-Commander is the de facto leader.
vii. Lumin; lo͞omən: A portable, artificial light source powered by Venulia Crystals.
viii. Though the foundational rhetoric of the Ghoula caste mandates that all Ghoulas are equal to each other and lesser than Assyrians, the long centuries of assimilation have led certain Ghoula peoples and cultures to flourish while others were exterminated. The Kota willingly joined the Empire in Cyrus's day, when Assyr was in its infancy. They donned the mantle of Ghoula and have served dutifully ever since, and thus they retained parts of their culture and even the name of their people: Kota.
ix. Luna: an extremely addictive substance and a thorn in the Empire's side. Originating from the sap of the ilaali lumay, its users develop what is known as "blue-tongue syndrome." Often equated to a "spiritual transcendence," it is said to offer a high so pleasurable that a few milligrams are enough to fry one's dopamine receptors permanently. Many spend their lives chasing their first high.
x.   Ilaali lumay: íl-LAH-li loo-mai
xi. M'ynhyvch: Men-have-AHK